Pr[illegible]
and her novels

"Mistletoe Reunion is a delightful story about the power of love and prayer."
—*RT Book Reviews*

"Lasso Her Heart does touch… on deeper issues…. God's message proves an encouragement to Bethany, and readers should get a kick out of this story of the late-in-life marrieds-to-be."
—*RT Book Reviews*

"Schmidt's top-notch story has a number of interesting characters."
—*RT Book Reviews* on *Home at Last*

"This is a wonderful story featuring interesting and likable characters, as well as excitement and lessons about forgiveness and acceptance."
—*RT Book Reviews* on *The Pastor Takes a Wife*

"A Mother for Amanda is another jewel by Anna Schmidt."
—*RT Book Reviews*

ANNA SCHMIDT

Lasso Her Heart

&

Mistletoe Reunion

HARLEQUIN® LOVE INSPIRED® CLASSICS

Recycling programs for this product may not exist in your area.

ISBN-13: 978-0-373-65166-5

This edition published by arrangement with Love Inspired Books.

www.Harlequin.com

Printed in U.S.A.

CONTENTS

Books by Anna Schmidt

Love Inspired

Caroline and the Preacher
A Mother for Amanda
The Doctor's Miracle
Love Next Door
Matchmaker, Matchmaker...
Lasso Her Heart
Mistletoe Reunion
Home at Last
The Pastor Takes a Wife

Love Inspired Historical

Seaside Cinderella
Gift from the Sea
An Unexpected Suitor
A Convenient Wife
Christmas Under Western Skies
"A Prairie Family Christmas"
**Hannah's Journey*
**Family Blessings*
**A Groom for Greta*
**Second Chance Proposal*

*Amish Brides of Celery Fields

ANNA SCHMIDT

is an award-winning author of more than twenty-five works of historical and contemporary fiction. She is a three-time finalist for a coveted RITA® Award from Romance Writers of America, as well as a four-time finalist for an RT Reviewers' Choice Award. Critics have called Anna "a natural writer, spinning tales reminiscent of old favorites like *Miracle on 34th Street.*" Her characters have been called "realistic" and "endearing," and one reviewer raved, "I love Anna Schmidt's style of writing!"

LASSO HER HEART

Blessed are those who mourn,
for they will be comforted.
—*Matthew* 5:4

For Serena—
Thanks for being my tour guide and my brainstorming buddy!

Chapter One

Cody Dillard was accustomed to being on the receiving end of admiring glances from women of all ages. He was tall and lean with an easy smile and eyes so deep blue that he'd been asked more than once if the color was his or tinted contacts. He'd been a high school junior and a wannabe athlete when his body had suddenly taken on the hard planes of manhood and his head had finally caught up with his ears—appendages that had caused him no end of teasing as a kid.

Basically shy and introverted by nature, as a kid Cody had not been sure popularity and admiration were much better than the old teasing and snickers. But as a grown man, he actually enjoyed the attention. He had learned that he could make some grandmother's day by returning her glance with a smile that bypassed the younger women around her. Cody was all about finding ways to lighten people's load. That was how he had decided to honor the lives of his mother and brother—two souls who had filled the world with laughter, joy and generosity of spirit during their far-too-brief stay on earth.

Too often he saw people rushing around, their faces set into hard frowns or exhausted blank stares as if they knew they needed to get somewhere but were not sure what they would do once they arrived at their destination. Cody understood that, better than most who enjoyed the many blessings of life might guess. Even now, five years later, Cody fought every day not to surrender to his grief—and his guilt.

He ambled through O'Hare Airport where no one ambled—ever—and focused on individuals hurrying past him. A businessman, cell phone to ear, brushed past. He was juggling a carry-on bag, laptop and shopping bag with presents for the kiddies back home judging by the teddy bear that had just fallen unnoticed to the floor. Cody picked up the bear and hurried to catch up with the man. He watched the man's expression go from annoyance at the interruption to appreciation. The man mouthed "thank you" as he turned so Cody could stuff the bear back in the bag.

Cody saw a security officer eyeing him suspiciously. Understanding that his leisurely stroll might be perfectly normal to him but stood out in a madhouse like O'Hare, Cody realized he'd better relieve the man's suspicions.

"Excuse me, Officer," he said. "I'm meeting someone coming in on the flight from D.C. Since I don't have a ticket and can't meet her at the gate, what do you suggest?"

The officer continued to check him out as he gathered information. Cody explained that he'd never actually met the woman he was meeting and was operating from a description provided by her aunt. Of course, Cody knew exactly what he needed to do, but asking the bored security guard for help gave the man purpose and an identity in the mad rush of the airport.

"If I were in your shoes," the officer said, "I'd find out where the luggage is coming downstairs, make a sign with her name on it and wait by the carousel. You could also have her paged…."

Just then the public address system activated and the security guard paused as he and Cody both listened to the garbled message. The words were effectively drowned out by the multiple conversations and competing announcements of flights boarding around them.

"Or not," the security guard added when the announcement ended. He grinned. "I'd go for the sign and baggage claim."

Cody thanked him and ambled off.

"Hey, buddy," the guard called, and a number of people—assuming trouble—stopped to gawk, wondering what Cody had done. Cody turned and the guard took an empty cardboard box from the candy kiosk vendor and waved it at him. "For your sign. She's got a marker, too," he added, nodding at the young woman managing the stand.

Cody grinned and retraced his steps, nodding to the gawkers on his way and causing one woman of a certain age to blush scarlet when he actually winked at her. "That's really nice of you," he said to the guard and candy vendor.

"What's her name?" The girl sat poised to write with a large red marker.

"Bethany Taft."

"Better just use first initial and last name," the guard instructed as the girl wrote the name in bold script letters. She quickly added a border of flowers and vines and handed the finished work to Cody.

"Thanks. I really appreciate the help," he said and continued down the corridor following the signs directing him to Baggage Claim.

Bethany Taft was having definite second thoughts about her latest decision. She was explaining all that to her best friend, Grace Marlowe, as the plane taxied for what seemed like the approximate distance that Grace had driven taking Bethany to the airport in Washington earlier.

"This was a mistake on so many levels," she said, cupping one hand around the receiver of her cell phone and her mouth to keep her seatmate from overhearing and commenting on her conversation. The man had introduced himself as a lobbyist for the pork industry. Just after takeoff, he had insisted they put the center chair arm up to give them more room and then proceeded to take over every inch of space that Bethany left available as she pressed closer and closer to the wall of the plane.

"Give it a chance," Grace replied. "Just remember what this is going to mean to your aunt Erika."

Grace had always been good at finding the core of

an issue and, of course, the core of this particular issue was that Bethany's favorite aunt—a spinster for all of her sixty years—was now engaged to be married to Ian Dillard, widower and nationally known businessman. Erika had insisted that only Bethany could help her plan the wedding and the multitude of events leading up to it.

"You did such a terrific job for me," Grace reminded her now. "No wonder Erika wants you to move in with her for the next several months while the two of you put this thing together. Besides it's good for you to get away—meet new people...."

Get on with your life now that Nick's gone.

Grace was a professional matchmaker by trade. She—and the rest of Bethany's circle of friends and family—had been extremely concerned about Bethany's change in outlook this past year. They understood that the sudden and unexpected death of her fiancé, Nick, a year earlier would have been enough to stun even the sunniest of souls—which Bethany had certainly been. But lately everyone had urged Bethany to move on—Nick would want that, they assured her.

"Did you set me up?" she asked Grace now. "Did you and Erika—"

"You're rambling," Grace interrupted. "I didn't even know your aunt, a woman I have met exactly three times, was seeing anyone, much less engaged to be married."

"So the fact that a couple of weeks ago you suggested that perhaps if I got away for a while—"

"Pure coincidence," Grace assured her. "Or perhaps God's handiwork?"

Bethany did not reply. God was not part of her life these days. Grace might not like it, but did not push the point. Bethany appreciated her friend's willingness to accept for now that Bethany had chosen to cope with Nick's tragic death on her own.

Turning her attention back to the conversation, she was glad to note that Grace had changed the subject. "Any sign of a gate yet?"

Bethany peered out the window. "We seem to be taking the grand tour as the pilot decides which one to choose. It's raining," she reported. "Another bad sign."

"Or it could just be raining," Grace replied with a laugh. "Give it a chance, Bethany. It means so much to Erika and why not immerse yourself in somebody else's life and happiness for a while?"

"While I try to unearth a life and happiness for myself?"

"You said it, I didn't," Grace said just as the plane finally stopped at a gate and the announcement came on about checking overhead bins, et cetera.

"We're here. I'll call you later, okay?"

Bethany clicked the phone off. Next to her the lobbyist had begun to stir. "What can I get you, little lady?" he asked as he struggled up from the seat and into the narrow aisle. He popped the overhead bin across from their seat. "This and the jacket, right?"

Bethany nodded as he wrestled her overstuffed carry-on out of the tight space while she bent to retrieve the large bag disguised as her purse that she had pushed under the seat in front of her. "You carry it all with you," he commented with a tight smile as he dropped the bag heavily to the floor with obvious relief. "Smart woman."

Bethany favored him with a radiant smile as she slid across the seat and stood in the space he'd made for her in the aisle. Then to forestall any further conversation, she flicked open her cell again. She had three text messages. The first from her mother—an address she wanted Bethany to be sure and give Erika. The second was from Grace. It read simply, Call any time—I'm here. The third was from her Aunt Erika.

Change of plans, sweetie. Ian's son, Cody, will meet your flight—probably at baggage. He'll find you—I gave him a full description. Ciao!

Erika had casually dropped the name of Ian's son before in the context of his being a major hottie, not to mention a brilliant businessman just like his father, and—by the way—single. Bethany groaned, closed the phone and shouldered her purse, makeup essentials, plus everything she couldn't stuff in the suitcase bag as the masses pushed forward up the jetway and into the chaotic terminal.

She followed the signs, passed through the security exit and glanced around. Not a soul seemed to be waiting to meet and greet unless she wanted to count the twenty-something guy holding a huge bouquet of red roses. He was a good four inches shorter than she was without her platform espadrilles.

"Couldn't be," Bethany muttered, but she made eye contact and the guy lit up like the sky over the Potomac on the Fourth of July. Bethany took a deep breath, plastered a smile on her face and started forward as she considered how she would manage to get through O'Hare carrying that bouquet without looking as though she were a candidate for Miss America.

Just then she heard an earsplitting squeal from just behind her left shoulder and a girl she recognized from her plane raced past her and into the waiting arms of the red rose guy. He swung her round and round and neither of them seemed to notice the cascade of rose petals that fell to the carpet to be trampled by the hordes as they made their way past the young couple.

Bethany stood frozen for an instant, unable to take her eyes off the couple. In the year since Nick's death she had thought she was making progress. Then she would see a couple, madly in love, like these two. When had she last known that kind of unadulterated joy? The truth was that with Nick's work that often involved traveling and her work, they had really not spent the kind of intense time together that some couples enjoyed. They had been the best of friends for years before becoming romantically involved. They had always assumed that once they were married there would be a lifetime for them to create memories.

They had even assumed that they had plenty of time to set a date and plan their wedding. They had been in love with the romance of being in love, but Nick had also been determined to achieve certain career milestones before settling down.

Bethany was tempted to go over to the couple and warn them, urge them not to take this gift for granted.

Then someone jostled her from behind, gave her an irritated frown and by the time she readjusted her luggage, the couple was lost in the crowd. Bethany flicked open her phone and hit speed dial for Grace.

"I'm being met by sonny-boy," she said without preamble.

"Really? What's he like?"

"To hear Aunt Erika tell it, he's Adonis come to earth, but since he's not here, I couldn't really say," she muttered.

"Well, usually when Dad is being met somewhere, the driver stations himself at baggage claim."

Grace's father was a United States senator and no doubt used to the protocol of drivers and such. "What if I didn't check luggage?" Bethany thought it was a perfectly logical question and was not at all amused when Grace burst out laughing and couldn't seem to stop.

"You?" she gasped. "Without luggage?"

"All right. It was a reasonable question—for most people." She surprised Grace as well as herself by seeing the humor in the idea of Bethany Taft traveling with anything less than the contents of a full closet.

"Well, at least you're still in fairly decent spirits," Grace commented. "Now don't take out your doubts about this whole thing on Ian's son. What's his name again?"

"Cody."

"Nice."

"If you like that sort of man-of-the-prairie thing. Okay, so here's the escalator to baggage. Descending now into the bowels of O'Hare. Looking around, not sure what for. What do you think a Cody looks like?"

"What does his father look like?"

"Haven't had the pleasure. Oh, my stars!" Bethany almost dropped the phone as she spotted the man holding a hand-lettered sign with a floral border and her name on it.

"Bethany? What happened? Bethany?"

"I'll call you back," Bethany whispered, not sure why she found that necessary since practically everyone surrounding her was jabbering away on their cell phones and oblivious to her and the incredibly gorgeous man holding the sign and grinning up at her.

Cody studied the women coming down the escalator, dismissing them one by one until he spotted the redhead attached to the cell phone and shouldering one large bag in addition to guiding a suitcase on wheels that must have just barely passed the size regulations for taking on the plane.

Erika had not oversold this one even if Cody had thought she might be more than a little partial. Bethany Taft was everything that Erika had promised and more. She had flaming red hair caught haphazardly in a topknot and set off by a pair of sunglasses at the ready should Chicago have a sudden burst of glaring sunlight at nine in the evening—as it was now. Her skin was lightly tanned rather than the alabaster white he might have expected given her coloring. Then there was the model's body that showed off to perfection the short jacket over a gauzy blouse and full print skirt that skimmed her knees. She was taller than most of the other passengers even if he discounted the ridiculous wedges of cork she was standing on and passing off as shoes. Why, he wondered, did women, beautiful women, do that to their feet?

He moved closer to the escalator and held up the sign. He saw her see it and then him. In that instant she snapped the phone closed and hoisted the bag more securely on her shoulder as she tightened her grip on the rolling suitcase and looked at him with a smile that was anything but genuine.

For an instant Cody was puzzled. Why wouldn't she be glad to see him—to see anyone representing the end of her journey? Well, not exactly the end. He wondered if Erika had told her about the change in plans. Maybe so. Maybe that's why she looked so…scared, he realized. She looked ready to bolt. That made no sense at all.

"Hi," he said as the escalator track disappeared beneath her feet and she fell forward. "I sure hope that you're Bethany Taft." He grinned as he steadied her with one hand while reaching for the carry-on with the other. He took a split second to enjoy the fact that she smelled as if she'd just stepped out of a shower rather than off a crowded airplane.

He made sure she was balanced on her platforms and then relieved her of the bag on wheels. He made a gesture toward the shoulder bag, but she tightened her grip and he assumed this mammoth thing was actually her purse. "I'm Cody Dillard, Ian's son." He offered her his hand.

She returned the handshake in a very businesslike manner. "Bethany Taft," she replied. "Nice sign," she added as if realizing that perhaps something more cordial was needed.

"I'd like to say I made it myself but the fact is..." Cody had started walking toward the exit expecting her to follow, then realized she was not moving.

"Ready?" he asked, waving away a porter.

"I have to get my luggage," she said.

What else could there be? Cody wondered but retraced his steps and took up the vigil with her and a hundred other passengers staring at the silent carousel and willing it to groan to life. It seemed as good a time as any to see if she knew of the change in plans.

"Did Erika call you?" he asked.

"I got the message—something about a change in plans. That she had to go somewhere with Ian and you would be here. Which you are. Thank you."

The carousel rumbled and started to turn.

"So, you know that we have one more leg of the journey." He breathed a sigh of relief. "The good news is that with the time difference, we'll be there at a decent hour. The bad news is that for you it will seem like the middle of the night."

She blinked, but said nothing. It was as if he'd suddenly started speaking in tongues. Finally she said, "The hour difference between D.C. and Chicago isn't really a big deal."

The crowd pressed forward as the luggage started appearing. "Actually," Cody said as he moved slightly to secure their position and protect Bethany from being jostled, "we're flying on to the ranch."

"What ranch?" she practically shouted, sounding borderline hysterical as she pointed to the biggest and most colorful suitcase Cody had ever seen.

The porter was still lingering nearby and he grinned at Cody when he saw the suitcase. Cody nodded and the porter went into action.

"There are two more," Bethany informed him. "Same pattern."

"Same size?" Cody asked and saw that it was exactly what the porter wanted to ask as well.

"Of course not," Bethany said. "One larger. One smaller." She pointed to the second piece as it trundled into view on the opposite side of the circle. "What ranch?" she asked again.

"The family ranch in Arizona," Cody replied without looking at her as he directed the stacking of the luggage. "Just outside Phoenix," he added and turned to find her gone.

"This is so not going to work," Bethany said as soon as Grace picked up. This time Grace answered her in a near whisper and Bethany regretted waking her friend. Grace was of the early-to-bed type while Bethany was the opposite. Bethany could not count the number of times she had awakened her friend with some disaster. Still Grace had promised to be there and it wasn't that late—even for Grace. "Sorry I woke you but—"

"No, it's Jud. Poor darling is exhausted. He just fell asleep on the sofa," Grace explained. "Let me get to the other phone." She covered the receiver with her hand and spoke tenderly to her husband. His response was a grunt.

"Jud's been working nonstop this week and he has an early meeting tomorrow," Grace said in a normal voice when she picked up the other phone.

"Sorry," Bethany said and meant it, but this was such a disaster and who else was she going to call? Grace was always so together. She would offer wise counsel and advice.

"You cannot back out at this point, Bethany," Grace said after hearing Bethany's abbreviated summary of events so far. "I don't care what the current situation might be. What's the problem? Does the son have two heads?"

"No, one quite gorgeous one with a body to match."

"Not that you noticed," Grace said, stifling something that sounded suspiciously like a chuckle but finally came off as a yawn.

"He's taking me to Arizona," Bethany said.

There was a pause on the other end that told Bethany that Grace fully understood the significance of this. "Arizona?"

"Arizona," Bethany confirmed and knew there was no need to add the obvious. *Arizona, where Nick died.*

"Well, honey, it's a big state."

Bethany knew she was doomed. Any time Grace called her *honey* it meant she was at a loss to offer advice. "Not big enough. The ranch is near Phoenix, which puts it near the mountains, which puts it—"

"Got it." Grace was quiet for a long moment.

Bethany saw Cody looking around for her while the porter waited patiently. "He's spotted me," she muttered. "What am I going to do?"

Grace took a deep breath. "You are going to go with him to the ranch and in the morning you can remind Erika why this setting is difficult for you. She'll understand and make sure you're on the first plane back to Chicago."

"You mean D.C.," Bethany corrected, not liking Grace's solution but knowing it was the only choice.

"I mean Chicago. Surely you can handle everything from there, and the change of scenery will do you good."

"Gotta go. My captor approacheth." Bethany shut the phone and turned to face Cody.

"Thought I lost you there for a minute," he said. She supposed that his smile made a defibrillator standard equipment for any woman within range of it. At least her heart was not in need of a jump start. It had died a year earlier.

"Let's go," she said in a tone that no one could mistake for enthusiasm. She waited for Cody and the porter to lead the way.

"I think we need to go up one flight if we're going to recheck the luggage," she said as they zigzagged through crowds of travelers and past the last escalator toward a long corridor that seemed to lead away from the main terminal.

The porter slowed and glanced at Cody. Cody spoke

to both of them as he explained, “We have to drive across town. My plane is at Midway.”

His plane? Did he say his plane?

Chapter Two

While Cody and the porter solved the puzzle of how to fit Bethany's mountain of luggage plus two people in the small sports car, Bethany walked around the parking structure hoping to find a decent signal on her cell and trying, without success, to reach her aunt Erika.

After all, she reasoned, this man calling himself Cody had offered no credentials—not that she had requested any. He could be anybody. He could have found the little sign and decided to see who would answer to his call. The fact that the license plate on the car read ID—as in Ian Dillard—meant nothing. The fact that a kidnapper wouldn't have the patience to retrieve her luggage and work up a sweat loading same into said vehicle… Okay, so he was probably who he said he was.

Bethany hit the speed dial for Erika once again. An impersonal recorded voice told her that the number she had dialed was not available. She could leave her number or a message. Bethany hung up. What was she going to say?

She heard car doors slamming and the murmur of an exchange between Cody and the porter as Cody handed him several bills. The porter laughed at something Cody said then trundled his now-empty cart down the aisle to where she stood. “All set, miss. You have a nice trip now.” He tipped his hat and headed back toward the terminal.

Wait! She considered shouting, but knew there was nothing the poor man could do to help. She turned and saw Cody leaning against the car. He was wearing a cowboy hat, and she couldn’t help noticing that it looked terrific on him.

“Any time you’re ready,” he called.

Was that sarcasm?

Bethany snapped her useless phone shut and strode back to the car, feeling fully in control until she got within two feet of where he still lounged against the trunk. Then she hit something on the uneven pavement and her ankle gave way. For the second time that evening he reached out and caught her.

“You might want to rethink those shoes,” he said as he set her back on firm ground with no effort.

Bethany made no comment, but walked—admittedly with more caution and a slight limp—to the passenger side of the car. Problem. Her overlarge bag-slash-handbag already occupied the seat.

“’Fraid you’ll have to hold that or stuff it on the floor under your feet. We kind of ran out of room,” Cody said as he climbed in, turned the key and backed out of the spot using the side-view mirrors. “Okay over there?”

“Just dandy,” Bethany replied.

He stopped the car and glanced at her. "I'm asking about the car next to you. Are we clear on your side?"

"Would you like me to get out and direct you?"

"Nope. Just look out that window there and tell me if I'm going to miss the guy's rear bumper."

When he stopped to pay the parking tab, she took the opportunity to study him again. She couldn't help noticing how he had the bored teller laughing and jabbering away with just a smile and a compliment.

"I like what you've done with your nails," he said as he handed her the money.

Bethany caught a glimpse of fingernails that were at least two inches long and painted in great detail.

"Let me see the full effect," Cody said.

The teller punched in the time on his card and then spread both hands for him to see.

"That's really something. Did you see this?"

This last was directed at Bethany so she leaned in for a closer look. "Amazing," she said politely as the teller revealed the silhouette of the Chicago skyline under a full moon spread across her two hands.

"You did that yourself?" Cody asked as the woman took his money and made change.

"My son," she replied. "He's a tagger—got himself in trouble a couple of times so I told him, if you're gonna paint, then make it useful."

"He's got talent," Cody said as he accepted the change.

The woman smiled and leaned out the window of the booth so she could include Bethany in the conversation. "You folks have a lovely night now."

Cody pulled the car forward and the gate opened. Bethany stared at him. Was this guy for real?

He maneuvered the car through heavy traffic and a maze of highway on and off ramps that made the complex street design of Washington seem almost simple. He made polite small talk about the flight, her family and living in the nation's capital. She was equally polite, if succinct, in her answers. She was still trying to digest the change in plans.

"How long are you planning on staying?" he asked after conversation between them had died.

Taking this as a comment on the amount of luggage she'd brought, Bethany bristled. It wasn't like her to take everything so personally but she was tired and this business of going to a ranch in Arizona when she'd prepped herself for life in Chicago was unsettling. Bethany did not deal well with change these days.

"I believe the wedding is to be set for spring. As soon as my aunt and your father are safely on their way to their honeymoon destination, I'll be on a plane back to D.C."

"To do what?"

Okay, it was an innocent question but it chafed because the truth was that she had no idea. In the year since Nick's death she'd been adrift, and the life she'd imagined living at this time was no longer available to her. And the truth was that she was not about to say any of this to a complete stranger. So she changed the subject.

"And what do you do?"

"I run the ranch."

"What about your father's business—I mean, what's your role in that?" she asked.

"It's my father's business. My business is managing the ranch." There was no hint of irritation in his comment. He was just offering information as requested.

Bethany's cell phone rang and she pounced on it as if it were a life preserver cast her way in the nick of time. When she saw that it was her aunt Erika's number she answered immediately.

"Hi."

"Hi, yourself. Did Cody find you?"

"He did," Bethany replied as she glanced at Cody and mouthed, "It's Erika."

Cody grinned. "Hey there, cowgirl," he shouted.

Erika giggled. "He's such a tease. Are you two getting acquainted?"

"More or less."

"Well, don't let him feed you anything—not that he would. He and Ian are single-minded when it comes to getting from point A to point B. Absolutely no stops unless you can prove a medical emergency."

"I ate on the plane."

"Peanuts or pretzels?"

Bethany smiled. "Pretzels," she admitted.

"Oh, Bethie, I cannot tell you what it means to me that you've come to manage this whole affair. I mean, I'm in a complete panic. Ian thinks it will be a cakewalk but what do men know? Are you at Midway yet?"

"Not quite."

"Well, tell that handsome cowboy next to you to step on it. We have a wedding to plan—not to mention at least half a dozen prewedding events. You're going to adore the ranch, dear. It will set your creative juices on fire with ideas."

"About the ranch—"

Erika laughed. "Not to worry, Bethany. *Crackle*… all the amenities…*crackle*…indoor plumbing and… *crackle*…breaking up…" The line went dead.

Bethany looked up and saw the signs for Midway airport. Cody took a side exit and drove directly up to a large hangar where a small jet waited.

In a flurry of activity, several men rushed around transferring the luggage from the car, driving the car away and ushering Bethany onto the plane. The man in charge assured her that they were cleared for take-off and, once they left Chicago, the weather was crystal clear all the way.

"Where shall I sit?" Bethany asked, glancing around the small interior.

"Might as well sit up front," the man replied. "That way Cody can point out the sights."

"He flies the plane?"

"It's his plane," the man said as if that were an answer. He helped her climb into the incredibly close quarters of the cockpit. "You might want to take off your shoes—it'll give you more legroom."

"I'm fine," she replied tightly. What was it with these people and her shoes?

The man nodded, handed her a headset and exited the plane. She watched as he conferred with Cody for several minutes, then took his leave—laughing, of course, at something the ever-cheerful Cody had said.

"Let's rock and roll," Cody said as he wedged his lanky frame into the pilot's seat and fired the small jet to life.

"You've been doing this for a while?" Bethany shouted over the roar.

"Maiden voyage," Cody replied deadpan and then he grinned at her stunned expression. "Relax. I've done over a thousand hours."

"In English, please."

"I'm an experienced pilot," he replied and taxied slowly toward the runway.

As they climbed smoothly above the earth, Bethany could not help but be impressed by the view below. Cody pointed out landmarks and Bethany relaxed as she enjoyed this bird's-eye view of the city. Maybe she could have a future in Chicago. The ranch was just temporary. Chicago was where Erika and Ian lived, where they had their life. She could deal with the ranch for a day or two, she decided and, as they left Chicago behind, she leaned her head against the window and fell sound asleep.

Cody had never met anyone as wired as Bethany Taft appeared to be. Anxiety and stress fairly oozed from her. It was as if she were fearful and certain at the same time that she would be blindsided by some unforeseen circumstance.

Not that he didn't understand that—he'd had a sense of subliminal panic ever since the day he'd gotten the call about his brother's accident. He couldn't help but wonder what might cause that look for Bethany. He'd first noticed it when he'd mentioned the ranch. Further evidence could be found in the way she tried to control everything and everyone. He'd done that in the first months after Ty died until he realized that all it did was feed his panic. What if he made the wrong decision, the wrong choice, as he had the day Ty died?

He forced himself to silence his inner voice and concentrate on Bethany. He could see the glint of her cell phone, still clutched in one hand. The thing was like an extra arm or ear or something. Personally he'd never been able to understand the constant need to be in touch with the outside world. What kind of person needed that? He preferred those times when he wasn't in touch with anything or anyone.

He hoped Erika knew what she was doing, asking this high maintenance, overreactive woman to take charge of the wedding. His father was anything but a snob. Still, there were certain expectations. Add to that the fact that Erika was nervous but also determined to make this the wedding of the decade in terms of surprises and memory-making events. Cody wasn't at all sure the redhead was up to the job.

On the drive between airports, he had made some attempt to get better acquainted. But her answers had been pretty monosyllabic and she had repeatedly allowed the conversation to die. Okay, so she'd had a long day. Okay, so traveling on to Arizona had not exactly been on her radar. But she was maybe thirty, in great shape—except for her penchant for foot-destroying shoes—and should not be so thrown by a simple change in plans. And where was her joy for her aunt and the fun of planning a wedding for this woman who clearly adored her?

With each thought, Cody's grip on the wheel tightened until the plane made a slight lurch, alerting him to what he was doing and waking his passenger.

"What?" she said, her eyes wide with fright as she peered out into the blackness of the night.

"Sorry about that." He raised his voice above the constant drone of the engine. "We're about twenty minutes out from Phoenix."

She nodded and flipped open her phone. He reached over and flipped it closed. "Might interfere with communications from the tower," he explained.

"I might have a message," she explained.

"It's waited this long," he replied and left the rest unsaid.

She stuffed the phone into the pocket of her jacket. She glanced around the cockpit as if looking for something to do. She drummed her manicured nails on her knee then reached for her seat belt. "I have to go to the bathroom," she announced.

Cody let go of the controls as he reached over to refasten her seat belt. "It's waited this long," he repeated with a grin and took some pleasure in realizing that up here, he was in charge, not Little Miss Cell Phone.

She squirmed in the seat.

"We'll be on the ground in another twenty minutes," he assured her and slowly turned the plane away from the lights of Phoenix toward the mountains.

"You're going to circle?"

"Nope. I'm going to land this puppy."

She glanced around wildly, twisting around to see the last of the lights and then leaning forward as a solid mass of mountains loomed larger and closer.

"Where?" she muttered and he read her lips.

He tapped her on the shoulder and pointed to a faint string of lighting at the base of the mountains. She looked at him wild-eyed as she clasped her hand over her mouth. For one terrible moment, he thought she might throw up.

"Bethany? Are you okay?"

She kept her fist jammed against her lips and stared straight ahead. As he banked the plane for the turn away from the mountains in preparation for his approach to the landing strip, she actually closed her eyes and planted her feet. It was clear that she thought they were about to crash. Cody was insulted. He straightened the plane's course and started the descent to the landing strip below, then tapped her on the shoulder and indicated the view of the ground rushing up to meet the landing gear.

He could see Erika and his father standing next to the golf cart used for moving between buildings on the large ranch. How would they fit all the baggage and three people on one little cart? But he was relieved to see them. It meant that he was free of hosting duties for the evening. He taxied to the hangar, cut the engine and in the sudden silence reached over and unsnapped her seat belt.

"Bathroom is just inside the front door of the house—if it's not too late."

"You scared me," she protested as he climbed out of

his seat and prepared to open the exit door. Her tone left no doubt that she thought he had done it deliberately.

"Ma'am, I was just flying the plane. You're the one who decided to panic for no good reason." He shoved the door open releasing the short flight of stairs and did not wait for her to go first.

Bethany took a moment to digest the fact that this cowboy son of her aunt's fiancé had just left her to crawl out of the cockpit on her own. Any gentleman would have helped her out—she was practically family, after all. Exactly who did he think she was? Some hired help brought in to manage the wedding?

"Bethany, dear."

Erika stood at the door of the aircraft, smiling uncertainly. "Is everything all right? Oh, I told Ian we should let you take a commercial flight tomorrow but he wouldn't hear of it. Waste of money, he said, since Cody was coming back anyway."

Bethany climbed out of the cockpit and bent to keep from hitting her head as she followed her aunt out of the plane. "I'm fine," she assured Erika, then mustered her last ounce of enthusiasm and gushed, "Chicago—now Phoenix—what an adventure."

Erika grinned with obvious relief. "It's called my life these days," she said happily. "Come meet Ian."

Ian was not as tall or hard-muscled as his son but he was every bit as handsome. They had the same eyes and the same smile—or at least she thought she recalled that smile from when she had first seen Cody holding that ridiculous sign. His smile and cheery outlook had definitely wavered as the evening went on. And was she being overly sensitive or had the man implied that this was somehow her fault?

"So this is Bethany," Ian said as he held out his arms inviting a hug. "You know, I've been telling Erika that it's time I met her family since she's already passed muster with all of mine. Welcome to Daybreak Ranch, Bethany."

Bethany smiled and accepted the hug.

"Where did Cody go?" Erika wondered as the three of them headed for the golf cart.

"He's making arrangements to get Bethany's luggage unloaded and delivered," Ian explained. "I hope he didn't give you too much of a joyride in that bucket of bolts of his," he continued to Bethany. "I've tried to get that boy to trade up but he loves that old piece of junk."

Oh, that was heartening, Bethany thought, glad all over again to be back on firm ground.

"Our Bethany is quite the little daredevil herself, Ian," Erika said as she wrapped one arm around her niece. "Remember, Bethie, that time that your brothers dared you to walk that fence at Grandpa's?"

Bethany grinned. "It was a wire fence with overhanging tree branches I could hold on to," she explained to Ian.

"She made it from one end to the other and then dared them to follow. Neither one of them would do it."

Ian laughed. "Well, little lady, I can see that you are going to fit into ranch life just fine."

Erika rolled her eyes. "Pay no attention to Ian, dear. Whenever we come to the ranch he turns into Clint

Eastwood. Anyone who has done business with him in Chicago is a little taken aback to say the least."

"Secret of my success," Ian said as he winked at Bethany, who found that away from the presence of Cody Dillard, she was feeling much more relaxed.

"Home sweet home," Ian announced as he pulled the golf cart to a stop in front of a rambling and deceptively massive house of glass, stone and adobe. Golden light spilled through windows that soared to a point three stories above the ground. A large, wide porch furnished with leather rockers and natural wicker tables and chairs wrapped itself around two sides of the house. The stained-glass panels of the front door reflected the light from within in a beautiful tableau of abstract desert flowers.

"Wow," Bethany whispered in awe as Ian held out his hand first to Erika and then her to assist them off the golf cart.

"Wow indeed," Erika agreed. "It was designed by an associate of Frank Lloyd Wright's. The first time I saw this place I set my cap for this man. He could have been from outer space for all I cared as long as he let me live in this beautiful desert palace."

"Ah, sweetie, you do say the nicest things sometimes," Ian replied and kissed her cheek.

Then he wrapped one arm around Erika and the other around Bethany and led the way up the wide stone stairs past columns sculpted to look like gigantic saguaro cacti. The front door should have been hanging in the National Gallery of Art as far as Bethany was concerned.

"Hi, Honey, we're home," Ian boomed as soon as they entered the house.

A short, heavyset woman of indeterminate age but with flawless skin, shining black hair pulled into a ponytail and a beaming smile hurried forward. She wiped her hands on her apron. "Hello," she said to Bethany. "I'm Honey Jorgenson. Welcome." She looked up at Bethany and frowned slightly. "Are you all right?"

Bethany had the oddest feeling that Honey had looked into her eyes and seen past everything she might do to disguise anything she was feeling. She blinked and forced a smile. "Fine," she said. "A little travel worn is all."

"Ah!" Honey snapped her fingers. "Powder room—" she pointed, indicating a small alcove off the foyer "—and then something to eat."

"Lovely," Erika said. "Honey makes the most incredible quesadillas, Bethany. I hope you like your food spicy."

"I love spicy," Bethany assured them all.

The supper was perfect. Honey served them in a small family dining room with stucco walls faux finished in shades of bright yellows and oranges. The table was set informally with multicolored striped place mats, bright Fiesta ware dishes and a centerpiece of red, yellow and orange gerbera daisies. In spite of her fatigue, Bethany couldn't help making mental notes as ideas for party themes and decor came to mind. She could bring the colors and atmosphere of Arizona to Chicago.

Erika and Ian were clearly devoted to one another.

This was no one-sided or even slightly lopsided romance. She had never seen her aunt happier and even though she had just met Ian, it appeared that he was operating in a similar state of bliss.

"So, what are your plans?" she asked after Honey had brought them large ceramic mugs of herbal tea and a platter of fruit.

"I'm afraid that all we have are dates and a start on the guest lists, dear," Erika said with a smile at Ian.

"Those would be *long* guest lists," he added fondly. "I think we may have to marry every year for the next ten or twenty in order to fit in everything Erika wants to do so our friends and family can share our joy." Then he squeezed her fingers and added, "Which would be fine with me."

"Well perhaps we could start with *this* year," Bethany suggested with a grin. "How many parties leading up to the big day?"

"Well, there's the engagement party in Chicago, for family and associates and friends there," Ian began.

"And the party for everyone here," Erika added.

"Two engagement parties? It might be less expensive to—"

Ian held up Erika's hand displaying a formidable emerald-and-diamond engagement ring. "Expense is not an issue, Bethany. If it becomes one, we can always hock this."

Erika giggled and blushed like a twenty-year-old. "Ian," she chastised. "Truly, Bethany, the parties can be fairly simple."

Bethany nodded and stifled a yawn.

"Oh, Ian, we're forgetting that it's the middle of the night for this young lady. We'll talk about this in the morning and let you get some rest, dear."

"No, I…well, if you insist," Bethany said with a smile. "I am a little tired."

"Honey!" Ian boomed.

"Don't shout," Honey admonished him as she appeared instantly in the doorway.

To Bethany's surprise, Erika, Ian and Honey walked with her to the front door. Erika promised to be along soon, but told her not to wait up. Ian kissed her on the cheek and wished her a good night while Honey waited by the open door. *Not another change of venue,* Bethany thought as she followed Honey out onto the porch.

"Hopefully all of your things have already been brought over to the guesthouse. If not, I can get you whatever you might need for tonight." She walked with surprisingly long strides for such a short woman. Bethany had some trouble keeping pace.

"Are those things comfortable?" Honey asked, looking down at Bethany's shoes.

Another comment on my shoes, Bethany thought wearily. "Yes," she replied and could not keep the edge of defensiveness from her voice.

"I love shoes," Honey said, sighing, "but I'm too chicken to try something like that. I'd probably topple right off them and look utterly stupid."

"Actually I did topple off them tonight," Bethany admitted, "and looked utterly stupid, but I am not about to give them up."

Honey grinned. "Perhaps you and I can go shopping

one day and you can help me find shoes and a little of your courage."

They had traversed a long stone pathway and reached a smaller version of the larger house. Bethany had noticed it on the ride in from the landing strip but never dreamed it was a separate guesthouse.

"Erika thought you would be more comfortable here than in the main house," Honey explained as she opened the door and led the way inside. "She hasn't said anything but it seems to me, meeting you, that you have suffered recently. It's in your eyes."

"I..." Bethany felt tears well. How could this woman know? "It's been a tough year," she said and then turned her attention to her surroundings. "Oh, Honey, isn't this wonderful?"

"It's pretty special," Honey agreed. "Erika's room is there." She motioned down a short hall off the kitchen as she moved about the spacious cottage, igniting the gas fireplace, pulling drapes closed and checking the refrigerator to be sure it was stocked with beverages and fruit.

"Your room is here," she said and led the way to a large bedroom where she opened the closet to reveal all of Bethany's clothes. "Good," she murmured as she turned back the duvet on the large cypress-framed bed.

"Good? It's incredible," Bethany said. "Who did all this work?"

"I sent my daughter, Reba, over to check on the luggage while you were eating. She must have put everything away." Honey smiled the smile of a proud mother and continued the tour.

"Bathroom is here," Honey indicated as she flicked on the light and visually checked to be sure everything was in place, "and in the morning you can breakfast on the porch off the living room. Best view on the ranch."

"It's all wonderful. Thank you so much, Honey. And please thank your daughter for me."

Honey grinned. "Get some rest. Erika has been on pins and needles waiting for you to arrive so the two of you can start planning parties. To hear her tell it, you are a master at this and frankly, we're all excited to see what surprises you come up with for Ian and his lady."

"I'll do my best," Bethany promised as she walked Honey back to the door and waved good-night.

Alone after a day of crowds and unexpected schedule changes, she let out a breath of utter exhaustion. The fire flickered and the oversize bed beckoned. Who would have thought a ranch could be so luxurious? She couldn't wait to call Grace and tell her that maybe things were going to work out after all.

"After all, it's a few days and then back to Chicago. I can handle that," she announced as she showered and changed into the nightgown Honey's daughter had left out for her. "I can handle anything for a few days." And for the first time in months, Bethany fell asleep looking forward to what a new day might bring.

Chapter Three

Unfortunately, the new day brought with it more than one unexpected problem. The first being the "best view on the ranch."

"Wake up, sleepyhead," Erika sang out gaily as she pulled open the drapes on the bedroom window, filling the room and Bethany's bleary eyes with sunlight brighter than she had ever before experienced.

But it wasn't the sunlight and Erika's cheery greeting that brought Bethany crashing back to the reality of why she had dreaded the change in plans that brought her to Arizona. It was the sight outside the window.

A cloudless blue sky and bright sunlight undiffused by smog and pollution brought every detail of the view into sharp distinction. But the focus of that view was none other than a range of immense and—to Bethany's eye—almost sinister mountains. They were closer than she might have imagined, had she considered it at all. She could actually see details—jagged cliffs and shadowy hollows that seemed to lead into nameless voids.

Voids like the one just miles north of here where Nick had fallen and died. She stood staring out at the scene for a long moment, then ripped the drapes closed again.

"Too bright. Too early," she explained when she turned and saw Erika's puzzled look.

"Coffee," Erika said. "That's what you need." She headed off to the kitchen and continued the conversation while Bethany dressed and made the bed.

"Did you sleep well?"

"Fine," Bethany called as she mentally rehearsed the speech she knew she must deliver before this thing went any further. She dressed in jeans and a white cotton T-shirt enhanced with the turquoise necklace Erika had sent for her birthday.

"Out here, Bethie," Erika called when Bethany headed for the kitchen. She followed the sound of her aunt's voice out to a small screened porch.

The bistro table was set with woven placemats, contemporary free form plates and tall red-and-black mugs that coordinated with the placemats and the striped black-and-red cloth napkins. Erika looked up, a pitcher of what could only be fresh-squeezed orange juice in hand.

"You look wonderful, dear. I knew the necklace would be perfect."

Bethany fingered the stones and smiled.

"Sit, sit," Erika invited as she filled the mugs and then set a basket of pastries and a bowl of fruit on the table. "Not there. Here—where you can see the view."

Bethany had deliberately taken the chair with its back to the mountains. "No, this is fine. I'm not used to the brightness. Too used to things being filtered through smog," she added.

Erika's expression sobered and she seemed to consider saying something and then rejected that idea. Instead she took a deep breath, closed her eyes and released it. "It is so wonderful to breathe truly fresh air, don't you think? I mean you can practically feel yourself getting healthier, stronger."

Actually, Bethany was thinking that absorbing the first cup of coffee intravenously might help clear her head. She was still fighting the unexpected twists of her journey and had not slept well, haunted by the usual dreams of Nick. She was going to need to be at her sharpest if she was going to find a kind way to tell her aunt that there was no way she could stay here.

"Auntie Erika," she began as Erika filled their mugs. She ignored the food in favor of breathing in the aroma of the coffee.

"Uh-oh," Erika said, helping herself to a sweet roll and a banana. "You never call me Auntie unless you want something."

This was going to be a lot harder than Bethany had imagined. How self-centered was she that she couldn't even let the woman have breakfast? She took a long swallow of the coffee and then smiled.

"I want you to tell me about this idea you have for not one but *two* engagement parties," she said and reached for a cherry-filled muffin.

Three small muffins, a substantial bunch of grapes and two more cups of coffee later, Erika was still dictating a verbal list of events and details that would need Bethany's expertise.

"Are you sure we can do all this in a few short months?"

"If anyone can, it's you." Erika glanced at her watch. "Speaking of which, the morning is speeding by. It happens here—you'll see. Now that I've given you plenty to think about regarding the party in Chicago, how about driving into town with me? I have a hair appointment and some shopping to do. Cody can show you the sights, or perhaps that ought to be *s-i-t-e-s,* since you'll need to familiarize yourself with venues for the party here in Arizona. Cody can fill you in on the best caterers and florists and such. He knows absolutely everyone in the area and, of course, they adore him. Cody is the nicest man—well, next to his father, of course." Erika reached across the round table and took the last bit of muffin from Bethany's plate and popped it into her mouth.

A car horn tooted in the background. "That'll be Cody. Go tell him I said to keep his boots on. We'll be there in a minute."

Bethany saw no way to refuse this request. When the horn sounded again, Erika laughed. "Never keep a cowboy waiting," she advised. "Especially not those named Dillard." She shooed Bethany toward the front door as she busied herself clearing the table.

The man was even better looking in broad daylight than he'd been the night before. He was standing next to an oversize pickup truck and was just reaching inside the cab to give another blast of the horn when Bethany opened the front door and stepped out onto the porch. "She's coming."

Cody grinned. He folded his arms across his chest and tapped one booted toe. He was wearing jeans and a denim shirt with the sleeves rolled back, revealing tanned and definitely sinewy forearms.

"Not good enough," he said. "I was promised the pleasure of squiring *two* good-looking women today."

"I'll see what I can do," Bethany replied and prepared to return to the house.

"Hey, Taft," he called.

She glanced back at him.

"I brought you something." He reached inside the cab and brought out a narrow-brimmed Stetson. He tossed it her way like a Frisbee with a flick of his wrist. The hat made a soft landing at her feet. "The desert sun can be brutal, and sunglasses aren't always enough."

Bethany bent and picked up the hat, surprised at its softness. "Thanks," she said.

"Try it on," he suggested, pushing himself away from the truck and making the short journey to the porch in less than half a dozen long strides.

She quickly perched the hat on her head. She had the oddest sensation that he might actually touch her and for reasons she could not fathom that was most unsettling. "It's great. Thanks. I'll get Erika," she babbled.

He reached toward her and adjusted the hat to an angle. "There," he said as he took half a step back to admire his handiwork. "Much better. I thought Erika said you knew something about fashion." The grin mitigated any insult she might have heard.

"I do," she replied with a sassy smile she hadn't used in months. "For example, you might want to...how did you put it...*rethink* those boots."

"Do you have any idea how long it takes to break in a decent pair of boots? These are just getting to the point of being ripe."

"I'll bet," Bethany said, unable to stop herself from laughing at the potential for double meaning in terms of *ripe.*

"Erika!" he called. "Your niece is picking on me."

Bethany could hear the rattle of china and a rush of water. Erika was just finishing the dishes.

"Some help I am," Bethany said, rushing to dry the last plate.

"Nonsense," Erika replied. "You're our guest, isn't she, Cody?"

Bethany wasn't even aware that Cody had followed her inside.

"Yeah, we pretty much give you a free pass for the first day. Tomorrow now, you'll be expected to be up at dawn and help with the chores." This last was delivered in the same Western twang Ian had fallen into the night before.

No wonder Erika loves him, Bethany thought. *Ian,* she mentally corrected herself. "I'll just get my sunglasses," she said and hurried off to the bedroom.

Cody dropped Erika at the beauty salon and promised to return in two hours. "Two hours? It only takes me twenty minutes to get my hair done," he teased.

"There's more involved than hair," Erika retorted and laughed when Cody held up his hands in surrender.

"I don't want to know," he said. "See you in two hours."

On the ride into town Erika had insisted that Bethany sit in the middle. Erika wasn't exactly being subtle in her attempts at matchmaking. Bethany couldn't help but wonder if Cody had noticed. When Bethany had suggested that perhaps she should go to the salon with her aunt, Erika had declined.

"For what? You look as if you just stepped out of the pages of *Vanity Fair*."

"We could talk some more about the wedding plans," Bethany said and hoped the hint of hysteria that she heard in her voice wasn't noticeable to Erika or Cody.

"Nope. Salon time is my time. You're stuck with Cody, poor girl."

After waving goodbye to Erika, Cody pulled back into the slow traffic. "Looks like you are indeed stuck with me," he said, "but I applaud the effort you made to avoid that."

"Not at all," Bethany protested.

Cody glanced her way and lifted one eyebrow.

The man had a way of making her feel flustered and her response these days was to become more than a little defensive. "Well, don't pretend like you were looking forward to spending your morning shepherding me around," she said.

"No need to get snippy."

"I am not getting 'snippy'—I don't even know what that means."

Cody drummed his fingers on the steering wheel. "Look, the way I see it we have arrived at a point of having to figure out how to best fill two hours without annoying each other—something we seem to be getting good at doing. Then in two hours we need to be back here to meet Erika. It would be nice if we weren't snapping at each other like a couple of ornery junkyard dogs."

Bethany considered and rejected several retorts. The man had a point even if his choice for illustrating that point might have been more flattering. "Look, I expect you see as well as I do what Erika is trying to do," she said.

"Erika is fabulous but subtlety is not her strong suit. She's harmless, though, and you have to admit that romance is something near and dear to her heart right now."

"Nevertheless, if you could just drop me at the nearest library or museum—whichever is closest—I can do some research."

"And what exactly am I supposed to do?" he asked as he pulled into traffic.

"That is entirely up to you. I'm sure you have better things to do than chauffeur me around. Besides, I'd really rather not feed into Erika's fantasy any further."

Cody observed her for a long moment—long enough for her to feel uncomfortable—and then he asked, "Have you always been this uptight, or are you just nervous about taking on this wedding thing?"

It wasn't a reprimand or sarcasm. It was more like idle curiosity. But what really set her off was the way he seemed to assume that she had always been uptight. If she cared about his opinion for one second, she would have him know that never in her life had she been described as uptight.

"Have you always been this rude?" she shot back and forestalled the answer he started to give. "It's a rhetorical question. And fascinating as this little point-counterpoint discussion may be I have work to do so please—"

Bethany grabbed for the dashboard to brace herself in spite of the fact she was wearing her seat belt as he pulled across three lanes of traffic and up to a curb. He reached across her and pushed open the passenger door. "Museum—right up those steps," he said. "I'll be back for you in ninety minutes. I'd appreciate it if you'd be out front here."

As soon as she was out of the truck, Cody pulled away.

"Of all the insufferable, arrogant, obnoxious, overbearing—" She was going to run out of adjectives before she reached the top of the steps so she started over.

Dinner was a stilted affair consisting of Honey's usual delicious fare interspersed with nervous chatter initiated by Erika to fill the silences that Ian seemed not to notice. Cody refused dessert and excused himself, citing the need to attend to some evening chores. That was only partially true. The thing he didn't say was that being around Bethany was—well, unsettling was the only word that came to mind.

After their first meeting at the airport and the flight

back to the ranch, he had been certain that he had her number. In spite of Erika's tales of a girl who kept the family laughing and a little off balance, the woman was pretty stereotypical for her age group and background. Pressed to describe her the evening before, he would have said she was into the latest trends and fashions, no doubt a slave to shopping, and a woman who hid any insecurities behind either her cell phone or a carefully maintained pose of superiority. In fact there were times when she reminded him far too much of his ex-girlfriend, Cynthia.

The truth was he hadn't liked Bethany very much on that first meeting. No, the truth was that he'd been disappointed—not selfishly, but for Erika and her fantasy of who her beloved niece was as an adult. Still, after gratefully turning her over to Erika, he had had second thoughts. He kept going back to that look in her eyes. He'd noticed it again earlier on the drive back to the ranch. Her eyes revealed a mind racing along at warp speed, constantly aware of all around her. It was almost as if she expected something unpleasant, and did not trust finding out that there was nothing to worry about.

Curiosity and his innate empathy for the pain of others—even when he really couldn't define that pain—made him reassess his initial reaction to Bethany. Early that morning after bringing her to the ranch, he'd been eating breakfast in the kitchen, keeping Honey company as was his habit, when he'd decided that perhaps Bethany deserved a second chance.

"What are you looking for?" Honey asked as he rummaged through the catchall closet near the back door.

"Nothing," he replied at the same moment he spotted exactly the item he'd remembered being there.

"That was your mother's," Honey commented when he emerged with a lady's straw Stetson. She said nothing more, but her eyes locked on his as she continued to knead bread.

"I know. I just thought that maybe—I mean Erika's niece didn't know she was coming here—I mean she probably didn't think about—"

"She'll need a hat," Honey said as she snapped open a damp tea towel and spread it over the bowl of dough.

"You think it's okay then? I mean, I could pick one up when we go to town."

"It's already over eighty degrees out there," Honey observed. "By the time you get to town..." She finished that observation with a shrug.

"Right," Cody said more to himself than to Honey.

So the hat had been a peace offering, a way of starting over for both of them without stating the obvious, that they'd gotten off on the wrong foot. And it had worked—better than he might have imagined. Maybe Bethany had had some second thoughts, as well.

Either way, the trip into town had started off well. Wedding chatter between the two women, with Cody occasionally managing to get in a word or two, made it easy. But once they'd dropped Erika at the salon, things changed dramatically. The thing that annoyed him most was the way Bethany needed to control everything. To Cody that was a clear indication of someone seriously lacking in confidence.

So how was someone like that going to handle several major social events plus a high society wedding? How was she going to bring to the table all the tact and diplomacy that would be required? His dad didn't need any hassles, and Erika deserved the wedding she'd been dreaming of all her life. In his eyes, Bethany Taft was not the person to carry that off.

After they'd picked Erika up from the salon and headed back to the ranch, Bethany had become subdued, even withdrawn. Her conversation had consisted of polite responses to Erika's comments. As they got closer to the ranch, she fell completely silent, staring out the window. He'd also noticed the way she fingered the turquoise beads on her necklace, almost as if they were some sort of worry beads or rosary. She'd had that same tension the night before as he'd maneuvered to land the plane.

"You okay?" he'd asked when they reached the outlying gate proclaiming the entrance to Daybreak Ranch and Erika had gone to open it.

The smile had been as phony as it was the evening before. "Fine."

At dinner, she seemed to be working overtime at playing the fascinated guest. She was quick. Cody would grant her that. She had apparently realized that the house was Ian's pet subject and soon had him giving her the entire story behind Frank Lloyd Wright's deconstruction-of-the-box approach to architecture.

"See," Ian said with a sweep of his arm to include the sloped ceiling of the dining room that led the observer's eye straight to the low glass walls surrounding them. "There are no corners—mitered glass makes corners disappear and the low placement of the windows brings the courtyard in. The outside becomes part of the space and the stone cantilevers not only form the mantel for the fireplace but give the building support without being obvious."

"Brilliant," Bethany agreed, then looked slightly panicked as she realized that the topic of the design of the house had probably gone as far as she could take it.

"Well, if you'll excuse me," Cody had interjected, "I have some unfinished chores."

His father frowned but said nothing. Erika was clearly surprised but, as usual, found a way to make it all seem like just what she had planned. "Of course, Cody. I'm sure Ian has calls to make and Bethany and I still have tons to discuss and plan."

Bethany said nothing.

Outside Cody sought the refuge of the barn where the prized Thoroughbred racehorses the ranch was known for breeding were housed. He picked up a grooming brush from the pristine storage area beneath the display of trophies and ribbons and moved down the row of stalls. He stopped at the next to last stall and patted the high solid rump of Blackhawk, a black Arabian stallion.

Blackhawk snorted a greeting and stamped one back hoof. He stepped to one side as if making room for Cody in the narrow stall. Cody began the rhythmic grooming routine, ignoring the fact that not a hair was out of place on the massive animal. Blackhawk let out a breath that warmed the cramped space, then shifted restlessly.

"Easy, big guy," Cody murmured, stroking the

horse's neck. "Just stopped by for a little company. We'll ride tomorrow."

He considered his father's suggestion that he take Bethany for a tour of the ranch. Ian rarely asked him for anything. Ever since Ty and their mother had died, it was as if Ian was constantly afraid that he might lose Cody, too. In the old days he and Ian had enjoyed debating each other on controversial topics such as religion and politics. No more. These days Ian would occasionally let slip a look of disapproval as he had at the dinner table when Cody rose to leave, but he would say nothing.

Sometimes Cody wanted to shout at his father. "I don't have cancer and Ty didn't die of a heart attack or because you said the wrong thing to him. He died because he got buried in snow and couldn't dig his way out. He died because *I* wasn't there to dig him out."

But this last was never uttered—not to his father, not to anyone he knew, not even to God. It was just there, deep inside, the drumbeat that accompanied him everywhere he went.

He forced his thoughts back to Bethany. If he did take her out to show her the ranch, then maybe the best idea would be using one of the ranch's off-road vehicles.

"I can't imagine she rides," he mumbled.

Blackhawk snorted.

Cody stroked the horse's mane. "There's something about the ranch that seems to set her off."

Having said it, Cody realized it was true. For somebody like her, all city sophistication and highbrow clothes, maybe the setting was just a little too rustic.

Some women were like that. Cynthia had only pretended she loved everything that he did about the place. The majesty of the setting. The peace and quiet. The distance from the woes and tribulations of life in the city. The sense of being a part of God's world rather than trying to fit God into the human world.

No, Bethany didn't strike him as a nature lover. She'd thought she was packing for Chicago with all its theaters, art galleries and shops. Now that he thought about it, she had really seemed to come alive the closer they got to Phoenix. It was on the way back that she'd gone silent with every mile they traveled across the desert and into the foothills, leaving civilization in the dust.

Blackhawk shifted and gave an indignant whinny as if reading his thoughts.

"You think maybe we could change her mind, Hawk?"

The horse flung his massive head from side to side. Cody laughed. "Yeah, go ahead and pretend you understand what I'm thinking. I'm not buying it."

"Do you always talk to the horses?"

Cody dropped the brush as Blackhawk repositioned himself for a view of the intruder. Bethany took an involuntary step back.

"I didn't hear you come in," Cody said, retrieving the brush and moving out of the stall to stand next to her.

She pointed to Blackhawk. "Is that your horse?"

Cody nodded, trying to gauge her mood. "Do you ride?"

She smiled. "I have ridden—as a little girl. My uncle

had a farm in Virginia. But it was a pony. Nothing like this guy."

"Horses come in other sizes," Cody said. "In fact," he continued, "I was thinking we might go for a ride tomorrow." *No, you were thinking about NOT going for a ride.*

"Really?" In the shadows cast by the low work lighting it was hard to read her expression, but her voice registered doubt.

"Sure. You've only seen about one-hundredth of the ranch. I could give you the grand tour." *In for a penny, in for a dollar, as Mom used to say.*

She looked up and down the row of stalls. "I'd need a horse that's gentle and slow and—"

"Leave it to me," Cody interrupted and realized he was excited about the prospect of showing off the place he loved. Maybe she'd like it once she saw it through his eyes. "Seven o'clock?"

"In the morning?"

"Best time," he assured her. "Before the sun gets too hot."

She sighed. "Okay, but you'd better have a thermos of hot, strong coffee in your saddlebags, cowboy."

Cody laughed and walked with her out of the barn. They strolled toward the guesthouse in silence.

"Did you come out to the barn for a reason?" he asked as they passed the main house and waved to Honey through the kitchen window.

"I wanted to apologize and thank you."

"For what—on both counts?"

"It was very generous of you to give up your day for me."

"We aim to please, ma'am," Cody said in his best Western drawl. "And the apology?"

They walked for several steps before she replied. "Look, it's not something I want to go into, but sometimes I'm—that is, I can be a little—"

"Unapproachable?" As soon as the word was out of his mouth he wanted it back.

"I am not unapproachable," she argued. "I may not be the constant life of the party—if that's what you're looking for—but I have always been open and—"

Cody held up his hands in self-defense. "That came out all wrong. Now I'm the one who's apologizing. It's just that at the airport and then again today, you seemed…" He mentally ran through a list of possible adjectives and rejected them all.

"Well, I'm not," she said firmly as if he had delivered the list. They had reached the guesthouse and she marched straight to the door.

"Look, all I'm trying to say is that if this is a bad time for you, Erika and Dad would understand," Cody explained, losing some of his own patience at the way she seemed always on the defensive. "There are at least half a dozen professional wedding planners in Phoenix and a gazillion in Chicago that they could hire."

She wheeled around on him and in the light from the multiple windows surrounding the entrance, he could see fire in her eyes. "I *am* a professional," she said through gritted teeth.

"Of course. I mean, that's not what—"

The door to the guesthouse slammed, leaving him alone on the stone porch.

"Does this mean we are still riding tomorrow?" he called through the closed door, knowing she was still there since she hadn't moved past any of the windows yet.

No answer.

"I'll take that as a yes. Seven with gentle steed and coffee as ordered, okay?"

Silence.

"Okay. Seven-thirty but that's my final offer."

The lights inside went out.

Chapter Four

Bethany waited in the dark until the sound of his boots crunching the gravel on the path assured her that Cody had left. She was still smarting from the remark he'd made about Erika finding another wedding planner—a *professional* wedding planner. What did he think she was?

Okay so the emphasis on the word had been hers, but why include it at all unless he was making a comparison? Cody Dillard might fool some people with his aw-shucks, ma'am charm, but she wasn't buying it. He had been raised with the best that money could buy and when it came to choosing goods and services, she was sure that he preferred name brands. Admittedly, in the world of event planners, she wasn't exactly a household word.

Well, she would show him. She wasn't some ditz whose only reason for working was to earn more money to spend on clothes and hand-beaded purses. He'd obviously based his opinion of her on false—well, maybe not completely false—information. But there was more to Bethany Taft than he knew and bright and early tomorrow he was going to meet the *professional* businesswoman.

She was so wrapped up in jotting notes and ideas for Erika's wedding and planning her strategy for her next encounter with Cody that it was well after midnight when she finally fell into bed. And it was dawn before she realized that she had failed to close the drapes that shut out the range of mountains framed in the wall of glass.

But she could hardly ignore the red-orange glow that woke her the following morning. She was anything but a morning person, and yet Bethany sat up and watched in fascination. The arc of the sun's orb seemed to ascend the dark side of the mountain range until it had conquered the mountain and moved on to chase shadows from the desert landscape, backlighting giant saguaro cacti in the process. She was intrigued by the way the silhouettes of the cacti resembled people waving or gesturing as if in conversation with each other. It gave her a new idea for the party invitations.

When Cody arrived on Blackhawk at seven-thirty, he was leading a second horse. Bethany took special delight in his surprise at seeing her sitting on the porch of the guesthouse dressed and waiting for him. She flung the last of her coffee over the railing and set the mug on a side table as she pulled on leather gloves and the hat he'd given her.

"Good morning," she called with just the right amount of cheer and professionalism. She glanced at the extra horse—a small palomino that side-danced impatiently as Cody swung down from Blackhawk still holding the reins. "And this is?" Bethany asked, approaching the horse that up close seemed far too high off the ground to be successfully mounted.

"Thunderbolt," Cody replied, handing her the reins. The shadow cast by his Stetson made it impossible to tell if he was smiling, but Bethany was certain that he was.

Gingerly she patted the horse's neck. "Well, Mr. Thunderbolt, we have a lot of ground to cover this morning. Are you ready?"

Thunderbolt snorted and tossed his head, then stood perfectly still as if inviting her to mount.

"That's my boy," she said as she reached for the horn of the saddle and prepared to put one foot in the stirrup. Problem was the stirrup was about six inches higher than she could gracefully manage.

"Here," Cody said, offering a bridge of his hands for her to step into.

"Thank you," she said as she gave him her sunniest smile and accepted his help. This time his face was fully exposed as he looked up at her mounted on the horse. She took some pleasure in the confusion that was mirrored in his eyes. Whatever attitude he had prepared to deal with this morning, this one clearly wasn't it.

"We aim to please here at the Daybreak Ranch," he muttered as he returned to Blackhawk and fumbled with the closing on his saddlebag. He pulled out a red aluminum travel mug and held it up. "I believe you ordered coffee—strong and hot."

The last thing she needed was more coffee, but this was business and she had requested it. "Wonderful," she said, leaning down to accept the closed mug. She flicked the lid open and took a sip. "Just right," she assured him as she closed the opening and tried to figure out where to put the thing.

"Here," he said, handing her a portable cup holder. "Hook this over your saddle horn."

She saw that the holder had been specially constructed for just that purpose. "That's really cool," she said and meant it as she placed the mug in the holder.

Cody mounted Blackhawk and took a swallow from the mug she hadn't noticed on his saddle. "Ready for the grand tour?"

Thunderbolt pawed the ground restlessly. Bethany hoped the steed did not intend to prove his name was accurate. "Ready," she replied and tried to hide her nervousness behind a sunny smile. She produced a small notepad and pen from her jacket pocket and held them up for him to see. "I hope you don't mind if I make notes, ideas that might come to mind for the wedding events."

Cody nodded and tapped Blackhawk's flanks with his boot heels. Blackhawk headed around the house and Thunderbolt followed. Thunderbolt's sudden movement made Bethany's pen fly out of her hand as she fought to find a rhythm that would not have her rising several inches in the air and then slamming back onto the hard saddle with every step.

In minutes they had put some distance between themselves and the buildings of the ranch and climbed to the top of a small rise. Cody reined Blackhawk to a halt and turned the horse to face the view below. Thunderbolt followed suit. Bethany fought to calm her racing heart and find a position on the saddle that didn't feel as if she were sitting on rocks.

"Bird's-eye view," Cody announced. "Down there is the hub of Daybreak—the house, guesthouse, stables, barn, paddock area, pastures, training corral. How about a rodeo?"

Was he serious? He certainly looked serious. "A rodeo?"

"For the engagement party here—could be a real hoot."

"Interesting idea," she said halfheartedly.

"Yeah. I can see it now—Erika could lasso Dad instead of a calf."

"You cannot be serious," she blurted.

Cody laughed long and hard. "Gotcha," he said, pointing his finger at her.

"Very funny," she said and even to her ears her voice sounded prim and petulant. She pretended an inordinate interest in her surroundings. "How far does your land go?"

"Far as you can see and then some." He turned in his saddle and motioned toward the mountain range behind them—mountains that were closer now than they had been from the guesthouse. "Our property stops at the base of the mountains there." He handed her a pair of binoculars for a closer look. "See that hollow over there just down from that first cliff? There's a cabin there."

She swallowed hard and peered through the binoculars, swinging them up and down and side to side until she saw the rustic cabin set into the curve of a solid granite fortress. "Very quaint," she said, handing the glasses back to him.

"That was Dad's first building here. When I was a kid we used to come here for family vacations and that was it. That little cabin at the base of the Superstitions."

Bethany thought she must have misunderstood. "Superstitions?"

"The mountains—that's the name of this range. Great, huh?"

"Perfect," Bethany replied without enthusiasm.

"Arizona is full of unique names. That spot where the cabin sits? It's called Bachelor's Cove."

"So is that where you live these days?"

Cody looked confused.

"Bachelor?" she prompted.

"Got it."

"You've never married?" she asked, more comfortable now that she'd turned the conversation to focus on him.

"Nope. Never married."

"You're what—thirty?"

"Thirty-four." His response was just to one side of testy. "I wasn't aware that there was an age limit."

She ignored his sarcasm and kept pushing. "You mean a wealthy good-looking guy like you has never even come close? The women must have been lined up at some point."

"Close only counts in horseshoes," he muttered and

readjusted his hat before urging Blackhawk a few steps closer to the edge of the bluff.

Bethany smiled. “So, there was someone. What happened—if you don’t mind my asking?”

It was pretty obvious that he minded very much. He tipped back his hat with two fingers and locked his blue eyes on hers until she had no choice but to look away.

“Some people—some women—are just born to be city dwellers. It’s really not their fault that they can’t see the beauty in a place like this, a life like this.”

The inference was transparent. Bethany shifted uncomfortably in her saddle in the knowledge that Cody Dillard had just described her. He seemed to have done so deliberately. He was watching her, those eyes boring into hers like lasers.

“Others,” he continued in that low quiet voice she’d first noticed last night in the barn, “like Erika, for example, can find beauty and a place to call home in the shadow of skyscrapers or mountains, metropolis or desert, so-called civilization or wilderness.”

“I suspect that’s because Erika long ago found her own inner peace and level of comfort,” Bethany said, surprising herself as well as she had apparently shocked Cody with her insight.

He blinked. “And now she has someone to share it with,” he added.

Bethany couldn’t help but wonder if the wistfulness she heard was actually there in his tone or something she had felt shift ever so slightly in her own soul.

The moment was heavy with unspoken understanding and unfathomable tension. Bethany cast about for a safer topic. "And what's the story behind naming it Daybreak Ranch?"

Cody relaxed and swung around in his saddle. He pointed to the mountains. "No other choice. Did you see that sunrise this morning?"

"It was impressive," she said and meant it.

He looked insulted. "Impressive? See, that's exactly what I mean. It was awe-inspiring. It's the kind of stuff that makes people understand there really is something bigger than us. Like there really is some grand plan for this earth, God watching over everything."

"As I said, it was impressive," she repeated.

Cody stared at her while she pretended to concentrate on the view below. He let out a breath, whether in exasperation or just releasing air, Bethany couldn't say. "Ready to press on?" he asked and she couldn't help but notice the hint of something she could only interpret as disappointment in his tone.

"Sure." How much more could there be? He'd given her the Big Picture. Surely that was more than enough.

Blackhawk picked his way over the rocky soil and deep ruts that Cody called dry washes. Thunderbolt followed. The slower pace was certainly a more comfortable ride, but after they'd ridden in silence for several minutes, Bethany couldn't help thinking, *And the point of this little jaunt across acres of the same boring dry desert landscape is...?*

"This is all very interesting," she said with false cheerfulness after they'd ridden for nearly an hour with Cody providing a travelogue of names of mountain peaks and desert plantings. "I think I've got the picture."

He reined Blackhawk to a stop, bringing Thunderbolt to a halt as if the two horses were wired to the same system. "You don't want to go on?"

"No—that is—I don't want you using your whole day again just to show me around. This has been wonderful and gives me lots of ideas, but—"

"Like what?"

Because she had no answer, Bethany took his words as a challenge. She forced a laugh. "Men usually don't get it."

"Try me."

Was he testing her? Still looking for proof that she could really pull this off?

Bethany glanced down to hide her panic at having no real answer. Thunderbolt pawed a cluster of stones. "Colors," she exclaimed, mentally promising the horse an extra sugar cube. "See those stones? The white marbly one with pink veins?"

Cody nodded. He actually looked impressed. "What else?"

The man was impossibly persistent.

"Okay, well—"

"How about that muted green color in the sagebrush there? Does that work?" He was getting into this.

"It does. Then there's that deeper, almost burnished orange color on the boulders up there—makes the pink less girly—more mature—like Erika and Ian."

Cody grinned. "See? Told you the place is a veritable artist's palette."

"Exactly. So, your work here is done." She gathered the reins and prepared to turn back. "Do we take the same route back?"

"Honey packed us a picnic. Thought we'd have it up there." He nodded toward the rocky path that, to Bethany, looked as if it climbed straight to the top of one of the lower peaks before dropping off into oblivion.

"On that mountain?" she asked, trying hard to form the words around the sudden cotton that seemed to fill her mouth.

"That's no mountain, Bethany, just a little rise in the desert." He turned in his saddle and pointed back toward the Superstitions. "*Those* are mountains."

"What's up there?"

"You'll see," Cody said and spurred his horse into action. "Come on. You'll love it."

"As if I had a choice," Bethany muttered to herself as Thunderbolt dashed after Blackhawk.

To her relief, the trip was shorter, the trail was wider and the horses were more sure-footed than she might have imagined. Besides, she was distracted by the sudden realization that she had made a huge mistake in selecting a fleece top instead of layers she could easily remove. Against her bare skin and under the scorching sun, fleece was doing a great imitation of goose down.

At the top of a flat bluff, Cody stopped and dismounted. "Here," he said, tossing her a bottle of water as he unhooked the saddlebags from Blackhawk. "Sun's getting pretty hot and you need to replenish fluids."

Bethany caught the bottle. "I think I still have plenty of coffee," she said.

Cody shook his head. "No more coffee. It'll just dehydrate you more." He dropped the saddlebag and held out his arms. "Swing your leg over and slide down," he instructed.

"I can do it," Bethany said, dismissing his open arms with a wave of her hand. She stood in the stirrups and tried kicking out of one so she could swing her leg over the horse's rump and dismount as she'd been taught by her uncle.

"Have it your way," Cody replied, dropping his arms but not moving away from the horse's side.

Bethany freed her foot and began the maneuver to dismount but accidentally kicked Thunderbolt's hind quarters in the process. The startled horse snorted and leaped forward a step, sending Bethany flying and straight into Cody's arms, her left foot still solidly planted in the stirrup.

"Great way to break an ankle," Cody mumbled as they both took a moment to catch their breath.

The combination of the heat, the fleece and the exertion—not to mention being this close to an attractive male for the first time in over a year—was catastrophic. Bethany felt her face flame red and sweat pour in rivulets down her cheeks and neck.

"Just put me down, okay?"

"Yes, ma'am." He disentangled her foot with one hand while balancing the rest of her between the hard planes of his body and a suddenly docile Thunderbolt. "There you go." He set her on the ground and walked away, grabbing the saddlebag as he went and heading for what seemed to her to be the very edge of the cliff.

"You know—not that I want to interfere with your choice of dress or anything—but you'd be more comfortable if you'd take off that fleece," he said.

"I..." All snappy retorts failed her. "I can't," she admitted.

He turned and squinted at her and she was sure she saw the beginnings of a laugh tugging at the corners of that handsome mouth. "Why not?" he asked, all innocence.

"Never mind," she huffed and thrust the sleeves up to her elbows.

Cody chuckled as he rummaged through the saddlebag, pulled out a neatly folded T-shirt and tossed it to her. "Here. Go put this on before I have to cart you out of here with heatstroke."

"I'm fine. Let's just head back to the ranch."

"Stop being stubborn for once and go change. It's clean, and I'm not looking." He turned his back on her as if to prove the point.

Bethany edged toward some low bushes—not that they would afford much cover, but they were the only choice.

"You might want to avoid those particular bushes," he said, as he knelt, his back to her, and started unpacking the picnic.

"I thought you weren't looking," she said, hugging the T-shirt to her unshed fleece.

"I'm not, but I figure you don't trust that and will seek cover."

"Gee, wonder why."

He said nothing.

"Okay, I'll bite, what's wrong with these bushes?" she asked irritably.

He turned and tossed a small rock into the cactus a few feet from where she stood. To her amazement the bush exploded, sending balls of sharp-needled foliage several inches in all directions.

"They're called shooting cholla. Nasty little buggers." He turned back to unpacking the lunch. "Probably a little safer back down the trail a bit."

Stepping gingerly around anything resembling one of the exploding cacti, Bethany edged her way back down the trail. She looked in all directions making sure she had no audience, then changed.

"One more thing," Cody's voice boomed from beyond the rise. "Sidewinders. They like to come out about this time of day and sun themselves."

"What are sidewinders?" Bethany called back as she tried to repair her hair.

"Rattlesnakes."

Bethany gave a little shriek and scampered back up the trail. Her hair would just have to do until they were back to civilization.

Lunch was a feast of tortilla wraps filled with fresh vegetables and cold barbecued chicken. There was also fruit and Honey's special trail mix chocolate chip cookies. Bethany could not believe how much she ate or how ravenous she was.

As they ate, Cody pointed out the sights below. In one direction they could see parts of the sprawling metropolis of Phoenix. In the other was the Superstition

Wilderness dotted with rock formations that seemed to spring right out of the ground, towering saguaros and the squatter barrel cacti all interspersed with sage, prickly pear and the seemingly innocent chollas.

It was plain to see that Cody loved this land and seeing it through his eyes, Bethany had to admit that it did have a certain unique beauty.

"Water," Cody ordered, motioning toward her barely touched bottle.

Obediently Bethany uncapped the bottle and took a sip.

"Drink it all," he said, draining his own bottle before lying back with his arms forming a pillow and his Stetson shading his eyes.

Bethany leaned against a boulder, relishing the warmth of the rock against her back. "Well, you've certainly provided the grand tour. Thank you."

"You're welcome. I'll say this, you've really got an unusual way of approaching this wedding planning thing."

Was that another dig at her professionalism? Bethany stiffened. "How would you approach it?"

He chuckled. "I wouldn't touch it with a ten-foot pole. That sort of thing is for—"

"Women?" She wondered why his opinion set her off like that—and why his opinion should matter to her at all.

He tipped his hat up with two fingers and squinted at her. "I was going to say *professionals*."

"Which you assume I'm not. But enough about me."

He scowled at her. "Don't put words in my mouth, Bethany."

This order was followed by an uncomfortable silence during which each of them looked around for something else to do. Finally Bethany sighed and made the first attempt at turning the conversation to a lighter topic.

"Speaking of weddings, let's get back to how you've remained a bachelor."

"I told you. I haven't met the right woman," he replied as if he'd answered that specific question more times than he'd like to admit. He pulled the hat forward again and folded his arms across his chest.

"Case closed?" Bethany asked, enjoying his discomfort more than she should have.

"Why? You interested?" came the muffled reply accompanied by that devastating grin.

"Cute."

Cody seemed content to drop the discussion. His breathing was even and for all she knew the man had dozed off. Bethany looked around for something to occupy her until he woke.

She could take a walk, but then those shooting things might attack—not to mention snakes. She shuddered. Then she walked over to where the horses were hobbled and retrieved her notebook.

"Cody? Do you happen to have a pen or pencil?" she asked in a near whisper in case he really was sleeping. "I want to make some notes."

Without sitting up or uncovering his eyes, Cody fished the stub of a knife-sharpened pencil out of his shirt pocket and held it up to her.

Bethany turned her back to him and began recording her thoughts. First she gazed down at the city, but her thoughts were on the sprawling landscape behind her—the desert leading up into the foothills and then on to the rugged country of the mountains. Slowly she turned until she was facing the wilderness. And thinking about Nick.

What had it been like that day? Sunny and hot like this? Nick would have loved that. She could almost see him striding across the rocky terrain, his eye on the summit he planned to conquer. She recalled the many times she'd watched him climb the fake rock wall at the gym where they worked out together. How long had it taken him to realize that while the footholds and handholds on the gym wall were conveniently available to take him to the next level, in the real world it was never that easy? She brushed away a tear.

"Anything inspiring or are you ready to move on?" Cody asked. The gentleness in his tone told her he hadn't been sleeping at all. He'd been watching her.

She snapped her notebook closed. "I'm ready," she replied.

Cody pushed himself up until he was facing her, leaning on one elbow. He picked up a shiny white rock with veins of pink and stacked it with another that was shades of mustard and gold and a third in the deeper rust brown. "It's called a cairn," he said. "Hikers use it to mark the trail—for themselves and for others. Of course, in our case, it could just mark a place where inspiration struck, right?"

Bethany did not miss the way he said "our" instead

of "your," nor could she ignore the ripple of pleasure she felt at the idea they were working together.

At dinner that evening, conversation was far livelier than it had been the evening before. Bethany even told Ian and Erika about Cody's idea for a rodeo engagement party.

"At first I actually thought that the man was serious," Bethany said.

"Well, it's not entirely out of the question," Erika replied. "I mean, it has just the right sort of unique flavor."

"Auntie Erika, you can't really—"

Erika waved Bethany's protest away. "Not a rodeo per se, of course, but you get the idea. That sort of informal, unusual flair. What other ideas did the tour inspire?"

Ian stood up. "I think this is our cue to leave, Cody." He kissed Erika's forehead as he passed her chair and nodded to Bethany. "Try to keep everything somewhere in the continental USA, okay, ladies?"

As soon as the men had left the room, Erika pulled her chair closer to Bethany's. "So, you had fun today. Good. I was certain that a new project and new environment would help you."

"Help me?"

Erika placed her hand on Bethany's knee. "Come on, Bethie, you know what I'm saying. Nick was—"

Bethany felt the familiar wave of disloyalty and guilt that came with any mention of Nick. "Cody was an excellent guide," she interrupted.

"But?" Erika was not going to let it drop.

"But I already have friends and I'm not ready for anything more," Bethany replied. She placed her hand over Erika's to soften the reproach. "So stop match-making, okay?"

"I just want you to be happy again," Erika replied.

"I know, but this is your time."

"You're right. Oh, Bethie, I never dreamed that love could come to me so late in life. I had all but given up, but it just goes to show that God works on His time-table, not ours."

Bethany studied the girlish rapture that lit her aunt's face. It was indeed Erika's time and Bethany could make a difference by planning the most spectacular calendar of events any bride-to-be had ever dared imagine.

"Then trust me to plan the dual engagement events and surprise you, okay?"

"On one condition."

Bethany frowned, expecting another attempt to push her toward Cody. "What condition?"

Erika grinned. "No rodeos."

Chapter Five

After using most of her cell phone minutes to gather information on possible settings for the dual parties, Bethany came up with a framework for all events leading up to and including the wedding itself. What if she planned events that followed the path of Erika and Ian's romance? A love story come to life?

"That ought to impress Mr. Cody Dillard," she muttered.

Bethany was determined to prove herself to Cody. She certainly did not understand why, but the fact was that she felt she had to win his approval.

I'm going to need help.

Unable to sleep, she confided her idea to Honey over tall glasses of orange juice the following morning. "But I need details," she moaned. "Like how did Ian meet Erika?"

Honey laughed. "That's an easy one. Erika taught Ian how to properly swing a hammer."

"You're kidding." It was difficult to imagine her stylish, never-a-hair-out-of-place aunt picking up a hammer, much less teaching someone like Ian to use it.

Honey got up to get more ice for their glasses. "Ever hear of Habitat for Humanity?"

"Of course."

"Well, it's a pet charity for Ian and apparently for Erika as well. The organization was building a house in Chicago and Erika had volunteered to take a group of youths from her church there to help."

Bethany rested her elbow on the breakfast counter and her chin in her hand. "What happened?"

"The way Ian tells it, Erika showed up in denim coveralls that looked as if they'd just come out of the store catalog—"

"Which they probably had," Bethany added.

"Her little group was assigned to nail down the plywood base for the flooring and Ian was assigned to show them how to do it."

"But you said Erika taught him."

"She took one look at Ian holding that hammer and tapping at the nail and couldn't stand it," Honey continued. "She gently removed the hammer from his hand, and in three swings had the nail hammered in place."

"What did Ian say?"

Honey started to giggle. "Erika says he stood up, faced the young people and said, 'And there you have it—the wrong way to hammer a nail and the correct way. Do it the correct way and we'll be out of here in time to go for ice cream. My treat.'"

"No wonder she fell in love with him," Bethany said wistfully as she made notes. "So, I need to get in touch with Habitat in Chicago." She shut the notebook, drank the last of the juice and carried her glass to the sink. "Thanks, Honey," Bethany said, trying to keep her tone upbeat. But her eyes brimmed with unshed tears as she ran water and washed her glass. The hammer story had triggered her own memory of a time when she and Nick had been trying to repair her bike. A time when they were still just friends. A time when she'd felt something beyond friendship for the first time.

"Ladies." Cody acknowledged both of them as he passed through the kitchen. "Need anything from Chicago?"

"Not me," Honey replied. "Will you be back before midnight?"

"Only if it means one of your fabulous midnight suppers."

Bethany suddenly had a thought. "You're flying up to Chicago now and you'll be back tonight?"

"That's the plan."

"Could I come along?"

Cody looked surprised. They were getting along in the polite way that people did when they were thrown together for a limited period of time because of relatives. But since the tour of the ranch neither of them had exactly sought the other out.

"Well, sure, if you want," Cody said.

Bethany turned to Honey. "I need you to keep it quiet that I went with Cody. Tell Erika that I went into town to do some research."

"And when you're not here for dinner?"

"Erika and Ian are going out tonight—some charitable thing at the museum in Phoenix. By the time they get home, Erika will assume I'm fast asleep."

Honey smiled. "Okay, go. Your secret is safe with me."

Bethany could see by the way Honey winked at Cody that the housekeeper thought she was advancing the cause of romance. It was also clear that Cody was equally in the dark about why she had suddenly come up with something that could only be accomplished by spending long periods of time alone with him in the close confines of his plane.

"I just need to swing by the guesthouse and get my bag," she said and headed across the yard.

"I'll pick you up," Cody called after her then turned back to Honey. "What's this all about?"

Honey shrugged. "Beats me. Maybe something to do with the wedding?"

"Yeah, maybe."

"Could also be something to do with you," Honey added.

"Now *that's* unlikely," Cody said.

Bethany rushed out of the guesthouse, large bag over one shoulder and cell phone to her ear when Cody pulled up in the golf cart. She climbed in next to him and kept talking.

"You do? That's fabulous. I'm on my way. I can be there by…three?" She glanced over at Cody for confirmation and kept talking. "Well, I'm in Arizona and we have to fly to Midway and then—" Cody nodded.

"Okay, see you at three." She clicked off the phone and grinned as she made notes in her dog-eared notebook.

"What's up?" Cody asked as he drove the golf cart down the winding asphalt path to the landing strip.

"Just some wedding business," she said and kept jotting notes in the notebook.

"In Chicago?"

She looked up. "Well, of course. After all, that's where the wedding will be, and there are a million details to—" Something in his expression told her she'd gotten some part of that wrong. "What?"

He shrugged and pulled the golf cart to a stop. "Nothing." He reached for her bag. "This it?"

"Yes, thank you."

"You're sure?"

Still lost in what his question about Chicago might have signaled, Bethany completely missed the fact that he was teasing her. "That's it," she said with a hint of irritation and then saw that he was holding the single tote bag with a couple of fingers and grinning at her.

"Oh, you mean, I usually don't travel this light?"

"You said it, I didn't," he replied and headed for the plane.

"Cute," she said, hurrying after him and grabbing the bag from him. "I can manage, thank you."

He tipped his hat then turned his attention to the plane. "Go ahead and board," he told her. "I just have to go through this checklist and file the flight plan."

In broad daylight Bethany was more aware of the age of the plane—the "bucket of bolts," as Ian had called it. It was clean and felt sturdy enough, but was it really safe? She tested the handrail on the short stairway into the cabin. It rocked slightly from side to side.

"Yeah, that needs tightening," Cody said from his position on the ground. He kicked the tires on the landing gear. "Probably could use some new treads here, as well. After this trip I'll get her into the shop for a real overhaul."

"After this trip?" Bethany swallowed hard. "You know, I really could do this over the phone." She shielded her eyes from the sun and smiled at him. "Really, this isn't at all—"

"Relax. I'm kidding around." He studied her for a moment. "You are one high-strung dame, Bethany Taft. Wanna tell me what's got you so wired?"

"Wanna tell me why you get such a perverse pleasure out of teasing me about things that have to do with life and death?" she shot back.

"Just trying to lighten the mood." He started up the steps behind her. "Are you coming or going?"

She marched up the remaining two steps and into the cabin. Instead of climbing into the seat next to him in the cockpit, she chose one of four passenger seats in the cabin.

"Ah, come on Bethany, play nice."

"I have work to do," she said and snapped open the notebook and her cell phone to make the point. He reached over and took the cell phone and pocketed it. "Thought we had this straight—inside these walls, I'm the captain, okay? That means no cell phones."

He pulled the door shut and secured it, then climbed into the cockpit and started the plane's twin engines.

Just before starting the plane in motion he reached back and pulled a curtain shut, leaving Bethany alone. She tried not to be annoyed. After all, she was the one who had insisted on sitting in back.

As they taxied down the runway so he could turn for takeoff, Bethany was surprised to hear his voice over the plane's public address system.

"Ladies and—or rather, lady, we'd like to thank you for selecting Dillard Airlines today. Now please turn your attention to our hostess who will do her interpretive reading of 'Ode to FCC Safety Regulations.' Oh, so sorry, our hostess is not on board today, so please bear with me while I go over said regulations."

And then in a monotone he gave a rendition of "your seat belt works by..." and "should there be a change in altitude..."

Bethany could not help smiling.

The takeoff was so smooth that she didn't even notice when they soared past the mountains and climbed higher into the brilliant blue sky.

The PA system activated again. "Now that we have reached our cruising altitude, please feel free to move about, although we strongly suggest that you stay inside the aircraft at all times."

This time Bethany burst out laughing.

The curtain between them opened and Cody looked back at her. "Well, *finally.* I mean, this is my best stuff, lady!"

She grinned. "Okay, you win." She released her seat belt and climbed into the seat next to him. He had the good sense not to gloat.

"Now then," he continued in his best tour guide's style, "for those of you on the right side, if you'll look out your window you'll have a perfect view of…clouds."

Bethany glanced out the window in spite of her determination not to and giggled.

"And here on the left side," he continued, leaning forward, blocking her view, "is it? Why yes, it is," he said excitedly.

Bethany rose halfway from her seat and closer to him as she strained to see what might cause such excitement.

"It's…" He leaned back giving her a full view. "It's more clouds," he finished triumphantly.

Bethany collapsed back in her seat and punched him in the arm. But she was laughing and it felt so good. How long had it been since she had allowed herself to fully enjoy this kind of silliness?

The combination of guilt and grief—both her constant companions since Nick's death—rose inside like bile and silenced her laughter abruptly. She settled into her seat and turned her attention to the clouds outside her window.

"So," Cody said after a long moment, "do I get to know what's so important in Chicago that you were actually willing to spend all this quality time with me?"

There wasn't a hint of irritation or reproach in his tone. Bethany glanced at him. His features were passive, his focus on flying the plane. He was just making conversation.

"I was trying to come up with some sort of theme for the many parties leading up to the wedding—something to tie everything together."

Cody nodded. "Isn't it enough that Dad and Erika are in love and getting married?"

"Well, yeah—I mean, turns out that's the perfect frame for everything—they fell in love and now they will be married."

"I'm with you so far. What's in Chicago?"

"Habitat for Humanity."

"Okay, but they have chapters all over the country. Besides, what does a charitable organization that builds houses for low-income people have to—"

"Erika and your Dad met while working on a house for Habitat," Bethany reminded him.

Cody smiled. "I'd forgotten that."

"Well, it's probably not going to work, but I thought, what if we did the Chicago engagement party at a Habitat project and asked the guests to help Erika and Ian get another couple started and..." She tried to read his reaction.

First he frowned, then he was shaking his head.

"Dumb idea," she said, resigned. "I mean for Ian's crowd—Erika's friends would love it but I can see that—"

"It's a great idea," Cody said softly, looking at her with something that might be wonder or might be disbelief. "And Dad's crowd—as you put it—will get into it if for no other reason than the sheer novelty of it. But how are you going to pull this off?"

For the rest of the flight she pumped him for information about Ian and Erika. He wasn't much help and she sighed in exasperation as yet another question was answered with an apologetic shrug.

"I wish I had more to offer," he said. "It's just that Dad spends most of his time in Chicago and my life is on the ranch. It's only since he met Erika that he's started to spend more time there."

"It's okay. I'm sure that Honey can fill in a lot of the blanks."

"So what's the plan with Habitat?"

She told him about her contact with the director of the Chicago chapter and the fact that there was a project in progress that might be perfect. "It's a house for a young newly married couple expecting their first child—well, children. She's having triplets."

"Weather might be an issue," Cody noted as they flew through the gray overcast skies above Lake Michigan in preparation for landing on a snowplowed airstrip.

"I checked on that. The house is a rehab so it already has a roof, and the wiring and plumbing are all in. Then they ran out of money so it's been on hold for the last three months."

"When are the babies due?" Cody set the plane on the ground as easily as he might parallel park a car.

"Sometime in the spring."

"Then the timing is perfect."

"Still, I don't really know if this is the kind of thing that—"

Cody taxied to the hangar and cut the engine, then turned to her. "It's perfect, but don't take my word for it." He pulled her cell from his pocket and punched in some numbers.

"Hey, it's Cody." Three "Sure's" and two "Got it's"

later, he snapped the phone shut and presented it to Bethany. "Hope you didn't have any plans for supper."

It was all perfect—the house and the young Hispanic couple each working two jobs and expecting their first children. Then there was the setting of the house in an older tree-lined neighborhood that had escaped the trend for gentrification. Instead it had become a haven for those displaced by the boom in downtown luxury high-rise residential building.

"Erika is going to love this," Bethany said as she walked through the small house. It was not a new house in the sense of being built from the ground up, but rather a total renovation of an old abandoned property. Erika had always had a passion for preservation.

"The project had to be put on hold a couple of months ago because we ran into a problem with mold," Amy Barnes, the local Habitat coordinator explained. "Fixing that was more complex than we imagined. There was a time when we thought we'd have to give up and find another property."

"But you were able to fix the problem?" Bethany asked and Amy nodded. "I'm so glad. It's a wonderful house." She ran her hand over the smooth wood of a built-in china cabinet in the small dining room. "Wonderful details you just can't have without spending a fortune these days."

She had explained her idea to Amy on the drive over from the Habitat office. Amy had been thrilled on many levels, not the least of which was being able to tell the young couple that they could possibly be in their new house for Christmas—maybe even Thanksgiving. "The wiring is all in and the plumbing," she told Bethany. "I could speed up delivery of the donated appliances if that would help."

"It would be nice—we could have beverages and snacks here while the work is being done," Bethany replied as she imagined the kitchen freshly painted with cabinets stained and hung. "I thought we should have the actual celebration at a restaurant, or maybe Ian's town house?" She directed this to Cody.

He seemed to be spending most of his time lost in thought, wandering through the rooms until some detail caught his attention. From the expression of abject sadness she saw—and recognized from her own experience—she knew that he was not considering the logistics of hosting a party in this tiny house.

"What do you think?" she asked.

He shrugged. "You're the party planner." He glanced around the unfinished kitchen that led to the unfinished living-dining room that led to the unfinished hall leading to the unfinished bedrooms and bath.

Now that they were actually here, Bethany was once again doubtful of the entire idea. What had she been thinking? What on earth made her imagine that the movers and shakers of Chicago society would find it charming to don coveralls and wield paintbrushes and hammers for an entire afternoon?

Amy was watching her and in the coordinator's eyes, Bethany saw that she understood that Bethany was reconsidering this whole plan. "Perhaps a donation in honor of the couple might be an easier solution," Amy said softly.

Cody turned from his inspection of the workmanship on the front door and waited.

I will make it work, Bethany thought. *Erika will love the idea and I'll just find a way to make everyone else love it, as well.*

"Well, of course," she said aloud. "You'll let me know what it will cost to complete the work—paint, finishing molding—the works."

She glanced at Cody and saw that he thought she was giving up. Was he relieved?

"And if you could have everything here on the twelfth of the month, we'll have a couple dozen people here to supply the sweat equity and get this house finished."

Amy smiled broadly. Cody turned back to flicking the light switches by the front door. It was hard to tell what he was thinking and Bethany realized that she really wanted him to get on board with this project. Perhaps on the flight back she would broach the subject, find a way to convince him that it would all work out.

That would be right after I convince myself it will all work out.

Instead of having Amy drop them back at Ian's offices, Cody directed her to a brownstone town house a block off Lake Michigan and two blocks from the posh shops of Michigan Avenue.

"I want you to meet someone," was all Cody said after he and Bethany had thanked Amy and she had promised to be in touch to finalize the details. He dashed up the worn stone steps, past a tiny garden surrounded by an ornate wrought iron fence.

An elegant woman dressed in corduroy trousers and a heavy beige turtleneck opened the door and threw her arms around Cody before he could touch the doorbell. She was about sixty, half-glasses perched on her nose, her snow-white hair cut in a cap that highlighted her perfect bone structure and soft gray eyes. "And you must be Erika's niece," she said, turning her attention to Bethany.

"Bethany, this is my Dad's sister, my aunt Susan," Cody said before heading down the long hall toward the back of the house. "You got anything to eat in this place?" he called.

Susan rolled her eyes and smiled at Bethany. "Have I ever not had food for you, Cody Dillard?" She took Bethany's purse and jacket and hung them on the newel post before following Cody into the kitchen. Cody was at the stove stirring a simmering pot of soup. The table was set for three.

"This is so kind of you," Bethany said, indicating the table.

"Nonsense," Susan replied. "Cody will tell you that I am a frustrated chef and he certainly gives me every opportunity to prove it."

"I do what I can," Cody said as he tasted the soup and gave the thumbs-up.

"Come, sit, Bethany," Susan said, "and tell me your idea for the engagement party."

"It's pretty unusual," Cody said.

Unusual. Not great. Not incredible. Unusual.

"Tell her," Cody urged as he made himself at home in the kitchen, serving up bowls of barley soup, slicing a loaf of Italian bread, getting butter from the refrigerator.

Susan pulled up a chair next to Bethany's and waited.

"Well, it's still in the planning stages," Bethany said hesitantly. She glanced from Susan to Cody, wondering what this was really about. Had he brought her here so his aunt could give the family's final say to her idea? She took a deep breath and forged ahead. "As you can imagine, there will be a number of events leading up to the wedding. So I was thinking that an overall theme to tie things together might be a good idea."

Susan nodded, her soft gray eyes encouraging Bethany to continue as Cody took down glasses from a cabinet.

"The theme I came up with is Erika and Ian, a Love Story."

Susan clapped her hands in delight. "Perfect. Cody, there's cold cider in the fridge," she added without taking her eyes off Bethany. "Go on, dear."

"Honey told me that they met while working on a house for Habitat for Humanity." She recounted the story of the hammer, earning herself a surprised smile from Cody, who had finally joined them at the table.

"I never knew that," he said.

"So, I was thinking that perhaps—knowing how giving the two of them are and how important it is to both of them to share their good fortune—"

"You're having a rehab party?" Susan guessed. "I love it!"

"I know it might not be the usual…"

She loved it? Had she actually said she loved it? Bethany glanced at Cody and saw that he was bent over his soup bowl but he was smiling.

"Tell me everything," Susan urged.

Bethany laid out the broad details of her plan. "I thought the invitations might be in the shape of a house—"

"Exactly. And I have the perfect party favor." Susan pushed back her chair and rummaged through a large drawer in the butler's pantry next to the kitchen. She returned holding up a small hammer painted in bright colors, then proceeded to take it apart to show that it was actually a mini tool kit complete with screwdriver heads and even a small pliers. "Ta da! Three dollars at the discount store—shall I pick up a couple dozen?"

"Uh-oh, I've created a monster team here," Cody muttered as he got up to refill his soup bowl.

"You don't think—I mean, might some people think that—"

"And what if they do?" Susan replied. "That's their loss, isn't it? Those of us who get into this are going to have the time of our lives. More to the point, Ian and Erika are going to be blown away with delight. You must keep this a surprise, Bethany. It will add to everyone's pleasure."

For the better part of an hour Susan and Bethany sat at the kitchen table discussing the details of the party. Cody had excused himself citing the need to make some calls and attend to the business he'd come to Chicago for in the first place.

An hour later, just after Susan had finished telling Bethany the story of Ian's fear that Erika would turn him down, Bethany heard Cody's step in the hall. He lingered near the pantry doorway until Susan had finished describing the coveralls she'd seen at an art supply store, then caught Bethany's eye. "We need to get going."

Susan reached for a pad of paper and a pen. "Here's my e-mail address and cell phone number. Let me know whatever you need at this end."

"Thank you," Bethany said, "for everything."

"You are entirely welcome, my dear. No wonder Erika put you in charge—such wonderful, fresh ideas. I do hope that once your aunt and my brother are married you might consider spending more time here in Chicago. I know of several charitable events that have grown tiresome and predictable and could definitely use your fresh ideas."

"I'll think about it," Bethany promised and realized that she wasn't just being polite. She was good at this. Maybe Grace and everyone else had been right. Maybe she *could* start over someplace new.

Bethany fell asleep almost before they had reached cruising altitude and Cody was glad. He needed some time to think about the day. About the way the Habitat house had brought back memories of his brother, Ty. Where Cody had strolled through the rooms taking in the attention to fine detail, the restoration of vintage touches, Ty would have raced from room to room. He would have led everyone on a frantic tour, exclaiming excitedly over the leaded windows, the custom-built china breakfront, the restoration of original light fixtures. "Awesome," he would have declared repeatedly. To Ty, the simplest things in life had always been "awesome."

In the blackness of the night sky, Cody could see Ty's face—eyes on fire and mouth open exclaiming the pure joy of life. Ty had always been alive in a way Cody could not ever imagine. Alive as if somehow he understood that his time here was short. Had he known? Or had he—like Cody—cried out at the stupidity of the accident that had killed him? Had he—like Cody—wondered why his brother hadn't stopped him from going that day?

Bethany shifted in her seat, drawing his attention away from the memories of his brother and back to her. The day had been fun. He'd seen the way she'd been in the city—alive, vibrant, confident. At first he'd attributed her high spirits to the energy of planning the party. But it was more than that. He'd seen the same thing that day when he'd taken Erika and her to Phoenix. It was on the ranch or out in the countryside that she turned tentative, wary, restless.

So she was a city dweller, born and bred. He'd made the mistake once of thinking he could make someone love the desert and the quiet life of ranching. He'd made the mistake of thinking he could change another human being. Never again. You either accepted a person for who she was or you moved on. No matter how interesting and attractive he found Bethany Taft—and today he had admitted to himself that she held a certain fascination for him—it wouldn't work. The best they could hope for was friendship.

He glanced at Bethany, her face relaxed and vulnerable in sleep, her lashes skimming her cheeks, her lips slightly parted. He found himself thinking about how it might feel to kiss her. In sleep she was approachable—unfortunately, wide-awake she was often anything but. In spite of several moments they had shared in laughter and good fun, she always seemed to close herself off again.

Like the trip down when he'd been kidding around with the PA system. It had seemed as if they might make a real breakthrough. She had laughed so hard and for one of the few times since he'd met her that deer-in-the-headlights look had been completely absent. But then it was as if she'd been caught giggling in church or something. She pulled away, went somewhere inside herself, shutting him out—not that he took it personally. He suspected she did it to everyone. What was it that made her unwilling to allow anyone to get too close? What would it take to bring out that lighter, easygoing personality that Erika had described, but that he had only seen in fleeting glimpses? The joy for life that was so much like Ty? The joy Cody was missing in his own life?

Chapter Six

Bethany woke with a start. She'd been dreaming about Nick. It was a dream she'd had many times over the last year, only this time…

"You okay?" Cody looked over at her, his features cast in shadow by the black night and the dimly lit control panel.

"Fine," Bethany said and knew she sounded anything but convincing.

"Nightmare?"

She did not want to recall the dream much less analyze it. "Just—it was nothing. Are we almost there?"

"Another hour," Cody replied.

Bethany nodded and stared out the window. There was nothing to see, of course, but she was still shaken by the dream.

In it she and Nick were together, laughing and kidding around as they always had. Then he turned and looked at her, his expression unusually solemn. She waited for him to deliver bad news, but instead of speaking, he took a step closer and held out his arms to her. In past dreams she had walked into the circle of his arms, felt them close around her, felt the closeness of Nick and the love they shared, and awakened in tears but still somehow comforted by the moment.

This time everything had happened according to her internal script of the dream. She had felt herself relaxing, anticipating Nick's comforting embrace. But when he turned and waited for her to come to him, she had moved backward, not forward, step by step, until she could no longer see Nick's features, only his outstretched arms. She was losing him, losing her memory of him. As she stared out into the night she tried to imagine his smile, his eyes, his touch. She failed on every count. She shuddered and forced herself to concentrate on the here and now.

"If you talk about it, maybe the dream won't seem so frightening," Cody suggested.

"I'm not frightened," she said and tried hard to include a note of laughter at the ridiculousness of that idea.

Cody took a long breath and let it out. "Okay, so you don't want to talk about it. Then let's get your mind on more pleasant topics—like the party for Dad and Erika. Aunt Susan was really impressed."

It worked. The memory of Susan's avid enthusiasm and attention over bowls of barley soup in her wonderfully homey kitchen lifted Bethany's spirits. "I'm so glad that both you and Susan agree with the idea. I was a little concerned."

"Dad's friends aren't that stuffy," Cody said and

laughed. "In fact, some of them are a real hoot. They're going to love this idea and your biggest job will be trying to accommodate *their* ideas for adding to the fun."

"Like what?" Bethany turned her attention away from the window and focused on Cody. She really did not want to plan this party by committee.

He shrugged. "Well, Barney Wellstone—that Dad's doctor and friend since college—is capable of pretty much anything. He's the ringleader in the group, loves pulling practical jokes. Maybe you should put him in charge of getting Dad and Erika to the site."

He had a point. Guests taking ownership of the idea would only increase their enthusiasm for it to be a complete success. "That's a wonderful idea, Cody. Will you ask him?"

"Sure."

Bethany stretched and yawned. "Long day," she said apologetically.

"Good day," Cody replied. "Will you be in church tomorrow?"

Bethany stiffened. She hadn't been in church since Nick's memorial service.

When she didn't respond right away, Cody glanced at her and stepped in to fill the silence. "It'll be a good opportunity for you to meet Reverend Stone and see the church where Dad and Erika attend whenever they're at the ranch."

"I have a meeting with the minister scheduled for later this coming week," Bethany replied evenly.

Cody looked over at her but didn't comment on the

obvious—the fact that she had not answered his question about attending services.

"Just a thought," was all he said as he concentrated on navigating the turn for the landing.

The silence between them over the next several minutes was uncomfortable. Bethany felt that it was up to her to ease the sudden tension and maintain conversation. It had occurred to her that perhaps she had been too quick to judge Cody. After all, he was only trying to help. If Grace or Erika had suggested she attend services, Bethany would have suspected the ulterior motive of bringing her back to God. Cody's invitation to come to church had been entirely innocent. It wasn't like her to jump to assumptions the way she'd been doing ever since she and Cody met.

The realization made her think of other ways she had not been herself since Nick died. Maybe the time had come to start mending fences—an appropriate image for communicating with a rancher, she thought, and smiled.

"You know, you're okay," she said.

"Well, shucks, ma'am, that's real nice of you to say," he drawled.

She waited a beat and when he said no more, released an exasperated sigh. "That would be your cue to admit that maybe I can handle this wedding thing after all," she coached.

He looked at her with mock surprise. "I never said that I doubted—"

"Come on, admit it. You said that there were plenty

of *professional* wedding planners who could handle the job."

"Semantics. To-*may*-to. To-*mah*-to. You *thought* I was casting doubt on your professionalism when I was really trying to reassure you that here in the backcountry we might be able to scrounge up an actual wedding planner if you weren't up to—I mean if, you decided the job wasn't for you."

"Uh-huh," Bethany said, not sounding the least bit convinced.

"Okay, I'll prove it. While you were sleeping, I was thinking about how brilliant the Habitat idea was and wondering what you might come up with for the party in Arizona."

"I'm still working on that one. The Habitat thing was easy because that's where they met. I need some history about how their romance blossomed here in the desert."

"Okay. Here's an idea," Cody said. "Dad proposed to Erika in the desert, right up there in Dutchman's Canyon." He pointed at the mountain looming in front of them as he smoothly made the turn to land the plane. "We could have the party there, backpack everything and everybody in. Have Honey recreate the picnic she made for Dad that day—only on a grander scale, of course. We—"

"It's an idea," Bethany said with little enthusiasm and as the plane touched down, she busied herself gathering her notebook and other belongings and stuffing them into her bag. "Thanks for letting me tag along today and for introducing me to your aunt and for—"

Cody cut the engine, but didn't move. She looked up

and, in the harsh light cast by the spotlights on the exterior of the hangar, saw that he was watching her with frustration that bordered on outright irritation.

"Well, it was just a thought," he said. "A pretty key piece of the love story, if you ask me. You might at least give it some thought."

Bethany placed her hand on his. "Really, it's a good idea, Cody," she said and meant it. "I just need to think about it some more, okay?"

He pulled his hand away. "Hey, it's your party," he muttered and concentrated on making notes in the flight log.

"No, it's not," she said when it was clear he intended to ignore her. The pencil stopped moving but he didn't look up as she climbed out of her seat and exited the plane.

As Bethany and Erika shared breakfast on the guesthouse porch the following morning, Erika was filled with details of the charity event she and Ian had attended the night before.

"Must have been quite a night," Bethany said, only half listening.

"It was. We didn't get home until after midnight and, of course, then you're so filled with the delight of it all that you can't go right to sleep."

"Is Ian sleeping in this morning then?" *And Cody?*

"Of course not. He and Cody were up with the rooster as usual, I suspect."

"Even on a Sunday?"

Erika laughed. "Oh, Bethie, the animals don't care

what day it is. But, more to the point, Ian and Cody like to get the chores out of the way and then shower and dress so they can make it to choir rehearsal before services."

"Choir?"

"Yes. Whenever we're down here we attend this lovely little country church. Honey's church, really. Cody started going there with Honey and her family after he took up permanent residence here at the ranch."

Bethany wondered what her aunt would say if she admitted that she had not attended church in over a year. It was an unimaginable feat for her. Although she did have to constantly remind herself that she didn't miss the quiet of an empty church or just talking to God whether she was happy or troubled.

Erika looked at her watch and then stood. "And speaking of church, we need to hurry if we're going to make it on time." She shooed Bethany away from the table. "Go on now and get dressed. Nothing fancy. These are just plain country people. I'll clear up here."

There was no arguing with Erika, who made short work of scraping and stacking their few dishes. "Go on," she urged as she disappeared into the kitchen.

They were late. Cody watched from the choir's position to the left of the pulpit as Erika hurried down the aisle to the second pew from the front. Honey made room as the congregation reached the final stanza of the first hymn.

Bethany followed more slowly, eyes downcast as she took the last place on the aisle. She started to sit, seemed to realize everyone else was still standing and accepted her half of the hymnal as the minister led everyone in the responsive reading.

Cody continued watching Bethany as he kept pace with the short and repetitive congregational response to the minister's litany of God's creation.

"And it was so," he said in chorus with the local farmers, ranchers and workers and their families that filled the small sanctuary.

Bethany's lips did not move.

"And God said, 'Let there be Light,'" Reverend Stone intoned.

"And it was so," came the response.

The reading continued for several verses with the last response being, "And it was good."

Bethany remained silent.

In the rustle that accompanied everyone taking their seats at the same moment, Bethany sat and almost immediately moved closer to the high carved end of the pew.

It's as if she wants to hide, Cody thought.

She glanced up for a second, focusing on the large rugged cypress wood cross that dominated the apex behind the pulpit. And in her eyes, Cody saw a look of such naked pain and anguish that he was the one who looked away. He was so caught up in wondering about Bethany that he almost missed the cue for his solo during the choir's anthem.

Reverend Stone's reading that morning was the story of a boy whose mother died when the boy was twelve. He prefaced the section by explaining that the boy had just learned his young mother had died suddenly and with no warning during the night.

"In this passage, the boy goes to the home of a neighbor." The pastor cleared his throat and began reading.

> "All afternoon our neighbor—Mom's best friend—listened while I poured out my grief, my anger at the unfairness of it all. She tried consoling me with words like 'God's will.' I shouted her down. I had no more use for God."

Bethany's head came up, her eyes alive with interest for the first time all morning.

"After that morning," Reverend Stone continued, "for years the boy refused to allow himself to love for fear that it would hurt too much."

Bethany was nodding—ever so slightly—but without question. And as the congregation stood for the second hymn Cody found himself hoping that Reverend Stone might have an answer to whatever Bethany had found to agree with in that twelve-year-old boy's anger toward God.

Bethany mouthed the words to the hymn as much to take Erika's attention and obvious concern away from her as anything else. Her mind was on what the minister had said in his reading. The words of the boy had given voice to everything that Bethany had felt since Nick's death. The minister understood—*finally,* someone understood her. She waited impatiently for the hymn to end so she could again hear from Reverend Stone.

She was aware that Cody was watching her. She'd come to realize that he had this way of looking at her as if he could see through her, inside her, into her mind… and heart. She'd tried to disguise her feelings from him on other occasions, an instinctive need to keep anyone from getting too close—as the boy had said—to divert any possibility of pain.

Now, she didn't care what Cody might see. She raised her face to the minister, felt the sun filtered through the watery amber of the stained glass window warm her face, and waited.

The sermon was about the need for trust—existential trust, as Reverend Stone called it. The idea of developing a sense of trust in God in spite of the pain and unpredictability of life. "In spite of the certainty of death," Reverend Stone urged.

Bethany tried to take it all in but her mind raced with counterarguments. "But," she wanted to protest until she realized that Reverend Stone had come to the close of his message.

"Would everyone please stand and join me in the Lord's Prayer?"

Bethany rose slowly to her feet. All around her people prayed the familiar words of the prayer. Bethany got to "Thy will be done…" and could go no further.

Her throat closed and her eyes were as dry as the wasteland landscape outside. Erika placed her hand over Bethany's, no doubt thinking this was Bethany's moment of breakthrough. Little did she know that all Bethany felt was defeat and disappointment. No one had the answer to the boy's question—"if God loves me, why did He let my mother die?" Certainly not Reverend Stone.

Bethany cleared her throat and stood tall and unbowed as the benediction was said. As the organist struck up the postlude, she turned to Erika with a bright and completely staged smile.

"I wish we could pack this place up and ship it to Chicago. It's the perfect setting for the ceremony, don't you think?"

Erika and Honey exchanged a look.

"Come meet Reverend Stone, dear," Erika said as she ushered Bethany up the aisle. Bethany couldn't help but notice that Erika had ignored her question.

Ian had arranged for the family to have lunch with the minister and his wife, Molly, at a local cantina. Over a feast of soft-shelled tacos, red beans and rice, Tom Stone entertained them with stories of his thirty years of service in the local church.

"How did you and Ian first meet?" Bethany asked.

"Mountain bike accident," Ian said. "The man rescued me. I was a novice then and not used to the sudden changes in terrain. I took this path, made a sharp left to avoid a sidewinder sunning himself on the trail and—"

"Ran out of trail," Molly and Erika chorused. It was obvious they had heard the story before.

"Well, she asked," Ian said with a grin. "Do you bike, Bethany?"

Bethany fingered the small silver charm of a bicycle on the chain at her throat. "Not the way you do," she replied. "Not mountain biking."

"Piece of cake," Ian boomed. "Cody will take you one day."

Bethany smiled to hide her discomfort with the very thought of being in the mountains on foot, much less on a bike. Besides, she and Nick used to bike. He had given her the charm the Christmas they started dating.

"The more interesting tale, Bethie, is how I met Cody," Erika said.

Bethany saw that her aunt had read her discomfort and deliberately turned the conversation to a new topic.

"Tell me," she said and smiled gratefully at Erika.

"Well, it was here in this cantina. You know how sometimes these places like to have strolling musicians?"

Ian laughed and took up the story. "I had arranged for Cody to join the musicians that night."

"Dad loves a good practical joke," Cody said. Bethany realized it was the first time he'd participated in the conversation.

Bethany waited for an explanation. "So? What was the joke?" she asked when everyone else seemed to know the end to this story as they had all the others.

"The joke was to see how much patience your aunt would have," Ian said, squeezing Erika's hand. "I couldn't believe this lady—so unfailingly polite and patient with everything."

"He had Cody and the others stay at our table singing song after song," Erika explained, shaking her head and smiling at the memory. "You know how usually they sing one song and move on? Well, the place was crowded that night but they just kept singing right at our table—especially this one," she added, poking Cody's shoulder.

Cody grinned. "We ran through every song we knew and some we only half knew and still all she did was nod and smile politely. Although you could see in her eyes that she really wanted us to leave them alone."

"Well, I was just beginning to hope that what I was feeling for Ian was something we shared—that we were both falling in love. I didn't need music for that."

Everyone at the table was chuckling now at the memory. Even the waiter serving them was smiling as he overheard their conversation.

"How did it end?" Bethany asked, ideas for the Arizona party starting to evolve.

"A real standoff," Ian said.

Cody nodded. "Finally I just signaled for the others to stop playing, stuck out my hand and introduced myself."

"I was so relieved," Erika said, "and so upset with this one for playing such a trick on me." She looked lovingly at Ian. "But I am proud to say that I passed whatever test there might have been."

Ian leaned closer and kissed Erika's cheek. "That's certainly true. It was that night that I resolved to ask your aunt to marry me, Bethany."

Everyone was smiling and looking fondly at Erika and Ian—everyone except Cody. He was watching Bethany and wondering if she was really that touched by the story or if it was something from her past that brought that closed *nobody's home* look to her eyes.

Chapter Seven

The Chicago party was coming together with Susan's help. The party in Arizona was another story altogether. After the lunch at the cantina and Erika's story of how she met Cody, Bethany had come up with a fun idea for the Arizona party. Set at the cantina, guests would be asked to compose and sing a song for the happy couple. It was perfect until the owner of the cantina called to say they had suffered a kitchen fire that would shut them down for four to six weeks.

"Is everyone all right?" Bethany asked.

"Fine," the owner replied. "But I'm afraid there's no way we can host the party now."

Bethany fingered the draft of the invitation—colorful drawings of jalapeño peppers representing notes on a musical scale. She had just hung up from promising the printer she'd have the draft to her that afternoon. "Can you suggest any other place?" she asked.

"Not really, but we could cater the food if that would help. We could use the kitchen there at the ranch or—"

"Let me see what I can come up with," Bethany said. She hung up and called the printer, promising to have the final mock-up of the invitation to her by the end of the week. Then she went to find Honey.

The kitchen was empty. Through the kitchen window she saw Honey and Erika waving to Cody as they drove away.

"No," she cried as she raced out the door. "Honey!"

They were gone.

"Can I help?" Cody walked toward her.

"I need Honey," she replied, watching the trail of dust from Honey's car in the distance.

"She's taking a couple of days off to visit her mother down in Tucson. Erika didn't want her to drive by herself. Her mom fell last night and fractured her hip. She's in the hospital there. You could call."

"That's terrible," Bethany said, turning her attention to Cody. "About her mother, I mean. Will she be all right?"

"She'll need surgery followed by physical therapy, but she should make a full recovery, according to what the doctors told Honey."

"Well, I don't need to bother her with this. I'll just—do you know where she keeps the Yellow Pages?"

Cody folded his arms across his chest. "Why don't you just tell me what you need? I might be able to help."

There was something in the way he said it, his expression one of curiosity mixed with concern. For a moment Bethany was stunned by the question. It was as if he'd seen past the carefully constructed facade and revealed everything she'd kept locked inside. She had needs on so many levels—levels far more personal than the immediate one of the party setting. Needs that she spent so much effort every day and night holding at bay.

"Bethany?"

"I—uh—well, there was a fire at the cantina. I had hoped to hold the engagement party there for the Arizona contingent. Now that's impossible because they won't be able to reopen for at least a month, but the owner said he could still cater the food using the kitchen here. Of course, that assumes we would even think of hosting the party here. I mean, it's a beautiful setting but just not right for what I had in mind for the party, you know. So now—"

The man was grinning down at her. No, he was laughing at her. "You really take this stuff seriously, don't you?" He shook his head in amazement. "It's a simple party—old friends getting together—not the marriage of royalty."

Men. What did they know? She turned on her heel and stalked back toward the guesthouse.

"Hold on," Cody called and she knew he was following her by the crunch of his boots on the path. "Don't go away mad. Let me help."

She wheeled around and retraced the two steps it took to be toe-to-toe with him. "Get this straight—this is *not* a simple party. It is a piece of an entire calendar of events leading up to and including possibly the most important day in my aunt's life. It will be as perfect as I can make it because she deserves no less. Is that clear?"

He smothered a grin and tipped his hat. "Yes, ma'am."

"All right then. Maybe you can help." It was downright annoying how attractive the man could be—especially when he was obviously amused by something she said or did.

"Sit," she said as soon as they had entered the living room of the guesthouse. She rummaged through her notes and papers and found the envelope with the invitation. She handed it to him and waited while he opened it.

He read the contents quickly and immediately started to smile. "I love it," he said, handing the invitation back to her. "So, what's the problem again?"

"The part about 'where' is no longer valid and I don't have a backup plan."

"And holding this shindig here at the ranch is out because…?" He seemed genuinely puzzled so she cut him some slack.

"Because," she began speaking slowly as if explaining algebra to a first grader, "it's not the cantina where the original event took place."

"Which is no longer a choice due to the kitchen fire," he added in an equally belabored voice.

"Bingo. So now I have to come up with a completely new idea, new invitation, new—"

"Maybe not," Cody said. "What are you doing for dinner?"

Bethany waved her hand impatiently. "Salad, maybe a pizza. Why?"

He stood and grinned down at her. "Be ready at six. I may just have the answer to all your problems. Oh, and wear something kind of dressed up." He picked up his hat and was gone before she could digest what had just happened.

Kind of dressed up? What was that exactly? More to the point, what did it mean to Cody Dillard, ranch manager and twenty-first century cowboy?

As it turned out, *kind of dressed up* for him at least was a perfectly tailored business suit worn with a blue shirt and red tie. Seeing Cody, Bethany was more confident of her own choice of a simple black sleeveless dress worn with stiletto heels and a rope of pearls. Apparently he approved, as well, because Cody released a long, low whistle of admiration when he saw her.

Okay, not exactly poetic, but there was no mistaking the sincerity.

"Thank you," she said, sounding a little prim even to her own ears. She picked up her black satin clutch and followed him out the door.

He hurried around his cream-colored SUV and opened the door for her, taking her elbow as he helped her into the seat. His touch on her bare arm was disconcerting. Warm, yet at the same time goose bumps snaked up the back of her arm.

"Where are we going?" she asked when he had taken his place behind the wheel and pulled away from the ranch, headed for one of the myriad of highways that tangled their way around the greater metropolitan area that was Phoenix.

"Scottsdale."

She was aware of Scottsdale only as a relatively ritzy area of the city, sporting fancy resorts with golf courses, swimming pools and lush tropical grounds in contrast to their desert surroundings. There were boulevards, some lined with impressive houses and others with wonderful boutiques and shops. Any other time she would have been delighted at the opportunity. Tonight she did not see how going to Scottsdale was going to solve her problem of what to do for the party.

"I thought you had an idea of a way we might salvage the original concept for the party," she said, trying to keep a positive tone in spite of her sinking feeling.

"Frank Lloyd Wright."

"The architect," she prompted. "What about him?"

"He started a school in Wisconsin. Then on a trip here when he was working on the Biltmore Resort, he decided to build a winter campus."

"Taliesin," Bethany said.

Cody nodded. "Taliesin West," he corrected. "That's where we're going tonight."

And this solves the issue of no place for the party exactly how? "Oh."

He looked over at her as if reading her mind. "I'm not patronizing you, Bethany. This does relate to our earlier discussion—to your perceived problem with the party here in Arizona."

"My *perceived—*"

"Yeah, as in could be but doesn't have to be."

Whatever that meant, she thought.

He turned onto a road that wound away from the lights and homes of Scottsdale and back into the foothills, pulled into a small parking lot already nearly filled with upscale cars and cut the engine. "I'm just asking you to keep an open mind, okay?"

"I always—"

The firm closing of the door on his side told her that he wasn't listening. She waited until he had come around and opened her door. "I always keep an open mind," she muttered as she ignored his helping hand and climbed down by herself.

Cody placed her hand in the crook of his elbow without further comment. He led her past a series of the kind of low, hugging-the-earth buildings that Wright had pioneered. They stepped through a slanted doorway where Cody actually had to bend his head to accommodate even the tallest part of the door.

"In Wright's day there weren't many men six feet tall, much less six-two," he said, unconsciously reaching to smooth his hair. "I've always thought that it would be fun to take the pro basketball team—the Suns—on a tour here and watch them try to maneuver their way around."

His attempt at disarming her worked and she forced herself to just relax and enjoy the evening. "Wonder what he would have thought of women in four-inch heels?" she asked.

"Probably would have been okay as long as you were the one wearing them," Cody said. "Rumor has it that Wright appreciated a good-looking woman as much as he did art and design." Bethany felt a rush of pleasure at the compliment.

Cody had stopped at a point where the pathway made a sharp right turn. Behind them was the main building of the campus. In front of them—in the distance—were the lights of the city.

"See those utility poles and wires?" Cody stood behind her and pointed toward a spot just below the horizon.

Bethany nodded, trying to focus on his conversation rather than on his being so near that she could feel the fine cloth of his suit brush her arm, could smell the light spiciness of his aftershave, could actually hear him breathing.

"When those poles—the old ones there—first went up, Wright was furious. He was ready to give up on the entire project and start over somewhere else."

"But obviously he didn't," Bethany said. "What happened?"

"His wife reminded him that he was ninety years old and starting over was no longer an option. He'd solved problems such as this in the past—he could solve this one."

"And?"

Cody took her arm and gently turned her away from the scene beyond them until she was looking at the buildings and the rising mountains behind them. "He turned the whole design around. One day he brought everyone out here, told them to look at the valley, then told them to turn around. Then he announced that from that moment on the mountains were to be the focal point for the campus."

Bethany looked up at him. "And the moral of this little tale would be?"

He grinned sheepishly as they walked on around the path. "If one thing won't work, you gotta turn around and look at it from another angle."

Bethany laughed. "Okay, point taken. I'll sleep on it and tomorrow—"

"Oh, I'm not done—Wright never just laid out a problem without having his own ideas about solutions. Come on, we don't want to be late."

Cody opened another door and out poured the sounds of conversation and utensils on china, all accompanied by soft music and the aroma of fine food. Inside Cody worked the room as he led her to a café table set for two. Everyone seemed to know him, which really didn't surprise her. What did surprise her was that everyone seemed to revere as well as genuinely like him, and the fuss clearly made Cody uncomfortable. She also noticed that no one was especially curious about her. That told her that these people were used to seeing Cody Dillard at various functions with a woman on his arm. They didn't take it seriously and why should they? Why was she even thinking about it? It was what it was, nothing more. Not that she would want it to be anything more. The very idea of Cody and her—

"Now, check this out," he said. His voice, low but still excited, interrupted her thoughts.

"What?"

"This," he said, indicating the greater space of the room with a slight sweep of his hand.

"It's—" She had been prepared to dismiss it and then she looked around, really looked. They were in a small cabaret theater. The floor sloped upward to the back of the long room. The performance area at the front was the lowest point in the room.

"Stadium seating," she said as the waiter—obviously a student—served them.

"Yes, ma'am," the student said. "Mr. Wright also came up with the idea of aisle lighting. He didn't like it when ushers carried flashlights and interrupted the performance, so he put in those." He pointed with pride to the cable of low lighting that ran the length of the sloped walkway.

The waiter took their order and left. Bethany continued to study the room.

"The acoustics are perfect," Cody told her. "Chances are even the worst song the guests write for Erika and Dad will sound fine in here."

"It *might* work," Bethany said softly as she continued to survey her surroundings making mental notes for the party. "We could do centerpieces to give it the feel of a cantina and the strolling musicians could work the room during dinner and then—"

"Told you." Cody was grinning, obviously quite proud of himself.

"Okay, smart guy, is it available for private parties?"

"I think for this party it would be," was his answer as the waiter delivered their salads.

The evening included musical entertainment by several of the students and members of the faculty. Bethany could not help being surprised at their talent. The closing act—a folksinging trio of faculty members—invited the guests to sing along with such standards as "Blowin' in the Wind." The evening ended with all performers on stage and the guests singing "If I Had a Hammer."

Bethany and Cody raised their voices along with the

other guests and Bethany had more fun than she'd allowed herself to have in months. More to the point, the few times she'd thought of Nick during the evening were when certain musical numbers or phrases triggered a memory, but it was without guilt. In fact, she felt more comforted by reminiscences than she had in a long time.

Cody excused himself after the concert and approached a woman he'd introduced to Bethany as an artist-in-residence for the season. Some of the other guests and staff members nodded and made small talk as they made their way to the exit, leaving Bethany alone in the cabaret.

She walked down to the performance area and looked back at the seating—the tables set with white cloths and flickering votive candles, the chairs that she could imagine covered with fabric in festive colors.

"Ask me a question—but turn away and speak low," Cody said, standing alone at the very back of the room.

Bethany turned away and murmured, "How did you know this would work?"

Instantly came the answer. "I didn't, but I wanted you to come here with me tonight, and the way you were going on about the party, I figured I'd better find some kind of a link."

Bethany took a moment to compose herself before she turned back to face him. She made no comment on his words to her. It was safer to focus on the exercise. "I barely whispered."

Cody grinned. "I know. Perfect acoustics, see?"

On the walk back to the car, Bethany kept up a running commentary on how they could make use of the various aspects of the setting.

"Oh, Cody, it's going to be fantastic," she gushed as she turned to take one last look at her surroundings. Then before he realized what was happening, she spontaneously threw her arms around him and hugged him. "Thank you *so* much."

Instinctively he hugged her back, then tightened his arms around her. That simple move—the prelude to going beyond a spontaneous hug to a kiss—was all it took to bring that startled look back to her incredible eyes. He took a moment to be sure and then gently loosened his hold on her and opened the passenger door. "You are most welcome," he said.

After that she was unusually quiet. Was she making mental notes for the party? Or was she still reviewing what had just almost happened between them, as he was? There was one certain way to find out.

"Tell me about your fiancé, Bethany."

Chapter Eight

Bethany took a long breath. She couldn't recall the last time anyone had asked her outright about Nick. Ever since his death, people—even close friends and family—avoided the subject unless she brought it up first.

She started to speak and couldn't seem to find her voice. She cleared her throat and started again. "Nick?"

Cody remained silent, navigating the turns that would take them away from the blocks of houses and out into the desert on their way back to the ranch.

"Nick was…very special," she finished weakly. In her peripheral vision she saw Cody nod, but he still didn't say anything.

"My friend Grace's husband is a reporter," she began.

The sudden change in topic got his attention. "What's that got to do with Nick?"

"Nothing, really. It's just that you reminded me of Jud just then. He has that same reporter's trick of saying nothing so the person he's interviewing will eventually fill the silence."

"I'm not interviewing you, Bethany. I'm trying to get to know you a little better."

"Oh."

They rode in silence for a few minutes before Bethany asked, "Why? I mean...well, why?"

Cody's smile was slow to come but so genuine that it made Bethany's heart quicken. "Two can play this game, Bethany—why not?"

"I'm really not all that complicated," she said. "What you see is pretty much what you get in my case."

"Yeah, that's kind of how Erika described you. But ever since we met—frankly you're pretty tough to figure out."

"So why bring Nick into it?"

Cody shifted slightly, rubbed his chin with one hand and steered with the other. "If you were ever the straightforward life-of-any-party woman Erika described, then something has changed since she spent time with you."

"I'm really sorry I haven't lived up to my reputation," Bethany said and could not keep the hint of defensiveness out of her voice. "But to put it bluntly, I'm really not here to impress you."

"Point taken. The problem is that you *have* impressed me."

Okay, get past that little bump of pleasure that he's impressed by you and focus.

"Not to mention the fact that once Dad marries Erika we'll be kind of like family."

"Family?" *As if he sees me as his little sister or something?*

Cody shrugged. "Face it, down the road, we're probably going to run into each other from time to time at family gatherings. I just thought it would be nice if we were—I mean, we're kind of going through this wedding thing together and well, it's not like you're hired help and someone that I won't see again after the wedding."

Hired help? Okay, he said not *hired help—stop being so defensive. What is your problem?*

"I see." *I don't see at all. I have no idea how we've come from discussing Nick to this. Frankly, it might have been easier to talk about Nick.*

"So I brought up Nick because it occurred to me that his death is where everything changed for you."

"You know, I really would rather not talk about that." *With you,* she almost added and wondered why the qualifier.

Cody's fingers tightened on the steering wheel. "Got it."

They were completely out of the city now. The road was lit only by the headlights of passing cars and there were few of those. Before leaving the parking lot, Cody had removed his suit jacket and rolled back the sleeves of his shirt. Bethany found herself watching the subtle movement of his forearms as he navigated the road to the ranch.

"Thank you again for tonight," she said, unable to bear the silence any longer. "It was fun in its own right, but the fact that I can stage the party there is a very special bonus."

"Anything I can do to help out." He glanced over at

her. "I mean that, Bethany. I want this to be as perfect as you do. Dad's been through a lot. Finding Erika—he deserves that happiness, so thank you."

Bethany laughed self-consciously. "Will you listen to the two of us? We sound like characters in a British farce. 'Thank you.' 'No, thank *you.*' 'But I insist. Thank you so very much.'"

Cody grinned, then reached over and took her hand, raising it high. "We could be quite a team, Taft."

"Odd couple might be closer to the truth," she said and gently eased her hand from his as he turned onto the gravel road leading to the house.

The party at Taliesin was every bit the hit that Bethany had imagined. Cody had done a masterful job of getting Ian and Erika there without revealing the surprise. In fact, it was far easier than it would have been to get them to the cantina.

The guests had gone the extra mile and dressed in festive South-of-the-Border style, taking their cue from the invitation. The trio of musicians from the cantina played during dinner and then the church organist took her place at the grand piano and expertly accompanied each improvised song the guests offered as their gift to the delighted couple. Bethany stayed behind the scenes coordinating everything from the serving of the food to the lineup of songs to the special toasts and desserts that came at the end of a perfect evening.

All she had to do was take one look at Erika and she knew that she had truly outdone herself. But if Erika and Ian thought this was special, wait until they found out what she had planned for them in Chicago.

It was an especially touching moment when Ian found his way to the kitchen and grabbed Bethany in a bear hug. "Sweetie, you have made your aunt so happy. Thank you so much for all the work you put into this. People are going to be talking about tonight for a long time, you know." He hugged her harder and his voice broke. "I really appreciate it, Bethany."

"Aw shucks, mister, 'tweren't nothin' much," she said, easing the emotional moment by dropping into Ian's familiar cowboy drawl. He laughed and released her. Just over his shoulder she saw Cody standing in the doorway observing the two of them. He smiled and gave her a thumbs-up before returning to the party. She felt more alive than she had in months.

The highlight of the evening was Cody's song to Ian and Erika. Most guests had used the limerick form or made up new words to familiar tunes. Cody took the stage last.

"It may surprise some of you who have heard me roast and toast members of my family before that tonight I intend to do neither."

Every guest leaned forward in anticipation of something very special. Bethany saw Erika glance at Ian as Ian focused all his attention on Cody.

Cody picked up a battered guitar and strummed it lightly, tuning the strings to the right pitch as he introduced his song. "I read some poetry recently that was written by St. John of the Cross. He was a sixteenth-century Spanish cleric and he wrote these words while imprisoned in a dungeon. It may be a leap of faith to go from a poem written in jail to love and marriage but listen to the words."

There was a general murmur of expectation among the guests as Cody took a seat on a high stool and played an introductory melody on the guitar. "Like Jonah in the whale, St. John of the Cross was in the depths of despair, but he found light again through his poetry, just as Dad has found light in life with Erika."

The room was silent except for the soft melody played on the guitar and Cody's fine baritone.

Love is like the mountains
Or the valleys alive with flowers
It speaks to us in the wind
And the sound of rushing streams
Love comes as the candle
Burning always in our heart
Carrying us through the darkness
Bringing us into the light.

Cody sang the verses he'd composed, always ending with the chorus. At the end he repeated the chorus and allowed the last note to die away in the perfect acoustics of the cabaret. For a moment there was silence and only the memory of the note. Then everyone gave a standing ovation as Ian and Erika came forward to embrace Cody. Bethany watched from the back of the room and wondered if she had only imagined that as he sang the words, he was looking right at her.

* * *

That night Erika was too excited to sleep. She and Bethany sat up into the wee hours of the morning dissecting every detail of the evening—including Erika's conviction that Cody was more than casually attracted to her niece.

"He really couldn't take his eyes off you," Erika said.

"Well, then he must have superpowers because I was in the kitchen or backstage for much of the evening." Bethany deliberately made light of her aunt's comment. "So tell me, what was your favorite song?"

Erika sighed. "They were all wonderful, funny and sweet, but Cody's was so touching. Now *there* is a man practically brimming over with a capacity for love and giving."

Bethany gave up. "Aunt Erika, I know that you've been hoping that there might be some sort of spark between Cody and me, but—well, it's just not right, for either of us."

"I would suggest you let Cody speak for himself."

"I have. He's made it perfectly clear that the woman of his dreams is someone who loves the desert and the solitude as much as he does. That simply isn't me—even if I wanted it to be."

Erika sighed. "Yes, Cynthia was a disaster."

Bethany's ears perked up. "Cynthia?"

"He met her at a conference in Chicago where he was speaking. She went after him like someone on a mission, but men often miss that. They take the attention to heart, especially when the woman falls all over herself to be anything he wants."

"Is that what Cynthia did?"

"Oh, my stars, the woman was relentless. 'My Daddy taught me to ride when I was just three.' Or 'I just love the outdoors, don't you, Cody?' and then having the audacity to look surprised when he said he did." Erika visibly shuddered.

"Cody doesn't strike me as being that gullible. Maybe he was just being polite."

"He's not gullible at all. I think he just wanted it to work. He'd been through a lot and was ready to move on." She gave Bethany a meaningful look. "Unlike some people I could name."

"But Cynthia? She sounds awful."

"I'm overstating things a bit. She wasn't right for Cody. They met a little over a year ago, after Ian and I had been seeing each other for several months. Ian was so concerned that Cody was trying too hard to move on with his life and that he was going to end up heartbroken."

"What happened?"

"Cody brought her here. All very proper—her out here in the guesthouse and all."

"And?"

"She made it for two days and then started suggesting they go into town, see a play, do some shopping, meet some of his friends." Erika giggled. "When Cody told her that the people here on the ranch and his neighbors are his friends, that was it. Next morning she arrived at breakfast filled with apologies but she had to get back to Chicago as soon as possible—some disaster at work."

"Poor Cody," Bethany said and meant it.

"No! He'd been rehearsing his 'this really isn't working out' speech all night. He was relieved."

"He and Cynthia must run into each other at functions in Chicago. It must be awkward for both of them."

"Within six months Cynthia married an oil industry executive twenty years her senior. She lives in Wyoming—on a ranch—" Bethany and Erika both broke into giggles at the irony of Cynthia's story. "Of course, she has her own private plane and pilot to take her anywhere she wants to go at any time."

Then Erika stood, stretching and yawning before gathering her evening shawl and beaded purse and heading for her room. "So you see, Cody is free of all entanglements."

"Oh, Erika, really—"

"And one thing more—" Erika's expression sobered. "He understands what you've been through. He found his own path out of mourning. He could be a friend if nothing more if you'd let him." She kissed Bethany's cheek. "Think about it."

Two days later Bethany and Erika left for Chicago. Their agenda included shopping for Erika's wedding attire and trousseau and organizing the Thanksgiving dinner that would include Bethany's entire family plus other members from Erika's side of the family as well as Ian, Cody and Ian's sister, Susan, and her husband, their grown children, spouses and three grandchildren. Bethany also needed to finalize plans with Habitat for the surprise engagement party that was scheduled to take place the Saturday after Thanksgiving.

"Oh, one thing more to add to your calendar," Erika said once they had arrived at O'Hare and been met by one of Ian's drivers. "There will be a special ceremony on Monday in the conference room of Ian's offices—a small gathering, but the press is sure to be there to cover it."

"What's the occasion?" Bethany continued adding notes to her list. The last thing she needed right now was one more appointment, so she hoped Erika would say that she really didn't need to be there.

"It's a special foundation that Cody has put together, with some major backing from Ian and others, to provide scholarships for aspiring architects."

Bethany stopped writing. "I didn't know Cody had such an interest in architecture." But it made sense, given the way everyone had received him that evening at Taliesin.

"He doesn't—but his twin, Ty, was just getting started in his own business when he died. And their mother, Emma, was an avid supporter of Taliesin."

Bethany put down her pen and closed her notebook, giving Erika her full attention. "You mentioned that Cody had lost a brother, but I'd just assumed it was in infancy."

Erika gave her a look that bordered on irritation. "Well, you've had a lot on your mind."

It was a gentle but stinging rebuke. More so because it was true.

"All right, tell me."

"Cody and Ian suffered a dual loss five years ago—one expected, one horribly unexpected. Cody's mother had been ill for some time with lung cancer. Her death was just a matter of time."

"And Cody's brother?"

"Ty died in a snowboarding accident about four months after the death of his mother. I never knew him, but Ian talks of him—always with great fondness—as Cody's opposite in every way. Where Cody is quiet and content, Ty was always seeking the next level of adventure. Where Cody is practical and studious, Ty partied his way through school."

"Still, he became an architect?"

Erika nodded. "A brilliant one, from everything I've seen. His death was a terrible blow not only for those who loved him but for those who would have benefited from his unique talent for design."

The driver had reached the narrow town house that Bethany recognized as being only a few blocks from Susan's home. Erika led the way up the front steps while the driver unloaded their luggage from the trunk.

"Cody has spent the last couple of years trying to put together the best tribute for both of them and came up with this marvelous program. I do hope you'll come for the dedication, Bethany—not that you need to. I know you have a great deal to get done, but still—"

"I wouldn't miss it," Bethany replied. How could she not have realized the depths of Cody and Ian's losses? More to the point, how had each of them found a way to come to terms with those losses and move forward? She thought of the song Cody had sung at the party—about his explanation of St. John of the Cross as someone who, like Jonah in the Bible, had escaped from the belly of the whale. In St. John's case, the whale had been a sixteenth-century dungeon. Bethany couldn't help thinking that her whale was almost as dark and depressing.

Thanksgiving Day was a movable feast between Ian's and Susan's town houses as well as a celebration of family, food and football. Bethany's entire family had come from Washington including her parents, her brothers, their wives, their children and even a couple of the children's friends, who'd come along to enjoy the spectacle of the holiday season in Chicago. Her nieces and their friends all studied Bethany's clothes, makeup and hair as if she were a supermodel. Her nephews paid close attention to anything and everything that Cody had to say. Here was a guy who knew sports and had played sports, and was a real-life cowboy.

The kitchens at both houses were happy, chaotic scenes filled with the sounds of laughter and shared culinary secrets, and the aromas of the season. Cody was both surprised and unexpectedly pleased to see Bethany right there in the thick of things, apron tied low on her hips. Her hair was pulled into a nonchalant topknot, her cheeks flushed with the heat of her simmering homemade onion soup as she stirred the pot and contributed more than her fair share to the women's conversation.

"Can I be of service, ladies?" he asked, snagging a pecan tart his aunt was adding to a dessert platter.

Susan slapped his hand and he danced away laughing as he stuffed the sweet into his mouth. "Out," Susan ordered.

"You wound me, madam," he said, hand to heart. "Do I get no credit for offering to help when all the other men are content to let you ladies do all the work?"

"Oh, you can help," Bethany said, winking at the others. "You and all your male friends in there in front of the television."

Cody grinned uncertainly. "Okay. How?"

Bethany looked at the other women and in chorus they shouted, "You get to clean up," before bursting into a fresh round of laughter at the expression on Cody's face.

"Be careful what you wish for, cowboy," Bethany said and turned back to stirring her soup.

"Now, get out of here," Susan said, waving a spatula at him as he reached for a second tart.

The adults lingered over dinner for nearly two hours. Long before that the children grew restless and were sent off to the attic to amuse themselves by dragging out the decorations for the Christmas tree Susan and her family would decorate later that weekend. Bethany could not help noticing that the holiday—at least *this* holiday—was easier than it had been the year before. Was that what happened? As time passed, would she slowly let go of the grief and the memories? Or was it being in this different place—this place that did not hold any memories for her? This place where she was making new memories?

"Enough of this grown-up stuff," Cody announced

after downing his last bite of pumpkin pie. “Bethany and I are going to check on the kids.” He stood and waited. “Come on, or did you eat so much that you need help getting up?”

That brought Bethany immediately to her feet. “Race you to the attic, Mr. Three Pieces of Pie,” she retorted and had reached the first landing before Cody could work his way past the others and out of the dining room.

Chapter Nine

Cody, Bethany and her nieces and nephews and his young cousins spent a delightful afternoon sorting through the boxes of decorations. Cody had them all laughing over memories triggered by an ornament he had made for his aunt Susan when he was in second grade. Bethany's nieces and nephews and their friends helped Susan's grandchildren fasten hooks to each ornament before placing them carefully back in the box.

Later, Cody led the children in a stampede on the kitchen where he and Bethany supervised as the children prepared turkey sandwiches, fruit and chips for a post-football game supper. It had been a long time since Bethany had enjoyed a day so much, especially a holiday. Holidays were the most difficult since Nick died. Everything seemed to remind her of what they had shared…or might have shared. But not this holiday.

After supper Cody announced his intention to walk off all that food. "Care to join me?" he asked and Bethany did not miss the exchange of knowing looks among the women.

"Sure," she said and tossed her dish towel to her sister-in-law, who gave her a none-too-subtle wink.

Outside the air was crisp and cold. Bethany and Cody both shoved their hands deep into the pockets of their coats as they walked along the narrow cobbled sidewalks, their breath coming in tiny white puffs as their booted feet crunched the last of the fall leaves.

"Cody, I owe you an apology."

"Stop apologizing to me, Bethany."

Bethany searched for the right words. "You have to admit that we kind of got off on the wrong foot when we met. All I'm saying is that most of that was my fault."

Cody said nothing so she felt compelled to continue.

"Usually I'm not that way—defensive and suspicious of everyone's motives and all."

Cody chuckled. "What made me a special case?"

"That's just it. You aren't. I mean, you are special, of course. It's just that lately I've been treating most people the same way."

"Not a problem. I know you've been through some tough times. It takes a while to work your way through the dark and come out in the light on the other side."

She wondered just how much Erika had told them. "Yes, but that's no excuse. So, officially apologizing, okay?"

"Apology accepted—unnecessary but accepted," he replied.

Once again he fell silent. The street was deserted and with the snow falling in fat flakes covering the tiny gardens and front stoops of the old brownstone town houses, they might have been walking through a scene in a movie or a Christmas card.

"I loved the family tradition of sorting the ornaments," she said, uneasy with the lack of conversation.

Cody chuckled, but offered no further comment. She'd noticed that about him. He was absolutely content with silence.

"It was wonderful to hear the stories and memories that each ornament brought back for the children—and for you. In our family, we kind of drag everything out at the last minute and put up the tree—no ritual or tradition."

Cody glanced at her. "Mom started it and after... When we started spending more time at the ranch, Aunt Susan became the keeper of the collection and carried on with the tradition."

"Your mother sounds like she was a very special lady."

Cody nodded, but said nothing.

"How do you feel about Ian marrying again?"

Cody glanced down at her and then turned his face back to the wind. "I think anything that brings Dad happiness is great—and your aunt brings him great happiness."

"Still—"

"Mom would have been the first to encourage him to find someone and fall in love again."

"But it's a passage—for you, I mean."

"I'm not a kid, Bethany. Life is full of passages. This happens to be one of the good ones."

She considered asking about Ty but for reasons she couldn't fully explain, did not. They walked along in silence.

"You really enjoy city life, don't you?" he asked after a while.

"I like the energy of a city, the rushing around and urgency of everything."

"You don't enjoy just being."

"Being?"

"You know, quiet, alone with just your thoughts."

Bethany shuddered and pulled her coat more tightly around her body. She laughed nervously. "I like people, activity. Being alone can get…well, lonely. Don't you ever find that?"

"Nope," he replied and picked up the pace. "Come on, you're freezing. Let's get you inside."

By Sunday Bethany had developed enough of a case of laryngitis that no one pressed her to attend church services. With Ian's spacious town house to herself, she called Grace. The time difference meant that Grace was just leaving services—probably in her office at the church.

"Church on the Circle, how can we help?" Bethany felt a wave of emotion wash over her at the sound of Grace's familiar lilting voice.

"It's me," Bethany croaked out.

"What's wrong?" Grace asked immediately.

"Nothing. Everything. I have a slight case of laryngitis." As if that explained anything.

"Where are you?"

"In Chicago, at Ian's town house. You should see this place. It's like a private museum. Full of art and antiques, and yet very warm and comfortable. Not intimidating at all."

"Sounds nice. So what's the problem? And don't say there's no problem. I can hear it in your voice."

"It's just—I don't know. Oh, Gracie, I just feel so… lost." She couldn't stop her voice from breaking.

"Then come home," Grace said softly.

"I am, for Christmas, but I really don't think that's the answer. What I'm feeling is something more complex than homesickness. I can't explain it. What's wrong with me?"

There was a long pause.

"Nothing is wrong with you, Bethany. You are grieving and it's a process. The fact that you are beginning to notice other things—other people—is a good sign."

"But it feels…I don't know…like somehow I'm losing Nick all over again—"

"You're no longer mourning Nick's death, Bethie. I think that what you're grieving for is the loss of the life you thought you would have with him. You had planned your future in terms of a life with Nick but that's no longer possible. So now you have to start over. That's going to take time."

"But—"

"All you can see right now, Bethie, is what you've lost, what can no longer be. In time you'll start to see new possibilities, and when that happens—"

"I don't want to start again. It's too hard." Bethany hated the petulance in her tone, but it was the truth.

There was a long pause before Grace said, "It would be easier if you would open the door to your heart again, Bethie—open it to God. Let Him back in your life."

Now it was Bethany's turn to stay silent. God was not a subject she was willing to discuss, not even with Grace.

"Bethie?"

"Oh, don't mind me. I'm just feeling sorry for myself. What's going on there? How's Jud, that handsome husband of yours?"

"He's great." A pause. Grace cleared her throat. "As a matter of fact, I was going to call you today. I wanted you to be the first—other than Jud, of course—to know."

"You're pregnant?"

Grace answered with a girlish giggle.

"You are! Oh, Gracie, I am so happy for you, truly. You are going to be such a wonderful mother. When did you find out?"

"This morning—I did one of those pregnancy tests and it came up positive. I know it's not official until I see the doctor, but—"

"Grace, this is the best possible news. Can I tell Mom and Auntie Erika?"

"Let's wait until Christmas and Jud and I will make it all official then, okay?"

"Perfect. We'll do a party. I have to go now. Call me as soon as you've seen the doctor, okay?"

"Wait, Bethany. Will you be the godmother?"

Bethany swallowed hard around the lump in her throat. "I'd be honored," she said and covered her emotion with a cough. "Have to go," and with that, she hung up.

What was the matter with her? Was she so far gone that she couldn't even share in her friend's joy? Was she so self-centered that all she could think about was herself? All she could wonder about was "ever a godmother, never a mom"?

On Monday Bethany had intended to make some excuse and skip the dedication ceremony, wishing she'd never said she'd go in the first place. It wasn't her place to be part of something so tied to the family, she told herself. But internally she knew it was more than that. It was a memorial for two vital people who had died in their prime—as Nick had. She wasn't ready for that. She wasn't sure she would ever be ready for that.

"Nonsense," Erika said when Bethany proposed that she use the time to check out potential caterers for the New Year's party Ian planned to host at the town club where he was a member.

"Ian wants the entire family there."

"But—"

"And don't say you aren't family. You are my family and in Ian's book, that makes you part of his."

Bethany frowned. "What should I wear?"

"That's better," Erika said with a smile. "You know exactly what to wear. Asking is just your roundabout way of agreeing to be there." She touched Bethany's arm. "Thank you," she said gently. "I know things like this bring back memories, but honestly, dear, that is the only way you are ever going to find your way back."

Bethany said nothing. She patted her aunt's hand and moved away. "I'd better change," she said and headed for her room.

The gathering for the ceremony was far larger than Bethany had imagined. The corporate auditorium was packed and people were even standing as she and Erika were ushered to their seats in the front row. Bethany saw Cody glance at her, saw his eyes widen before he looked back at his notes. Was he surprised to see her, and if so, was he pleased?

Ian stepped to the microphone and the chatter that had dominated the room ceased immediately. There was a rustle as people turned in their seats to face the podium and then silence. Ian smiled.

"Thank you for coming today. All of you were close to either Emma or Ty or both. You knew—as Cody and I did—their charm, their gentle spirits, their sharp wit, their laughter. You mourned with us when they left us far too soon. And now Cody and I ask that you join us in establishing this program that Cody has envisioned. A program that perhaps more than any bronze statue or memorial of bricks and mortar will carry on their zest for life—for bringing people together regardless of their history or background, for giving young people a fresh start. But I've gone on too long. This is Cody's project—his way of making sure that it will be their lives, not their deaths, that we remember. And now it's time for me to sit down and let someone who knows this topic far better than I do talk—something Emma always admonished me that I did far too seldom."

There was a murmur of laughter as Ian took his seat behind the podium and nodded to Cody. The room was hushed as Cody smiled at Ian and then stepped to the microphone, adjusting it to accommodate his greater height. He cleared his throat, took a sip of water and spread out his note cards.

"Unaccustomed as I am to public speaking," he began and everyone chuckled, "I hope you won't mind if I check my notes from time to time. I need to get this right because this is about my mother, Emma Browne Dillard, and my brother, Tyrone—Ty—Dillard. This is, as Dad has said, about finding a way to celebrate the life each of them lived. This is about finding a way to honor all that they gave and all that they would have given had their lives not been cut short."

Bethany was aware that people along the front row were nodding. Their faces were turned up to Cody, anticipating his next words. He had them in the palm of his hand. She had never seen a seasoned politician do a better job and she knew that the difference was Cody. For this was no speech sprinkled with platitudes that the audience wanted to hear. There was no double-talk and no need for considering the political correctness of his words. This was straight from the heart and Bethany sat enthralled as she drank in the stories Cody told about his mother and brother.

"Ty and I were not always model children," he said. "Well, *I* was—" he gave the audience a grin and they laughed "—but Ty loved testing boundaries. Once when we were in high school, he kind of forgot to study for an exam. In fact, several times he forgot to study, but this one time he persuaded me to switch places and take the test for him. I did and we were both pretty pleased with pulling it off until Mom saw the test score. Immediately she knew what had happened. Our teachers might not be able to tell us apart—sometimes even Dad couldn't—but Mom always knew. We could never fool her—not that we didn't try."

Like a minister building gently to the point, Cody allowed a moment for the audience to appreciate the story before moving on.

"She not only made Ty take a different exam, but she volunteered both of us to tutor elementary students for the entire summer."

Bethany smiled.

"I, of course, protested that it wasn't fair to punish us the same. Her answer? 'Life isn't fair. You boys have more than your share of blessings. It's past time for you to learn that lesson.'"

He turned a note card and looked out at the audience. There wasn't a sound. "And we did," he said quietly. "Ty learned it—as he did everything—more quickly and more completely than I ever could."

He went on to outline the things his brother had done behind the scenes for others even as he gained a reputation as a rebel and agitator. He told the story of how, after their mother died, Ty had quietly taken his own trust fund and established a school for disadvantaged women in Chicago—single mothers trying to work and raise their children.

"And now," he said, "that torch of their benevolence and caring has passed to us—those who knew them and loved them and now seek to honor their memory."

He turned and pulled the covering from an easel behind him revealing a large engraved sign that read The Emma and Tyrone Dillard National Scholarship Fund. Referring to the impressive booklet now being passed out to guests by the ushers, he outlined the plan for the program.

Bethany felt the hard knot of her grief tighten in her chest—not because she was thinking of Nick, but because of Cody and what he must have suffered these last few years. Yet he had found a way to give meaning to his dual losses. His plan would make such a difference for so many young lives. She looked up at Cody and found him looking directly at her. In that moment it was as if they were the only two people in the room.

"When my mother died and a few months later my brother followed, I knew my life would never be the same. But my parents had always taught us that life is about choices. Through prayer and the dedicated work of so many people who loved them, I believe we have made a perfect choice in how best to celebrate the lives of two wonderful, generous people. Thank you for your support and enthusiasm for this project. Thank you for coming today. Thank you for everything each of you meant to the life of my mother and my brother."

He turned and sat down as the room echoed with applause. Ian and Erika were both dabbing at wet cheeks and lashes, as were several others in attendance. So many people moved forward to talk with Cody that it was impossible for Bethany to say anything to him. She wanted to tell him how moving his tribute had been. She wanted to ask more about the project. She wondered if she might not find some similar way to honor Nick's memory—perhaps establish a fund or scholarship in his name. Maybe that was the way she would finally escape the bonds of her grief. After all, it seemed to have worked for Cody. She would talk to Grace and to Nick's parents about the idea when she saw them over Christmas.

Bethany had been looking forward to being back in Washington for Christmas. She could see her family and spend time with Grace, filling her in on all the details that did not translate through e-mail or phone calls. But she found that within a couple of days of returning home to Washington, she was restless. It was not about missing Nick, she told herself, for she had already been through those first holidays without him—Thanksgiving, Christmas, New Year's Eve. That had been last year—the year when she thought she would never recover from the shock of Nick's being taken from her so suddenly and cruelly.

Perhaps time did heal all wounds, but she knew that she had a long journey before her grief was truly healed. Still, on this Christmas Eve as her family gathered with Grace's for the annual Christmas Eve supper they shared before heading off to services at the church, Bethany realized that she felt quite the outsider. Her thoughts were elsewhere. She thought of Erika and Ian—and Cody—on the ranch and wondered what Christmas would be like in that sunny desert climate. What would Honey serve? How would they exchange gifts? What were the traditions that were carried on from before when Cody's mother and brother were alive? What new traditions would Erika gently introduce?

"Bethany?"

Bethany glanced up blankly. Her mother had just shut the front door and now held a large box. "It's for you," she said, bringing the box to the table where everyone watched expectantly.

"Well, open it," Grace urged.

"I should wait until we open gifts in the morning. See? It's from Arizona. I'm sure it's something from Erika." She did not say that the handwritten label wasn't even close to Erika's flowery style of printing. It was masculine.

"That's not my sister's writing," Bethany's mother said. "Open it. If nothing else, get down to the actual gift-wrapped package and let's get rid of this packaging. The thing looks like it's come via Pony Express."

Bethany could not argue that point. The corners of the box were battered and the packaging tape was beginning to come loose in several places. "All right," she said and placed the box on the floor.

One of her brothers produced a pocketknife and slit through the tape. Wadded bunches of newspaper surrounded a large round box—a hat box tied up in vivid green tulle with a gold ribbon.

"Wow!" Grace said and grinned at her.

Bethany's father gave a low whistle. "Impressive," he added. "Who's it from?"

Before Bethany could react her niece reached for the gift tag and read aloud:

> You forgot this, so just thought I'd send it along. Erika and Ian send holiday greetings and remind you not to forget to come back. Cody

"Well, well, well," Bethany's sister-in-law murmured and exchanged looks with Bethany's mother.

"And who is Cody?" Grace's father asked.

"He's—that is, he—I mean, Ian is his father," Bethany managed, although inside she tried to answer the deeper question that she knew was on everyone's mind. *Who is Cody to you?* was the real question.

Bethany gathered the gift, the packaging and newspaper and stuffed it all back inside the shipping box. "I'll just put this under the tree," she said and fled the room.

In the living room, she set the gaily wrapped box at the edge of the piles of presents already there. Then she took the shipping box and packaging out to the garbage. The blast of fresh air that hit her as soon as she opened the back door told her just how flushed—not to mention flustered—the gift had made her.

Cody had sent her a gift. Well, not a real gift according to the note. Something she'd left behind. She ran through her packing and could think of nothing she'd forgotten. Back inside she could hear the others still in the dining room talking and laughing. They had moved on to another topic.

She picked up the box, amazingly light for such a large container. She shook it gently, then harder.

"You'll never change," Grace said, laughing as she came into the room.

Bethany quickly set the box under the tree and pretended to admire its place among the other gifts.

Grace moved closer and picked up the box again. "As long as I've known you, Bethany Taft, you have never been able to wait for a surprise."

"I was just—"

"So, open it," Grace said as she handed her the box. "What are you? Twelve again? You're a grown woman and can certainly choose when and where to open a gift."

Bethany grinned. "You're right," she said as she pulled the streamers on the gold bow. "It's my present and it's not like he's here and I need to wait to open it in front of him."

Grace glanced around. "Nope, he's definitely not here." She nodded encouragement and Bethany allowed the tulle wrapping to fall to the floor as she tugged at the tight-fitting box top. "It's a hatbox," she said as if needing to explain.

"I can see that," Grace said, smiling. "Question would be, is there a hat?"

"There is," Bethany said as the top of the box pulled free, exposing the crown of the straw Stetson. She lifted it from the box and put it on. "It belonged to Cody's mom, but I've been wearing it when I'm at the ranch.

The sun can be brutal even this time of year, not to mention the glare."

"He gave you his mother's hat?" Grace was looking at her strangely.

"Well, it wasn't like that," Bethany stammered.

"Like what?"

"You know, like he was giving me an heirloom or something."

Grace arched one eyebrow and smiled. "Right," she said softly. "It's just a hat."

Bethany saw her point. It was not just a hat at all. It was his mother's hat that he had now given her twice. "I'm not ready for this," she muttered as she replaced the hat in the box.

"What's that?" Grace asked, pointing to an envelope taped inside the lid.

Bethany reluctantly pulled the envelope free and opened it. Inside was a CD. Bethany held it up for Grace to see.

"Did you bring your laptop home with you?" Grace asked.

Bethany shook her head. "And I don't want to use Mom's. She's already asking too many questions."

"Never mind. We can use mine at the church after services."

They could hear the others leaving the dining room. "We'd better get going," her mother called in the general direction of the living room while everyone else pulled coats, gloves and scarves from the hall closet.

Bethany hesitated and Grace said, "It's been a year, honey. Come to church, if for no other reason than it will be a gift to your family. They've been so worried about you."

Grace was right. Whatever Bethany's personal feelings with regard to God and His part in taking Nick from her, Christmas Eve services were a family tradition. One she had broken the year before. She recalled the look on her parents' faces that night when everyone but Bethany left for church. She did not want to see that look again, because it had hurt her already shattered heart.

"Coming," she called and linked arms with Grace as they flicked off the lights on the Christmas tree and joined the others in the hallway. In the general confusion about who would ride in which car, no one but Grace noticed when Bethany placed the envelope with the CD in the side pocket of her shoulder bag.

The service featured the children's pageant telling the story of the birth of Jesus. Everyone joined in the singing of carols and the lighting of candles. With the exception of the previous year, Bethany had sat through the same ritual for years. Her mother reached over and squeezed her hand as the minister gave the benediction and Bethany was glad that she had come. Not because the service meant anything to her these days, but because Grace had been right. It had meant everything to her parents that she had come.

"I have to get something from my office," Grace said to the others as everyone gathered in the fellowship hall for the reception following the candlelight service. "Bethany, come with me. I want to show you something."

Bethany smiled and followed her friend. "Thank you," she said when Grace had unlocked the office, booted up the computer and turned to go.

"Don't be long," Grace said. "I'll wait out here." She softly closed the door behind her as Bethany slid the CD into the tray and waited for it to load.

The title of the piece appeared—"A Christmas Message From Us To You!"

Then there appeared a grainy image of Ian, Erika and Cody standing together wearing silly grins and ridiculous matching red sweaters emblazoned with snowmen.

"Ready?" Ian asked, glancing at the others.

Erika nodded and blew a note on a pitch pipe. The three of them mimicked the note, then Cody cleared his throat and they all began to sing to the tune of "Blue Christmas."

"Tiny lights and some trim on a green cactus bush won't be the same, Bethie, when you're not here with us. So hurry back, Bethany, we miss you. We send good tidings to those around you. But while you're doing all right with that Christmas not white, in Arizona it's a blue, blue Christmas."

Bethany was laughing aloud but very close to tears. Unable to stem her curiosity, Grace had quietly reentered the office. "Everything okay?"

"Yeah. It's so sweet. I'll play it for you. I—"

"Wait, there's more," Grace said as Bethany reached to replay the CD.

Cody was on the screen alone. He was wearing a tuxedo, and he was crooning the song, "What Are You Doing New Year's Eve?"

"Whoa!" Grace was beaming. "You've been holding out on me."

Flustered, Bethany shut down the computer and pulled the CD from the tray. "It's a joke, Gracie. He knows very well what I'm doing New Year's Eve. Apparently every year Ian throws a major party for friends and business associates. This year he asked me to plan it. I'll be working New Year's Eve."

Grace looked skeptical. "And Cody?"

"He's like a host," Bethany said. "It's a joke," she insisted as she put the CD back in her bag. "Now let's go before they send out a search party."

Chapter Ten

Bethany went straight back to Chicago the day after Christmas and took a room at the town club where the New Year's gala would be staged. She told Erika that by being on-site she could be assured that everything would go according to the plan. Erika and Ian had protested, but Bethany had been firm. So Ian had insisted on booking a suite for her. It had panoramic views of the Chicago skyline, a sitting room large enough to accommodate a grand piano, two bedrooms plus phones, televisions and wireless Internet service in every room, including the two bathrooms.

As Bethany dressed for Ian's gala, she could not help remembering other New Year's Eves. Especially strong was the memory of the New Year's two years earlier, when Nick had first kissed her. After years of friendship, that kiss was the start of their admitting their love for one another. That was the start of the journey they both thought would end in marriage, children, happily ever after.

She stood before the mirror seeing the woman she'd been then—happy and carefree, with everything good to come. She blinked and studied her face, tried a smile, tossed her hair. Nothing had really changed—except the eyes. The eyes told the real story. She had never imagined she would come to this state of utter loneliness. And that was what it was. She was surrounded by people, but so alone.

Her cell phone played its merry tune. The sound was so incongruous with her mood that she answered it only to silence the sound.

"Hello." Her voice was low and impatient.

"Uh-oh," Grace said.

Bethany sighed. She was so tired of people assuming the worst—and of Grace knowing instantly. She pulled herself up to her full height, swallowed and forced a laugh. "I can't get my hair to behave," she moaned and knew that Grace would be relieved that it was something so trivial.

"Your hair is glorious whatever it does," Grace told her. "Are you wearing it up or down?"

"Both—trying to get those little tendril thingies you see in the magazines. How do people do that? Mine just hang there limply." She studied her hair in the mirror and fingered an errant strand.

"Hair spray, gel, whatever works," Grace said. "But why don't you leave it down? It looks so wonderful around your shoulders, especially when you wear something formal—as I assume you are tonight?"

"The aquamarine strapless," Bethany replied and released her hair. "You're right. It looks better down.

This is serious, Grace. I have fallen so far as to be taking fashion advice from *you,* of all people."

Grace laughed. "Okay. Want to know what I'm wearing?"

"Sure."

"My flannel jammies," Grace said. "I can almost see the look of horror on your face, but before you start the lecture let me assure you that Jud is away on assignment and I'm spending New Year's Eve with a good book and a fairly substantial piece of Belgian chocolate."

"Cravings?"

Grace groaned. "Like you wouldn't believe. I am going to look like a two-ton gorilla by the time this kid arrives if I keep going like this."

Bethany laughed. She realized that she felt better. Grace could always do that for her. She was grateful Grace was her friend.

"Hey," Grace said, her voice serious, "I just called to wish you a very, very Happy New Year, my friend."

"Right back at you—and Jud and the kid. It's going to be a very special year, Gracie."

"Maybe for both of us?"

"You're pushing it."

Grace did not laugh. "I'm serious, Bethany. It's time, okay?"

They wished each other Happy New Year and Bethany promised to call the following day with all the details of the gala. She turned off her phone and slipped it into her silver beaded evening bag. Why did everyone assume that grieving could happen on a timetable? It wasn't like a sports event, where you got so much time to work it out and when time was up you were either a winner or a loser.

She took the private elevator down to the ballroom, where the hotel staff was scurrying around attending to last-minute details. Everything was perfect—the centerpieces in tall crystal vases with swimming goldfish among the floral arrangement of Birds of Paradise, orchids and long-stemmed roses were every bit as elegant as she had imagined. Three busboys were lighting hundreds of white votives in the clear glass bowls that circled each centerpiece and lined the food station tables. Large freestanding candelabras stood watch at every column in the large room. Three small gold chairs were arranged close to the grand piano as the musicians unpacked their instruments and began tuning them. A trio of singers ran through scales warming up their voices.

"Oh, Bethany, honey, it is simply magnificent," Erika said as she and Ian arrived.

"Fantastic," Ian agreed and bent to kiss Bethany's cheek. "Thank you. Like you needed this on top of everything else you're trying to plan," he whispered.

"I'm so pleased that you like it," Bethany said.

"And just look at you," Erika exclaimed. "You're beautiful and so completely unruffled. I would be a wreck."

Bethany smiled. "You look great, Aunt Erika—like the proverbial radiant bride."

She showed them where they should stand to welcome their guests once the doors to the grand room were opened. She went over the seating arrangement with her aunt one last time.

"And you, dear, where's the place for you?"

"Oh, I'll be behind the scenes. I need to be able to keep an eye on everything and make sure—"

"Nonsense," Ian boomed. "You there," he called to a passing hotel staff member and motioned him over. "This table needs one more place setting and chair."

"Yes, sir," the man replied without question. "And the name on the place card, sir?"

"Ms. Taft," Ian replied and spelled the last name. "Now where's that son of mine?" he asked, looking at his watch. "The boy operates on ranch time, I'm afraid."

Cody had stayed at the ranch after Christmas while Ian and Erika returned to Chicago. Bethany had not seen or talked to him since returning from her own holiday in Washington. In some ways it had made it easier to concentrate on planning the party. In other ways, it had made it hard not to imagine him in his worn Stetson, denim shirt and jeans riding Blackhawk across the vast acreage that was the ranch.

The time raced along as each phase of the party came off without a hitch. Guests arrived and soon filled the large room with their chatter and laughter and the scent of expensive perfume. They feasted on gourmet appetizers, toasted one another with flutes of nonalcoholic sparkling pear cider and then took their places at the dozens of round tables for a five-course dinner. All the while the musicians played and the singers entertained with pop and Broadway tunes that were always crowd-pleasers. By the time the dessert tables were in place, many of the guests had gathered closer to the pianist and other musicians to call out requests and sing along. And through it all Bethany moved around the room, checking every detail as she smiled at the guests, made small talk and finally sat down for the main meal.

Ian had placed her between Cody and himself. Cody's aunt Susan was to his left and Erika was to Ian's right. The rest of the table was filled with Susan's children and their spouses.

"To you," Cody said when everyone else was otherwise engaged in conversation. He raised his glass to Bethany. "I thought I had seen your best work in the engagement parties, but this is really very special—elegant and yet so comfortable for everyone."

Bethany smiled and didn't try to suppress the flush of color she felt redden her cheeks. "I had a wonderful staff to work with," she said. "I—"

Cody frowned slightly. "Why do you do that? Defer a compliment to others?"

"I don't. It's just that a party like this doesn't come together because of one person."

"Maybe. But it doesn't come together at all without the right person in charge."

Bethany smiled. "Thank you," she said softly and clinked her glass to his.

Cody glanced around. "So, when everything is set, do you think you might be able to get away for half an hour—the half hour before midnight?"

Bethany laughed. Surely the man was joking. Midnight was the climax—the moment when everything had to be perfectly coordinated—the music, the refilled glasses, the release of balloons and confetti.

"You cannot be serious," she blurted but could see that he was completely serious.

"I can be and I am," he said. "Well?"

"I don't think you fully appreciate what all has to come together at midnight."

He shrugged. "Balloons, confetti, music—it'll happen or it won't. Either way, you've done all you can unless you plan to personally pull the release for the balloons or go around refilling glasses."

It was maddening the way he could take the most complex thing and simplify it down to its very core. He stood. "I'll be waiting over there at half past eleven." He indicated the side door. "I'd really like you to be there."

"I don't have a coat with me. I—"

He picked up her evening bag and opened it, pocketed the key to her room. "I'll get it for you," he said and walked away. It was ten past eleven.

Cody stood by the exit and watched as Bethany gave final instructions to the staff. She gestured at the ceiling, walked around to every food station apparently to assure herself that the feast of desserts had been delivered as promised.

As he watched her fussing over the final details of the party, he wondered what he had been thinking—inviting her to go with him. This was a tradition he had always followed alone. Even when he'd been seeing Cynthia, he had not included her in this. So, why Bethany?

Asking her had been purely a spur-of-the-moment thing. The words had escaped before he realized it. Of course, she had no idea where they were going so he could easily choose something else—perhaps the top of the John Hancock Center for a view of the city at midnight. But that would mean abandoning a tradition he had held to ever since his Mom had received her diagnosis—a tradition he had kept to himself and shared with no one.

Ty had always been suspicious. "Where do you go? It's like you have this secret life that you only pursue on midnight of December thirty-first."

Cody had never told Ty. His brother would have laughed at the sentimentality of it all. "You are seriously losing it, bro," he would have said, shaking his head in amusement.

So why her? After all, he barely knew her, even after all this time at the ranch. Maybe that was a part of it. In spite of an external persona that was all overly bright smiles and quick-witted chatter, she kept her thoughts and true feelings to herself. It was there in those incredible eyes of hers. He'd noticed it, although he hadn't understood it, at the airport when he first met her. He had seen it again when they toured the ranch, when he sang at the Taliesin party, and once more during the dedication of the scholarship program. He saw it now as she lifted the hem of her gown and maneuvered her way through the tables to where he stood.

He held out her coat and she smiled when she saw that he had also taken her wool scarf and mittens.

"Don't I make a fashion statement?" she said as she buttoned the coat and wrapped the scarf around her throat.

"Somehow on you, everything seems to work," he replied, handing her back the key to her room. "Ready?"

He offered her his arm. Outside he nodded and the doorman gave a sharp blast of his whistle. A car she recognized as Ian's pulled up immediately and Cody held the door while Bethany climbed in. He got in after her and gave the driver an address—an intersection. He still had no idea what he was going to do.

"Okay, so what's all the mystery?" Bethany asked as the car wove in and out of crowded avenues and side streets. She was nervous. She had never liked surprises. And yet, she had come.

"You'll see," he replied. "It was a wonderful party, Bethany."

"The party's still going on. There's still a lot that needs to come off well before we can really call it a success."

He covered her hand with his, stilling her from fussing with her scarf, which was suddenly far too warm. "It's a success," he assured her.

"And we had to leave because..."

He smiled, patted her hand and released it. "Nice try. This is fine," he told the driver, who had stopped at a light.

Bethany thought about her shoes. They had cost her a fortune but they were not exactly appropriate for a winter walk in Chicago. "Uh, Cody—"

Cody laughed. "Come on. The walks are clear and dry. If the shoes get ruined then I owe you a pair, okay?"

She could not help noticing that he was not only nervous, he was also in a hurry. Bethany climbed out of the warm car, repositioned her scarf and attempted to match his long strides as they hurried across the street and around the corner.

"Any other time I would be happy to take you on in a walkathon," she called when she had fallen several steps behind, "but this dress and these shoes put me at a distinct disadvantage."

"Sorry," he mumbled. "Oh, let's just forget it. Let's just walk and wait for the New Year, okay?"

Bethany stopped, forcing him to stop, as well. "Do you want to tell me what's going on here?"

Cody stared at something over her left shoulder for a long time before answering. "I'd like you to go to church with me."

Instinctively Bethany bristled. This was the second time he had suggested that she attend formal services. She wasn't ready, wasn't sure she would ever be ready. How could she explain that? Why should she need to explain anything at all?

"I have this tradition of always starting the New Year at that church over there. They have this incredible youth bell choir and every year at midnight they perform. The bells echo throughout the high, thick stone walls of the sanctuary. They vibrate inside you. They always seem to me to peal out such joy, such hope, such promise for a better year to come."

"I'm sure it's lovely," Bethany said, trying hard to insert some sincerity into the words.

"But?"

"But I'm not exactly into church-type things these days."

"Because?" he pressed.

She was trying hard to maintain her composure. "Look, Cody, you of all people should understand why this is difficult for me. Nick died—unnecessarily."

"And you blame God."

She started to speak and he held up his hand to stop her. "You know what I think? I think this isn't about Nick at all. It may have started out that way but now it's beyond mourning Nick."

"I am still—"

"Now it's about guilt—something I know a lot about. In my case not a day goes by that I don't wrestle with guilt over not stopping Ty from going on that ski trip."

He was getting too close to something that felt like a truth Bethany had not allowed herself to contemplate. Sarcasm was her only defense. "And I suppose you think you know all about my feelings?"

"Not really. You like to keep those under wraps. If I had to guess," he said more calmly, "I'd say it has to do with the fact that when the going got rough—when God wasn't giving you your usual perfect life, when you came face-to-face with maybe your first ever serious challenge—you looked for someone to blame. And God was right there."

He hailed a passing cab. "I'm going to church, Bethany. It's what I do on New Year's Eve. I would have enjoyed sharing it with you, but I can see now that you're not even close to being ready, and I won't force you."

The cab pulled to a stop, splashing slush onto Bethany's sandals. Cody opened the door, gave the driver the name of the club and some cash, then shut the door after Bethany was inside.

The cab took off. Bethany turned to peer out the back window. Cody crossed the street and went inside the church. She could hear bells ringing.

"Stop," she said and the driver squealed to a halt at the corner.

"I'll get out here," she said.

The driver stared at the twenty-dollar bill he still held in one hand.

"Keep it," Bethany told him. "Happy New Year."

She lifted the skirt of her gown and walked quickly back toward the church. Inside the enormous and mostly empty sanctuary people sat in small, isolated groups. There were families and couples and people alone. From their clothing, it was clear they came from all walks of life. Some sat with faces lifted to a stained glass window above the altar. Others sat with heads bowed, shoulders slumped. Cody had taken a place on the aisle of one of the rear pews.

Bethany stood near a pillar in the back of the sanctuary. If he turned he would see her, but the pillar was large enough that she could easily hide. She watched him. He sat with his head bowed for a long moment, then raised his head and watched the choir enter down the center aisle.

The bell ringers were dressed in brilliant red robes, their brass bells gleaming in the flickering candlelight. They walked the length of the large church, up stairways to either side and took their places in the balcony that surrounded the main floor on three sides.

It began with a single bell—high-pitched and stunning in its clarity. Just as Cody had described, Bethany felt sound fill her and reverberate through her. Then gradually more bells joined in and with each new sound her heart raced faster.

She forgot about everything—the party, the argument with Cody, the fact that she was once again inside a house of God. She felt the pounding of the bass tones in her chest, felt the sound chip away at the hard rock of her grief. She wrapped her arms around her body.

"Are you cold?" an usher whispered.

"No," she murmured more to herself than him. It was not intended as an answer to the usher's concern. She had not even heard the question. Her *no* was a defense against the small break she felt in the carefully constructed dam that had kept her grief at bay all this time.

She felt panicky, her heart beating so fast she thought it might shatter. She gripped herself tighter. She'd had panic attacks shortly after Nick died, but not recently. She could get through this. She *must* get through this.

As the last pure chime of the inside bells died away, the bells in the church bell tower pealed out the joy of a New Year. Slowly people made their way to the exits. Bethany moved farther into the shadows, intending to stay until Cody had left and then leave. Cody passed very near where she stood, but she was certain that he had not noticed. It wasn't until he pulled the white handkerchief from the breast pocket of his tuxedo and handed it to her that she realized he'd known she was there.

She accepted it and dabbed at her face, knowing the effort was hopeless.

"Come on," Cody said, taking her arm. "Let's go."

Outside Ian's driver was waiting. Cody held the door for her, asked the driver to take her to the club and then shut the door.

Bethany was surprised. She rolled down the window. "Aren't you coming?"

"No. I'll see everyone tomorrow." He leaned down and touched her cheek. "Happy New Year, Bethany Taft." Then he tapped the roof of the car and the driver took off. Bethany twisted in her seat. Cody was walking back toward the church, his shoulders square in spite of the cold. He moved like a man at peace, Bethany thought, despite everything he'd been through. She envied that.

Cody and Ian were gone by the time Bethany checked out of the club and met Erika at the town house the following morning.

"Ranch business," Erika said, but Bethany couldn't help wondering if Cody's sudden departure had something to do with her.

"We really need to finalize plans for the ceremony this week," she reminded her aunt, trying hard to put Cody out of her mind.

Erika frowned and then sat forward on the edge of her chair before taking Bethany's hands in hers. "Bethie," she said and her voice caught. She cleared her throat and began again. "I have the most enormous favor to ask of you."

Erika looked so distressed that Bethany grasped her aunt's hands in return. "Anything. You know that."

Erika smiled ruefully. "Be careful what you promise, Bethie," she said with a soft laugh.

"Just ask," Bethany said.

"Okay. Ian and I have been discussing the ceremony and we have come up with an idea. Actually, you inspired the idea with your wonderfully innovative and thoughtful themes for our engagement parties."

Bethany felt a rush of pleasure that she had delivered even more than they had anticipated.

"Of course you've already reserved the Town Club here in Chicago and the church in Arizona," Erika said.

"The deposits have been paid on both and are nonrefundable," Bethany reminded her gently. It had not been easy getting Erika to agree to a site so she had decided to secure the two most likely venues just in case.

Erika waved a hand as if the lost deposits were of no matter and stood. She walked to the window and looked out. "The thing is that it has occurred to us—Ian and me—that it would be lovely to stay with this theme of following our love story."

"All right," Bethany said.

"There is a perfect setting for the wedding—it's where we began this journey, really."

Bethany's mind raced with possibilities and relief. She knew that Erika and Ian had met right here in Chicago. That must mean the ceremony would be here, not on the ranch. "I think we can pull off anything you want here in Chicago," she said and reached for her notebook. "Tell me what you and Ian have decided."

To Bethany's surprise Erika did not seem relieved. Instead she began pacing the room, a worried frown marring her otherwise flawless skin.

"That's just it, you see. I know that you have been thinking of the ceremony here or perhaps in a more traditional setting near the ranch even—like the church there, but—"

Bethany's heart sank as quickly as it had risen seconds before. "Another venue may not be available on such short notice," she prodded. "I'll need to make some calls and the sooner the better."

"This venue is available," Erika said, turning to face Bethany. "We want to be married in the canyon where Ian proposed, in the mountains behind the ranch with just family and close friends present."

"Oh." Bethany was speechless, nearly breathless with panic at the very idea.

"I have explained to Ian that the mountains—well, about Nick's death. He understands—we both do—and if you aren't ready yet then we can…we could… It's just that—" Erika started to cry. "Oh, I know it's selfish of me, Bethie, but it's my wedding day and it's a day I never dreamed would—" Her tears had evolved into serious sobs.

Bethany stood and pulled her aunt into a hug. "We'll work it out," she said. "It *is* your wedding day and you should have everything you've ever dreamed for that precious moment when you and Ian say your vows. We'll find a way, okay?"

"But I don't want to lose you," Erika sniffled.

Bethany laughed. "Lose me? Just you try to get rid of me. I might never have another opportunity to plan an event where money is no object."

Erika choked out an attempt at laughter and pulled away. "You're such a special young woman, Bethany," she said, gently touching Bethany's cheek. "I have to admit that inviting you to come here and plan my wedding was something of a ruse to get you out of Washington. I hoped—well, we all did—that being in another setting would be just the thing to help you move forward."

Bethany studied her hands. "I didn't realize that I had become such a burden," she said softly.

"Oh, no, dear, not at all. You could never be anything but this wonderful, high-spirited creature that we all love to pieces."

"I know everyone wants only the best for me," Bethany said.

"And that was exactly why I asked you to come here. But then as things have evolved Ian and I find ourselves more drawn to the desert as the place we want to start life together as man and wife. Even though he lived there with Emma, it was more of a vacation home for them. Ian is ready for the ranch to be our main home and I like that idea, as well. Can you understand what I'm saying?"

Bethany was at a loss for words and admitted as much with a shake of her head.

"I am saying that although when I asked you to come it was all about helping you, now as my wedding day draws nearer I am not too proud to say that it is all about me."

Bethany could not help but smile. Erika had never put her needs ahead of those of others. She was incapable of putting herself first—even on an occasion such as this. But this was what Ian wanted, too, and forced to choose between Ian and her niece, she would choose Ian every time—and rightly so.

Bethany held out her arms to her aunt. "So, how soon can we get a flight to Arizona, lady? We've got a lot of planning to do."

The relief she saw in Erika's eyes was worth everything. They would find a way. She would find a way. She would not spoil this once-in-a-lifetime dream for her beloved aunt.

After a three-year drought in Phoenix, everyone seemed thrilled when it rained every day for two weeks and seemed destined to continue for another two weeks. Everyone except Bethany. Every morning she awoke to a view of the mountains shrouded in gray. Somewhere amidst those ominous cliffs and shadows was the canyon that Erika and Ian had chosen for their wedding.

It was impossible for others to understand why these mountains represented everything she feared. She didn't understand it herself. But somehow that forbidding pinnacle had come to stand for everything she'd tried to hold at bay since Nick died—her anger, her loss, her loneliness.

For some time now she had felt as if she were destined to make her way through life as a solitary traveler.

She was surrounded by the love and caring of family and friends and yet she couldn't seem to feel anything. No, she couldn't permit herself to feel—if she lost someone else it would hurt too much. She knew that now.

As she stood on the porch of the guesthouse waiting for the rain to let up, she saw Cody dash across the yard on his way from the main house to the stables. He had on a black rain slicker and a black Stetson. The rain ran off the hat in rivulets and he pulled it lower as if to keep the pelting rain off his face. He did not see her, or if he did, he gave no sign.

Ever since he'd put her in the car outside the Michigan Avenue church, he'd gone back to the kind of polite distance they had settled on before Thanksgiving. In the presence of Ian, Erika or Honey he was charming and even talkative. But if he encountered her alone, he found some reason to keep moving.

Bethany had begun to understand that the invitation to share the bell choir concert had been far more than a gesture of simple kindness. For her, it had been a battle to keep her own trauma at being in the church in check. But as she had listened to the peal of the bells, her thoughts had turned to Cody. How quiet and at peace he had been. How had he come to that peaceful place? How had he overcome his grief not once but twice and found his way back to God? Perhaps that night he had taken her to the church hoping to help, wanting to show her that he understood. And once again, her instinct had been to turn away, to reject anything that might ease the pain she carried with her like a boulder, like those mountains—hard and unyielding.

She pulled on Erika's bright pink slicker, retrieved the one thing that might penetrate the barrier Cody had erected between them and ran across the yard to the stables.

The rain pelted her from all sides and in spite of the rain gear she was soaked by the time she reached the shelter of the stables. She took off the slicker and hung it on a hook, ran her hand through her hair—a lost cause—and followed the low murmur of Cody's voice as he talked to Blackhawk at the far end of the row of stalls.

She was acting purely on instinct now—something she had not allowed herself to do for some time. Before Nick died, spontaneity had been her byword. Since he died, she had pulled inside, protecting herself from any possibility of something going wrong. She had spent every waking moment planning for any contingency.

But this time things were different. Instinct had led her to grab the pair of evening sandals. Instinct told her to keep this initial contact light—gauge the mood, test the waters.

Cody had obviously decided that he needed to back off and who could blame him? After all, he'd made several attempts to break through the barriers she'd thrown up whenever anyone got too close. Maybe he regretted the things they'd shared over the holidays—Thanksgiving with their families, sending the hat, not to mention the New Year's fiasco.

No, instinct told her to keep it light. Maybe they could find their way back to what she understood now had all the promise of a valuable and lifelong friendship. And then maybe someday that might evolve into something more than friendship.

Chapter Eleven

Cody hated the distance he forced himself to keep from Bethany but he saw no other choice. They were oil and water and any fantasy of some kind of real relationship he might have entertained at various times over the last few months was just that—pure illusion.

Not that she was like Cynthia. Not at all. Cynthia had been calculating in everything she did. Bethany was anything but. He might not fully understand her, but her emotional pain was there in her eyes for the world to see—fear, sadness, insecurity and doubt. And on the very rare occasion, a glimpse of the happy, carefree soul she must have once been.

Cody was drawn to her because of that vulnerability that lay beneath the tough exterior she tried so hard to present. In spite of his frustration with her, he could not help but want to reach her, to make things easier for her, to bring out her smile and that delightful sense of humor he caught glimpses of now and then.

The truth was that Bethany Taft fascinated him. At first he had thought his interest was no more than the normal interest he showed in people who were in obvious distress. But almost without his realizing it, his feelings for Bethany had become far more complicated. With others, he could be objective. He could offer his help or advice and whether or not the other person chose to take it was not the point. He had tried.

But when Bethany turned a blind eye to his attempts to help, he felt rejected. No, sometimes, he felt downright angry. Didn't she get it? Couldn't she see that she had come to mean something to him? That he looked upon her as more than just some stranger in need. She was—

What?

Family? Not really.

A friend?

More?

The idea rocked him. Is that where this was headed? Was he developing feelings for her that went beyond friendship?

Major mistake.

"Look, she's here to do a job and then she's out of here. She's made that clear from day one. Keep it simple. A friendship that can sustain itself across the miles, that can survive on seeing each other two or three times a year. That'll work, right, Hawk?"

The horse made no response, not even a swish of his tail.

"You're a big help," Cody muttered.

* * *

Bethany heard the low murmur of Cody talking to his horse as she walked past the long line of stalls.

"Hi," she said a step before she reached Blackhawk's stall. She didn't want to risk startling the horse—or Cody.

Cody glanced up and there was a second when he couldn't disguise the mixture of surprise and wariness he obviously felt at seeing her. "Hi," he replied and continued grooming the horse. "What's up?"

"It occurred to me that you might have some time this afternoon to make good on a promise," she said.

He frowned. "Promise?"

She dangled the strappy silver shoes she'd worn New Year's Eve in front of him. "Something about if these got ruined, you'd buy me a new pair?"

To her relief, he smiled. The slow lifting of the corners of his mouth that she'd come to recognize…and like. She hoped this meant that the tight-lipped, suspicious grimace that had passed for a smile these last weeks was gone forever.

He took the shoes and examined them. "They look fine to me," he said.

"How can you say that? There are water marks and salt stains all over them. I can't possibly wear these again."

"So, you want to go shopping?"

"I want to go shopping with your credit card," she said.

"I go where my credit card goes," he warned, but he was smiling.

"Works for me. How does now work for you?"

Cody gave Blackhawk's mane a final sweep of the brush. "Let's go."

Ten minutes later he turned his SUV onto a narrow dirt road and stopped in front of a ranch-style building that stood alone in what Bethany could only describe as the middle of nowhere.

"What's this?" she asked warily as Cody swung down from the cab and came around to open the door for her.

"This, my lady, is boot paradise." He bowed and swept one arm toward the entrance as if a red carpet awaited her.

"As in cowboy boots?" Her heart sank. Not exactly her cup of tea.

"Yup. If you're gonna hang out with the Dillard clan, you're gonna need yourself some boots, ma'am."

"Cody!"

A small dark-haired boy of about eight bolted from the shop and threw himself at Cody. "Where ya been? Who's this? Your girlfriend?"

"Whoa! Hold on there!" Cody caught the child and lifted him so that the boy was eye level with Bethany. "Jimmy Boxer, this is Ms. Bethany Taft."

Jimmy offered her his hand and she shook it, charmed.

"She your girlfriend?" he asked Cody again, sizing Bethany up.

"Not this week," Cody replied.

Jimmy giggled. "So, where ya been?"

"Around. Mostly in Chicago."

Jimmy's chocolate-brown eyes grew wide with excitement. "Did you fly there and back?"

"Yeah." Cody's eyes twinkled and Jimmy pressed a fist to his mouth to stem the tide of giggles and then together they shouted, "And boy, are my arms tired!"

It was the corniest joke that Bethany had heard in months. It was ridiculous. But their laughter was contagious and soon she was laughing as hard as they were.

"I like her," Jimmy announced as Cody set him down and he took off for the store. "I'll tell Dad you're here."

"He's adorable," Bethany said as she wrestled with the urge to get lost in the depths of Cody's eyes, focused on her with no hint of teasing.

"He's my godson," Cody said then cleared his throat and glanced around as if trying to remember why he'd brought her here in the first place.

"You did promise shoes," she reminded him.

Cody grinned and took her arm.

As soon as Bethany stepped over the threshold, the aroma of expensive leather hit her. She paused, closed her eyes and breathed it in as if it were the finest perfume. "Oh, it smells wonderful in here," she whispered and opened her eyes.

The shop's pale cream paneled walls were the perfect backdrop for a veritable art exhibit of boots. Bethany squealed with delight and headed straight for a pair of silver-studded suede ankle boots. "These are magnificent," she cried.

"I'm glad you like them," a man she hadn't even noticed said. He was standing at a curtained door that led to a back room.

"Bethany, meet Sam," Cody said. "He's the designer and boot maker, not to mention my best friend."

"You're a genius," Bethany gushed and pumped Sam's hand enthusiastically. "Have you ever thought of opening a store in the D.C. area?"

"Nope," Sam replied. "Got all I can handle right here. Now, what can I show you—size seven, right?"

Bethany nodded and started pointing to various styles. "That one and this one and oh, that red one there."

Sam pulled boxes from the shelves and placed them in front of a long wooden bench.

"Why don't I play the role of shoe salesman?" Cody suggested, pulling up a smaller stool in front of Bethany. "Looks like you could be busy for a while."

Bethany sat and started opening boxes. "Oh, this is so wonderful," she said as she held up a moccasin-style boot in a pale cream.

"Dress boot," Cody assured her. "Guaranteed appropriate for the most formal gathering."

He took the boot from her and spread the laces, then held it for her. "Is it not to the lady's liking?" he asked when she hesitated.

"No. Yes. I love it," she said, taking the boot away from him and putting it on. "Oh, it's like wearing silk on my feet," she squealed, quickly grabbing the mate and putting it on as well.

"Wrap 'em up," Jimmy shouted.

"Hold on, pal," Cody said, "I think she's just getting started."

* * *

Cody hadn't been fooled for a moment when Bethany suggested the shopping trip. The tension between them had become almost palpable and he felt a little guilty that she was the one who had made the first move.

The shopping expedition had been fun and had definitely achieved its purpose—easing the tension between them and bringing with it a return of Bethany's high-spirited side.

After they had said their goodbyes to Sam and Jimmy and headed back toward the ranch, though, Bethany withdrew. The rain pelted the windshield and for a mile or so the only sound was the rhythmic slap of the wipers on the windshield.

"How about some coffee?" Cody asked.

"Sure. Sounds nice."

He took a side road to a café he knew on the reservation. "Ever try fry bread?"

She turned her attention from the rivulets on her side window and looked directly at him. "Sounds fattening," she said and smiled.

"Definitely, and guaranteed to clog an artery or two if you make a habit of it, but you really can't come to Arizona and not try it once."

He parked and produced a giant golf umbrella, which he opened as he came around to open her door. He stood blocking her way for a moment and considered her shoes. "This isn't going to cost me another pair of shoes, is it?"

To his relief, she laughed. "Nope—just coffee and this fry bread thing."

In spite of the umbrella the rain spattered them and they were laughing breathlessly as they entered the small café. The place was deserted. A Native American woman looked over at them from her place at the counter.

"Sit anywhere you like," she said as she pushed herself away from the counter and picked up a couple of menus.

"Coffee and an order of your fry bread," Cody called to her as he led the way to a small table near the window.

"Honey? Powdered sugar?" the woman asked.

"Both," Cody replied.

They shrugged out of their wet slickers and Cody hung them on hooks near the door. They made small talk about the shopping experience. She asked a couple of questions about Jimmy. The waitress delivered their coffee. Silence reigned.

Cody considered his options. He had this feeling that she needed to talk, that this whole day had been about testing the waters, wondering if she could confide in him. He wondered why she had picked him and not Erika. Must be something to do with the wedding.

"How are the wedding plans coming along?"

"Fine. Everything is really falling into place." She laughed nervously. "It's almost scary how smoothly everything is coming together."

The waitress brought two orders of fry bread sprinkled with powdered sugar. She removed a syrup pitcher filled with honey from the pocket of her apron and set it between them. "Anything else?"

"No, thanks," Cody said and the woman walked back to the counter where she resumed reading a magazine.

"This is incredible," Bethany said as she savored the first bite of the light pancakelike bread.

"Try it with a little honey," he advised, drizzling honey over his entire slice.

"It's already so sweet," she protested.

"Trust me," he said and handed her the syrup pitcher. He wondered if she understood the dual meaning of his words. He wanted to add, *trust me to understand.*

They quickly devoured the plate-size servings of the bread. Conversation consisted mostly of murmurs of appreciation for the taste and Cody explaining the recipe.

"More coffee?" the waitress asked. They both nodded. She refilled their mugs, picked up their plates and left the bill. "Take your time," she said.

Bethany sipped her coffee and looked out the window.

"How about talking about it," Cody said softly. "Instead of keeping it all inside. Maybe I can help."

Her expression told him that he'd hit the nail squarely on the head and that his perception had caught her by surprise.

"I…" Her tone was at first a prelude to denial that there was anything to discuss, but then her expression changed and she took a deep breath. "It's going to sound so selfish and self-centered," she warned.

"I try not to judge people," he promised. "I figure even when we're being selfish we have cause. You don't strike me as the self-centered type. In fact, just the opposite. I would be willing to bet that you often put others first to your own detriment."

She looked into his eyes long enough that he felt the color rising on his neck. "Honest," he said with an uneasy laugh. "I'm a good listener."

She began by changing the subject. She talked about Jimmy and Cody's friendship with Sam. She talked about the people at the ranch—how they seemed more like part of the extended family than employees. She talked about the way the people at Taliesin had welcomed him that night.

"You have a life," she said finally.

"As do you, and a good one," he agreed. "We're both blessed as far as I can see."

Her head shot up and she stared at him in disbelief. "How do you see that?"

Cody faltered for a moment, taken aback by the sudden look of anger and bitterness in her eyes. "Well, it seems that we both have been blessed with a loving family that extends beyond our immediate circle of parents and siblings to include others."

She said nothing so he kept going.

"And beyond family we both have work we love and an extended community of people who care about us and are there for us in various ways. We both have wonderful friends—you have Grace, for example. I'm looking forward to meeting her and Jud at the wedding."

Bethany ignored this last. "Look, I know that I'm fortunate. I have friends and a loving family. I have work that I'm good at. I have—"

"Many blessings," Cody interrupted.

Bethany scowled. “Good fortune in most ways,” she corrected.

“But?”

“But sometimes it feels as if I don’t have a *life,*” she said, her tone wistful. “It’s like I’m just marking time.”

“Until what?” he asked.

“That’s the problem. I don’t know. Meanwhile, everybody is moving on and I’m…not.”

“It takes time,” Cody said, trying to be reassuring.

She shook her head and ran her forefinger around the rim of her coffee cup. After a minute she said softly, “After your mother and brother—after losing them so unexpectedly, so young—weren’t you angry at the unfairness of it all?”

Cody relaxed, understanding finally where this was going. “Unfair to who?” he asked, his gaze steady on her.

“To them—they had so much life yet to live, so much left to give. And what about Ian? What about you?” Her voice shook. She started to say something else but waved away the thought.

“And where should I direct that anger?” he asked, knowing that it was the wrong place and the wrong time, but also knowing that now that she’d let him in he had to push the door wider before she slammed it shut again.

She looked out the window, her lips locked in a tight line.

“Bethany?” he prompted.

She turned back to him, her eyes flashing. “Well,

clearly it wasn't God since you seem perfectly at home in church."

"For me the church is another part of my extended family—God is the head of that extended family, I guess," Cody said, keeping his voice calm.

"God took your mother and brother," Bethany reminded him, her voice laced with bitterness.

"No. Cancer took my mother and a terrible, unnecessary accident took Ty."

"So where was God?" It was obvious now that he had found the chink in the dam behind which she held all of her grief and despair at what had happened to Nick, and she was incapable of stopping the swirling flood of her rage and bitterness.

The woman at the counter glanced their way as Bethany's voice rose and then fell to an enraged whisper.

"Tell me, where was God when they needed Him? When *you* needed Him?" She drained her coffee and set the mug on the table with enough force to make the woman look up again. "Can we get out of here?" Bethany asked, already standing and moving toward her coat.

Cody laid money on the table and nodded to the waitress. By the time he retrieved his jacket and the umbrella, Bethany was already out the door.

The rain had stopped and she was striding down the dirt road toward the highway. Cody sighed and got in the car. He pulled alongside and kept pace with her.

"It's a long walk back to the ranch," he said.

She ignored him.

"If I promise not to talk, will you get in?"

She stopped, waited for him to stop then walked around and got in.

"Seat belt," he said and she shot him a look. "Okay, just a reminder."

Neither of them spoke a word all the way back to the ranch.

"Thanks for the boots," she said quietly when he stopped in front of the guesthouse. "Would you let Honey know I won't be at dinner tonight?"

Cody nodded. "Hey, Bethany?" he called to her as she started up the walk. "Can I say one thing?"

She nodded.

"It just seems to me that you've got an awful lot of questions you've been carrying around for a long time now. Is it possible that you're so busy asking the questions, that you're not listening for answers?"

She blinked and just stood on the walkway for a moment staring at him. Finally she gave a slight nod. "Maybe," she said and then turned and went into the house.

Bethany could not get over the speed with which everything that she had so carefully repressed for months had come rushing to the surface under Cody's gentle probing. She was embarrassed by the way she'd acted with him. After all, this wasn't someone who had no experience in loss of a loved one. This was a man who had lost not one but two beloved people in the span of a few months.

Perhaps that was why it had come so easily, the anger and bitterness of it all spewing out of her like a sickness.

Perhaps that was why it was so hard to ignore his words. He hadn't offered any direct advice or counsel. He'd reminded her of all she had in her life and what had she done? Rejected it because she couldn't see a life in all of that. What kind of person had she become that she could so easily reject her family's love, her friendship with Grace, her ability to do work that she loved and do it well? Cody was right. Everyone and everything that had been there before Nick died still was.

She picked up the phone and called her parents. She told her mom all the details of Erika's wedding dress, sought her opinion on the menu for the reception, and asked her to send a couple of recipes. When her dad got on the line, she gave him tips on making travel plans for the family to come to Arizona for the wedding, told him about the boot store and promised to take him there.

"You sound good, Bethie," he said as the call wound down to its inevitable end.

Bethany swallowed around the lump in her throat. "Busy," she said with a laugh. "Like father, like daughter. I like being busy."

After she'd hung up, she thought about calling Grace but knew that Grace would see through to the core of the reason for the call. "What's wrong?" she would ask and Bethany was so very tired of being asked that question.

No, what she was weary of was having no answers.

Chapter Twelve

The following day Bethany was all business—wedding business. At breakfast she spelled out a long to-do list for Erika. Topping the list was her need to see the site for the wedding for herself so she could figure out the logistics of moving a small wedding party and the two hundred guests in and out of a mountain canyon.

"It is a bit ridiculous when you put it that way," Erika sighed. "Perhaps just Ian and I—and the minister, of course."

"Not!" Bethany said. "This is your wedding and the setting you want is the setting you will have. Others may need to make choices and accommodations, but definitely not you or Ian."

Erika reached over and hugged Bethany. "You are such a special young woman, Bethany. Do you know how delighted I am to claim you as my niece?"

Always uncomfortable with a compliment, Bethany returned Erika's hug and then turned her attention back to her notes. “The question is, how best to do this?” She tapped the eraser end of the pencil against her teeth.

“There are maps,” Erika said. “Ian has detailed trail maps in his desk. I’ll get them for you.” She was up and out the door before Bethany could protest.

The maps might be all she needed. If they showed the topography, she could see if her plan might work. Several of Ian’s friends had already laughed nervously at the idea of the wedding being at the ranch. “Just wait’ll they find out they’re going to the ceremony on horseback up the side of a mountain,” she muttered.

“There are other ways into the canyon,” Cody said, his deep voice startling her since she’d been oblivious to anything but her notes.

She composed herself and looked at him with a frown. “Such as?”

“Why don’t I show you?”

“Now?”

He shrugged. “I’m not doing anything. You sound like you’re stuck. Now sounds good to me.”

“Erika went to get the maps.”

“Ever try to read one of those topographical maps?”

Reluctantly Bethany had to admit she had not.

“Hard to get the real picture from a bunch of elevation numbers.”

“And your suggestion is?”

“How about taking the helicopter view?”

“Is that a business term?”

“It can be a synonym for what’s called the ‘big picture.’ In this case, though, I’m talking an actual helicopter.”

"You have a helicopter?"

He nodded. "Can be a big help in covering a place as big as this one is."

"You drive it?"

"Pilot it," he corrected without judgment. "Sometimes. Mostly I let Danny do the honors. He's great at getting in and out of tight places."

She hesitated.

"You know, Bethany, at the risk of starting World War Fourteen between us, I'm going to say something here—sometimes if the mountain won't come to you, you really do have to go to the mountain."

"I thought we were discussing logistics for the wedding," she said.

"That, too." He turned and opened the front door. "Coming?"

The helicopter ride was noisy as the ranch foreman, Dan Lawford, pointed out various places of interest. "There's the trail," he yelled above the whupping of the blades outside the open doorway.

Bethany pushed her hair out of her eyes and raised her digital camera for a shot. "Can you get any closer?" she yelled back, ignoring Cody's raised eyebrows.

"Sure," Danny said with a grin. "I can land this baby there if you like."

"That won't be necessary. Just a little closer—got it. Now what's that down there?" She pointed toward the bottom of the canyon.

"Creek," Cody said. "It'll dry up in about six to eight weeks."

"Where does it go?"

"Go? It gets hot and dry and there's no rain so it just dries up."

"I know that, but now it must be headed somewhere—a river or lake?" She could see that Cody and Danny were both impressed with the question.

"Lake," Danny said. "I'll show you."

The lake was a nice size. "Is there a road and a place to launch boats?" Bethany asked.

"It's seasonal," Cody said.

"Okay. Could we bring the guests for the ceremony down to the lake and into the canyon by boat?"

Danny glanced over his shoulder at Cody.

"By raft maybe," he said and Cody nodded.

Bethany made a note and next to it did a small sketch. "So we could hire a flotilla of rafts to carry the guests in and out."

"A flotilla?" Cody repeated and had trouble hiding his amusement.

"A bunch of rafts," Danny translated, earning a wide smile of gratitude from Bethany.

"Exactly. Will it work?"

"Don't see why not," Danny said in spite of Cody's obvious reservations. "Wanna take another look?"

"Sure," Bethany agreed. "After all, as someone told me recently, if the mountain won't come to you—"

"Cute," Cody muttered.

Two days later her cell phone rang. Erika and Ian had gone out for the day and would not be back until late. Bethany was looking forward to having the entire afternoon and evening to herself. Given that she'd just seen Cody at breakfast that morning, she was surprised that he would call instead of stopping by as he sometimes did.

They exchanged the customary phone greetings and then Bethany was sure her cell battery had gone dead. She was always forgetting to recharge the thing. She checked the screen. Plenty of power.

"Cody? Are you there?"

She heard him clear his throat.

"I was wondering," he said before clearing his throat again. "I mean, since we seem to be getting along pretty well these days—if you might like to go out somewhere?"

Bethany was surprised at the hesitation she heard in Cody's voice.

"You mean like a date?" she asked.

He paused. "Yeah, something like that."

She couldn't help laughing. He sounded like a teenager calling the girl he'd never imagined asking out.

"Or not," he added when she laughed. She heard him draw in a breath and then in his normal confident voice he said, "Bad idea."

"Hold on," she said. "Give a girl a chance to answer."

He waited.

"What kind of date?" she asked.

"One that has nothing to do with researching stuff for the wedding," he answered immediately.

"Oh." Now she was the shy one. Without the wedding to spark conversation, what would they talk about? She really didn't want to relive Nick's tragic accident anymore. In fact she was certain that she'd told him far too much. She'd never told anyone the things she'd admitted to him.

"We could go for a ride—Thunderbolt seems to like you."

"Am I going on this date with Thunderbolt?" It slipped out. It was the kind of sassy response that came naturally to her. At least, it had up to a year ago. She regretted it the moment the words left her lips, but to her surprise, Cody chuckled.

"No, ma'am. Thunderbolt can do his own asking."

"Are there other options?" she asked. "In case it rains…again."

"Good point. There's always dinner and there's a concert you might enjoy if you like country music."

"I love country music."

This news seemed to cheer him enormously. "Me, too."

They were both silent for a moment, then he cleared his throat once more. "Okay then, I'll pick you up at six-thirty."

"Tonight?" Her hand flew to her hair, which was an impossible mess.

"Unless you have to wash your hair or something," he said in a teasing tone. "That's when the concert is—tonight at eight."

Bethany glanced at the clock on the fireplace mantel. It was already after four. A little more than two hours. She never got ready to go anywhere in that kind of time. "I can make it," she said, more to herself than to him.

"Great. Casual, okay? The place we'll eat is no-frills and the concert's in the church fellowship hall." He paused then added, "I hope that's not a problem…being in the church and all?"

It was and it wasn't. Bethany was well aware that her stomach still tightened at the idea of anything to do with being in God's house. Still, it was way past time for her to get over such nonsense. God—if a person believed in Him—was everywhere. And if you didn't believe? He was still there, so what did it matter?

"No problem."

"Okay then. See you at six-thirty."

"I'm looking forward to it."

Bethany was clicking the Off button on the phone as she walked quickly to her closet. She pulled open both doors and stared at the vast selection of clothes. There was absolutely nothing to wear.

Once again she remembered her hair, gave a shriek and headed for the shower. When she came out forty-five minutes later, Erika was sitting on her bed.

"I thought you and Ian were going to be out late," Bethany said.

Erika shrugged. "He received a call about some business deal that could not wait until tomorrow. He's taking care of it now and then we'll have a quiet evening here."

"Sounds nice," Bethany said.

"I heard that you and Cody are going out," she said and could not hide the twinkle of delight in her eyes.

"News travels fast," Bethany said as she whipped off the towel she'd wrapped around her wet hair.

"Honey is my source. Apparently Cody made the call from the back porch, just outside the kitchen window."

Bethany nodded absently as she combed through the

tangles of her hair. "This will never dry in time," she moaned, "even with the hair dryer."

Erika laughed and came to stand behind her. "Of course it will, but I have an idea. What if I do it into a French braid for you? It would be the perfect look for a casual dinner and the concert."

"Will you and Ian be there?"

"Why, Bethany Taft, I never thought I'd see the day when you got nervous about a date."

"I am not nervous. It just seemed like a nice idea—the four of us out for the evening."

"Not our cup of tea, dear. Now about your hair—" She gently removed the comb from Bethany's hand and started raking it slowly through the tangles, working them out to the ends until Bethany's hair lay smooth against her back.

"The braid might work," Bethany said, "if I had anything to wear that would be appropriate."

This time Erika could not seem to stop laughing.

"What?" Bethany said testily.

"You know what," Erika replied. "You have an outfit for every occasion, with several spares in reserve." She turned Bethany so that she was facing the open closet. "You sit there and put together the perfect outfit while I do your hair," Erika said.

"He said casual," Bethany grumbled, "so normally I would think a nice pair of jeans but you can't wear jeans in a church."

"Why on earth not?"

Bethany considered that. "Okay, I'll start with my

embroidered jeans," she said and fell silent as her eyes roved the rack of clothes before her.

"All done," Erika announced half an hour later.

Bethany turned to the mirror and gasped. She looked different, her pulled-back hair only served to accent her cheekbones and eyes. She looked…great. She grinned at Erika. "Fabulous," she said and gave her aunt a hug.

"Now get dressed," Erika ordered and left the room.

Bethany had tried on and rejected several different outfits when she heard Erika's happy voice welcoming Cody.

"Why, Cody, don't you look terrific?" she exclaimed. "Bethany should be out any minute. How about a glass of lemonade?"

"How about several glasses of lemonade?" Bethany muttered as she studied her latest getup in the full-length mirror and rejected it.

"Bethie? Cody's here," Erika called out as she tapped softly on the door and entered the room. She took one look at the mound of rejected clothes on the bed and then at Bethany tearing off yet another outfit and closed the door.

"Nothing is right," Bethany moaned.

"Oh, Bethie," Erika said as she dug through the clothes and found the original jeans. "These with that—" she pointed at the rose-colored T-shirt Bethany still had on "—and that wonderful suede cropped jacket you got in Mesa last week."

Bethany followed her directions and had to admit the outfit was perfect. "Shoes?"

"Boots," Erika corrected. "Preferably the ones you conned Cody into buying for you."

"They have a three-inch heel," Bethany said.

"And fortunately for you, Cody still tops that in his stockinged feet." She presented Bethany with the boots. "Perfect," she pronounced after Bethany pulled on the boots and stood up. "Now get out there before one or both of you changes your mind."

When she entered the living room Cody was standing by the window looking out at the mountains. Bethany suddenly realized she had nothing to say.

Cody turned and the look that crossed his face was everything a woman hopes to see in the eyes of a man she—what? Likes? Is attracted to? Impossible.

"Hi," she managed. "Sorry to keep you waiting."

"Worth every minute," Cody replied and handed her a single orchid.

"Oh, it's so unusual—the color is—"

"Matches your eyes," he said.

"Doesn't it, though?" Erika said as she entered the room. "I'll put it in some water for you, Bethany. And, my, look at the time. You two had better get going if you're going to eat and make it to the concert on time."

Once again Erika herded Bethany toward the door. "Have a wonderful evening," she called as soon as the two of them were outside.

She closed the door firmly and they found themselves alone with the sun setting and streaking the sky with an incredible display of pink and purple clouds.

"Oh, my," Bethany said as she looked up at the sky.

"Come on," Cody said. "If we hurry there's a great spot for seeing the full effect."

He drove out into the desert and up into the foothills, then swung the car around and pointed. "Look."

The sight was so awesome that it took Bethany's breath away. Below her was the ranch, the lights in the house a golden glow in the twilight. Above her was a sunset like none she had ever seen before. An endless sky streaked with mauves and reds and gold-tinged pinks. And below that the mountains were purple.

"It's like the song," she said.

Cody started to hum the tune to "America, the Beautiful," and Bethany heard the words echo in her head. Purple mountain's majesty—it was the first time she had been unable to take her eyes off the mountains.

All too soon it was over as the orange sun disappeared.

"Wow," Bethany murmured. "Thanks for showing me that."

Cody smiled, but said nothing. He turned the key and headed back toward the paved road that led to the highway.

Until they were actually at the restaurant—a lovely little French bistro with seating in an outside garden—Bethany had put the idea of this being a date firmly out of her mind. But once they were seated and the conversation slowed to a stop, she had to deal with the fact that she was out with a man—a man who wasn't Nick. She searched her heart for feelings of guilt and disloyalty, and found both sensations lurking there.

"The seafood crepes are good if you like seafood," Cody said. Bethany had been studying the menu as if she might be called on to recite it from memory.

"That sounds good," she replied and could not think of anything more to say.

The waiter came for their orders, relieving her of the need to make conversation for the moment. He was charming without being obtrusive. Bethany found it easy to make conversation with him.

"What would you recommend?"

"The seafood crepes are excellent and so is the veal."

"I'll have the veal," Bethany said, and Cody nodded and seconded the choice. The waiter smiled, took their orders and left.

"He's very good," Bethany said, relieved that the exchange with the waiter had given Cody and her a point of conversation.

"The owners have done a good job of training the staff," Cody agreed. Once again, the conversation died.

The waiter brought their salads and a loaf of warm bread on a cutting board. Bethany cut the bread more for something to occupy her hands than her desire to taste it. Cody poured olive oil onto a side plate.

He dipped his bread, took a bite and then set it down. "How's this working for you?" he asked.

"The bread? I—"

"The date," he said.

"Fine," Bethany said in a falsetto voice she barely recognized. "Really. I'm having a wonderful time."

"Too soon?"

This time she had no doubt what he was asking. "Maybe."

"Tell me something. If Nick could see us right now, what do you think he'd be thinking?"

"That's ridiculous," Bethany said and took a piece of bread she didn't really want.

"No. The question is, would Nick approve?"

"Of you?"

"Of this—you out with another man."

"Nick wasn't the jealous type," she said.

"It's not about his being jealous. It's about what he would want for you since he can't be here."

The waiter chose that moment to deliver their entrées. He followed that by refilling their glasses with iced tea and asking if they needed anything else.

Bethany took the first bite of the veal. "Fabulous," she said.

Cody nodded. "So, answer the question—what do you think Nick would want for you?"

"What would your Mom and Ty want for you?"

"To get on with my life and live it fully—which I *am* doing, to the best of my ability," he replied immediately. It was clearly something he'd thought about.

Bethany concentrated on her food. "Well, of course, anyone who loves someone would want that for the other person. This sauce is incredible."

Cody looked at her for a moment. "Okay, I get it. Change the subject," he said without rancor. "I'll get the recipe for the sauce if you like. The chef is a friend."

"It seems as if everyone we meet is a friend."

Cody shrugged. "In many ways it's a small community. People take the time to get to know each other—especially those who've made this their home."

Bethany nodded. "Washington is like that. You wouldn't think so but it has a real small-town atmosphere in many ways." She was relieved to have the conversation move away from Nick. "My family has been there for generations, living in the same neighborhood. One of my brothers just bought a house down the block from my parents."

"So, will you go back there when the wedding is over?"

It was an innocent question—a natural one following the path their conversation had taken. "I…maybe."

They were back to Nick.

"Must be hard," Cody said.

Bethany didn't pretend not to understand what he meant. "No more than your living on the ranch. That must be filled with memories of Ty and your mother."

"Not really. For Mom and Dad, the ranch was something they looked on as more of a vacation place. Their life was in Chicago."

"And Ty?"

"City boy all the way. He came down here more for the sports—mountain biking, skiing, anything that required him to test himself." His voice trailed off and he had a faraway look in his eyes.

"My turn to ask you a question," Bethany said.

"Okay."

"Why did you ask me on this date?"

He bought time by taking a long swallow of his tea. "Why not?"

Bethany laughed. "That's not an answer. Come on. Why would you ask out a woman who is clearly—at least in your opinion—city born and bred when by your own admission city girls are not your type?"

"Maybe it occurred to me that city girls could change." He was flirting with her now, his eyes twinkling, his smile irresistible.

"Right."

He called for the check and paid with a credit card. Bethany saw that he gave their waiter a substantial tip—a fact the waiter did not miss.

"Thank you, sir," he said, his eyes popping.

"You are a really nice person," Bethany said as they drove to the church for the concert.

"Why shucks, ma'am, I was just trying to impress you."

"You were not. You would have done that even if I hadn't been there."

"But it did impress you?"

"Yeah."

"Good."

He pulled into the church lot and had to drive around a bit before he found an open spot. As they walked to the church they could hear the musicians warming up.

Cody handed the usher two tickets and took Bethany's arm as he led the way to two seats in the front.

Toward the end of the concert, the group onstage moved from country to gospel and got the entire audience singing along. Bethany liked the way Cody's rich baritone resonated without dominating. No, Cody Dillard was no show-off. He just loved to sing and he did it with genuine joy.

"Come on, Bethany, you must know this one," he said as the group launched into "Go Tell It on the Mountain."

"I can't sing," Bethany said softly.

"Of course you can. Everybody can sing a little."

"Not me. I'm tone deaf," she replied as the opening music built and everyone prepared to join in.

"Humor me," Cody insisted.

"Okay. Just remember, you asked for it." Bethany took a deep breath and sang the chorus with gusto.

Cody glanced at her several times as if trying to decide if she was putting him on. Bethany sang louder. Cody grinned, then started to laugh. That started Bethany laughing and even the performers onstage caught on to the joke. They kept singing but they were chuckling and nodding at Bethany.

"One more time," the lead singer called.

Cody put his arm around Bethany's waist and the two of them swayed back and forth as the audience belted out a final chorus.

After two encores, the group left the stage, the lights came up and there was the general buzz of people leaving a concert that they'd enjoyed enormously. Bethany was one of those people. She was feeling none of her usual guilt or anger. She felt as if something inside her had opened and allowed this little piece of happiness to enter.

As they crossed the parking lot, she spontaneously

linked her arm through Cody's. "Thanks so much, Cody. I had a really terrific time."

"Better than a bell concert, I take it," he said, his tone light.

"Oh, no, just different. Just…different," she said again, realizing that she had been about to say, "I was just more ready."

"I really did enjoy the bell concert, as well," she said on the drive home.

"It upset you."

"It touched me," she corrected.

"Either way, it was probably bad timing," he said. "I didn't think it through."

"But you asked me to go there for a reason, didn't you?"

"Yeah."

"And?"

"It just seemed like something I wanted to do."

"For me? Ever since Nick died people are always trying to…help. They mean well, but—"

He shook his head. "Nope. That was for me."

Bethany was a little taken aback at the idea that he might have seen her as being capable of helping him. "Tell me why," she said.

He drove for a minute longer before answering. "That church in Chicago holds a lot of memories for me. Of my parents. Of growing up. Of Ty."

"I'd love to hear about it—if it's not too painful."

He began with stories of his mother—how in her quiet, gentle way she had opened people's minds to the idea of women doing more in the work of the church than putting on bake sales and potlucks.

"She was the first female president of the congregation," he said with pride.

"And Ty?"

Cody laughed. "Well, most adults had pretty well counted Ty out as a lost cause. He'd slip out of Sunday school, play practical jokes. Once he even set off a firecracker in the choir loft."

Bethany laughed. "How old were you then?"

"Thirteen. Of course, I got part of the blame. Ty could always charm most people into believing that he was just the twin who went along. I was the smart one who came up with the ideas."

"That wasn't very fair."

"Oh, in the end, he would own up to being the ringleader. Mom and Dad were never fooled so he usually got his punishment at home and more than once he had to stand up before the entire congregation and offer his apologies."

"What happened as you grew older?"

"Amazingly, Ty decided he wanted to teach Sunday school and he was brilliant at it. He made faith cool at a time when most kids weren't paying much attention. He actually started the bell choir with a group of street kids. Can you imagine a bunch of tough guys willing to put on red choir robes and ring bells on New Year's Eve?"

"Nick did something like that at our church in D.C. The neighborhood was going through a real transition. It was a big time for gangs, lots of homeless people in the streets, just a bad time."

"What did Nick do?"

"He organized a shelter near the church in a former school building. Then he got a judge he knew to consider sentencing gang members to community service at the shelter. Over time, there was an incredible connection between the homeless adults and the teens—they bonded, and the adults encouraged the young people. Nick never took any credit, of course. That's just how he was."

"Ty was that way, too. He always seemed surprised that anyone would make a big deal out of the good things he did. It was the only time I saw his confidence falter."

"But you're that way," Bethany protested. "At Taliesin and then at the launch of the foundation, I saw the way you reacted when people wanted to give you credit. You passed it on to others."

"Really? Well, what about you? I haven't exactly seen you taking credit for all the wonderful events you've put together since you got here," he teased.

"Those are just parties. What you and Ty and Nick have done—those things make a real difference."

"Don't sell yourself short, Bethany. You make a difference, for all of us."

"Okay, nice avoidance of the question that started all of this. Why did you want me to go with you to the bell concert?"

"It was the first time I had ever wanted to share the experience. Before it had always been a kind of personal ritual—a way to start off the year by reminding myself of the responsibility I have to live fully."

"I'm glad I got out of that car and came back."

He looked over at her as he parked in front of the guesthouse. "I think that was the first moment that I fully understood that the connection between us was something bigger than just friendship. I tried to fight it, but I wanted you to share that with me. Not just anybody."

She didn't know how to answer that so she let herself out of the car, then waited while he came around and walked with her up to the porch.

"Coffee?" she asked.

"No, it's late." He bent and kissed her lightly on the cheek. "Thanks, Bethany. I had a good time tonight."

"Me, too," she replied resisting the urge to touch the place where he had kissed her. "See you tomorrow." She turned the handle on the front door.

"Hey."

She looked back at him, her smile expectant.

"I have to go out of town for a couple of days. Would you think about something while I'm gone?"

"Sure."

He paused, obviously reconsidering.

"What?" she prompted, taking a step closer.

"Well, I'd like you to think about the possibility that maybe we could…I don't know…keep in touch after the wedding. Go out now and then."

"I'd like that," Bethany said.

Cody frowned. "Don't answer right now. Think it over."

He bent and brushed her lips with his. "I'm not asking about a casual friendship here, Bethany."

When he kissed her she had instinctively placed the palm of her hand on his chest. She could feel his heart beating and the speed of it matched her own.

"I'll think about it," she whispered.

He took a deep breath and a step away. "Okay then. See you in a couple of days." And he was gone.

Chapter Thirteen

Cody couldn't imagine what had possessed him to bring up the idea of a relationship. There was no question that it was exactly what he was asking her—in spite of his awkwardness in doing so. And halfway through getting the words out he'd been sure it was a bad idea—like asking her to come with him to the bell concert had been.

She'd agreed too quickly. She might regret agreeing just as quickly.

"Cody?"

Cody hadn't even seen his father sitting at his desk. "Hi. It's late. I figured you'd be in bed."

"Nice evening?"

"Yeah." *If you don't count the fact that I may be falling in love with a woman who is not ready to be in love and who—even if she were—would not exactly jump at the chance to match herself with me.*

"Bethany is very special," Ian observed in that quiet

way that Cody recognized as laden with unspoken messages.

"She is that." He made a show of stretching and turned to go.

"She's not Cynthia," Ian said.

Cody paused. "Not even close," he agreed. "Good night, Dad."

That night Bethany had lain awake long after she and her aunt had said their good-nights. Of course, Erika had pressed her for details of her date with Cody, but Bethany found she was reluctant to share very much about the evening. She needed time to think about it, to think about how things had shifted for her in terms of Cody.

She worked up enthusiasm by telling Erika about their dinner and then about singing at the concert, and Erika seemed satisfied that the date had been a success.

"You're starting to come back to us, Bethie. I'm so relieved and happy to see that," Erika had said.

The next day Grace had called her. And although she was less blatant about seeking details of the evening with Cody, she was clearly no less relieved. It seemed that everyone saw this as a pivotal moment for Bethany's "recovery," as Erika called it.

But for Bethany there was no healing pill she could take to make everything all right in her life. Frankly, it scared her to find herself moving on without Nick. It felt disloyal to realize that she'd gone through an entire evening barely thinking about him or the times they had hoped to share.

Even now, two days later, it was most disconcerting to find herself lying in bed after yet another restless night as she thought about Cody Dillard. Over the course of the time he'd been gone, she'd moved from considering the possibility of the two of them starting to date to things becoming more serious to the point where now she was actually imagining what sharing a life with him might entail.

Confused and restless, she got up and wandered through the common rooms of the guesthouse. She flicked on the television and muted the sound as she watched a program on the home and garden network. Five minutes after it ended she could not have described one thing she had seen. She turned off the television and wandered out onto the porch.

Cody would be back today. He'd be expecting to talk about this. Or maybe he had reconsidered. Perhaps she should make it clear that they could be friends but nothing more. That way—

What? That way she wouldn't risk being hurt? That way she wouldn't risk losing someone again? What was going on with her? Cody was offering her the very thing she had been trying to find—a way to move forward, to get on with her life and stop living in the past.

Being with him had made her understand that building new relationships was not being disloyal to Nick. It was, as everyone had reminded her, what Nick would have expected, what he would have wanted for her.

So, why the hesitation? After all, Cody wasn't proposing anything permanent—just taking things to the next level. Just seeing where that might lead for both of them. No promises and no strings. In so many ways it was perfect.

She trusted Cody. His losses had given him a special empathy that she would be hard-pressed to find with any other man. But it was more than that—it was *way* more than that.

Over these last two days she had begun to understand that she could fall in love with Cody Dillard. She was half in love with him already in that she had experienced that first burst of emotion when she had to ask herself, “Hold on—what’s this?”

No, the problem was that she had nothing to offer him. He deserved more than her anger and confusion. That was no way to start a relationship. He was a man of faith, a gentle soul who had taken the deaths of two loved ones and found ways to turn tragedy to triumph—for them and for him. She couldn’t begin to measure up to that.

Bethany shuddered. The predawn was cool and calm. A star-filled sky formed a magnificent backdrop for the darkened buildings of the ranch. She heard a horse whinny and wondered if it might be Thunderbolt. That thought made her smile. Over the course of half a dozen rides, she and Thunderbolt had bonded. The horse no longer took his cues from Blackhawk. He waited for Bethany’s direction.

She turned her attention to the one sight she had avoided from her arrival. She looked directly at the mountain before her, and focused without really being able to see it, on the point where she knew the trail led back along the narrow cliffs and down into the canyon where Erika and Ian would be married.

Plans for the wedding were moving along smoothly. She and Erika had worked out the details of how guests would arrive for the intimate ceremony and how Erika and Ian would make their way into the canyon. Bethany had even flown over the site a second time with Danny. Ian had provided her with maps of the trail and the canyon that she had gone over repeatedly. There was nothing to fear—after all it was just a canyon, not the canyon where Nick and her faith had died. Not ominous after all.

But now as she stood facing the solid bulk of the mountain she realized that her resistance to the mountain had never been about Nick's death. It had never been about fear. It had always been about anger—her anger at God for taking a wonderful man in his prime. This mountain—any mountain—had come to represent that solid rock of rage that had taken its place at her very core the day they buried Nick. This mountain—any mountain—had come to represent the solid wall of her resistance to the idea that she could ever again operate in her life on the basis of faith.

And yet how she missed the comfort of her faith—the solace that came with prayer, the acknowledgment that there could be no beauty greater than that found in God's creation, the belief in a higher power—a creator.

With Nick's death she had been unable to find a way to reconcile life and creation with death and despair. It had been Cody's understanding and gentle probing that had started her on the road to recovery. Now it was up to her.

What she knew for sure was that she wanted to move forward—Nick would have wanted that for her and she did nothing to honor his memory by burying herself in her anger and stubborn resistance.

But how to do that? How to face her fear that the whole idea of a divine plan, a higher power guiding her life, was nothing more than a child's Sunday school lesson? What if she tried finding her way back to God and couldn't?

She studied the mountain for several long moments and understood what she needed to do. She would go to the mountain, she would cry out her agony, and—as Cody had advised—she would then be still and listen for an answer.

Cody had barely landed the plane before he was out of the cockpit, striding up the path toward the house. If he hurried he might catch Bethany in the kitchen with Honey.

She'd taken to spending the mornings there sometimes, enjoying Honey's stories about her three children, now grown, and six grandchildren. He had often heard the two women laughing together or speaking in the low, serious tones women had when they were sharing ideas and seeking advice.

In the weeks since returning to the ranch from Chicago, Bethany had used her visits with Honey, along with some lessons in preparing Southwest cuisine, to escape the cold and damp weather. She had become more at home on the ranch, moving among the many rooms of the house more as a member of the family than a guest. At meals she was less reserved, kidding around with Ian and sharing inside jokes with Erika.

Cody took the stairs to the back entrance of the main house two at a time, slapping his wet hat against his thigh to shake off the rain that had just started to fall. He was sure he would find Bethany and Honey bent over some cookbook or sharing a cup of herbal tea as they discussed menus and venues for the events of the wedding.

The kitchen was deserted. The house was silent. He moved quickly through each room until he found Honey cleaning his father's office.

"You're back early," Honey said.

"I finished everything I needed to do last night so there really wasn't much sense to hanging around. Aunt Susan sent you this." He dug in the pockets of his jeans and handed Honey a paper with his aunt's recipe for lemon bars.

"Oh, good. Bethany's been waiting for this. And speaking of a certain young lady from Washington, that wouldn't be the real reason you've rushed back here, would it?"

Cody grinned. "And what if it is?"

"You're out of luck. Erika stopped by earlier and said that Bethany was up and gone before dawn this morning."

Cody's first instinct was to wonder if Bethany was trying to avoid him. She knew he was due back this morning. Had she gone somewhere to dodge a discussion of the question he'd ask her to consider—the idea that they might explore a relationship that went beyond friendship?

Almost as quickly as his doubts formed they were gone. Bethany was not that kind of person. She wasn't coy when it came to the feelings of other people. The proof of it lay in the way she was willing to put aside her own fears and feelings about the canyon and mountain setting in order to make her aunt's dream come true.

"Where did she go so early?" Cody asked.

"Erika wasn't sure. Apparently she left a cryptic note—something about if the mountain wouldn't come to her, she'd go there."

Cody's heart lurched. It couldn't be. She wouldn't head out on her own into the backcountry before daylight. Would she?

"My guess is that she rode over to the church to see Reverend Stone. We've been talking about things—her boyfriend dying so tragically and all—and I told her what a terrific listener Reverend Stone can be and—"

"She rode?"

Honey looked blank.

"She took Thunderbolt?" Cody asked, his heart hammering now.

Honey nodded. "Mario said Thunderbolt was gone when he got to the stables this morning."

Mario was Honey's husband and always got to the stables before sunrise. Cody headed for the door.

"I'm sure she's fine," Honey called after him, but her voice shook as if she'd just begun to realize that Bethany would not have left before dawn if her destination was the church. Even on horseback, it wasn't that long a trip.

Cody picked up the pace as he headed across the yard for the stables. The message Bethany had written played over and over in his brain. Go to the mountain.

She wouldn't. Not alone. Not on a day like this when thunderclouds were rolling across the sky. Of course, it would have been dark when she started out and she wouldn't have seen the clouds.

If the mountain won't come to—

Cody stopped dead in his tracks. He had said those very words to her the day he flew her over the site for the wedding. He had been joking about finally having found a way for her to view the site without panicking.

The same way he had joked around with Ty the day he'd gone off on his own. The day he had not come back.

"God, don't let this be happening again," he prayed to himself as he ran for the stables. "Don't let me lose her, too."

"Cody!"

Mario was standing just outside the stables. He motioned toward the foothills.

Cody blinked and tried to focus on the horse picking its way over the rocky terrain. Was it Thunderbolt? Was there a rider?

The rains came faster and harder making it impossible to see. Mario started running toward the horse and Cody followed. There was no rider.

"Get Blackhawk," Cody ordered and Mario reversed his course and headed back to the stables.

"You want me to come with you?" Mario asked as he passed Cody.

"No. I'll go. You organize a rescue. Have Danny do a flyover as soon as the storm passes. You and the others can come as soon as we locate her."

Mario nodded and kept running. Just then Thunderbolt, perhaps having spotted the stables where he would be dry and warm, picked up the pace.

Cody caught the dangling reins and spoke soothingly to the horse.

"It's okay, big fella. You're okay."

All the while he examined the evidence before him—the loosened saddle cinch, the saddle sloping crazily to one side, the sopping wet papers clinging to the open saddlebag.

He carefully opened the paper and knew immediately what he would find. It was the map Ian had given Bethany to show her how the wedding party and guests might approach the canyon and enter it for the wedding. It showed the trail marked by certain cacti clusters and rock formations.

He stared for a moment at the scene before him—a stretch of desert leading into the foothills, then the rugged climb and beyond that the canyon. He swiped at his wet cheeks and could not have said if it was the rain or his own tears he wiped away.

"No," he whispered. "Please, no."

He turned at the sound of hoofbeats behind him. Mario rode up on Blackhawk, slid to the ground and handed Cody the reins. "She'll be okay," he said as he gently removed Thunderbolt's reins from Cody's clenched fingers. "She's a fighter, that one."

Cody nodded and with the practice of years of riding, mounted the horse and turned its head toward the mountain in a single motion. He glanced down at Thunderbolt's lopsided saddle and knew that Bethany had—as usual—not sought help but assumed that she could saddle a horse herself, even though she had never done so before.

He dug his heels into Blackhawk's sides and took off across the soaked desert, pushing Blackhawk more than was safe on the soggy and uneven terrain, but not caring. The only thing was to reach her before…before it was too late.

Bethany pulled herself tight against the mountainside, under the scant protection of an overhanging rock. Two hours had passed since she'd left the ranch. It had been pitch-dark then. It would be light soon. *And then what?* she thought as the rain came at her from all sides and the thunder crackled and echoed across the canyon below her.

Cody was going to be upset with her. Of course, he had every right to be. It had been beyond stupid to head off by herself like this. But she'd known with such clarity that if there was ever going to be a chance for her to even consider the possibility of a future with Cody, she must first face her fears and make her peace with God. The mountain—the symbol of how she saw God's abandonment of her—had seemed the perfect venue.

Thunder rumbled ominously as she recalled her father's way of telling how close the lightning was. Count the seconds from the time the thunder sounds until the lightning appears.

"One, one thous…"

The lightning flashed before she could get the word out. She rested her face in her hands. She was wet, wounded and weary. Most of all, she was terrified.

"Okay," she shouted defiantly. "So You're right here. You've certainly got my attention, so now what?"

She had never dared to speak to God in anything other than reverent or pleading tones. But here she was, out here a gazillion miles from civilization; her horse had abandoned her after throwing her inches from a shooting cholla cactus and frankly, her backside hurt, big-time.

After her fall, she had realized the rocky trail was too slippery for Thunderbolt. So she had tied the reins loosely around a jutting rock and continued on foot. She hadn't gone ten yards when she heard Thunderbolt give a yelp. She turned just in time to see a snake slither off into the rocks and Thunderbolt take off down the trail.

"Wait," she called. "Whoa," she amended, but the horse kept going.

At that point she had had two choices: go back herself or keep going. She was nearly there, just up to the top of that slope, then a left turn and there would be the path into the canyon. How hard could that be?

She'd made it to the top and turned left and started down. Her first step had landed her on a loose rock that had slid out from under her foot and she'd gone down, sliding several feet to the outcropping of rock, and twisting her ankle in the process.

She pressed closer to the rock behind her and stared at the abyss before her. She laughed at the obvious between-a-rock-and-a-hard place scenario and even to her ears the laughter bordered on the hysterical. The rain continued to come at her in sheets. She closed her eyes.

Listen, the wind and rain seemed to whisper. *Listen,* Cody had advised. "Stop talking and listen," she chided herself.

She waited.

Only her own thoughts filled her brain. Thoughts about how upset Cody was going to be with her, about whether or not Thunderbolt was okay, about how confused she was, how disloyal she felt to Nick's memory now that she'd finally admitted her growing feelings for Cody.

"I'm listening," she yelled. "I don't hear anything but the rain and wind and thunder which, by the way, is pretty scary. Could You turn it down a notch?"

The rain swept over her, driven by a strong wind, and the sky was alive with lightning and the crash of thunder.

Bethany held up her hands in surrender. "Listening," she said in a weaker voice. "Really listening," she promised.

It had been reckless to come out here alone, even on the best of days. But she had become so used to pushing others away and doing everything herself that the idea of asking for help had never occurred to her.

On the practical side, it had been downright lunacy

not to at least check the weather forecast before starting out. And what had made her think she could properly saddle Thunderbolt just because she had sort of watched Mario or Cody do it a dozen times?

"Pride," she muttered to herself. "Stupid pride."

She picked at a nail she'd broken in the fall. "Okay, so I was impetuous," she admitted. "So, now what? Thunderbolt bolted—every pun intended—and I'm pretty sure I can't climb out of here again on this ankle."

She reached down and pulled off her boot with effort. It slipped out of her hands and tumbled over the edge of the cliff into the canyon. "Oh, that's nice," she muttered.

She glanced around, trying to figure her next move. She was exhausted, in pain and no one knew where she was.

The rain settled into a steady downpour as the storm finally passed. Bethany turned up the collar on her jacket and tugged the brim of her hat—Cody's mom's hat—more firmly onto her forehead. She pulled her knees close to her chest and closed her eyes again.

She tried not to surrender to the hysteria that was building inside. What if no one came? What if she couldn't get out of this mess? What if this was it for her?

Was this what it had been like for Nick? This incredulity at finding himself in such a situation? And as the hours passed had he realized that he would not be getting out of this? Was that how he'd spent his last hours? And if so, what had he thought about?

She knew without doubt that Nick had prayed. She knew it as certainly as if he'd told her himself. He had not railed at God in fury. He had prayed for those he loved. He had prayed for her. He had thought of her and about what her life would be without him.

And suddenly Bethany felt the one thing she had been seeking ever since she had learned of Nick's accident. She felt surrounded by Nick's spirit—the comfort of it, the certainty that he was with her, that a part of him would always be with her in some sense. And in that moment it was as if she released a breath she'd been holding for months. She gulped in air, breathing deeply, then blowing it out and with it the pain and anger that had poisoned her soul for too long.

She found herself remembering the sermon Reverend Stone had preached—the one about the boy who had been so angry at God. The sermon had not been about the boy at all, although Bethany had seen it that way then. That boy and she had shared the same anger at what had happened to someone they loved. But Reverend Stone's message had been about trust as the essence of faith. Trust that even those things that seem incomprehensible happen for a reason. She hadn't been able to comprehend that then. Now, she could find some meaning in the minister's message. The very fact that it had come to her out of the blue when she hadn't given it a thought for weeks was enough to make her pay attention.

"Thank You," she whispered as she began to cry. "Thank You, God, for bringing me to this place…this peace."

In that moment she understood that whatever might happen to her now, it was right. There was purpose in everything. Nick's death had meant different things for different people. For her it had forced her to take charge of her life in a way she'd never been pushed to do before. For all her life she had lived her days by going along with others—her family, Grace, Nick. She had never really looked for her purpose—for God's purpose for her. She had been secure in God's love without ever thinking about what it really meant. She had assumed she would always feel that wonderful sense of well-being and happiness. She was blessed.

Sure. She had thought she understood her role—to be the clown, the one who could lighten any mood, spark any gathering, plan the very best parties. But was that all she was? Was that all that God had wanted for her?

She had always thought that once she and Nick were married she would find her true calling—as his wife, the mother of their children. But again she had been seeking it through Nick—always through someone else's life.

"Living life externally through others," she said, fully understanding why she had spent the last year wandering in the desert of her grief. Grief that had moved without her realizing it from the loss of Nick to the subconscious realization that she had no clue of God's plan for her life.

So, she had done what she always did in a crisis. In the choice of fight or flight, Bethany had almost always chosen flight.

"Not this time. If You will show me the way out of this, I will not back down from whatever challenges come before me."

She looked around, considering her options. She was

huddled on a narrow cliff, her ankle badly sprained if not broken, her horse gone, and no one knowing where she was.

"Okay, so next challenge is to get out of here, right?" *To get back to Cody,* she added silently.

It was all the motivation she needed. She would find a way, with God's help, to begin to live her life with purpose. And she would start by accepting the gift God had given her—the possibility to rediscover love with Cody.

"Dear God, I have missed You so much," she prayed and felt God's answering comfort in her soul. He had always been there. She was the one who had turned away. God always gave His children choices. "Please forgive my stubbornness, my rage, my turning away."

She thought of her favorite psalm and murmured the words, words she had refused to say with the others at Nick's memorial service. Words she now understood... and embraced.

"'The Lord is my shepherd, I shall not want,'" she whispered and then skipped to the crux of the matter. "'Yea, though I walk through the valley of the shadow of death, I will fear no evil.'"

She moved to the edge of the path and shouted down into the canyon, "'For Thou art with me!'"

The words echoed up and down the narrow canyon and Bethany laughed at the sound of her own voice ricocheting off the steep walls.

Chapter Fourteen

Cody had reached the point where the risk of a mud slide or loose rock made it dangerous to go farther on horseback. He hobbled Blackhawk and caught the glint of something metallic on the ground a few feet away.

He bent and picked up the slim silver chain Bethany wore every day. He searched the ground and finally found the small bicycle charm. Had Thunderbolt thrown her? And if so, what had spooked him? A slippery rock? A sidewinder?

Cody pocketed the chain and charm and started up the rocky trail at a near run. The rain had settled into a fine mist and there were breaks in the clouds that promised better weather within the hour. The problem then would be the heat. Knowing Bethany, she had not taken water and even if she had, the bottle would have left with Thunderbolt. If the temperatures reached the predicted high, it wouldn't take long for Bethany to become seriously dehydrated.

He pushed himself harder, his breath coming in the

even gasps of exertion as he followed the turns of the trail. Finding her was his only thought. Reaching her before—

He pushed aside the thoughts of Ty—the memory of the day Ty had gone off on his own, of the hours Cody had spent with the rescue team searching. Climbing and searching and praying.

He paused. What if he was going the wrong way? What if instead of climbing higher, she had started back after Thunderbolt ran? Worse, what if she had slipped and fallen? He glanced over the edge into the canyon below, his eyes searching each jut of rock, each cliff for signs of her.

He was paralyzed by fear, by the possibility he might choose the wrong way and lose precious time.

"Help me," he pleaded. "I love her. Please give us this chance."

And then he heard the faint echo.

"With me…with me…with me…"

The faint echo of her voice came from above and below him. It surrounded him. He pushed his way to the pinnacle.

"Bethany," he shouted through cupped hands, but the sound was lost in the beat of the chopper's blades as Danny rounded the peak above Cody.

Bethany licked her dry lips—another thing Cody was going to chastise her for. She should have brought water. Well, even though the rain had stopped and she could feel the heat building as the clouds broke above her, there was water caught in the cups of the rocks.

Using her hand as a spoon she scooped some water and brought it to her lips. It was cool and soothing. She gathered more and wet her cheeks and throat. She removed the scarf she had tied around her neck and soaked it in the water. And all the time she was looking around considering her next move, her eyes and ears on alert for signs, for she was fully confident that God would help her find a way out of this.

The moment she recognized the sound of the helicopter, her heart pumped hard with a mixture of adrenaline and joy. She pushed herself to her feet and, using the ledge of rock for support, hobbled out from under her shelter. She scanned the sky trying to determine where the chopper would be as the sound of it echoed around the walls of the canyon.

Cody. It had to be Cody, looking for somewhere to land.

"Hey," she yelled as the helicopter passed overhead. "Cody!"

For a second she thought he had spotted her, but then the engine's drone faded as she watched the chopper fly away. Had he seen her?

"Be calm," she ordered herself. "He'll be back. If he didn't see you on this pass, he won't give up."

She continued to reassure herself by playing out the rest of her imagined scene. No doubt Erika had realized the real meaning of Bethany's note and alerted everyone. There must have been a moment of general panic before Cody took charge. In that quiet, calm way she had come to rely upon, he would organize everything. He would come for her. She only had to wait—preferably in the shade since the sun was out now in full force, hot enough to have nearly dried her soaked clothing. She hobbled back to her shelter and lay down. A little power nap was all she needed. Then they would be there. Erika would cry as she always did when things turned out well. Ian would be solicitous and probably insist on taking her to the hospital for a complete checkup. And Cody?

She tried to imagine his expression. Fear, anger, relief all mingled together. She imagined him taking her in his arms and holding her close. She imagined him telling her he loved her.

She rolled to her back and looked up.

There above her was a small green shoot, a single leaf pushing its way out of the stone, not a crevice but the hard solid rock itself. She reached up and gently touched the leaf. It was real and impossible at the same time. As real as Cody's suggestion that they might find something beyond friendship and as impossible as the realization that she could love and be loved again.

She felt the solace of her tears rolling freely down the sides of her face onto her neck. For the first time in over a year she opened the floodgates of her soul and found comfort in that release of all she had forced inside for this last year. In that stream of emotion, she finally accepted Nick's death.

"Thank you," she whispered as she looked at the leaf again. It was a sign. She was certain of that. A sign so filled with simple hope that she had no fears for what might come next. Whatever time she and Cody might have—for friendship or something greater than that—

she would not waste a moment of it. She would declare her feelings to him and if he did not return those feelings, she would accept that, accept whatever he might be ready to offer.

In the distance she could still hear the rhythmic beat of the chopper blades. The sound was steady and reassuring—like Cody himself. She closed her eyes and was asleep before she fully realized that the helicopter had come back.

Cody watched as Danny made the wide circle of the canyon, went away and returned for a second pass. This time he flew the chopper straight toward a place near where the trail turned and widened on its descent into the canyon. At the last second he pulled up and Cody understood that Danny had located Bethany.

Cody waved his hat in a wide arc and Danny flew away. The sun was merciless now, beating down on him, heating the stone he touched as he continued his way along the trail. He shouldered the saddle pack he'd surprised himself by remembering to bring along when he left Blackhawk farther back down the trail. It contained a first aid kit that included sunscreen. Bethany would need that sunscreen. He hoped that was the most important thing she would need.

He reached the top of the trail and followed it around an outcropping of rocks. This was the tricky part. For the wedding, Mario would guide the horses through this part. The guests would arrive by raft via the creek at the base of the canyon and be waiting on the banks of that creek. The plan was brilliant in its conception for it addressed both Erika's desire to make the grand entrance by horseback as well as that of guests who might be less than thrilled at the idea of mounting a horse and traversing a narrow, rocky trail. The idea had been all Bethany's.

Cody tested a couple of stones that the weeks of rain had loosened, then eased his way around the boulders where the scene before him opened to a spectacular view of the jagged canyon walls and the trail meandering like a river until it reached the small creek at the base. The creek that would be dry as dust in another couple of months but that now cascaded over boulders and rocks with such fervor that he could hear the pulse of it even without being able to see it.

In a couple of weeks the rains would be over for the season and the trail would be dry and easily navigated. The desert would be in full bloom. It was going to be an incredible scene for a wedding.

But Cody thought of such things subliminally as he worked his way down the trail. He was glad he'd left Blackhawk behind. He was even thankful that something had spooked Thunderbolt because if he hadn't run, Bethany might have tried riding him all the way into the canyon.

"Thank You," he murmured with a glance upward toward a now-cloudless sky. "Now please lead me to her. Please don't let her be badly hurt. Please be with her until I can get there."

A hawk circled overhead. The sun was blinding. Cody pulled his hat lower to shade his eyes and started down the trail. "Bethany," he called and her name echoed across the canyon. "It's Cody. I'm coming."

Coming…coming…coming…

Silence. No answering call.

He had almost reached the area Danny had indicated. He hoped Danny was back at the landing strip and had joined Mario in organizing the rescue team. Even now they should be making their way across the desert and up into the foothills.

"Bethany!"

A rare breeze stirred a wayward piece of sagebrush and it rolled beneath an overhanging ledge. Something stirred beneath that ledge. It was Bethany.

Oblivious to risk or personal safety he half ran, half slid down the trail to her. "Bethany," he said hoarsely when he reached her and saw that she was curled on her side, one boot missing, her hair a mass of damp tangles covering her face.

He knelt next to her, touching her cheek, watching for the rise and fall of her breathing, his heart beating so loud and fast that it drowned out everything else.

"Cody?" She blinked several times and then her eyes opened fully. "Oh, Cody, I thought I only dreamed you."

She reached for him and he was only too glad to pull her into the protective circle of his arms.

"What were you thinking?" he murmured as he kissed her eyes, her forehead, her cheeks.

"I wasn't," she replied, clinging to him and letting his strength restore her own. "I just wanted—needed—"

She started to cry; breath-depriving sobs tore at her, fighting for release.

Cody held her, stroking her hair as he uttered soothing words of reassurance. "I'm here," he said. "I got to you before—it's over. You're safe." He could not control the shudder that racked him at the memory of all that he had imagined. At the memory of finding Ty's lifeless body.

She heard the catch in his voice, felt the shudder and looked up to see tears glimmering on his thick lashes. "Oh, Cody, you thought—this must have come at you like Ty all over again."

He nodded. "I'm so sorry, Bethany. So sorry that I said that about going to the mountain. So sorry that I drove you to—"

"No," Bethany interrupted. She stroked his face. "Stop this. You are *not* to blame for this. I came up here because I needed to find my way, literally and spiritually. It was what my grandmother would have called 'my come to Jesus moment.'"

Cody looked doubtful, but he smiled.

"I am not Ty," she said softly and his eyes immediately lost their light. "And even if I were, you did not cause this any more than you caused Ty's death."

Cody blinked and tears drifted along the haggard planes of his face. "Rationally I know that," he assured her. "I do. It's just that—"

"We make choices. You reminded me of that, Cody. Ty did and Nick did. Even your mom did when she continued to smoke."

"I know."

"You did what you could for Ty but in the end he made his choice—and so did I."

"Are you all right?" he asked, suddenly aware that he hadn't even taken the time to examine her, so relieved was he to find her conscious...and alive.

She laughed. "Well, we may have to figure out a way to get me out of here on one foot. Seems this one is pretty useless at the moment." She held up her left leg.

Cody gently pressed her swollen ankle, watching her face for signs of tenderness or pain. "I don't think it's broken," he said.

"There's more," she said.

His expression was one of alarm mingled with fear—the expression she had imagined. "Nothing huge," she assured him. "Seems I lost a boot down there somewhere." She nodded at the place where the edge of the trail dropped off into the canyon. Cody shuddered. "I love these boots," Bethany said, seeking any possible way to get his mind away from what could have happened. "I think we might have to go shopping again."

Cody visibly released his breath. "I don't know, lady, you've been pretty careless with these."

He opened the saddle pack and took out the first aid kit. Inside he found the sunscreen and an elastic wrap for her ankle. He tossed the sunscreen to her.

"Here. Put this on." He began wrapping her ankle, concentrating on his work as if it were the most important thing he would ever do.

"Cody?"

"Hmm?"

"What would you say if I told you that I think I love you?"

His hands stilled but he did not look at her. "When do you think you'll know for sure?"

"I—it just seems like it's so soon and—"

"What if I told you *I'm* sure?"

"Of what?"

"That I love you. In spite of everything I've done to avoid it, it seems to be fate."

"Fate? Or God's plan for us?" she asked gently.

This time he turned. He locked his gaze on her. "Are you saying that you believe in God's having a plan? That you've—"

She smiled. "Well, a girl can do a lot of thinking—*and* a lot of listening—up here."

"And Nick?"

"Being with Nick showed me my capacity to love and be loved. Nick wouldn't want me to make that love some sort of shrine—and neither does God."

"Nick will always be a part of you," he warned.

"I understand that and it's a lovely feeling knowing you can always carry those you love inside you through memories. My problem was that I wasn't open to anything but painful memories."

"You're sure? I mean, sometimes when people have a scary experience like you've had today, it can—"

She put her hand over his. "Cody, this is not some emergency room conversion here. God has been with me every step of the way—as He was with Job and Jesus—both of whom, by the way, did a bit of ranting of their own in their darkest hour."

"'Why hast Thou forsaken me?'" Cody quoted.

"Exactly. I realized that to get answers you do have

to raise the questions. I did and let me show you something."

She tugged at him until he had pushed back beside her. Then she pointed to the leaf growing through the rock. "There's my answer," she said softly as the two of them leaned against the sheltered stone and looked up at the wonder of the tiny shoot making its way through the solid stone.

Bethany turned to Cody. "I love you, Cody Dillard," she whispered just before they kissed.

In novels, the story might have ended with them declaring their love, Bethany thought as she rested her sprained-not-broken ankle on the pile of pillows Erika had insisted on building for her. But this was real life and this was Cody, ever practical.

He had first raised the issue on the mountain as he held her and told her repeatedly that everything would work out. That they would find a way. She had assumed he was speaking of the predicament of the moment—the two of them on the side of a mountain, her with an injured leg. It was only later that she understood that he was already considering the possible barriers to their love.

"We're very different, Bethany," he said one night as he sat with her, helping her fill small tulle bags with birdseed for the wedding.

"They say opposites attract," she had teased, barely noticing his serious expression.

"That's what they say," Cody replied and there was no hint of joking in his voice. Only doubt.

Bethany paused and looked at him. "What?"

Their love was so new, so untested. Was Cody already having second thoughts? "Tell me," she said.

"It's important to me that you be happy," he said.

"I am. For the first time in months, I am truly happy and content. Everything is falling into place for me."

"You're a long way from home, from your friends and family."

"Not so far and besides, most of them will be here for the wedding."

"I'm talking long term."

She put down the box of seed and touched his face. "If you're having second thoughts, just say so, Cody." She pressed her palm into his cheek, hoping he would not notice how it trembled.

"No." He turned his face to her palm and kissed it. "No," he said more softly.

"Then what is all this?"

For an answer he stood and scooped her into his arms.

"Cody," she protested, laughing now. "What are you doing?"

"I want to show you something." He carried her out to the porch and set her down on a chaise longue built for two. He sat next to her and pointed to the mountain, the star-filled sky.

"Look," he whispered, his mouth close to her ears, his arms around her. "This is the world I've come to love. This is where I have lived most of my adult life. Listen."

He said no more as the silence of a desert night engulfed them both, wrapping itself around them like a comforter.

Bethany turned to him, cupping his face in her hands. “Cody, whether it’s happiness or grief—it isn’t a place. I learned that here. The first time I saw that mountain I wanted to get right back on your plane and fly out of here.”

Cody smiled at the memory. “Still, you can’t deny that—”

“Cody, here is what I’ve come to understand over these last weeks. Happiness is not the place—it’s the ebb and flow of life that makes it worth living, that brings true happiness. It’s the people and the pleasure and the purpose that we bring to our lives.”

Cody smiled. “When did you get to be so wise?”

“When a very *wise* man suggested I stop questioning long enough to actually hear what God was trying to tell me.”

“And what is that?”

“That our time here on earth is a gift.”

“And that’s exactly why it’s important that you live the life you want—surrounded by people and activity and the bustle of the city.”

Bethany let out an exasperated sigh. “You are impossible.” She kissed him. “Now get out of here and let me do some work. In the morning I want you to saddle up Blackhawk and Thunderbolt and meet me at the main house at nine.”

“Not on your life. You are supposed to stay off that ankle.”

“The ankle can be taped. Either you saddle Thunderbolt or I will, and we both know saddling a horse is not exactly my strong suit."

The following morning it was Bethany and Thunderbolt leading the way across the desert and up the trail to the rise where she and Cody had first picnicked.

"Watch out for those cacti," she said, pointing to a nearby exploding cholla. "They can be a pain—literally."

At the top of the rise, she dismounted and expertly hobbled Thunderbolt before unpacking a picnic lunch from her saddlebags.

"Sit," she instructed as she offered him a sandwich and large bottle of cold water.

He sat facing the wilderness and the Superstition Mountains. She sat opposite him facing the skyline of Phoenix.

"Okay, here's the way I see it. We have the best of all worlds right here. The wilderness you love and have taught me to love." She gestured toward the scene before him. "And down there, a city with all of the opportunity for activity and involvement anyone could possibly want. As a matter of fact, regardless of whether or not you decide to back out of this, I already am committed to organize three major charitable events in the coming year. So I'm going to be here."

He stared at her, his expression one of alarm. "What do you mean if I decide to back out?"

"Just calling it the way I see it. Seems to me you're working overtime trying to analyze everything to death. The only thing I can figure is that you declared your love in a moment of high emotion and now you're having second thoughts."

"I am not," Cody protested.

Bethany calmly took a bite of her sandwich.

"How can you even suggest such a thing?" he fumed, getting up and pacing around the perimeter of their picnic.

Blackhawk and Thunderbolt both snorted.

"You two stay out of this," Cody muttered. "I'd just like to know what's so wrong with wanting to make sure the woman I love is happy."

"Nothing at all," Bethany said as she uncapped one bottle of water and offered it to him. "Here, drink this. You're becoming seriously overheated."

"Very funny," he replied but he took the bottle and drained half of it in one long swallow. "Well?"

"There's nothing at all wrong with wanting happiness for someone you love—"

"In this case that would be you," he reminded her.

"In wanting *me* to be completely happy," she amended. "All I'm suggesting is that you rethink how you're going about it."

"Meaning?"

Now it was Bethany's turn to get to her feet. She limped over to stand toe-to-toe with him. "Meaning I've already wasted a lot of time—that's my fault for being so stubborn. I don't want to waste any more. I love you. You love me. Where we spend our time together doesn't matter to me. The only thing that matters is not wasting a single moment of it with silly details like you being country and me being city."

"All right. Marry me then." The words came out more like a dare than a proposal.

"All right," she replied, equally defiant. "I will."

And then realizing what had just happened, they both burst into laughter. Cody grabbed her in a bear hug and swung her around and around as the mountains and desert and city skyline melded into a dizzying whirl.

Chapter Fifteen

Erika and Ian's wedding day was everything anyone could have dreamed of and more. The weather was perfect and the weeks of rain had brought the desert alive with a rainbow of colorful flowering cacti and wildflowers. To Bethany's relief, the guests found the idea of the raft trip to the ceremony exciting.

Led by Susan's example, most of the women had chosen to dress à la Katharine Hepburn in *The African Queen*. The variety of wide-brimmed hats and Edwardian lace blouses was a show in itself.

But the star of the day was Erika. Radiant was the only word anyone could think of to describe her. She wore a high-necked ecru lace blouse with loose flowing sleeves that caught the gentle breeze. The blouse topped a calf-length flared skirt of caramel suede so soft it felt more like silk, and boots—a gift from Cody. They were hand-decorated with crystals and beads on cream-colored leather. For her headpiece, she wore a narrow-brimmed Stetson trimmed with layers of tulle and a single orchid.

Ian and Cody waited with the minister on the banks of the creek as Erika descended the canyon path on Ian's wedding gift to her, a chestnut mare that Erika had named Daybreak.

Father and son wore Western-style suits over crisp white shirts trimmed with bolo ties of turquoise and silver. Bethany's breath caught when she saw Cody. It still seemed impossible that she had made her way through the long dark night of grief and anger to come into the light to find this incredible man in love with her.

She had not missed the Biblical parallels of their journey—her wandering in the desert, so to speak—nor had Cody, who took obvious delight in teasing her about the fact that at least it hadn't taken her forty years. She, in turn, reminded him that she would still be waiting for a proposal if she hadn't pushed him. And underneath the good-natured teasing was the relief and delight they both felt that she had found her way back to God and God had led them to each other.

Sometimes it amazed her how easily she had returned to her lifelong habits of praying aloud or humming snatches of a hymn as she went about her day. As she contemplated the life they would share, it was different than it had been with Nick. Neither she nor Nick had had any thought of the finite nature of time. They had taken it for granted that just because they were both young and healthy they had decades ahead of them.

After all she and Cody had been through, separately and together, they knew better. They had both suffered the pain of loved ones dying. They had both found their way along grief's lonely and desolate path to the understanding that grieving was about those left behind, not about the person who had died. And they had each learned that there was a vital life lesson in reaching the truth of losing a loved one far too soon—the importance of living in the moment, not the future.

At the brunch following the wedding, the church hall was filled with laughter, toasts and such utter joy that Bethany found herself standing quietly in a corner observing the day unfold. It was as if everything she had dreamed for Erika and Ian's special day had come to life before her.

"You okay?" Honey asked as she passed Bethany on her way to get Erika's traveling clothes from the car.

"Couldn't be better," Bethany assured her.

"Or happier?"

"That, too."

Honey studied Bethany closely for a brief moment, then nodded. "Yes. The pain and sadness I saw in your eyes that first night you came to us are gone. You are no longer frightened."

"Frightened? I was never—"

But she had been. Frightened to take any risk. Frightened to make a decision. Frightened to live now that she had seen death.

She smiled at Honey. "You're right. I feel as if I'm free—free to make a life again."

"You were always free, Bethany. The walls were created by you. The rest of us just had to find a way in."

Bethany hugged Honey. "Thank you. You have become such a wonderful friend." Then she took a step back and looked at Honey. "And taller. You are definitely taller. Let me see those shoes, girl."

Honey lifted the hem of her gauze ankle-length skirt to reveal a pair of sandals with two-inch platforms. She giggled. "I had to practice for hours to get the hang of them."

"They're fabulous," Bethany exclaimed. "I want a pair. Tomorrow we'll go shopping, okay?"

"And some things never change," Erika said wryly as she joined them. "I know that Bethie is fine if she's got shopping on her mind."

The three women laughed and hugged until Ian reminded Erika that it was time for them to change and head off for their honeymoon in Hawaii.

"Hawaii." Erika sighed, then pinched her forearm. "I can't believe this is really me."

"Believe it," Ian said, kissing her cheek. "And it's only the beginning. Now get changed."

Erika and Honey hurried off to the classroom that was serving as a changing room for the wedding.

"I should check on—"

Ian stopped her by putting his hand on her shoulder. "Bethany, I may not get a chance to say this before we leave, so indulge me for a moment."

He offered his arm and when she took it, he led her out to the desert garden behind the church. They sat on a cypress bench and Ian took both her hands in his.

"Young lady, you blew in here several months ago like a desert storm, blinding in your energy and your almost manic need to be constantly doing something, planning something."

Bethany's heart pounded. "I'm sorry if—"

"You charmed us all in a way I don't think any of us had ever experienced before. You took some getting used to before we all realized that you were covering your own pain."

"I was—"

"By the time we all realized that—me, my sister, not to mention Honey, Mario, Danny and everyone who works here—we all loved you. The very idea that you would arrange this event and everything leading up to it and then go back to some other life became unacceptable."

"Oh, Ian, everyone has been so incredibly warm and welcoming and made me feel so much a part of everything here—almost like family."

"You *are* family, Bethany. You always were because of Erika, but what you have given my son—" His voice shook and he cleared his throat. "Cody is a strong man inside and out, but in losing his mother and brother, he changed. Oh, outwardly he was the same—confident, caring, a model son and citizen. But inside it was as if a piece had broken away from his heart. He just wasn't whole."

Bethany was so close to tears that she could only nod.

"When I first met you," Ian continued, "there was something so familiar about you. It took me several weeks to recognize it but then I knew. They say the eyes are the window to the soul and when I looked into your eyes I saw the same thing I saw every time I caught Cody unaware. That same sorrow."

He patted her hands, unable to continue.

"I know," she said softly. She couldn't imagine where this might be leading.

Ian took a long breath, looked at her and smiled. "What I'm trying to say here, Bethany—and doing a pretty poor job of it—is that I am so proud and happy to know that you're going to be my daughter-in-law—that we *will* be family."

Bethany had no choice. She threw her arms around Ian and hugged him hard. "Oh, Ian—Dad—thank you. I'm going to treasure this moment forever."

The two of them were hugging and laughing when Cody came out to the garden. "Hey, Dad, go find your own bride. This one's mine," he said with mock seriousness.

Ian picked up Bethany's left hand and turned it over. "Funny, I don't see a ring on this finger. Seems to me she's still available."

"Well, you're not," Cody said. "There's a beautiful lady waiting just inside there to toss a bouquet and get out of here."

"I forgot to hand out the birdseed," Bethany shrieked and headed back inside the church at a run.

Bethany was exhausted, but it was the best kind of fatigue. Everything had gone perfectly. The ceremony, the brunch afterward, the send-off for Erika and Ian as the guests boarded horse-drawn wagons to follow a carriage carrying the happy couple down to the landing strip. Danny had the plane ready to take them to Chicago, where they would spend the night before flying off to Hawaii.

After all the guests had gone back to their hotels, Bethany and Cody walked arm-in-arm back up to the main house. She couldn't help noticing that Cody seemed nervous.

"I think everything went well, don't you?" she asked, trying to imagine why he would be anxious at this stage of the day.

"It was perfect and you know it," he said, chuckling as he put his arm around her waist and pulled her closer.

"Still, you seem…distracted."

"I was wondering if you might be up to taking a ride?"

Bethany grinned. "Plane, car or horseback? There are so many choices around here."

"I was thinking horseback."

"Sounds great," Bethany said. "I'll get changed and meet you at the stables."

The guesthouse felt strangely empty now that Erika was gone. Bethany wandered through the rooms as memories of the days and nights she had spent in this house surrounded her. She wandered out onto the porch and stared at the mountain. In the late-afternoon sunlight it was deep purple in color and had lost any semblance of threat or danger for her.

On that mountain she had said goodbye to Nick. She had rediscovered her faith. She had found love. And most important of all, she had found the inner peace that had now replaced fear and anger as her constant companion.

"Thank You," she whispered as she studied the light and shadow playing over the planes of the peaks that she had once found so intimidating and hateful. "Thank You for bringing me to this place, for leading me through this valley, for bringing me back into the light."

She bowed her head for a moment and then hurried to change. Cody would be waiting.

They rode into the desert, and Bethany realized how much she had come to love the unusual and changing beauty of the landscape. As she had expected, Cody led the way up the trail toward the mountain, but instead of following the way to the canyon, he turned toward another trail.

"Where are we going?" she asked.

"You'll see." He urged Blackhawk to a trot and Thunderbolt followed.

It wasn't until they rounded a curve in the trail that Bethany realized where they were headed. "Bachelor's Cove?"

Cody nodded. "But we're changing the name."

Up close the cabin was charming and far larger than Bethany had imagined. "Wow," she said as Cody dismounted and came to help her down. "This is impressive."

She turned and took in the view. The house was set higher than she had thought. To one side was the desert; below, she could see all the buildings of the ranch

and off to her right was the city, its twinkling li
just beginning to come alive as the sun began to set.

"I have something for you." He handed her a small gift wrapped box. "Open it."

Bethany grinned and tore away the wrapping. Inside the box was a key. "To your heart?" she said hopefully.

"My heart is never locked where you're concerned," he assured her. He led the way to the wide front porch and it was only then that Bethany noticed the laser-cut sign over the door.

Bethany's Cove.

"Oh, Cody," she murmured as she fit the key into the lock and turned it.

"You don't have to use it—we won't live here or anything. I just thought you'd like someplace where—"

"Why don't we live here?" Bethany said. "It's wonderful." She pushed the door open and walked inside expecting to see the usual rustic furnishings common to such outposts. The place was empty. She looked around, confused. "It could use a chair or two," she said.

"I wanted you to fix it up the way you want," Cody explained. "Check the gift box, under the tissue."

She reopened the box that had held the key and lifted the paper. There was a credit card and the name on it was Bethany Taft Dillard.

Her eyes filled with tears of joy. "You've got a unique way of popping the question, cowboy," she said, her voice catching.

"Aw shucks, ma'am. That's not the proposal—this is."

She turned to find him down on one knee offering

iously old velvet ring box. "Bethany,
?"

e box to discover a beautiful diamond
by small gems of pink, sage green and
violet. the colors of the desert," she whispered as she held the ring box to the light to see it better.

"It was my mother's ring—I had it reset. Answer the question."

Bethany got down on both knees and handed him the ring, then presented her finger. "I will," she said, "on one condition."

Cody frowned.

"We live right here in this wonderful house in the hollow of this great protective mountain overlooking everything we both love—the wilderness, the city, and best of all, the ranch where family and friends are right here whenever we need them."

"You don't have to do this," Cody warned. "We can have a place in the city and here if that's what you want."

She placed her arms around his neck and rested her forehead on his. "What I want, Cody Dillard, is to spend as much time as we have together. I really don't care where, but this place has a connection to everything we've gone through to find our way to each other and I don't ever want to forget that journey. So, here's the deal. I'm living *here,* with or without you."

Cody laughed. "Bethany Taft, has anyone ever told you that you are impossible sometimes?"

"Not impossible, just irresistible in my crazy sense of logic. Now, do I get to wear that ring or not?"

He slid the ring onto her finger.
“A perfect fit,” she murmured.
“Just like us,” he said and kissed her.

Epilogue

Cody leaned on the fence and watched as Mario put the colt Blackhawk had sired through its paces. For the first time since he'd gotten into the business of raising horses, he had found one he thought might actually be capable of running in the Kentucky Derby. Of course, that was down the road, but the idea was exciting and had put a whole new light on the breeding business he had started soon after his mother's death. He had needed a career that would allow him to make his life on the ranch. Breeding and selling Thoroughbreds had become that career. It was Bethany who had suggested getting into the racing business, and to Cody's surprise, he loved it.

"It will certainly only add to your reputation for having the best stock," she had reasoned. "Besides, it could be fun."

Fun—no, *joy*—was what Bethany had brought to his life in the year and a half since they'd gotten married.

Every day was an adventure. He was never quite sure what she might say, do or suggest.

Like the way she had elected to tell him she was pregnant just eight months earlier. She'd been standing in the middle of their now furnished great room when he came home that evening. She had been looking at the upstairs loft and frowning.

"We need a bigger place," she muttered as he hung up his jacket and hat in the hallway.

Uh-oh, he had thought. Here it was. Life on the ranch was too isolated, too confining. Well, it had been a good year and to be fair she had been a real sport about the whole thing. Now it was her turn.

"I have to run up to Chicago on Friday. You could come along and see what's available."

"I don't want to live in Chicago," she had replied, her eyes wide with surprise. "What on earth would have made you think such a thing?"

Cody shrugged. "I thought you said we needed more room."

"Well, we do. We're about to double the occupancy in this place and frankly—"

Cody had started to protest and then the light had dawned. On their wedding night they had decided that knowing what they knew about time, they did not want to wait to start their family. But in spite of numerous false alarms, Bethany had not gotten pregnant.

"Are you—?"

"I am. And guess what?"

"You're okay?"

"I'm fine. Come on. Guess. I gave you a great hint already."

"I don't know." Then he mentally rehashed her words. *"Twins?"*

"Twins," she confirmed.

Their joy had had to be shared with everyone they knew. They had spent hours on the phone calling friends and family, telling everyone the news. Over the next several months Bethany had taken on that glow that comes with impending motherhood. Together they had designed and overseen construction of an addition to the house, declining Erika and Ian's invitation to move into the main house.

"Not our style," Cody had assured his father, and Bethany had agreed.

"We're just plain folks," she had drawled, to Ian's delight. "You keep this fancy place for you and the missus."

But at the beginning of her seventh month, Bethany had had some spotting and her doctor had ordered bed rest for the duration. Bed rest was not something that came easily to Bethany and Cody had asked Honey to stay with her during the day to assure that she didn't try to get up.

The two women played endless games of Scrabble, read books aloud to each other and watched old movies. Overall, Bethany was a model patient but one night when Cody commented on his surprise that she was adapting so well to her confinement, she had burst into tears.

"I am so scared," she had mumbled as he held her and stroked her back and swollen belly.

"Don't be," he said, although his own heart had barely gone below a steady hammer since the day she had first seen bleeding. "Whatever happens, we can get through it, right?"

"I know," she replied and then added defiantly, "but I'm still scared."

As am I, Cody thought now as he watched Mario still the colt before moving the animal through its paces again. Cody stared across the desert to where he knew the cabin sat in the cove of the mountain. He blinked and looked again.

A trail of dust was all he saw at first and then as his eyes focused he saw the SUV growing bigger as it covered the distance between the cabin and the ranch.

"Mario." Cody nodded at the dust cloud. Mario nodded and led the colt away, tossing Cody the keys to the truck as he went.

Cody caught the keys and headed for the truck at a run. He rammed it into gear and started across the desert, ignoring marked roads in favor of the shortest possible distance.

As he got closer, he saw two people in the SUV—Honey behind the wheel and Bethany on the passenger side.

"Labor," Honey shouted as soon as he was close enough. "Get in."

Cody shut off the truck's motor, left the keys and ran for the SUV, cell phone in hand.

"You should have called me. You should have called

911. You should have—" He was near hysteria as he climbed into the backseat and barely got the door closed before Honey floored it.

"Your phone was off," Bethany said calmly. "The contractions are still fifteen minutes apart. We have plenty of time to make it to the hospital. Now stop yelling at poor Honey and hold my hand."

She reached her hand toward him and he grabbed it like a lifeline. Just then another contraction hit.

"Ten minutes—less than," Honey muttered and looked over at Bethany.

"Plenty of time," she assured them both through gritted teeth.

Cody punched his cell to life and hit speed dial for Danny. "Fire up the chopper. Yeah, it's Bethany."

He knew that Danny would take things from there.

"Hang on, Bethany," he said and wondered if the words were more for him than they were for her.

The hospital staff was waiting when Danny set the helicopter on the roof of the building. A team raced to the door and in seconds had Bethany on a stretcher and on her way inside.

"Don't forget to bring that bag I packed," Bethany told Honey as they rushed her away. "I can't stand those hospital gowns."

Cody ran alongside, holding her hand in spite of swinging doors, passing people and packed elevators.

"The doctor's here already," a nurse assured them. "He's scrubbed in just in case you need a C-section."

"No C-section," Bethany protested.

"We'll let that be the doctor's call," Cody answered

as she squeezed his fingers to the breaking point with the onset of another contraction.

"Your children are in a rush to get here all of a sudden," she said with a weak smile as the contraction passed.

"They get that from you—*I'm* a very patient man." He glanced around as the elevator doors opened. "Where's the doctor?" he shouted and Bethany laughed the kind of laugh that can't be denied in spite of intense pain.

In minutes she was settled into a birthing room, and had been examined by the doctor, who pronounced her "coming along nicely."

"Sounds like I'm a turkey roasting for the holidays," she muttered.

"Doctor?" The nurse sounded worried and both Cody and Bethany looked at her in alarm. "There's a head," she said.

The doctor moved to the foot of the bed and lifted the sheet covering Bethany's raised knees and spread legs. "So there is," he said and Cody really considered decking the guy for his calmness.

In what seemed like no time at all the doctor was handing a baby to the nurse. "And here comes number two," he announced. "Push, Bethany. I know you're tired but one more big push and—"

The second baby wailed in protest.

"That one's yours," Bethany said, her eyes brimming with tears of joy and exhaustion. "I get the quiet one."

"Two healthy boys," the nurse gushed as she and

another nurse wiped them and wrapped them in sterile blankets.

"Boy and a girl," Bethany corrected. "Ty and Emma."

They had spent almost no time coming up with the names once they had known the gender.

"Nope, two big boys," the doctor corrected. "Better come up with another name. This guy doesn't look like he'll take kindly to being called Emma."

He placed the crying baby on Bethany's chest as the nurse handed the other child to Cody.

"Hey, little Ty," Cody crooned.

"Hey, little...what?" Bethany looked up at Cody.

"How about naming him after your dad?" he suggested.

Bethany blinked. "How about *both* our dads? Thomas Ian?"

"Good names," Cody said as he rocked Ty in his arms. "From good men."

"Hey, Tommy," Bethany whispered and the baby stilled. "He likes it," she said, her eyes glistening with tears.

The christening was held the following Sunday in the Chicago church where Cody had taken Bethany for the bell choir concert. Grace and her husband, Jud, were there along with Honey and Mario as godparents for the boys. And Erika and Ian, along with Bethany's parents, took their places alongside as the proud grandparents.

Bethany stood with Cody at the altar and listened as the last clear notes of the bells faded. Then they turned their attention to Reverend Stone as he performed the time-honored ceremony that would dedicate their children to God.

As she listened to the minister's incantations and watched him sprinkle the boys with consecrated water, Bethany said her own silent prayer of thanksgiving and promise. She looked up at Cody and knew that he was doing the same. As their children snuggled more securely into the protective embrace of their parents and Cody wrapped his free arm around Bethany, she knew that she had indeed made it through the valley and out into the light.

"My cup runneth over," she whispered and Cody answered, "Amen."

* * * * *

Dear Reader,

Special thanks to all of you who asked for Bethany's story after reading about her in *Matchmaker, Matchmaker*... In her role of best friend, Bethany was often called upon to be the strong one, the voice of encouragement and hope. As a best friend she was filled with advice and great humor. But, I wondered, what would happen if Bethany's world was rocked by an event that she could never have imagined? How would she work through the challenges and, more to the point, how would it affect what she considered to be a faith that she had thought was unshakable?

Many of us have had to face such challenges in our own life—times when the future we had planned and dreamed of was no longer available. How would we find our way out of the darkness and back to the light? How could we understand God's plan for us when it brought such pain? I hope you found Bethany's personal journey inspiring and a path for understanding challenges you may be facing or working through in your life.

All the best,

Anna Schmidt

Questions for Discussion

1. Early in the story you realize that both Bethany and Cody have suffered the loss of loved ones, but each is dealing with that loss in different ways. How do their approaches differ, and what role does time (one year for Bethany and five for Cody) play in that?

2. Bethany's best friend, Grace, and her aunt Erika have both taken a hands-off approach to trying to get Bethany past her anger at God. How do you think a best friend or family member might approach someone who is clearly blaming God for the death of a loved one?

3. Why do you think it's so difficult for Bethany to understand that faith is a two-way street—God's faith in us and ours in God?

4. How was God's faith in Bethany to weather this storm and come back illustrated in the story?

5. Name two struggles/fears in your life and consider what your response should be to these if God is both *good* and *all-powerful.*

6. Think about a time in your life when you were in the midst of a great struggle. Maybe that's true for

you now. How can you learn to put your future in God's hands?

7. Discuss your thoughts on the symbolism of the mountain throughout the book.

8. What event might prevent someone from knowing God's love and experiencing it in their hearts?

9. Why doesn't Cody give up on Bethany?

10. What do you think the future will be for Bethany and Cody?

MISTLETOE REUNION

Except the Lord build the house, they labor
in vain that build it: except the Lord keep the city,
the watchman waketh but in vain.

—*Psalms* 127:1

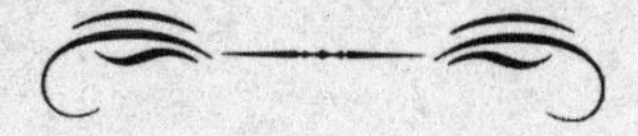

To everyone who knows the true power that growing up in a small town can have no matter how large the place you end up calling home.

Chapter One

"It's snowing!" Isabella crowed as the flight from Phoenix landed in Denver. "Look at the roof of the terminal. It's like snow-capped mountains. How totally cool!"

Norah Wallace could not help smiling. Was it just a mere forty-eight hours earlier that her thirteen-year-old daughter was fighting the very idea of a trip to Wisconsin to visit her grandparents for Thanksgiving? Obviously she'd changed her mind, but Norah was quickly learning not to spend too much time questioning the logic of teenagers.

While Isabella reveled in the sight of the unique fabric tension roof of the terminal, Norah noticed snow falling in huge flakes that covered everything—including the runway—in a duvet of white. "Hopefully it won't delay our connection to Chicago," Norah said.

"Oh, Mom, you worry about the weirdest things. What could be so bad about getting stuck in Colorado? We could go skiing."

"No one is going skiing—at least not in Colorado," Norah said. "And I don't worry about everything. I just want things to go smoothly." She felt the familiar twinge of guilt that came with her impatience and covered it by rummaging through her carry-on. Did her daughter think she wanted to be the one always throwing cold water on Izzy's flights of fancy? No. But she was raising Izzy on her own—well, not on her own. Her father—Norah's ex—was still very involved. But Izzy lived with her in Arizona, not with Tom in California.

She checked their schedule. "We have an hour layover here and it looks like our connecting flight is in the same concourse, so we should have time for something to eat." It was an attempt at conciliation, but Izzy was slumped down in the seat, staring out the window.

"Whatever," she muttered.

The minute the flight attendant announced permission to use cell phones, Isabella went to work. Norah marveled at the way her daughter's thumbs danced on the keypad as the plane taxied to a gate. Everyone scrambled to gather belongings as if life itself depended on their quick exit from the plane. She stood in the aisle and watched Izzy transcribe messages to all her friends. Norah could barely manage e-mail. How did these kids learn these technically complicated things so quickly?

When their turn came to exit, Izzy dropped her phone in her pocket and hefted her backpack over one shoulder as they entered the concourse and joined throngs of other travelers making their way to and from restrooms, shops and gates. Norah couldn't help noticing that Izzy seemed to be looking for something and took some comfort in the fact that her daughter's annoyance was short-lived. But then as usual Izzy threw her a curveball she wasn't prepared for.

"Are you ever sorry you divorced Dad?" Isabella asked as they wove their way through crowds of passengers and dodged electric carts.

"First of all, the decision was mutual," Norah replied, fighting her natural instinct to remind Izzy an airport was neither the time nor place for this discussion.

"And second of all?" Isabella asked.

"Oh honey, you know the story. We each wanted different things." *Quell the impatience,* she reminded herself. She draped her free arm over Izzy's bony shoulders. "Well, actually we wanted the same thing—to make sure you had the best possible life."

"So how come the two of you couldn't figure it out together?"

"Timing—meant to be." Norah tossed off clichés as she searched for an answer that would end the conversation. The older Isabella got, the harder that challenge became.

"Yeah, so Dad took off for San Francisco like opening a branch law office there was a good idea or something," Isabella said wearily, "and you stayed in the desert because working on the reservation was somehow so important." She frowned. "So will one of you please explain how doing what you wanted was best for me?"

"Trust me. It was. We've remained friends—your father and I—not like some couples."

"Friends see each other now and then. When's the

last time you actually saw Daddy? Not talked on the phone, but were face-to-face?"

"It just hasn't—that is—" Norah stumbled for words. *Five years ago.* She considered whether or not to tell Izzy that she remembered the exact moment she'd last seen Tom. He'd been walking away from her to get in a cab and head for California.

"Ooh—soft pretzels." And Izzy was off. Obviously the moment had passed.

"For lunch?" Norah shifted her bag and hurried after her daughter.

"Mother! We're on holiday. Live a little," Isabella said hooking her arm through Norah's and steering her toward the pretzel stand.

As soon as his plane touched down in Denver, Tom called Isabella's cell phone. He wanted to be sure she'd let Norah know he was going to Normal for the holiday. Voice mail. Knowing his daughter, she had forgotten so just to be sure Norah got the message, Tom decided to call the house in Arizona.

He waited for the beep of the old-fashioned answering machine Norah still used even though Isabella had tried to persuade her that voice mail was ever so much more efficient. "But we have the machine and it's paid for," Norah had explained according to Izzy, "so why would I incur a monthly expense to switch to voice mail?"

Tom smiled as he recalled Bella's growl of frustration at her mother's well-known practicality and maddening logic. For his part he had always admired Norah's determination not to jump on the technology bandwagon, although he couldn't help believing that as time went by and technology continued to advance, it was at least partly her stubbornness that had made her avoid such conveniences. Norah could be very stubborn.

"Norah?" he said when he realized the beep had sounded. "Tom here." *Like she wouldn't recognize your voice?* "In case Bella forgot to pass the message, just letting you know—well, Clarc called and you know my sister. She had this brainstorm for us to celebrate Mom and Dad's fiftieth this weekend instead of for their actual anniversary in January, so I'll be in Wisconsin if you need to reach me. I'll be back late Sunday night. Bella was a little vague on your plans for the holiday, but I hope it's a good one." As always when he left messages for her, he paused. It seemed as if he wanted to say something more, but in five years he had not been able to figure out what. "Bye," he added quickly and hung up.

He picked up messages his assistant had left him as he walked to his connecting gate, then called back to answer her questions. The plane from California had spent several precious minutes circling the airport and now he just hoped he wouldn't miss the flight to Chicago.

As he hung up, the gate was in sight and packed with people waiting. He scanned the rows of chairs for a place to drop his luggage and spotted an empty one right next to a girl waving wildly at him.

Bella? Here? In Denver?

"Dad!" Isabella stood on the chair. "Dad! Over here."

Tom eased his way through the disorganized parade

of people, his smile meeting Isabella's while his eyes searched for Norah.

"Dad," Isabella cried for the third time as she catapulted her way into his arms. "Surprise! How cool is this?"

Tom laughed and eased his daughter back to a standing position. "What are you doing here?" He glanced around again. "Where's your mother?"

"Bathroom. She is going to seriously freak," Isabella predicted.

"Where are you two headed?" Tom was pretty sure he knew. Norah rarely took time off and when she did, it was to go to Wisconsin to see her parents.

"To see the grands." The response was muffled and Isabella was looking somewhere over his left shoulder.

"Bella, you didn't tell your mom that I was also going to Normal?"

Isabella had the good sense to look slightly abashed. "I kind of forgot."

Tom raised his eyebrows.

"Look at it this way—now we can all celebrate Thanksgiving and the anniversary together. How cool is that?"

"What do you think your mom will have to say about this?"

Isabella's expression tightened and she sighed dramatically. "Did it ever occur to you guys that the longer you keep up this thing of never seeing each other like up close and personal, the harder it's going to be when it actually happens?"

Tom considered the best response to that, but Isabella was on a roll.

"I mean the very fact that neither one of you has found someone new should prove something," she added. "Like maybe splitting up was a mistake of astronomical proportions?"

"I thought you said your mom was dating."

"Well, she didn't join a convent after you two split, Dad." Isabella rolled her eyes at him. "And you haven't exactly been without your share of female companionship. What was the last one's name? Tabitha?" she added.

"Tamara," he corrected, "and she was—is a business associate."

"Whatever. She's a lot younger than you. What was that about?"

"We work together on various projects. Her age has nothing to do with it."

Isabella's smirk said she was not convinced. "You want to know what I think?"

"Why do I feel you're going to tell me whether I want to know or not?"

"I think that you and mom both miss each other, but you're both too stubborn to admit it and try again. That's why you've spent the last five years finding ways not to see each other."

"Bella, it's been a long time," Tom explained, hating the fact that he was throwing cold water on her hope for a reconciliation. "We're different people now."

"Ya think?" she said with a dramatic sigh as if grown-ups were just dumber than dirt. "Okay. I didn't forget," she admitted, casting her eyes heavenward. "Forgive me," she whispered, then turned her attention back to her father.

On the occasion of her twelfth birthday Isabella had joined the church and her passion for her faith had blossomed from there. She sang in the youth choir, provided child care for toddlers for church events and was very active in the social action committee of her youth group.

"I'm surprised at you, Isabella," Tom said now. "I thought it was important to you to abide by the rules of your faith."

"Our faith, Dad. You used to belong to the same church and Mom still does."

"You know what I'm saying. How could you lie to your mother?"

"I didn't," she protested. "Not really."

"A lie of omission is still a lie," Tom reminded her.

Bella sighed and slumped back in her chair. "But where's the harm? I mean, how cool is it going to be to surprise Mom with the fact that we're all going to Normal together? Even I never imagined we'd actually be able to hook up here—though I have to admit I hoped we might."

"As I recall, your mom is not overly fond of surprises," Tom reminded her as he set his carry-on and computer bag on the small table next to her chair and tried to figure out the next steps in the farce his only child had created.

Isabella blinked. "Yeah, well… Too late now—she'll be back any minute." She eyed Tom warily. "Are you going to like disappear?"

"No, I'm here. You're here. Let's see how it goes."

Isabella grinned and stood up to clear a chair for him. "Okay, so come over here and sit down," she instructed. "Have you got something to read? No, better yet, open your computer—that's good." Isabella danced around him choreographing the surprise for Norah. "Here she comes," she whispered and giggled as she buried her face in a fashion magazine.

Norah was still several yards away, but he instantly picked her out of the masses and time reversed as he recalled the moment he'd realized he was in love with her. She had been a high school junior and he was a senior. She had lived just down the block from him her entire life. They had waited together at the same bus stop, attended the same church, seen each other countless times in all seasons because their parents were the best of friends. And yet, had he ever really looked at her until that winter's day when he stood shivering next to his broken-down car waiting for his dad to come and rescue him?

She'd been with a gang of her girlfriends, laughing and gabbing the way teenaged girls did, when one of them had spotted him. That girl had nudged Norah and nodded in his direction. Norah had peeled away from the others and headed his way.

"Problem?" The way she said it he thought she was getting a kick out his misery.

"Not if you've got a set of jumper cables in your backpack," he fired back.

Her eyes had widened in surprise. "You don't have jumper cables?"

Tom had seen no reason to respond to the obvious. Instead of moving on, she had leaned against the car with him. "Want me to call my dad?"

"No."

"Well, no need to be rude," she'd muttered, then, "Oh, you called your dad."

His father had pulled up then and produced the necessary cables to jump-start Tom's car. "You okay from here?" he asked when the car fired and continued to idle. "I have to get back to work."

"Yeah. Thanks, Pop."

Norah had still been standing there after his dad drove away. "You need a ride or something?"

"Are you going home?"

Tom had sighed. "No, I thought as long as I got the thing running I'd take a drive to California. Yes, I'm going home. Get in."

She had and then just after he'd pulled into traffic, she started laughing. This girl was laughing at Tom Wallace—student council president, varsity quarterback, on his way to university. "What?" he'd barked.

"Your ears are like Rudolph's nose," she'd managed. "I mean they are seriously red. They have these things now called hats, you know."

He'd glanced at himself in the rearview mirror. She had a point. He found himself grinning and then they were both laughing.

"Here," she said and pulled off her own knit stocking cap and pulled it over his hair and ears. Her warmth was still there in the yarn.

He'd dropped her off at her house, handed her back

her hat and asked if she had a date for the winter dance. And she had answered by asking a question of her own. “Are you asking me to go with you?”

“Yeah.”

“Then ask,” she’d said.

That was Norah—straightforward, self-confident, and sometimes too sure that she was in the right. *Like when she refused to even consider the move to San Francisco.*

“She’s coming,” Bella hissed. “Look busy.”

Over the open cover of his computer, Tom watched Norah approach. *Five years.* Suddenly it seemed like forever. What would he say to her after so much time? It wasn’t as if they hadn’t spoken. The one thing they had both agreed upon was that Izzy’s welfare and happiness came before any conflict or battle scars they might have with each other. But what to say face-to-face?

It had been so long since he had seen her and yet he would have recognized that graceful walk anywhere. The smile given so freely to total strangers. It suddenly struck him how much he had missed that smile. It had been hard to come by as their marriage had crumbled. Not that he had been giving her his best either. He’d been angry and hurt and looking hard for somewhere to lay the blame and guilt he felt creeping over him. He felt a little of it now, but maturity made him recognize it for what it was. Trying to make the fact they hadn’t seen each other for five long years her fault.

And now here she was not ten feet away, stopping to retrieve a child’s toy and return it with a goofy face that made the kid laugh. He had less than a minute to figure out some snappy line. His hands were shaking slightly. She looked great. She was one of those fortunate women who would age beautifully. He saw a couple of male passengers in the waiting area glance her way and felt a prick of the jealousy mixed with pride he'd always felt whenever they went somewhere together.

"Any updates?" she asked as she moved Isabella's backpack to the floor and started to sit. He could smell the familiar perfume of her hair, her skin. He could see the little scar that ran just in front of her left ear. She glanced at him and was prepared to nod pleasantly when her eyes went wide and her body froze.

Tom gave her an uncertain smile as he basked in the sheer pleasure of being near enough to touch her after all this time. Same dark hair—different style. Sort of a tousled cap of curls. Skin—unblemished except for the two spots of high color that currently dotted her cheeks. Eyes? Ah, those eyes. The blue-green color of a clear water lake—deep enough to swim in, get lost in.

"Surprise," he said quietly as he closed the cover of his computer.

Chapter Two

Norah could not have been more surprised if the president himself had been sitting next to her. Her lips twitched, but her voice seemed frozen as a number of catchy comebacks rocketed through her brain.

Gee, obviously the last five years have been great to you—you look...

Well, imagine this—

Tom Wallace, how long has it been? Let's see, must be five years, three months and twelve days or something like that.

Izzy bounced to her knees on the chair to Norah's left and rescued her. "Do you believe this? I mean what are the odds that we'd all end up in the same airport at the same time and waiting on the same plane?"

"Pretty good given the fact you knew I was coming this way, young lady," Tom said, but his eyes never left Norah's face.

Her gaze shifted to Isabella. "You knew?"

"Sorta, kinda," Izzy said and looked down.

Norah blinked, her thick black lashes feathering her cheeks. "Isabella Wallace, I am surprised at you." She realized she could not avoid acknowledging Tom's presence forever, so she took a deep breath and plastered on her biggest smile. "How are you, Tom?" she asked as if they were former classmates who had run into each other unexpectedly.

"Good. Fine," he said, clearing his throat. "You?"

"Fine," she said.

Isabella made a face and they both heard her sigh of frustration. The sigh brought Norah's attention back to her daughter. "You should go to the restroom," she said.

"Mom," Izzy moaned. "Stop treating me like I'm eight. I know when I do and don't have to go, okay?"

Isabella had been just about to celebrate her eighth birthday when the divorce papers arrived. Norah had had the phone in hand ready to call and put Izzy on the line so she could tell her father all about the party that Norah had arranged. In those early weeks and months she had remained in shock. It seemed impossible that she and Tom—of all people—had gone their separate ways.

The airport public address system crackled to life. "They're calling first class," Norah translated the garbled message and nodded toward the open door leading to the jetway.

He smiled. "I'm in coach. Busiest travel day of the year—you know how it goes."

"You can sit with us," Isabella said.

Simultaneously Norah and Tom opened their mouths to object to that idea.

"The plane is packed, honey," Norah said.

"We're running late, Bella. Let's not complicate things," Tom said.

Norah glanced his way, acknowledging with a slight nod of her head that he had backed her up. But then they had always been a team when it came to their daughter. The one thing they had both held sacred was that whatever differences they had, those would not affect Isabella any more than they had already.

She's still so young and lots of her classmates have divorced parents, they had both rationalized. In time, surely....

"Why did you decide to travel under such circumstances?" she asked. "No one's ill, are they?" she asked alarmed and saw that familiar flicker of irritation because he took her comment wrong. No doubt he thought that she was implying that the only thing that could drag Tom away from his work on a moment's notice had to be something to do with his parents. Most of their arguments in those last months together had been about his devotion, or as she saw it obsession, with his career.

"Clare and Liz got this idea that we should all surprise Mom and Dad over Thanksgiving for their fiftieth," he replied. "You know Clare. Once she gets an idea it's easier to let her have her way than try to debate the timing of the idea."

"Aunt Liz is coming, too? And the cousins?" Isabella clapped her hands in delight. "I mean is this the best Thanksgiving or what?"

The gate agent called Norah and Isabella's row.

Norah busied herself gathering her things and organizing Izzy's belongings in her backpack.

"We could share a car when we get to Chicago," Tom said.

"I've already reserved one," she replied and then immediately added. "Of course, I could cancel it. Yes, sharing a car would be nice. Thanks."

"Okay, so see you in Chicago," he said as he hugged Izzy.

"You and your father can talk more there," Norah promised Izzy as she hurried her toward the gate.

You and your father...meaning what? She didn't intend to say anything?

She glanced back wanting to apologize for what he might have thought she was implying, but Tom was packing his computer, his back to her.

"I have to go to the bathroom," Isabella announced as soon as they had located their seats and she had stowed her backpack under the seat nearest the window leaving Norah with the middle.

"I warned you," Norah said, but stood aside, blocking boarding passengers so Isabella could make her way to the rear of the plane. She sat down again and bent to rearrange their belongings so that she would have some legroom. When she looked up Tom was standing in the aisle waiting for other passengers ahead of him to get settled.

"I'm in the back," he said, making a face.

Norah shook her head sympathetically. "I'm in the middle," she replied, indicating the obvious. It was the kind of banter they'd always been good at and a little of the initial tension between them eased. During their marriage they'd had a long-running debate about which was worse—back of the plane with its noise and turbulence or crushed between two passengers who seemed to think they had claim to all armrests.

"Trade you?"

Norah smiled. "Not a chance."

Tom moved on just as the crew chief announced another slight delay to allow passengers on a late-arriving plane to make their connection.

A large man carrying a briefcase, carry-on luggage and an overcoat opened and slammed several filled overhead compartments. Norah pulled the airline magazine from the seatback pocket and flipped through it hoping he had the vacant seat across the aisle.

No such luck. He forced the luggage into an overhead bin two rows ahead of them, then threw his coat onto the seat and sat down heavily, his bulk and the coat spilling over into Norah's space as he jammed the briefcase under the seat in front of him.

Norah nodded at him as she gently pushed his coat off the armrest they shared. The man ignored her.

"Hey, Mom," Isabella said. "Guess what?" Izzy was accompanied by a young woman with a toddler in tow and what looked like a newborn cradled in her arms.

"This is Emma and she's got the two seats next to Dad and she'd be willing to switch, so I said that would be great—I'll even take the middle."

Norah tried not to take perverse pleasure in the look

of pleading horror the businessman gave her. "You'll take the middle?"

"Yeah, come on."

"Excuse me," Norah said sweetly as she recovered her purse and Isabella's backpack and stood.

"But," the man protested as Norah slid past him.

"Everything all right here?" the male flight attendant asked.

"Perfect," Isabella exclaimed. "My dad's back there and this nice lady traded so that now we get to sit together and—"

"Okay, I just need everyone to get settled as soon as possible. We're about to close the cabin door."

Tom was standing in the aisle waiting for them. Norah tried not to stare at the way his hair—brown streaked with copper—was still thick and silky. She did not meet his chocolate-brown eyes, fixed on her as she slid next to the window and Isabella took the middle without protest.

"You put her up to that—switching," Norah said.

"What?" Tom's eyes were wide with innocence.

"It was my idea, Mom," Isabella said. "Honestly."

Norah had her doubts.

"How are your folks?" Tom asked politely once they were buckled in.

"Fine," Norah answered equally as polite. This was going to be interminable. Suddenly she was glad to be in the back where the engine noise would surely make conversation impossible.

"This is going to be so great," Isabella exclaimed, ignoring the tension between her parents. "I mean, just wait until we all show up together. They are going to seriously freak."

"How's work?" Tom asked Norah.

"Fine," she said and looked out the window as the plane slowly taxied toward the runway. She wondered if she could be capable of more than that one-word response to anything Tom might ask.

"Ladies and gentlemen, we apologize for the short delay, but we should be airborne in about twenty minutes."

There was a ripple of muttered comments. "It's sleeting," Norah said.

Tom leaned across Isabella's lap to look out. Norah could not help but be aware of the scent of his aftershave—familiar and at the same time exotic. "From the looks of that sky we just need to get going," he said as the plane inched forward in line. "You okay?" He glanced up at Norah and she knew that he was remembering how nervous she got when flying. She couldn't help being touched that he had remembered.

"Fine," she replied and then grimaced. "I seem to have the same answer for everything, don't I?"

"Well, yeah," Isabella said before Tom could answer. "You're acting like you're on a first date or something, Mom."

Tom leaned back in his seat. "And just what would you know about first dates, young lady?"

Isabella blushed and giggled. "Oh, Dad."

Norah reached for her purse and pulled out a Sudoku puzzle book.

"Mom!" Isabella protested, casting a sidelong look from the book to Tom.

"Are you any good at those puzzles?" Tom asked, ignoring Isabella.

Norah shrugged. "Not really, but I can usually manage the simple ones."

"Can I try?" Tom asked, holding out his hand for the book.

Norah passed him the soft-covered book and held out her pencil.

Tom pulled a pen from his pocket and grinned. "No guts, no glory," he said and settled in to work the puzzle with Isabella's help.

Norah watched as he clicked the pen on and off—his hand tan against the pale cream starched cuff of his shirt. He wore dark brown casual slacks and a pullover sweater in a sort of copper shade that accented his tan and highlighted the gold flecks in his eyes. She heard his deep voice consulting with Isabella on an entry, his laughter when Isabella stopped him from making a mistake. He bent forward and ran his free hand through his hair. When a lock fell over his forehead, she literally had to tighten her grip on the armrest to resist the urge to smooth it back into place as she would have before.

Before. When they were married. When they were—

"Mom!"

Norah blinked. "Sorry," she said softly, still caught up in the fantasy of who she and Tom had once been to each other.

"I said, can you see what's happening? Why aren't we moving?"

Norah turned her attention to the window. It was coated with sleet. "I can't see," she said and just then the plane made a slow turn to the right. "I think we might be—"

"Ladies and gentlemen, weather conditions have changed. We need to de-ice the wings before we can take off. Please feel free to move about the cabin for the time being. We'll be on our way as soon as possible."

This time a chorus of groans rolled through the cabin as passengers crowded the aisle, rearranging the contents of overhead bins, stretching as they commiserated about the inconveniences of modern travel. Tom took advantage of the extra space afforded by being in the last row across from the galley. "Come on, Bella, stretch your legs."

Isabella followed her father's lead in a series of calf stretches and knee bends. The crew toured the cabin offering packages of pretzels and promising full beverage service once they were airborne.

"Your turn," Tom said and held out his hand to Norah. Norah slid across the row and stood in the aisle without taking his hand. "Feels good," she said as she stretched her arms high over her head, her fingertips grazing the ceiling.

Isabella lifted the armrests on their row and stretched out across all three seats, her MP3 player earphones in place. She closed her eyes and bounced her head and shoulders to the music they couldn't hear.

"I'm going for a little walk," Norah said, suddenly uncomfortable to find herself standing next to Tom—far too near to Tom for comfort.

He grinned. "Just stay inside the plane," he called as she edged forward.

The truth was she needed some time to think about the impact of spending Thanksgiving three blocks away from Tom and his family. In fact, there was no doubt that they would be thrown together often once they were back in Normal. His parents and hers belonged to the same church and were still close friends. Isabella would move easily between the two houses. Izzy's aunts and cousins would surely want to include Isabella in whatever extravaganza they were concocting for the anniversary. They would certainly include Norah's parents—and Norah—in the invitation as well.

The aisle was crowded with other passengers and the plane was not nearly long enough for Norah to stay away indefinitely. She glanced back and saw Tom talking to another passenger. Ahead stood the businessman glaring at her as the young mother tried in vain to soothe the newborn and the toddler, both of whom were crying now. The scene gave new meaning to "between a rock and a hard place" but by far the lesser of the two evils was to return to her seat.

Isabella had dozed off, so Norah perched on the aisle armrest. Tom finished his exchange with the passenger waiting to use the restroom and turned. He was standing toe to toe with her, his forearm resting against the overhead bin. He'd removed his sweater and rolled back the sleeves of his shirt.

"How was your walk?" he asked.

"Fine," she replied and then blushed. "Uneventful," she added with a slight smile.

Tom did not return her smile. Instead he studied her closely. "You look great, Norah," he said.

Norah ran a self-conscious hand through her hair. "I've been up since four and my—"

"Why do you do that?" he asked. "You never used to do that."

Norah fought a twinge of irritation. *I never used to doubt that a marriage I thought was forever could fall apart in a matter of months.* What did he know about her these days? "Do what?" she asked.

"Put yourself down. Someone pays you a compliment and you—"

"You know, Tom, it has been a number of years. I might have changed in that time."

"I expect we both have, but—"

"Izzy tells me you're seeing someone new," she interrupted, determined to turn the focus from herself to him.

"Izzy doesn't approve of my choice in female companionship," he said with a glance at their sleeping daughter.

Norah shrugged. "She just needs time."

"Speaking of time," Tom said clearing his throat. "Five years and not once seeing each other, Norah—it's a long time. How did that happen?" He leaned in to allow another passenger to pass. His face was closer to hers now. His eyes locked on hers and she saw that he looked tired.

"It's not like we weren't in touch," she countered. "I mean we were always on the phone or leaving messages about Izzy. I think we've done well by her, don't you?"

"Stop changing the subject. You didn't want to see me. Why?"

Norah shifted uncomfortably. "That was just at first. I mean it was all so fresh and we were both so vulnerable and I thought that maybe—"

"But to let not one, but five years pass?"

"It just happened, Tom. I didn't plan it and you could have just as easily—" She was whispering, keenly aware of others around them but equally aware that she could have been shouting and few other passengers would have cared. They were all that wrapped up in their own problems.

"Ladies and gentlemen, please return to your seats and fasten your seat belts."

This time the general chorus of commentary was filled with relief and even laughter as passengers returned to their seats and buckled up.

Norah tapped Isabella's leg. "Turn that off and fasten your seat belt," she instructed.

Isabella swung her legs around and did as she was told, only she took the obvious seat—the one by the window.

"I'll take the middle," Tom offered.

"No, I've got it," Norah said as she sat down, lowered both armrests and fastened her seat belt. She picked up the puzzlebook Tom had left on his seat, waited for him to sit down and then handed it to him.

"Thanks." He took out his pen and concentrated on the puzzle as Isabella stared out the window.

After several moments she reported their progress. "I think we're going back to the terminal."

"That's impossible," Norah said, leaning across her to look out the window. But her daughter was right. "Now what?" Norah muttered.

"Ladies and gentlemen, we are returning to the gate area. We regret that the airport is being closed for the time being. A major winter storm is passing through the area and we had hoped to get away in front of it, but it's coming too fast. Once we are at the gate you may deplane and there will be airline personnel inside the terminal with more information. Please feel free to make use of your cell phones to notify those who may be meeting you in Chicago of this unexpected situation—and thank you once again for choosing—"

Chapter Three

Even before the announcement ended, Tom had his cell phone out dialing his office. When he got voice mail, he glanced at his watch and realized that everyone had already left for the holiday.

"I was hoping to get my assistant to work on finding us an alternate flight," he explained, noting Norah's raised eyebrows.

"I didn't ask," she said.

But you questioned, he thought. *You always used to think I was putting work ahead of you and Bella.* He covered his irritation by pulling his sweater back on as they waited their turn to leave the plane.

If the country's fifth busiest airport had seemed crowded before, it was in total chaos when they emerged from the jetway. Harried airport personnel tried in vain to reassure passengers. Most passengers were accepting their fate, while a few like the businessman who'd shared a row with the screaming babies were demanding to speak with higher authorities. "You have to do something," he shouted, his mouth inches from the face of the gate agent. "From the looks of things we could be here for hours."

"Sir," the gate agent explained, "look at that weather." She pointed to the large windows where visibility was near zero. "Unfortunately none of us is going anywhere until this storm passes and we can get the runways cleared."

"And how long will that take?" the man demanded.

"I don't know, sir. Only God knows the answer to that one."

"She's right," Isabella said as she and her parents edged past the angry man. "This is God's work. He's got something in mind here and I think I know what it is." She looked up at her parents, then linked arms with them to either side of her. "Now let's get some food. I am so starving."

"You and your mother take care of getting us something to eat," Tom said handing Isabella money. "I'm going to see about getting us a hotel room—rooms—" he clarified when Norah's head shot up and her wide eyes met his. "There is no way we're going to get out of here tonight."

"We'll meet back here then?" Norah asked and realized she was glad that Tom was there. Tom had always been able to make things happen without berating people to get what he wanted.

"Give me half an hour," he said and strode away.

"What should I get for Dad?" Izzy asked when they were finally close to ordering.

"Turkey wrap with brown mustard, no mayo, tomato,

lettuce, no sprouts," Norah said as she gathered bottled drinks from the cooler. "Pasta salad if they have it. No chips unless they're baked." She glanced up to find Izzy grinning at her, her eyes wide with surprise. "What?"

"How do you know that? I mean the details?"

Norah shrugged. "Lucky guess," she murmured.

"Right," Isabella said softly and smiled as she repeated the order verbatim and multiplied it by three.

The cashier rang up the sale and Isabella peeled off two twenties from the bills Tom had given her, then waited for change.

Tom was waiting for them at the assigned spot. "Well, here's the deal," he reported. "The airport is bringing in buses to take people to hotels. I was able to book us one room—two queen beds," he assured Norah.

"But what about the party in Normal? The grands?" Isabella protested.

"Honey, be thankful your father was able to get us a room." *One room—with two beds, but still one room.*

"We do have another option—staying here," Tom said as if he'd read her mind. "It might be something we want to consider."

"All night?" Isabella exclaimed. "Now let's see—on the one hand we have a reserved hotel room with TV, room service and our own bathroom and on the other we could bunk down here. Gee, tough one, Dad."

"Staying here means we are here when they get a runway cleared. The hotel room I got is at least twenty-five miles away and in this weather getting here from there—"

"—could take hours," Norah finished his thought,

then focused her attention on Isabella when she caught the look in Tom's eyes. When they'd been together they had laughed about the way they used to finish each other's sentences on a regular basis. *Is the next step that we start to look alike?* Tom had teased. Norah focused on Izzy. "Staying here gives us the best possible chance for getting to the grands," she explained.

Izzy rolled her eyes. "Whatever."

"Bella, attitude," Tom warned. "Hey, it'll be an adventure—like camping."

Isabella gave him the wide-eyed grin of a six-year-old. "Oh goody, can we build a campfire and tell ghost stories and make s'mores?"

Tom laughed and wrapped his arm around her. "Come on. Let's see if we can snag a couple of those cots." He nodded to the area where people had lined up as skycaps wheeled in carts with folding cots loaded on top.

"Maybe Izzy should wait here with me," Norah said, eyeing the desperation of the stranded mob.

"You don't think I'm going into that, do you?" Tom said, his eyebrows raised in mock surprise.

"Well, how else—"

"Come on, Bella."

Norah watched as Tom steered Izzy to a corner on the outskirts of the crowd. She saw him approach a man and his wife—each with a cot in tow. A conversation ensued and next thing Norah knew Tom and Izzy were coming her way each hauling a cot.

"But, how—" Norah stuttered.

"We made a trade," Izzy told her. "Dad gave them

the hotel room. They handed over the cots. No problem." She looked adoringly at Tom as if the man had suddenly sprouted a cape and tights.

As Norah followed them down the concourse, she saw Tom nod pleasantly to gate agents and other passengers as if spending the night at the Denver airport was no big deal. At the airline's private lounge he punched in a code and opened the door, holding it for Izzy to wrangle her cot inside and then waiting for Norah. "Over here," he added, spotting a pair of chairs in the corner.

"Do you think they'll unload the luggage?" Norah asked as Tom and Izzy set up the cots and she distributed the lunch.

"Not likely," Tom replied, following her glance toward an older woman at the desk who was explaining that her husband's medications were packed in their checked luggage.

Norah watched the woman leave the desk as she bit into her sandwich.

"Hey," Tom said softly, "leave the social working to the airport staff, okay?"

You can't save the world, Norah, he had once shouted at her when they were arguing. But he wasn't shouting now. His tone was gentle and sympathetic and his eyes told her that he understood that she really wanted to help.

"This looks great," Tom said, turning his attention to the sandwich. "And you remembered the mustard," he said.

"Mom remembered," Isabella replied before Norah could.

"Did you remember your father's change?" Norah asked.

Isabella dug one hand into the pocket of her jeans. "Oh yeah. Here." She handed him a wad of crushed bills and some coins. "That's it," she said when Tom stared at the money. "Airport food equals inflated prices."

"I wasn't counting," her dad said with a chuckle. "I was just wondering how this fist-sized wad fit into the pocket of those jeans. What did you do? Have Mom sew them on you this morning?"

"Dad! They aren't that tight."

"They're pretty tight," Norah agreed. "You might wish you'd worn something more comfortable before this journey ends." She pulled at the leg of her own stretchy trousers to illustrate her point.

"Mom dresses like an old lady these days," Izzy explained to Tom as if Norah had suddenly disappeared.

Now it was Norah's turn to protest. "Isabella Wallace!"

"Well, it's true. I've been thinking of nominating you for that show where they make you throw out your entire wardrobe and go shopping for a new one."

"My clothes are fine—serviceable. Comfortable."

Izzy took another bite of her sandwich and continued to study her mother. "On that show they completely change your hair and makeup too. They can make the person look ten years younger."

Norah saw Tom mask a smile by taking a swallow of his bottled water.

"Do something. She's your daughter too."

Tom cleared his throat and spoke to Izzy while looking at Norah. "I think your mother looks—*fine,* Bella. Especially the way she's wearing her hair now—and the color—"

Norah's hand flew to her hair. "What about the color? This is my normal color. I do not—"

Tom and Isabella both burst out laughing and Norah smothered a grin. "So this is the way it's to be," she said sternly. "The two of you ganging up on poor defenseless me?"

Tom gave a hoot of laughter. "Defenseless? That'll be the day." He turned to Isabella. "One time there was this neighborhood bully. Your mother was—what, Norah? Nine—ten?"

"I was Izzy's age," Norah replied.

"But smaller than you. The bully must have easily outweighed her by fifty pounds or more. What was that kid's name, Norah?"

"Oscar," Norah said.

"So Oscar starts picking on this new kid and your mom had had it. She marched up to him, stood toe to toe between him and the new kid and told Oscar that—you finish it," Tom said, looking at Norah.

"You're telling it."

"Said what?" Isabella demanded.

Her mother sighed. "I simply informed the young man that if his name was a problem for him he should change it."

"Or words to that effect," Tom said.

"And what did Oscar do?"

"He asked me how he could change it when it was the one he was born with."

Tom took up the story. "She asked him what name he would choose for himself."

"And?" Izzy asked, glancing from one to the other. "What name?"

"Bruno!" Tom and Norah said in unison then chuckled.

Izzy took obvious delight in seeing them sharing a memory, looking at each other with no reservation, then Norah looked down and away. "And that's when you fell in love with Mom, right?"

Her father began clearing the trash from their lunch. "Uh—"

"I thought you said those paperbacks you've been reading were stories of inspiration and faith," Norah said, turning the focus on Izzy and away from her and Tom.

"Well, even God loves a good romance, Mom," Izzy replied as she took the trash from Tom and stuffed it into the paper bag that had held the sandwiches.

"We should see if there's been any change in what's happening," Norah said and Izzy watched as her mom relieved her of the trash and they headed off in opposite directions—her to deposit their trash and him to check in with the woman at the desk. When they returned Izzy had pulled her novel out of her backpack and settled into one of the chairs.

By late afternoon Norah had called her parents and Tom had spoken to his sisters. They whiled away the endless waiting by reading, working, or—in Isabella's case—listening to music. Around five, Tom shut his laptop, stood and stretched. "Come on, girls, let's go for a walk and see about getting something hot for supper."

It had been several hours since the announcement had come through that the airport would close. Airport personnel had put the contingency plan for such situations into operation. But as night came on and the storm gathered force, it became clear that no one was going anywhere at least until morning and maybe not then.

The first thing to hit Norah as they entered the concourse was the sheer level of the noise—people shouting at each other, babies crying, toddlers and their siblings fighting in loud shrieks over some toy or snack, bleary-eyed parents slumped on the floor or on chairs ignoring their children's pleas for mediation. In spite of the fact that shopkeepers and other airport employees were as stranded as the passengers, several restaurants and shops had shut their doors. The desks at every gate stood empty of airport personnel and the arrival and departure boards had simply been turned off.

"Dad?" Isabella edged closer to Tom's side and put her hand in his. "Everybody's so mad."

Norah put her arm around Isabella's shoulder as she looked up at Tom. "This place is turning into a powder keg."

"It'll be fine. The governor has declared a state of emergency and the National Guard is handling things along with airport security."

"Still, maybe we could organize some child care. These parents need a break."

"A camp," Izzy suggested. "Camp Stuck-in-the-Snow."

"It's not a bad idea," Norah told Tom. "We could take over the play areas along the concourse—there are slides and blocks and all sorts of activities."

"And don't they have coloring books and stuff on the planes to keep the kids entertained?" Izzy asked, scooting closer to her parents so that the three of them formed a tight ring.

"We could have the kids bring their blankets and pillows for nap time," Norah said, her voice growing with enthusiasm for the idea.

Tom looked from his wife to his daughter and back to Norah. "Aren't you exhausted?"

"I could sleep," she admitted.

"But, Dad," Izzy said, "this is Mom's thing. I mean she is practically an expert when it comes to setting up stuff for helping others. Right, Mom?"

"Right." Norah raised her eyes to Tom's. "A regular wizard."

"Well, I guess it beats wearing the turkey costume I'm sure my sisters have waiting for me back home at Mom's," he said.

"Don't underestimate me," Norah told him with a shy grin. "I've been known to come up with a turkey costume myself."

Izzy threw her arms around Tom's neck and squealed, "This is such a cool adventure we're on."

Norah saw Tom glance at her over the top of their daughter's head as he said, "Yeah. Pretty cool."

On Thanksgiving morning Norah opened her eyes and blinked several times as she tried to get her bearings. Airport. Denver. Vintage military cot where she had spent a good part of the night trying to remember this wasn't even half the width of her bed at home. She grimaced as she stretched her back and legs.

"Coffee?"

Tom was standing beside her looking as if he'd just stepped out of a shower even though he was wearing the same clothes he'd worn the day before.

"Intravenously, if possible," she muttered as she struggled to a sitting position with her back against the wall. "Where's Izzy?"

"Out recruiting." At Norah's blank stare he added, "Counselors? For Camp Stuck-in-the-Snow?" Then he grinned and sat on Izzy's abandoned cot. "You never were much of a morning person, were you?"

Norah chose to ignore that as she sipped her coffee. "So what are the chances we're going to get out of here today?"

"Slim and none—take your pick. It snowed all night and hasn't let up—twenty inches and counting. Last I heard this is just the front side of an entire line of storms."

Norah groaned. "I need a shower and a toothbrush."

"Can't help with either of those. How about an after-dinner mint?" He produced a cellophane-wrapped red-and-white candy from his pocket.

"Thank you," Norah said. As she sucked on the mint she studied him. "How come you look as if you just stepped out of *GQ* magazine or something?"

He ran one hand through his hair self-consciously. "I washed up a little."

"Tom!" A woman at the door of the club waved to him. "We're all set," she said, rushing forward and handing him a yellow legal pad with a list of names and numbers. "Every gate area has a representative."

Norah gave Tom a questioning look.

"I met with the airport manager," he said. "They thought it might be helpful to see if we could have a volunteer communicator for each gate area. Kind of cuts down on everyone trying to gain information. Also cuts down on rumors that can cause panic."

The woman had reached them now and Tom beamed at her as he took the notebook and scanned the list. "That's great work, Patty. Oh, Patty Martin, this is my—this is Norah."

Patty shook Norah's hand. She was close to forty, but with a face and body and manner of moving that made her look at least a decade younger. Norah felt old and dowdy as she accepted the woman's handshake.

"Now don't forget you promised me a ride in that sports car of yours when we get back to the world," she said turning her attention back to Tom.

The woman is flirting with my husband, Norah thought. She glanced at Tom and saw him watch the slim, fashionably dressed, perfectly made-up Patty stride back toward the door in her three-inch heels. *And he's enjoying it.*

Not your husband, she reminded herself.

"You okay?"

Tom was looking at her curiously.

"Fine," she replied tightly.

Tom sighed. "We have got to work on your vocabulary for social conversation, woman."

Woman—"my woman" he'd called her back when they were first married. "I love you, woman"—he used to say.

"I have to—" She struggled awkwardly to her feet, untangling herself from the twisted airline blanket and ignoring Tom's offered hand. She grabbed her purse and Izzy's backpack, certain that Tom would never think to keep an eye on it. He was far too busy running things, not that he'd exactly leaped on board when she'd suggested they get organized. But now that perky Patty had appeared, well—Norah headed for the women's restroom without finishing her thought.

"Hurry back," Tom called. "The gate reps can help you organize the camp."

Like I need help—is that what he thinks?

She was a mess. Her rumpled clothes screamed "slept in them" while her face was a road map of every one of her thirty-eight years. She was probably the same age as the ever-so-effervescent Patty—maybe even younger. She dug through her purse and found her hairbrush and attacked her hair with it. Then she paused and took a deep breath as she met her image in the mirror eye to eye.

Honestly, Norah Wallace, what kind of example is this to set for your daughter? There's her father out there saving the world and looking great doing it. Pull yourself together, girl. If you think he's falling into memory land with every word out of your mouth, think again. It's been five years—he's moved on and until you saw him yesterday—so had you.

Spotting Izzy's backpack, Norah rummaged through the contents, selecting items from her daughter's portable cosmetics counter and laying them out on the counter next to the sink. She opened the small tube of toothpaste that nestled with equally small bottles of lotion and foundation in the required plastic sandwich bag to get them past security. She squirted toothpaste onto her index finger and scrubbed her teeth. Next she smeared lotion on her face and wiped it clean with a tissue from the pack in her own purse.

Better already, she thought as she leaned toward the mirror.

This wasn't about impressing Tom or anyone else, she told herself. This was about taking pride in her appearance and setting an example for her daughter. It was about Izzy. Ever since the divorce her entire focus had been Izzy's upbringing and well-being. And just because Tom Wallace had suddenly reappeared in the flesh—in all his gorgeous, charming, glory-oozing memories she thought she had long ago laid to rest—there was no reason to start acting like a teenager with a crush.

Chapter Four

Tom did a double take when he saw Norah emerge from the restroom. Patty was introducing him to the gate reps, but Tom could not take his eyes off Norah. The cap of black curls framed her subtly made-up face. She had tucked the rumpled green T-shirt firmly into the waistband of her black slacks—slacks now belted with the long, slim scarf he'd seen Izzy stuff inside her backpack as they boarded the plane the day before. Over her shoulders Norah had tied the shapeless black sweatshirt he thought he might recognize from when they were married. Only now the contrast between the black sleeves and the green shirt highlighted her blue-green eyes, making them seem luminous.The finished look was both casual and sophisticated.

"Excuse me," Tom said to Patty and the others. "Wow, you clean up nice," he said, moving close enough not to be heard by the others.

Norah smiled. "You know, Tom, we are really going to have to work on your compliment-giving skills," she said as she walked past him toward the group. "Hello, I'm Norah Wallace and it would be great if some of you had the time to help me organize a day camp to keep the little ones entertained until we can all get out of here."

Five or six of the reps raised their hands to volunteer.

"Excellent," Norah said. "Let's get started. Ideas?"

And with that she exited the room with her band of volunteers trailing after her. The rest of the gate reps turned their attention back to Tom and Patty.

"Okay, where were we?" Patty said. "Ah, yes, Thanksgiving dinner."

The group had finally settled into serious planning for the holiday meal when Izzy burst into the room followed by seven tall, gangly male teenagers. "Where's Mom?" she asked as soon as she spotted Tom.

"Out there organizing the day camp. I thought you were helping her."

"Oh, right," Isabella said, looking slightly abashed. "I kind of got caught up in something else."

Tom turned his attention to the young people with Bella. "Hi, I'm Bella's father, Tom Wallace."

"Oh, sorry," Isabella said as she quickly introduced the teens. "And that's Mike. They're with the basketball team I told you about?"

"Sorry about the tournament, guys," Tom said. "So what's going on?" he asked, turning his attention back to his daughter, who looked diminutive in the circle of giants.

"Well, we were talking about the day camp and you know how on the last night at summer camp we always do this talent show?" Mike explained.

Tom nodded but couldn't ignore the fact that Bella was staring at Patty. He'd seen Isabella watching him the evening before after Norah had fallen asleep, and he—restless as always these days—had taken a chair some distance from Isabella and Norah where Patty was also fighting insomnia. He and Patty had connected immediately, exchanging war stories about their high-powered careers well into the night.

New girlfriend? Isabella's look seemed to ask as she shifted her gaze to him, and for the first time since meeting Patty, Tom realized that she was a clone of every woman he'd dated and introduced Bella to over the years.

"This is Patty Martin," he said including the basketball players in his introduction. "She's the public relations director for Teen Town." That got Bella's attention. Teen Town was a popular media conglomerate with a glossy fashion magazine, a popular Web site and its own show on cable television.

"Cool," one of the giants said and the others mumbled their support.

"Bella, why don't you and your—committee—sit down with Patty here and map out a plan," Tom suggested.

Isabella frowned. "I should go help Mom."

"I'll go help your mom. This is a great idea and you and your friends are the very ones to pull it off."

As always Isabella blossomed under his praise, and he felt the familiar kick of guilt that he wasn't around to boost her confidence on a regular basis. "Okay," she said. "You're sure you'll help Mom."

Tom gave the scout's honor signal. "Promise," he said.

"Were you ever really a scout?" she asked, her eyes darting to Patty who had the entire basketball team laughing and eyeing her slim figure.

"I was not," Tom replied. He took a step closer and placed his hands on Bella's shoulders. "What I am and always will be is your father and if I make you a promise, you can count on it, okay?"

He saw from the look she gave him that they both knew he couldn't always guarantee that, but she grinned and stood on tiptoe to kiss his cheek. "She's not your type," she whispered just before she turned and hurried back to where the boys and Patty were waiting.

Tom didn't have to look far to find Norah. The woman had always been a bit of a Pied Piper when it came to getting kids to follow her lead. Her eyes sparkled as she listened to the children shout out ideas for how this day camp thing might work. An admiring group of teenaged girls and boys all dressed in matching polo shirts with the logo of their church embroidered over the one breast pocket had gathered behind Norah, no doubt awaiting their assignments. Tom took advantage of the fact that Norah had her back to him and joined the circle of teens.

"Well now, Robbie, snowball forts are a wonderful idea, but we'll have to ask the people here at the airport if that's okay."

"They've got security issues," a worldly girl of ten informed everyone.

"Exactly," Norah replied. "Now these young men and

women are members of a very special choir," Norah explained, turning to indicate the teens. She spotted Tom among them and faltered.

"Is that man their leader?" a child called out.

"No," Tom replied stepping forward. "I'm Mrs. Wallace's assistant."

The children looked mystified.

"I asked them to call me by my first name," Norah explained softly. "Where's Izzy?"

"Putting together a talent show," he replied, then turned his attention back to the children. "We've got a lot of work to do, kids. Who wants to help work on the set for tonight's performance?" Tom asked.

Several of the children waved their hands and Tom selected half a dozen. "Oh, and we're going to need a stage manager," Tom said.

"Me!" The girl who had spoken earlier about airport security waggled her hand furiously at Tom.

Tom had his doubts about others being willing to follow this girl's lead. She was something of a know-it-all and in his limited experience that trait did not inspire leadership. He glanced past her hoping for more hands.

"Excellent," Norah said as she put her arm around the little girl and ushered her over to Tom. "This is Elizabeth."

"Well, Lizzie, let's—"

"It's Elizabeth," the girl informed him. "That is my name."

Tom met her look. "Elizabeth," he said solemnly. "Would you be so kind as to join the others over there?"

When the girl marched off, he rolled his eyes at Norah who covered a smile as she went back to the choir practice.

The morning flew by and the children were barely aware of the continuing storm. Furthermore, with the children occupied, the adults seemed to have calmed down considerably. Norah, on the other hand, was far too focused on Tom. By the time the children's parents had come to bring lunch and help settle the younger children for their afternoon nap, it had been over an hour since she had seen Tom and his crew.

Hurrying along the concourse, she could not help but notice more changes from the previous day. One man had apparently taken it as his responsibility to walk the length of the concourse, calling out the latest weather conditions at each gate like a town crier. "Snow has stopped for now, but warming trend means sleet and icing." He just shrugged when his news was met with good-natured boos. "Don't shoot the messenger, folks."

As Norah neared the dead end of the concourse, she blinked, unable to believe what she was seeing there. The semicircular backdrop behind the desks that served the last three gates had been covered with flattened cardboard boxes cut and colored to resemble a holiday village.

Norah walked past a group of children and adults seated cross-legged on the floor, then stopped. There in the middle of them was Tom, his fingers jammed into the child-sized handle of a pair of scissors, his tongue locked between his teeth as he concentrated on cutting a piece of folded white paper. The memory of their first

Christmas in Arizona hit her like a snowball to the back of the head. Suddenly she was back in that apartment where she and Tom had first learned that she was pregnant and where her doctor had dictated no travel for her.

On Christmas Eve, devastated that they would not be in Normal for a traditional Christmas, Norah had curled up on the bed and cried herself to sleep. And when she had awakened just before midnight, Tom had been sitting on the rocking chair he'd bought her when they'd gotten the news they were pregnant. He'd been wearing one of those Santa hats available at any drugstore at that time of year, and he'd handed her a headband of reindeer antlers.

"Time to make the rounds, Rudolph," he'd said, tweaking her nose, red from crying.

She hadn't felt much like playing, but while she'd slept she'd felt worse about the fact that she wasn't the only one missing Christmas at home. How selfish was she to think only of herself when Tom was missing out as well? She'd put on the antlers and followed him into the tiny living room. At the doorway, she'd stopped and gasped for the room was lit by dozens of votive candles and a snowstorm of crudely made paper snowflakes hung from the ceiling. In the background, the radio was tuned to an all-Christmas-music station.

"Come on," Tom had said, leading her to the loveseat he'd turned into a sleigh using the colorful fleece coverlet his mother had sent them.

"Aren't I supposed to pull the sleigh," she'd asked, indicating her antlers and red nose.

He'd grinned. "I put it on autopilot for tonight."

Together they had settled into the sleigh and sung along with the carols. Between songs, Tom had produced milk and cookies. "Perks of the job," he'd assured her, "unless you'd prefer reindeer food?"

"What's reindeer food?"

"Carrots, lettuce—healthy stuff."

Norah had curled her nose in disgust and Tom had laughed and pulled her into his arms and sung "Blue Christmas" along with Elvis as he fed her cookies.

At dawn they had exchanged gifts, but she no longer remembered what. The best gift had been Tom's recreation of a Normal holiday. The following year, Tom had placed several sheets of white paper and a pair of scissors in front of her.

"Teach me to make a proper snowflake?" he'd asked.

And through the years of their marriage the tradition had continued—even after they'd moved into their first house and then on to the grand house that Tom had insisted on buying. And even when their arguments or stony silences had become almost an everyday occurrence—some time in December they called a truce and the tradition continued.

"Hey, Norah? Check this out."

Norah blinked, aware once again of her surroundings. Tom was holding up one perfect paper snowflake and grinning triumphantly.

By the time the sky darkened into night, pretty much everyone still confined to the concourse agreed that everything they could reasonably expect was being done to make them as comfortable as possible.

"But we can hardly be expected to ignore the future," Dave Walker, the airport director of operations, said to Tom. "The airport will reopen—possibly as early as tomorrow. My people are exhausted, too. They've been here—away from their families, I might add—for the same number of hours as everyone else. Some of them longer. Some were at the end of their shifts when this thing hit."

"We appreciate that," Tom assured him. "It's Thanksgiving and we're just trying to make it special—for everyone."

"Still, you can't expect our vendors or the airlines to keep shelling out—"

"How about this?" Norah said. "How about if we take an offering for the meal and then divide it between the vendors according to their contribution. It might not completely pay the bill but—"

"I'll cover the difference," Tom said quietly.

Dave scratched his head and frowned. "Are you still going to want my staff to serve as waiters and—"

"No one is asking that," Norah told him. "We have volunteers ready to set up the buffet and others willing to clear away any leftovers afterward. The employees here at the airport should feel that they are as much a guest at this table as anyone else."

"Sort of like the first Thanksgiving," Tom said with a grin. "Come on, Dave, help us out here."

Dave glanced over to where the food vendors and airline managers stood. They were lined up in a show of solidarity, their arms folded across their chests. Earlier they had marched down the concourse with Dave to where Norah and Tom were setting up for the evening's meal and performance and made it clear—via Dave—that they had had it. "I'll talk to them," Dave said. "You'll pay the difference?"

Tom nodded. "I'll need receipts and invoices, but yes, tell them if they will give us access to whatever food supplies they may have on hand, they will be fully reimbursed."

Norah watched Dave approach the others. "Tom, this could be a lot of money."

Tom shrugged. "Look at these people, Norah," he said turning her away from Dave and his group to where groups of passengers were busy moving waiting-area benches into impromptu auditorium-style seating in front of the stage the children had created. "Look at their faces," he said, his hands still on her shoulders. "Close your eyes and listen."

Norah did as he asked and she heard laughter and snatches of the kind of conversation that takes place when strangers are getting to know one another. From a distant corner she heard the soft strum of a guitar and from somewhere behind her she heard the younger children busy at play in the children's area now dubbed Camp Stuck-in-the-Snow.

And through it all she was most aware of Tom's familiar strong hands resting on her shoulders, his deep quiet voice reverberating in her ear, and the rhythm of his steady breathing as predictable as her own. "We always were a good team, woman."

"Okay, you've got a deal," Dave said having returned

from his huddle with the others. "Get your people organized and follow me."

Half an hour later the food started coming—an unorthodox cornucopia of hot and cold sandwiches, pizzas, oversized pretzels, prepackaged salads, single-serving containers of yogurt, fresh apples, oranges and bananas, bags of chips, pretzels and nachos, and bottled water, soda and juices. The "guests" lined up on either side of the buffet and without anyone so much as suggesting they be mindful of the numbers of people to be fed, limited their selections so there would be plenty for everyone.

"Mom, over here!"

Norah saw Isabella waving to her from the position she'd staked out near the stage. Tom was sitting on the floor next to her.

A family Thanksgiving, she thought as she made her way to them.

"Pull up a piece of floor and join us," Tom said with a grin. He started to bite into his sandwich when Isabella stopped him.

"We haven't said grace," she reminded him.

Norah could see by Tom's expression that saying grace was not exactly a regular thing for him. The truth was that if it weren't for Isabella's devout faith, saying grace probably wouldn't be a regular thing for Norah either.

"You say it, honey," she suggested.

Isabella held out one hand to either parent and then indicated with a nod that they needed to complete this little circle by taking hands with each other. When they hesitated, Isabella sighed impatiently. “We’re giving thanks,” she said, “not making a lifetime commitment.”

Tom laughed and grabbed Norah’s hand. “Good point, Bella.”

Isabella closed her eyes and bowed her head and her parents did the same. Norah could not help noticing that nearby, other small groups of passengers had observed them and paused to put down their food and join hands as well.

“Thank you, God, for this food we are so blessed to receive. Millions of people are starving tonight and we ask for your help in showing us the way to relieve such suffering even as we celebrate this day of giving thanks. Amen.”

“Amen,” Tom and Norah murmured together.

“That was lovely, Bella,” Tom said as he released Norah’s hand and leaned over to kiss his daughter’s cheek. “Thank you.”

“You can eat now,” Bella instructed, every bit as shy about receiving a compliment as Norah had ever been.

“Kid gets more like you all the time,” Tom whispered as he reached past Norah for a packet of ketchup.

“So how did we spend our first Thanksgiving together?” Isabella asked when conversation among them faltered.

“You didn’t eat much—you were still a little peanut inside Mom’s tummy.” Tom tweaked Isabella’s nose.

“We were still in that tiny little studio apartment,” Norah added and saw Tom frown.

“It wasn’t that tiny.” Tom had always been especially sensitive about the material environment he had provided for Norah and Isabella. Even though when they split they were living in a McMansion in a gated community with hired help to tend the grounds, the pool and clean the house, Tom had wanted more.

"Cozy," Norah amended, not wanting to open the door to old wounds and arguments. "It was our first home together."

Appeased, Tom laughed as he continued the story. "Your Mom had bought this turkey—what was it, forty pounds or something?"

Norah blushed. "Twenty," she murmured.

"Frozen," Tom added as they both started to laugh.

"And it wouldn't fit in the oven," Norah said, snorting with giggles and the memory.

"Your mom had invited the immediate world to come for dinner."

"Just a few neighbors and people from work who had nowhere else to go that day," Norah protested.

"Twenty people in all," Tom reminded her.

"Where were you going to put them all if the apartment was so small?" Izzy asked.

"The apartment building had a flat roof," Norah explained, "so your father got this idea that we could have everyone bring lawn chairs and we'd set things up on the roof."

"Except there had been this prolonged drought and heat wave and the floor of the roof was coated with some kind of asphalt substance that not only held the heat but tended to stick to your shoes."

"But everybody was such a good sport. Remember Kyle?"

Tom grinned. “I haven’t thought about Kyle in years.” He turned to Isabella. “Kyle lived across the hall from us and somehow he got his hands on a child’s wading pool, brought it up to the roof and filled it with ice.”

“For the sodas,” Izzy guessed.

“For our feet,” Norah explained.

“How did you make the turkey?” Isabella asked, her eyes darting excitedly from one parent to the other.

“Mrs. Goslin,” Norah said. “She was the neighbor upstairs—she seemed old then, but she couldn’t have been more than—what?” Norah glanced at Tom.

“Mid- to late-sixties.”

“How’d she get the thing thawed in time?”

Once again Tom and Norah burst into laughter. “We ate a lot of appetizers that evening. The turkey was finally pronounced ready around—what? Nine?”

“Closer to ten,” Norah confirmed. “I remember because that’s about the time that her nephew—that Paul got there.”

“Wait a minute,” Isabella said, putting the details together. “Paul Goslin? As in the guy you went into practice with? As in the guy who sent you off to California to open a branch office?”

Tom took a swallow of his bottled iced tea. “He didn’t send me, Bella. It was a great opportunity—for all of us.”

“Yeah, right,” Isabella muttered. “Changed our lives.”

Conversation died as Isabella got to her feet. “I’ve got to go. It’s almost time for the program to get started.”

Norah half-rose to follow her, but Izzy was already

gone, so she sank back to the carpet and picked at her salad.

"Sorry," Tom said.

"You still think that—you still believe that—" She was feeling so defensive all of a sudden that it was hard to put words to her thoughts. Memories could be easy and comforting, but they could also be a reminder of harder times.

"Yeah, I still believe I was just trying to do the best I could for you and our daughter, but it's ancient history, Norah, right?"

Apparently not.

"And can you understand that I only did what I thought was best for all of us as well?"

"I guess I don't get how splitting up our family was the best thing for any of us," Tom said as he got to his feet and walked away.

Chapter Five

"Ladies and gentlemen, and boys and girls of all ages," Patty announced from the center of the make-shift stage in the voice of a circus ringmaster as soon as the dessert had been served. "It is our great pleasure to present for your entertainment this evening a program in three parts. For our opening act, may I present—" She gave a nod to one of the choir members who pounded out a drum roll on one of the gate counters, then shouted, "The kids from Camp Stuck-in-the-Snow!"

The audience applauded and cheered as the smallest of this little community of stranded souls made their way to the center of the backdrop. The children sang three numbers, their voices growing stronger and more confident with each. By the time they reached their finale—a rendition of "Let There Be Peace on Earth"—they were shouting out the words as if they wanted to be heard around the planet they sang about. As they moved into the final verse, Patty urged the audience to, "Please sing along with us."

Norah stood behind the last row of seats and watched as everyone stood and joined hands, going so far as to reach across aisles and around the ends of rows so that the chain of hands was unbroken as they belted out the chorus with the children. She felt someone move closer and take her hand and looked up to find Tom standing next to her, swaying in time to the music as he looked down at her and mouthed, "Sorry."

When the song ended there was a moment of silence and then the crowd erupted into cheers and whistles and calls for encores as the children ran off the stage to their waiting parents.

"Well, that's going to be hard to top," Patty shouted into the microphone. "But we aren't done yet. It's time for our very special version of—drum roll please! Stranded Americans with Talent!"

After the last talent act left the stage, Tom prepared to announce that a volunteer offering would be taken to help cover the costs of the meal.

"Change of plans," Dave told him. "We got together and decided nobody was out that much and we could certainly afford to donate this one meal. Take your offering, but we'd like it to be for charity."

"Thanks—thank everyone for us," Tom said as Patty handed him the microphone. He looked out over the crowd of people still buzzing from the excitement of the evening's entertainment. He gave himself a moment to soak in the sheer magic of what had happened over the last several hours. He searched the audience until he saw Norah, standing at the back with the basketball players, each of them holding one of the plastic bowls used at security checkpoints to collect loose change, watches and other small items that might set off the alarm. Tonight those bowls would be used as offering plates.

He cued the musicians and as the trio quietly played the chorus to "Let There Be Peace on Earth" Tom announced the generous gift of the airport vendors and then the collection for charity. He motioned for the church choir to take the stage and as the plastic bowls made their way up and down each row, the choir sang. By the time the last row had been served, there wasn't a dry eye in the house.

Afterward several people stayed to help reset the furnishings into the usual seating pattern at each gate. Others cleared away the remains of the food and took down the buffet tables. The teens dismantled the backdrop and stage area and by a little after ten, everything was back in its normal place as people settled in for another night.

"Have you seen Izzy?" Norah asked Tom when she found him in the airline club helping to count and record the money from the collection.

"She went off to call her friends," he said and moved away from the group, leaving them to attend to the finances. "She was pretty pumped about the evening, cheeks all rosy and eyes sparkling."

Norah tried to ignore a sense of foreboding as the two of them hurried down the concourse in the direction Tom had last seen their daughter. "It wouldn't be the first time she's lost track of time. I just hope the battery on that phone you gave her holds up."

But when Norah saw a group gathered around the entrance to the women's restroom, something told her to quicken her step.

"It's Isabella," Elizabeth's mother told her. "We just found her. She's been throwing up and—"

Tom pushed past them all. "Bella!"

Norah was close behind as Tom pounded on the locked door to the stall. Behind her she could hear people calling for a doctor. From under the stall door she could see the soles of Izzy's sneakers. Izzy heaved and heaved and between heaves, Norah could hear her shuddering sobs.

"Mommy," she called weakly.

"I'm here, baby," Norah called as she watched a frustrated and near manic Tom decide against trying to force the door to the stall open. Instead he went to the empty stall next door, stood on the toilet seat, and stretched down to release the lock.

Oblivious to the stench and dirty floor, Norah fell to her knees beside her daughter. She held Izzy's forehead and tried to calm her. "I'm right here, Izzy. Daddy too. A doctor's coming."

Somebody thrust a package of premoistened towels toward her and blindly Norah accepted them and began wiping Izzy's mouth as she smoothed back her daughter's perspiration-soaked hair.

"Better?" she whispered when it seemed as if the nausea might have run its course.

"It hurts," Izzy moaned, cradling her stomach with her arms as she leaned back against the wall of the stall.

"I know. I know."

But Norah didn't know. She didn't know why suddenly her vibrant daughter was weak as a kitten, seemed to be running a fever and was as colorless as the towel Norah used to clean her face. She looked up and saw Tom standing in the doorway of the stall, his face almost as pale as Izzy's.

"She'll be okay," Norah promised him, but again she felt the emptiness of that vow.

"Somebody need a doctor in here?"

A man with a mass of white hair, ruddy cheeks and a neatly clipped, short white beard, eased his way past the bystanders. If he'd been wearing a red shirt he would have been a prime candidate to play Santa at the mall. As it was he was wearing wide yellow suspenders over his Oxford blue shirt.

"Ted Roth," he said, offering a handshake to Tom. "You the father?"

Tom nodded. "Are you a doctor?"

"Pediatrician." He stepped to the sink and scrubbed his hands thoroughly, then turned to the scene in the stall. "How about I take a look-see?"

He didn't wait for permission but squeezed his bulk into the tight space as Norah pulled Izzy closer.

"You look like Santa Claus," Izzy said, her voice hoarse from vomiting.

"That's the plan," Dr. Roth replied as he gently began his examination. "Helps put the kids at ease," he confided. "Is it working?"

Isabella nodded and Norah felt a little of the tension that had riveted Izzy's slim body ease away.

"When did this all start?"

"A little while ago—"

"Okay, let's see what's going on here." He gently probed her abdomen. "That tender there?"

Izzy nodded.

"How about when I stop pressing? Any pain?"

Izzy shook her head.

Dr. Roth removed a thermometer from a case he carried in his shirt pocket and shook it out. "Open," he said and placed the thermometer under Isabella's tongue. "No talking or laughing allowed," he warned as he checked her pulse against the second hand on his large Mickey Mouse watch. When Isabella started to smile weakly, he held up a warning finger. "No laughing at the doctor."

Norah saw Tom move closer. He was frowning and his hands were clenched into fists.

"Now then," Roth continued as he removed the thermometer and pushed his reading glasses into place to read it. "So let's run through this one more time." He pressed around her abdomen on her left side. "Hurt?" he asked with each probe.

Izzy shook her head.

He moved more to the right side and pressed. Izzy grimaced.

"I'll take that as affirmative."

"She had supper with us from the buffet," Norah said, trying to provide information that might prove helpful. "She had a chicken panini, carrot sticks and—"

"What was on that sandwich?"

"Chicken," Izzy replied.

Roth grinned. "You don't say." He continued examining Izzy but spoke to Norah and Tom. "I don't think it's food poisoning if that's what's coming to mind. We've got a couple of diagnostic candidates here," Roth muttered as if consulting with some invisible assistant.

"Candidates for what?" Tom asked through gritted teeth.

"Best guess without running some tests would be the appendix—assuming that organ hasn't been removed," Roth replied as he used the door to pull himself to a standing position. "Her symptoms are pretty classic, but let's not jump to conclusions until we have a little more information. The good news is that if it is her appendix, it's a relatively mild attack. No rebound tenderness."

"Meaning?" Tom asked.

"Her right lower abdomen is tender to the touch. If releasing my fingers quickly had caused an increase in pain, we'd have ourselves a situation."

Tom let out a frustrated sigh. "In English?"

"Rebound tenderness is pain that worsens when I release my hand after probing the tender area—could indicate that the infection has spread. Since Isabella isn't experiencing that, then it's likely the inflammation is localized—could heal itself with antibiotics." The doctor washed his hands again and appeared to consider several options as he dried them on a fist full of towels. "First step is to get her off that filthy floor and some place where we can make her more comfortable."

"I can't leave," Isabella protested. "I can't be away from the toilet."

"You've pretty well cleaned yourself out," Dr. Roth said kindly. "I think we can find a makeshift basin that will meet your needs."

"But," Isabella protested, then glanced up at the crowd of concerned people still crowded around and looked away. She seemed about to cry again.

"Hey, folks," Tom said, "thanks for your concern, but we've got this under control." He actually started herding people out the door who had eased their way into the bathroom. "Really appreciate everything. We'll keep you posted," he assured them and then allowed the bathroom door to swing shut.

Someone knocked lightly on the door and Tom opened it a crack as Isabella shrank farther into Norah's arms. Tom exchanged a few words with the visitor, thanked the person and when he turned back to them he was holding one of the plastic containers from security like the ones they had used as offering plates earlier.

Roth took the container and washed it thoroughly, then handed it to Isabella. "Think you can make it to your feet?"

Isabella nodded as Tom moved into position to lift and support her.

"I'll start making the arrangements to get her out of here and over to the hospital," Dr. Roth said as he extended a hand to help Norah to her feet.

"No one seems to be using the chapel," Tom said.

"Good. I'll go start putting the wheels in motion. You folks okay?"

Both Tom and Norah must have looked shocked that

he could possibly think they were "okay" when Isabella was obviously so ill.

"Let me rephrase that," Roth said with a wink at Isabella. "Are you okay with getting our patient down to the chapel or should I ask somebody to bring a wheelchair?"

For an answer, Tom swept Izzy into his arms. Isabella nestled her head on Tom's shoulder and wrapped her arms around his neck.

"Mom?"

Norah was next to her in a millisecond, eager to attend to whatever need she might have. "What, baby?"

"Phone," Izzy said and nodded toward the floor of the stall they had all just vacated.

"Oh, Izzy," Norah said, but felt the first hint of a smile since the nightmare of finding her daughter sprawled on the bathroom floor had begun. She heard Tom chuckle as he shook his head and followed the doctor down the hall. Norah took the time not only to retrieve the phone and clean it off, but to also send up a silent prayer—first of thanks for sending them Dr. Roth followed by a plea that their daughter would be all right.

After Dr. Roth stopped by to assure them that he'd reached the hospital and a helicopter would be sent to transport Isabella as soon as the storm lifted.

"That could be hours," Norah objected.

"The weather reports show that the storm is almost past us. Should be able to get her moved first light. In the meantime, if she shows any signs of the pain spreading or worsening, come get me, okay?"

As Tom took his turn sitting with Isabella, he

couldn't help remembering the time when he and Norah had decided to divorce. In his anger and frustration, he had wanted to—needed to—lash out and try to control the dream he felt slipping away. He had told his lawyer to demand equal custody.

Norah had been stunned. "Do you hate me so much that you would use our child in your fight against me?"

By that stage of things they had been traveling their separate paths for months and Tom was as tired of the fight as she was. He wanted it over, but he also wanted to—needed to—win. "This is not about you," he'd told Norah, fighting to maintain calm in the face of her emotion.

"Please don't take that professional tone with me," Norah had said. "I am still your wife and this is still your daughter we are discussing."

That had brought him out of his chair and around the large ornate desk she'd bought at an antique auction for his new office when he'd made partner. "It is exactly because she is my daughter that I am doing this. You and I may not have a future together, but I will not abdicate my role as a father and surrender the total raising of Bella to you."

"Are you thinking at all about what you're asking of an eight-year-old?" Norah had shouted. "Two houses in two different states. Two different schools, teachers—sets of friends. Six months can make a huge difference in the world of children, Tom."

"Oh, come down off your social worker high horse. Bella is a people magnet. She'll make friends no matter where she is."

"I know she can do it, Tom—the question is why would we ask her to when she's not the issue."

"And you are just dying to tell me exactly what you think the issue is," he'd said, turning away from her.

She'd touched him then, her hand light on his arm, her tone gentler. "The issue is us, Tom. We find ourselves going down different paths and we're scared because we're not sure what that means, but the one thing I thought we had agreed upon was that the best thing for Izzy was to stop pretending we could work things out between us."

"I love my kid," he'd replied tightly.

"I know that and she adores you. Look, we both want the best possible life for Izzy—on that at least we are still on the same wavelength. How about this? How about you go out to California, get the office going, get yourself settled and then if you still think it's the best thing for Izzy that we share custody, I won't fight you. In the meantime, we'll go on with the original plan to alternate holidays and have her spend the summer with you."

He'd walked away from her, he remembered now and, for the first time, realized that it had not been so much wanting to turn away from her. It had been because the thing he'd wanted most was to turn to her, to take her in his arms and beg her to help find a way through this so they could all be together.

Unable to sleep, Norah abandoned her cot and collapsed onto one of the straight-backed upholstered chairs facing the small altar. It had been a long time since she had prayed—really prayed. Oh, she had her moments, sending hasty prayers of gratitude heavenward when Izzy made it safely home after being out with friends. She'd also sent up more than her share of on-the-spot requests for patience with her coworkers, for the energy to keep going when her work and home life collided, for the right words to say whenever she had to discuss things like drugs or dating with her growing teenager.

But truly praying as a deliberate act? She really couldn't remember the last time. Not that she didn't attend church. Especially since Izzy had begun to take her faith so seriously, Norah had been there every Sunday morning. She'd even volunteered to help out with the youth group. Still, religion for her—and for Tom—had always been more of a Christmas and Easter kind of thing. In the years before their marriage had fallen apart, they would attend services on the holidays and occasionally in between—as long as it fit into their plans for the weekend.

She wondered if that had changed for Tom. She didn't think so. More than once, Izzy had returned from spending time with him and sighed dramatically at what she called his failing to understand the importance of a community of faith.

Norah folded her hands, closed her eyes and bowed her head. She waited for the words to come, but none did. Surely she shouldn't just start in begging for Izzy to be all right. And what about Izzy's idea that this entire snowstorm had been some grand plan? Ridiculous, right?

Help me understand, she prayed silently. *Show me the way—for Isabella, for myself—and yes, for what seeing Tom again after all this time means. Maybe it was just time? Or is there something I'm missing? Help me.*

Norah opened her eyes. The altar table was decorated with a Thanksgiving arrangement of flowers and produce that spilled out from a straw cornucopia over the brown linen table runner. She stared at the flowers and had the thought that while they might have been fresh a day or so earlier, they were tired-looking and beginning to fade while the produce was shriveled and dotted with the first signs of decay.

Tom sat in the chair next to her. "That flower arrangement looks like I feel," he said, his voice cracking in spite of his effort to make a joke.

Norah said nothing.

"Want me to go see if I can scrounge up something to eat or drink?" Tom asked after several seconds had passed.

"No. Thank you," Norah murmured.

Tom nodded, stood up, then sat down again, his left heel tapping steadily on the carpeted floor.

Norah placed her hand on his knee, stilling it, but she didn't look up.

"Norah?" Tom's voice was gentle and filled with concern. When she felt his hand on her shoulder and then stroking her back, she could no longer hold back the wave of fear, exhaustion and relief that Tom was at her side. But it was Tom who started to cry.

She had never felt so helpless. Her only child was lying not five feet away, curled into a fetal position, reminding her of how tiny and fragile she had seemed that day they brought her home from the hospital. Together they had placed her in the crib that Tom had spent all of one Sunday afternoon assembling for her.

Now Tom—the father of her child—was leaning forward, face in hands, sobbing as if his heart had suddenly split right down the middle. "Hey," she said, leaning toward him as she continued massaging his back. "She's going to be fine," she added, scrambling for words that could stem the tide of his tears.

"We don't know that," he said. "You don't even believe that," he added, his voice challenging her to deny it.

"I just want to get her to a medical center where she can be checked out properly," Norah said. Sheer exhaustion swept over her in a tsunami and it was her turn to bury her head in her hands. "What if..."

"What if what?" He sat up and placed one hand on her shoulder as he swiped at his tears with the other. She wanted—needed—more. She wanted him to wrap his arms around her and tell her everything would be all right. "What if you hadn't been here?" she whispered and this time the tears were hers.

"Come here." He held out his arms and gave her the choice of accepting the comfort of his embrace or not. She wrapped her arms around him, burying her face against his shirt. "Shh," he whispered against her ear as he stroked her hair.

Eventually her sobs abated into the occasional shuddering aftermath. She felt herself go perfectly still. Was it that she had finally found a safe haven or that she had suddenly realized the position they were in? She leaned back and looked up at him. Without a second's hesitation, he bent his head to meet her upturned face and kissed her.

In an instant his kiss erased everything they'd used to build the wall between them over all these years. Even through the fog of her exhaustion, worry over Izzy and the miracle of leaning once again on Tom's strong chest and feeling his lips on hers, Norah's brain fought to sound the alarm.

Fantasy! Not real life! Danger!

But her heart beat so hard and loud that it drowned out everything but the instant memory of all the years of Tom's arms around her, his lips on hers, his body her comforter and protector against life's storms. She placed her palms on his cheeks, savored the familiarity of the stubble of his unshaven face.

And when he deepened the kiss, wrapping his arms more tightly around her as if he would never let go, Norah felt a bubble of joyous laughter replace the agony of her tears.

Oh dear heavenly Father, was this Your plan? Is it possible?

She was kissing him back when she heard a faint call.

"Daddy?"

Chapter Six

When Tom felt Norah push away from him, he suddenly remembered one night when they were teens, kissing on her parents' front porch. Norah's father had called to her from the living room and Norah had pushed Tom away and gone running for the screen door. Now it was their daughter calling out to them.

"Right here, Bella." He shielded Norah to give her the chance to regain control. Control was very important to Norah. Always had been.

Isabella squinted up at him, then cast her eyes toward her mother. "Mom?"

Norah moved quickly to Isabella's cot and knelt, her hand automatically cupping their daughter's forehead and cheeks, searching for signs of temperature change. "You slept a little," she said softly.

Isabella yawned. "I had a great dream," she said.

"Really? That's a good sign," Norah said. "What was the dream?"

Tom saw Bella glance up at him again, then back at her mother. "Nothing. You've been crying."

Norah backhanded her cheeks—dry now but her red-rimmed eyes told the story. "Yeah, well, you know me when my baby gets sick."

"Oh, Mom, I am not a baby." Isabella collapsed back onto the cot and closed her eyes. Then she sat up suddenly and grabbed blindly for the plastic bowl.

Tom joined Norah next to the cot, one hand on Isabella's back while Norah held her head over the bowl. But all that came out was a hiccup, followed by another and then another.

"Oh, honey, like you need this," Norah sympathized, but there was a little bubble of laughter underlying her words.

"It's not funny," Isabella protested between hiccups.

Tom patted her back in a motion reminiscent of burping her as a baby. "Yeah, actually it is," he said and made no effort to conceal his grin.

Isabella shot him a look of pure fury, but then she hiccupped and the three of them started to laugh.

"Well now, that sounds like things are a little better," Dr. Roth said as he entered the chapel. "Got some news," he continued. "Your ride will be here at dawn."

"That's wonderful," Norah exclaimed, relief evident in every feature of her face.

"I've made all the arrangements for this little lady to be checked out as soon as we reach the hospital. If as I suspect we can treat this thing with antibiotics, then you folks can take her home and work with your own doctor."

"Thank you," Norah said.

"But if the appendix needs to come out?" Tom asked.

"We're ready to handle that at the hospital. Let's just see how it goes— Prepare but Don't Project has always been my motto." He turned his attention to Isabella. "Think you can hang in there for another hour or so, young lady?"

Isabella nodded.

After the doctor left, Tom watched Norah focus all of her attention on Isabella. They had kissed and she was acting as if nothing had happened. Worse. She was acting as if kissing him had been a mistake.

"I'm going to get my laptop. You need anything?"

"No. Thanks," Norah replied, her voice lowered to a whisper as Isabella fell almost instantly asleep. "You go ahead. We'll be fine here."

"I'm coming back," Tom said, fighting to keep the edge from his voice.

"There's really no need," Norah said.

"She's my daughter too, Norah."

Finally she looked at him. Her eyes were wide and her mouth was drawn into a pucker of surprise. "Of course she is, Tom. I just thought—I just—"

Tom turned on his heel and wrenched open the chapel door. "I'll be back," he muttered and pulled the door closed behind him with a firm click.

The concourse was quiet. Here and there a few people were still awake, reading or talking softly. The televisions in each gate area had been muted so that breaking news was still immediate but without the intrusive sound of the talking heads.

Tom entered the lounge and headed to the corner where they'd spent the night before. Across the room Patty Martin's manicured nails clicked away at her computer keyboard. She glanced up and raised an eyebrow.

"She'll be fine," Tom mouthed, but made no effort to go over and fill her in on the details. He was well aware that Patty Martin was attracted to him. He was also aware that she was a bright, energetic and good-looking woman. Under other circumstances—like two days earlier—he would have considered getting to know her better. But now when he looked at her, he couldn't seem to stop comparing her to Norah.

Who was he kidding? He couldn't stop thinking about kissing Norah, having her back in his arms. Being together again—the three of them like old times. Better times.

Clearly the kiss hadn't meant that much to her. She'd practically dismissed him. He should stay here while she kept watch? Why not both keep watch? Why mightn't Bella need him as much as she might need Norah if she took a turn for the worse before they could get her out of here? And what if Norah needed him as she had earlier? No one could convince him that she hadn't made a conscious decision to come into his arms, to kiss him. She might regret it now, but if Bella hadn't called out, what might have happened?

Norah was still trying to work through Tom's earlier reaction when he returned. He stopped next to Isabella's cot.

"How's she doing?"

"A little better, I think."

Tom moved to a far corner of the chapel and unpacked his laptop. "Are you going to work?" Norah asked, trying to smooth the awkwardness between them.

"I'm going to see if I can get flights out of here after Bella is checked out at the hospital. I'm assuming you want to head back to Phoenix instead of continuing on to Normal?"

Norah was confused. He was being so formal, so overly polite. History had taught her that both were symptoms that Tom was upset about something.

"Norah?"

She tried to decipher what could be seething beneath his calm exterior. "Yeah. I have to be at work Monday morning and by the time we actually make it to Mom's we'd practically have to turn right around and start for home and with Izzy not—"

"Okay," Tom said and began tapping information into the computer.

Okay? Norah thought as she watched him. *What is going on here? It's the kiss. He regrets the kiss and now he's embarrassed. He always got angry whenever he was embarrassed or whenever he made a mistake.* Norah felt her own prickle of irritation. *Maybe I regretted the kiss as well. Did you ever think of that, Thomas Wallace?*

"There's a commuter flight from Denver to Phoenix at seven on Saturday morning. Assuming they get the runways cleared and traffic moving that's probably your best bet."

"Saturday?"

Tom could not let out an exasperated sigh. "It's the best choice, Norah. By the time we get Bella to and from the hospital—assuming there's no need for her to actually be admitted—it's going to be late. Traffic will just be starting to get untangled. Flights out of here tomorrow are going to be jammed and—"

"Don't lecture me, Tom. I understand the logistics. I was simply repeating the day." Norah forced herself to remain calm and took some pleasure in the fact that Tom clearly noticed the difference.

In the old days whenever they had an argument, Norah would shout at him, instantly certain that somehow he was accusing or blaming her.

"So should I book the flight?"

"Please," Norah said, reaching for her purse. "I'll get you my credit card number."

"I'll use mine."

"Tom, I—"

"Just stop it, Norah. I want to get her home as much as you do."

"Stop what?"

"Stop trying to do everything by the book—by the rules we set up five years ago. You pay for this and I pay for that. Well, I want to do this for my daughter and—"

"*Our* daughter," Norah corrected as she folded her arms across her chest to hide her clenched fists.

Tom looked down at the keyboard. "You know what I'm saying, Norah." He completed the online transaction, then took out a yellow legal pad from his briefcase and scrawled some numbers on the top sheet. "This is your confirmation number and e-ticket numbers," he said as he tore off the sheet and handed it to her.

"Thank you," Norah said primly as she folded the paper in quarters. She was going to put the paper in her purse, but hesitated. "Tom?"

He gave her that half look that he used to think passed for attention whenever he was working and she wanted to talk about something important.

"Look at me," she whispered.

He looked down first, then closed the cover of the laptop and set it aside. He placed the palms of his hands on his knees and finally raised his eyes to her—without really raising his head.

Aware that Isabella was sleeping only a few feet away, Norah pulled one of the upholstered chapel chairs close to Tom and sat knee to knee with him.

"Look, everything about these last two days has been surreal," she began, keeping her voice low.

To her relief Tom visibly relaxed slightly. "You could say that."

"And neither one of us has had a lot of rest and then there was the excitement of the Thanksgiving program and then Izzy getting so sick."

Tom nodded as she ticked off each item. He was looking at the floor now and she almost didn't hear him mumble, "I never want to be that scared about Bella again."

"I know," she whispered. "And the worst part is, I mean, even if it does turn out that she needs to have her appendix removed, it could have been something so much worse."

"Yeah."

"I was thinking about all of that earlier," Norah continued. "Sometimes it hits me out of the blue—I mean how helpless I really am to protect her from everything that could happen."

"Me, too," Tom said. "Sometimes I just want to put her inside some kind of magical bubble where nothing can ever hurt her."

"When we saw her lying there, so sick and miserable, I was so—grateful—that you were here. That I wasn't facing this alone."

Tom glanced up and then back at his hands. "I'm always here, Norah, for whatever Bella needs."

And me? Norah thought and quickly stuffed that selfish need back inside as she had for years. "Hey, what I'm trying to get to here is that earlier—when I fell apart—" She swallowed.

"When we kissed?" Tom asked, his eyes meeting hers directly now, holding her there, each of them unable to look away. "Is that what you're trying to say, Norah?"

"Yes," she whispered. "I just didn't want you to think that—I mean, it was a moment—a wonderful moment—but I just—"

Tom stared at her for a long moment and then to her surprise he stood up. "I know. Don't sweat it, okay? We both were overwrought with worry and exhaustion." He stretched. "I'm beat and you must be exhausted. How about you get some rest?" He started arranging chairs into a makeshift bed. "You can lie down here." He handed her a blanket he'd brought from the club.

Norah stood as well. "There's no reason we can't both get some rest. That is if you'll stop being so cavalier about this whole thing."

This whole thing? Was she talking about getting through the night or was she still on the kiss? Norah really didn't want to think about the answer to that question.

"Fine," Tom said and kicked off his shoes as he settled onto the four chairs he'd lined up.

Fine, Norah thought. They were right back where they'd started.

Friday morning dawned clear and sunny and the public address system woke anyone still sleeping with the news that the airport would reopen as soon as at least one runway could be cleared. A cheer echoed up and down the concourse.

"So, what's the plan?" Isabella asked, her voice thick with sleep.

"Well, first we're going to the hospital to be sure you're really all right," Norah said as she bustled around realigning chairs in rows and folding the blankets she and Izzy had used.

"I feel okay," Izzy protested.

"Nevertheless, Dr. Roth—"

"Aka Saint Nick," Isabella said with a grin.

"He's made all the arrangements and we're going to the hospital."

"Where's Dad?"

"I don't know. Probably washing up or making arrangements for you and me to get back to Phoenix."

Izzy's eyes widened. "You mean we're not going to Wisconsin after all?"

"We need to get you home."

"You mean, you have to get back so you can be at work Monday."

"That's not fair, Izzy. Assuming you don't need surgery to remove your appendix right away, we need to find out what's happening and how to watch for symptoms."

Isabella frowned and refused to meet Norah's pointed look. She tried getting up only to sit down immediately. "Whoa," she whispered.

"Are you dizzy?"

"Just a little lightheaded," Isabella admitted. "I'll be fine. Really, Mom, just help me change and fix my hair. I can't let anybody see me like this—especially after last night." She moaned. "That was so embarrassing."

The door to the chapel opened. "Is there a princess in here?" Tom called as he wheeled a chair into the room. "Oh, you must be the Princess Bella," he said. "I have your chariot, Your Highness, and your public awaits."

"I am not leaving this chapel until I've made myself look at least halfway decent."

Tom frowned. "Gee, that could take some time," he said, shaking his head sadly as he looked pointedly at her rumpled clothing and tangled hair. "On the other hand, I see you have called upon your fairy godmother here to work her magic. Good luck," he said winking at Norah.

We're okay, she thought with relief. *Everything's going to be okay.*

"You just step outside and guard the door," she instructed Tom. "You'll see what a hairbrush and a touch of lipstick can do."

Tom did as she asked but periodically opened the door a crack and called in comments. "Anything yet?"

"Daddy!" Isabella would squeal each time and Norah would just laugh. It felt so good to be getting back to normal. Already Norah was thinking ahead. It was a habit she'd developed after Tom left. Always trying to second guess what might come up. If God had a plan, then Norah was sure she understood it. Now that the ice of a five-year separation had been broken, they could go their separate ways. Only now she could imagine many times like this—times they would share as Isabella's parents—and as the good friends they had always been.

"Mom?"

Norah continued brushing Izzy's hair, scooping it into the high ponytail she preferred and anchoring it with a wide barrette. "Hmm?"

"You know that dream I mentioned?"

"Tell me," Norah said as she watched her daughter apply lip gloss like a professional.

"I dreamed you and Dad kissed."

"Really?" Norah heard her voice crack. Izzy had seen them after all.

"It wasn't a dream, was it?" Izzy asked quietly.

Norah sat next to her and pulled Izzy into a hug. "No, but honey, it's also not what you think."

"You still love him," Izzy said, her voice muffled against Norah's neck.

Norah gently took Isabella's shoulders and held her

so that they were face-to-face. "I know you don't want to hear this, but one day when you're older—"

Isabella grimaced. "Not the 'when you're older' speech."

"Someday when you're older you'll understand that it is indeed possible to love someone even though the two of you have gone down different paths. Daddy and I love you and because of that shared love for you, we will always respect and care for each other."

Isabella pulled away and flung herself into the wheelchair. "Keep on telling yourself that, Mom." She grabbed her phone. "The princess is ready!" she bellowed toward the door as she checked for messages.

But the scene that greeted Norah and Isabella outside the chapel was enough to make Isabella forget all about connecting with her friends back home. As Tom wheeled her through the double chapel doors a chorus of applause, whistles and cheers greeted her. The members of the church choir and the basketball team were there, as were several of the younger children and their parents. In a flurry of handshakes and hugs the other teens said their goodbyes and promised to stay in touch.

"Where's Dr. Santa Claus?" Isabella asked, her good spirits restored.

"He's waiting with the helicopter team."

"Like one of those flight for life things?" Isabella said. "Hey, I feel fine—well, a lot better," Isabella assured them. "Let's just stay here. We'll miss our flight to Chicago."

"We're not going to Chicago, honey. Remember?"

Norah explained as Tom navigated his way through a door marked Employees Only and down a ramp.

Isabella's face tightened into the same "I'm not happy" expression she had used to good advantage since she was two. "I don't see why not."

"Because it is already Friday. The chances of our getting a flight out today are not that good and even if we did, this weather is moving toward Chicago. Dad has already made arrangements for a flight back to Phoenix tomorrow."

"You know that place you work can operate without you," Isabella said, every syllable a challenge to Norah to deny it.

"And they will if I can't be there." She turned to Tom to explain. "We're meeting with this major foundation on Monday to make our presentation for some key funding. Without it—"

Tom nodded sympathetically.

"When it comes to putting your job ahead of everything—and everyone—else, you're as bad as he is," Isabella announced, folding her arms tightly across her chest.

"That's uncalled for," Tom said. "Apologize to your mother."

"Sorry," Izzy muttered.

Norah met Tom's look and shrugged.

As promised, Dr. Roth was waiting for them on board the helicopter. "How do you like my sleigh?" he joked.

"Pretty twenty-first century," Isabella assured him.

When they arrived at the hospital, Isabella was whisked off for blood tests, an abdominal X ray and ultrasound. "Looks to me like you dodged a bullet this time," Dr. Roth announced later after he'd gotten all the results.

"We can go home?" Norah asked.

"Just in time to get back to school bright and early Monday morning."

Isabella did not see the humor in that. "We're supposed to be on our way to see my grands—both sets," she said with an accusing look at Norah.

"Well now, you still need to take things a little easy," Roth replied and Norah could see that he had taken in the tension radiating between mother and daughter. He wrote out a prescription for antibiotics and handed it to Tom. "You can get that filled in the hospital pharmacy," he said, then turned his attention back to Isabella. "Frankly, I'd rather see you back at home where you can get to your own doctor if these horse pills don't work."

Izzy rolled her eyes. "Boy, you grown-ups do stick together, don't you?"

"Isabella!" Tom said, his voice soft but no less of a warning.

"Sorry."

"No harm. Lots of folks had their plans spoiled, I expect," Roth said cheerfully. "On the other hand, you and your folks here sure made a difference. You should take some pride in that."

Norah saw Izzy's bad mood start to crack at the edges. "Everybody pitched in," she said, but it was clear that she had absorbed the doctor's praise.

"That's the way of it," Roth said. "Someone steps

up to lead and then others fall into line and before you know it, you've got something." He studied the final test results the nurse had just brought him.

"Well?" Tom asked.

"Everything looks good," Roth said, then helped Izzy down from the examining table. "Sorry I can't offer my sleigh to get you back to the airport."

"That's okay," Isabella replied.

Tom shook Dr. Roth's hand. "Thanks for everything, doc."

Roth accepted the gratitude, then turned his attention to Norah. "You're looking a little peaked, Mom. How about letting Dad here take the first shift once the three of you get home while you get some rest?"

The three members of the Wallace family froze. Isabella recovered first. "They don't—we live in Phoenix and Dad's in—"

"Oh, well, then, my prescription is for *both* of you ladies to get as much rest as possible over the next couple of days. Can't have Mom coming down with something now that you're on the mend, can we?" He put his arm around Isabella's shoulder and walked her to the door.

They stopped by the pharmacy on their way to the exit where the town car Tom had hired waited. Dr. Roth hugged Isabella again, then held his arms open to Norah. An invitation Norah found herself accepting as if her own father had suddenly appeared and offered her the comfort she needed. Her eyes welled with tears as she blubbered her thanks.

"Now then, everything's going to work out," Roth promised and while Norah understood he was speaking in terms of the medical situation, she had a moment's fantasy that perhaps he had seen into the future and was assuring her about that.

"I can't imagine what's got into me," she said as she stepped away from the doctor and saw Tom watching her closely.

"You're exhausted and it's been a grueling couple of days," Roth replied. "Get some rest and make sure she takes those pills—all of them even if she's feeling better. Doctor's orders."

Norah nodded and followed Izzy into the backseat of the car, while Tom went around to the passenger side. By the time they reached the airport, Tom had completed arrangements for changing flights for Norah and Isabella so they would be home as quickly as possible.

"Are you still going to Normal?" Isabella asked as Tom walked them to their gate the following morning.

"No. Hey, how about you and I go for Christmas—a good old-fashioned Wisconsin white Christmas?"

Isabella wrinkled her nose. "Actually I've about had it with the snow thing," she admitted. "Hawaii sounds good all of a sudden—or how about Cancún?"

Tom laughed. "Now what would you know about Cancún?"

"I know it has beaches and beautiful sunny weather," Bella replied. "Not to mention boys—*cute* boys."

"Give the Wisconsin idea some thought," Tom said as he kissed her forehead and handed her the backpack he'd been carrying for her. "We are not going to Cancún—at least not until you're several years older."

"That's our zone," Norah said as the gate agent called for passengers to board. She took her time gathering the last of their things, shy now that the moment of departure was actually at hand.

"You were terrific, Norah—with everyone," Tom said in a voice that was false and overly hearty.

So that's how we'll play this, Norah thought. She turned and gave him a bright smile. "Don't be a stranger," she said gaily as she started edging toward the jetway door along with dozens of other passengers.

Tom frowned. "Five years wasn't my idea," he said softly, his eyes riveted on hers, daring her to look away.

Instead she laughed nervously. "Well, no but it wasn't a contest, Tom. I mean neither one of us—either one of us could—"

They were at the doorway. Norah fumbled for their boarding passes and when she looked up, Tom was giving Isabella a final hug. Norah froze, remembering his arms around her the evening before, remembering his kiss, remembering…the feeling of having come home at last.

"Ma'am?"

Norah opened her eyes and saw the gate agent leaning toward her, a concerned look on her face. "You need to board now," she said gently, as if talking to a passenger who just might be a problem.

Norah nodded and stepped back to allow Izzy to head down the long hallway ahead of her.

"Norah?"

When she turned, Tom was standing at the door. "Call me when you get home," he mouthed.

Norah nodded and swallowed another wave of emotion similar to the one that had hit her when Dr. Roth hugged her. *Admit it,* she ordered herself as she made her way past passengers jockeying for overhead bin space to where Izzy was already curled up in the window seat, her head resting against the window and her eyes closed. *Dr. Roth was right. It's been an emotional roller coaster these last two days. Time to get back to normal—not the town—the status.*

"Izzy?"

The teenager frowned but did not open her eyes.

"Are you feeling all right?"

"Physically, yes," she replied tersely.

"Well, at the moment, that's the important thing," Norah replied.

Izzy's eyes flew open. "Oh, you mean my emotional and mental health don't count?"

Now it was Norah's turn to sigh. She simply was too exhausted to deal with teenage drama at the moment. "Of course they count, Isabella. But right now, could we just concentrate on getting home? I promise you we can have a long discussion about anything you like once we've accomplished that."

"Whatever." Isabella twisted in her seat and closed her eyes again as Norah smiled up at the elderly woman about to take the aisle seat.

Chapter Seven

First thing Monday morning Norah took Isabella to the pediatrician. After a second round of tests and a thorough examination the doctor recommended waiting before going ahead with surgery. "It could be years before she has another flare-up and you never want to subject a patient to surgery—even routine surgery—unless it's absolutely necessary."

She had delivered this recommendation in her office with Norah and Izzy sitting across from her and Tom on speakerphone.

Norah could tell by the extent of Tom's questions that he was not convinced and she completely understood why the doctor suggested they might want to get a second opinion. "But after talking things over with Dr. Roth, the two of us concur that surgery at this point just is not indicated."

"So, Dad, technically we've got a second opinion," Isabella said. "I'm fine. Really. Okay?"

Tom finally agreed to the doctor's suggestion that

Isabella come in for regular checkups over the next several months. "If there is any change—any new flare-up," the doctor assured him, "we'll take immediate action."

"Dad," Isabella begged.

"Sounds like a plan," Tom said finally. "Norah? Could you be sure an appointment gets scheduled right before Christmas so when Bella is out here—"

"I'll take care of it," Norah promised.

And while Isabella's physical health had definitely improved by the time she returned to school after the appointment on Monday, her disposition had not.

"We could *all* spend Christmas in Normal," she suggested that night at supper.

"It's your time with Dad," Norah reminded her.

"Yeah? So?"

Norah sighed. "Honey, stop matchmaking."

"Somebody has to," Izzy grumbled as she left the table and stormed off to her room. "Because you and Dad are beyond hopeless," she shouted just before the door slammed.

For the remainder of the week they coexisted in a state of silent tension. Norah because she had so much work to catch up on and the presentation on Monday had not gone well. Izzy because she'd bought into the fantasy created by their adventure in Denver and now had to come to terms with the reality of their situation.

Norah's commute to work was half an hour at best in the off-season. Once the snowbirds arrived—and more often than not they came as early as November these days—the commute was doubled. That meant that depending on how her day went, it could be seven o'clock before she made it home. The minute she entered the offices of the White Horse Social Services Agency on Friday morning, she knew this was going to be one of those days.

"Staff meeting at ten," Abby Driscoll said as she hurried down the hall and out to her car. "If I'm not back, take good notes."

Norah watched Abby, marveling at the young woman's ability to navigate on the stiletto heels she insisted on wearing. Norah had to wonder if she had ever been that young, that sure of herself. She shook her head and headed for her cubicle where the message lights on both her phone and her computer were blinking. Five calls and several dozen e-mail responses later, she picked up her notebook and headed down the hall for the staff meeting.

To her surprise everyone else—including Abby—had arrived ahead of her. Their faces told the story.

"We didn't get the grant," Norah guessed. Her heart sank. When they'd completed the presentation on Monday, the foundation's representatives had responded with only polite interest.

"Same story," Luke Randolph said, speaking to the entire group. "As long as there's gambling on the reservation, it doesn't matter how strong our business plan—no foundation is going to fund the program."

"But it's exactly because we don't want to use the profits from gambling—it's because some of the very people most in need of our services have been wiped out by their addiction to gambling, it's because—" Norah could not seem to stem the tidal wave of her protest.

Luke held up one hand to stop her. "We are all frustrated and disappointed, Norah. Still the facts are there—have always been there. Outsiders believe that with all the profits the nation earns through the casino, we shouldn't need money. We just need to find another way."

"In the meantime, we've got bills and we've put off paying them waiting for this funding," the finance manager reminded them.

"For now the program goes on hold until we can get back on firm financial ground." Then Luke pounded the table firmly with the side of one fist. "This is a good program," he said, his voice rising. Everyone on the small staff knew that voice. It was his "pulpit" voice. Before replacing Norah's friend and mentor, Dr. Stan Morrison, as head of the agency, Luke had been a lay minister and this was the voice he'd used to spur his congregation to action. "Let's all take the day to think and consider alone and then come together here at four to brainstorm new ideas."

As chairs scraped against the worn linoleum floor, Norah gathered her notebook and pen and prepared to follow the others back to their cubicles.

"Norah, could you stay a moment please?" Luke was looking down at his clipboard—his blank clipboard, meaning he was avoiding looking at her.

They had a brief but sticky history—she and Luke. Shortly after coming to the agency, he'd asked her out for coffee, telling her that he needed to be brought up to speed on the agency's history and mission and Stan had suggested he talk to Norah. Somehow the talk had turned to their personal lives—her divorce, the end of a long-term romantic relationship for him.

Over the next several weeks Luke surprised her by stopping by the house unexpectedly—originally with the pretense of something related to work, but after a couple of weeks just showing up unannounced. Norah had been flattered. Luke was handsome and charming. He showed an interest in Isabella and her activities. He began coming to their church, slipping into the pew next to Norah and Isabella. There had been kisses and one very uncomfortable grappling session in his car after he'd brought Norah home one night.

Luke had told her of his grandiose plans for the agency and he had persuaded Norah to abandon her fieldwork in favor of becoming the agency's full-time fund-raiser and grant writer. That's when he'd hired Abby—and in time he'd stopped dropping by, taking Norah on dates, and coming to church—at least her church.

She sank back into her chair as Luke moved to close the door behind the others. "I'll call Carol Williams—the foundation director." Action was Norah's immediate response to any sign of trouble. "Maybe if I—"

Luke took his time pulling out the chair across from her and pulling his clipboard and pen over to his new position. "Whatever happens, Norah, you know better than anyone here that we have to make some cuts—at least in the short-term. Once we find the funding, it would be my hope that we could return to full staffing, but for now—"

"You're firing me?"

"We've exhausted all reasonable possibilities for getting a grant, Norah. You've written brilliant proposals, but surely you must understand that the agency cannot afford a full-time person to write grants."

"I thought I was the agency's fund-raiser, that grant writing was just one of my responsibilities. Are you saying you no longer need to raise funds to sustain the work?" Norah forced herself to maintain a tone of calm and reason that she was far from feeling.

"Of course not, but—"

"Luke, you asked me to take this position—to give up my fieldwork. I can understand revising staff responsibilities, but surely you don't plan to simply abandon the program for families and individuals affected by gambling addiction. Put me back in the field. I can still offer counseling and—"

"And what would Abby do?" Luke asked. "She's the mother—the single mother of three small children, Norah—"

"I'm a single mother," Norah reminded him.

Luke smiled. "I know, but you have far more resources than Abby—a master's degree in social work for starters and an impressive résumé. Finding another position will be far more likely for you than Abby, with her bachelor's and the fact that this is her first job. Besides, your daughter is older and you've mentioned how supportive her father is—financially as well as emotionally. Abby has no one."

How dare you use what I told you in confidence against me? How dare you play on my friendship with Abby and my sympathies for her situation?

"Shouldn't any change in my position here relate to the performance of that work?" Norah reminded him.

Luke frowned. "I'm asking you to do what's necessary to make sure the work you've helped us do can continue, Norah. This isn't easy for me, you know. You've been here right from the beginning. I value your friendship, your contributions, your—"

I need this job but I will not beg you for anything, Norah thought. She closed her eyes. Suddenly she found herself thinking of how Tom might handle such a situation. *If you know you're right, then fight.*

"So let me be clear about this," she began, knowing from all the times she and Tom had argued that his first ploy was always to lay out the facts. "You find no fault with the work I've done here?"

"This is purely a strategic move to save the agency. Once we are on solid footing again I—we would be thrilled to have you come back."

"And earlier you instructed the staff—myself included—to take the day to come up with ideas for regaining that footing?"

Luke looked away.

"But now you are in fact making decisions without allowing me the same opportunity you're willing to offer every other staffer all of whom joined the agency after I did?"

"Well, now—"

Norah stood. "I deserve that opportunity, Luke, and

unless you want to find yourself—and the hiring and firing practices of this agency—under scrutiny by the media, I suggest that you wait until after our meeting at four to fire me."

Luke stood as well. "Don't threaten me, Norah."

"That wasn't a threat, Luke. That was a promise. I'll see you at four."

When she left the conference room, the others peered at her over the low walls of their cubicles. A moment after she sat down at her desk, Norah could hear keys tapping all around her and knew the e-mails were flying back and forth along with speculation about the future—hers and the agency's.

She looked down at her own hands and knotted them into fists to stop them from shaking. Her heart hammered as she realized that she had probably just sealed her fate. *Not without a fight,* she thought and reached for the phone.

Her first call was to Carol Williams. Without asking for specifics on why the foundation turned them down, she asked Carol for tips they might use as they approached other funding sources. And with Carol's permission she recorded every suggestion—even though there was little in what she heard that they didn't already know. On the other hand, Norah had the feeling Carol was holding back.

Next she typed up a transcript of Carol's comments and forwarded it to the other members of the staff with a note saying that this information might provide some valuable insights as they thought about possible direction for the future. She copied the e-mail to Luke. Almost immediately she hit the link to compose another e-mail and typed in Tom's address, then stopped.

What was that about? She hadn't contacted Tom for advice about her job in all the time they'd been apart. Why now?

She canceled the message and instead called a neighbor to ask her to let Izzy stay there until Norah finished work. Next, she left a message on Izzy's cell phone with instructions to go home with her friend, MJ. Then she absently fingered the phone keypad, tapping in eight of the ten numbers needed to reach Tom before she put her phone on voice mail, grabbed her sunglasses and headed for the door. "I'm going for a walk," she said. "I'll be back for the meeting at four."

She walked to the trailhead behind the agency and began hiking up the path. When she reached the top, she sat on a large boulder that overlooked the valley below. *Please help me know the right thing to say and do,* she prayed silently. *I am so unsure of how things are going. Everything about my life seems to be topsy-turvy all of a sudden. Izzy is still upset about there being no complete reconciliation between me and Tom and if I'm completely honest with myself, I admit that I bought into the fantasy myself. Now my job is in jeopardy. Not questioning Your plan, just need to know what You want of me.*

"Help," she whispered aloud as she looked up at the line of clouds gathering on the horizon. Then she pushed herself to her feet and trudged back down the path. But when she reached the office, the others told her that Luke had left shortly after she did with no explanation. He'd gotten a phone call that seemed to upset him and rushed off. In answer to their question about rescheduling the meeting, he'd told them Norah would handle rescheduling the meeting.

"Well, since I assume we've all made arrangements to stay late tonight, I see no reason why we shouldn't go forward," she said. "We can brainstorm, build a plan of action and give our report to Luke when he returns."

Tom stared at the computer screen. He'd finally wrapped up the Osbourn project, but now there were several new—and equally complex—cases in need of his attention. He glanced at the clock. Midnight.

There had been a time when the challenge of his work had energized rather than exhausted him. But ever since he'd returned from Denver… He flipped open his cell. No messages. He scrolled down the numbers and stopped on Norah's.

He put down the phone, surprised that he'd even reached for it in the first place. And where had that thought come from? He hadn't been thinking of Norah and certainly would never call her at such a late hour. It was Bella he was concerned about. Bella he had called daily or Norah he'd phoned two or three times to check on Bella's health in the two weeks he'd been back.

He forced his attention back to the computer screen. Ten minutes later he felt his cell vibrate against his hip. He flipped open the lid. *Norah?*

It was one o'clock in the morning in Phoenix. This could only be bad news.

"Norah?"

"Oh, Tom, hi. I thought you'd be asleep, so I was going to just leave you a message. I mean—it's—"

"Is it Bella?" Tom felt his heart hammer as he relived the moment when he had first seen his daughter pale and limp on the airport restroom floor.

"No—well, yes. I mean it's not what you think. Physically she's fine."

"But?"

"I don't know—you know teenagers. Their mood swings can be hard to track. She's barely speaking to me and then when I got home from work today, she was filled with news about this 'life satisfaction and outlook' survey she'd seen in some magazine. She left it out for me to complete."

"Maybe I should take that survey," Tom said and then wondered why. He had exceeded his wildest expectations when it came to achieving the career goals he'd set for himself. He had a beautiful daughter who was kind and loving and seemed to have inherited some of his flair for leadership. An ex-wife who had embraced the idea of a parenting partnership. He—

"Tom?" Norah's soft voice brought him back to the conversation at hand. "There is one thing that worries me."

"What?"

"Well, ever since we came home from the Thanksgiving fiasco, Izzy has—I don't know. It's like she's pulling away—not just from me but everything."

"She's probably still getting her bearings. She was pretty sick and that's got to have taken a lot out of her. Maybe it's just an energy thing."

"No," Norah said. "I can't put my finger on it, but there's a definite shift in her attitude."

"Toward you?"

"Me, her schoolwork, everything. Remember how excited she was about all her activities at the church?"

Tom chuckled. "Yeah. There was a point there when I thought she was going to tell me that she wanted to be a minister when she grew up."

"She did," Norah said. "That's just it. I used to have to practically drag her out of there on Sundays and it was imperative that we arrive at least half an hour before Sunday school started. These last couple of Sundays I've had trouble just getting her out of bed."

"Have you asked her what's going on?" Tom had not achieved the success he enjoyed by beating around the bush. Norah, on the other hand, had always been overly sensitive—in his opinion—about not upsetting other people.

"Of course I've asked," Norah snapped.

"And?"

"And either I get the fake smile and the wide eyes and something along the lines of, 'I've just got so much on my plate right now,' or I get the scowl and the silent treatment punctuated by dramatic sighs."

"Do you want me to talk to her?"

Norah paused for longer than was normal for a phone conversation as if she were wrestling with her decision. Finally she let out a long breath. "No, that might just make things worse. Thanks and thanks for listening. It helps. This is ridiculous. I shouldn't have called—now there will be two of us not sleeping."

"I wasn't sleeping, Norah, and I can do more than listen," Tom said. "I am her father."

"Maybe when she's with you for Christmas, you can see what you think—see if you notice any change. I'm probably just overreacting."

"Speaking of Christmas, the more I think about it, the more I think Bella and I should forget Hawaii and go to Wisconsin. What do you think—I mean, about going? The three of us? It might be a chance for us to both talk to Bella—present a united front."

Another long silence. Tom tried to imagine Norah's face, the way she was probably curled into a corner of the sofa, her bare feet tucked under her, one finger tracing the pattern of her nightgown.

"I don't think that's a good idea."

This time Tom sighed—in exasperation. "Please don't tell me it's going to be another five years before you're comfortable being in the same place with me, Norah."

"This isn't about you," she replied, her voice edged with defensive irritation. "This is about what's best for Izzy—it's always been about that and you know it."

"And the problem with our daughter being able to actually have both her parents on site for a major holiday along with all four grandparents who aren't getting any younger would be?"

"Oh, Tom, don't play dumb. You know what she wants—what she's always hoped would happen." Then he heard her breath catch and very softly, almost inaudibly, she whispered, "That's it."

"What?"

"Remember when we were in Denver?"

"Hard to forget."

"Well, everyone was making the best of it, but Izzy was relishing the entire situation. Think about it. She was settling in—making friends and organizing talent shows and in between she was making sure the three of us ate together and caught up at the end of the day before we went to sleep. She was pretending we were a family, Tom."

"I don't know. She's pretty savvy, don't you think?"

"She is, but remember—she even suggested that the blizzard was part of God's plan?"

"Yeah, but—"

"She wasn't talking about God's grand plan for the universe, Tom. She truly believed that God put us all there and sent the storm to keep us there so we could become a family again."

"Oh, come on, Norah. That's pretty far-fetched even for a thirteen-year-old's imagination."

"No. You didn't see her in the weeks right after she joined the church, Tom."

Because I was working—at some conference in Europe, Tom thought and felt the stab of guilt that had been his constant companion during that trip.

"She was inspired," Norah continued. "It was like she'd gotten some grand new insight into life. Everything was suddenly about discovering God's plan for her life. Everything became a symbol—a sign."

"And now?"

"Now, she's leaving me surveys on life satisfaction. It's like she looks at me sometimes with pity and concern. It's like she thinks she needs to parent me—us." Norah's voice rose with excitement.

"Okay, honey, slow down."

Honey. How long since he'd called her that?

Tom cleared his throat in the sudden silence between them that indicated she had heard the term of endearment and been equally surprised. "But if we do the Christmas trip, we can work this out when we're all together."

"No. Don't you see? If I'm right, she would see that as our 'correcting the error of our ways,' but when nothing came of it she'd be even more disappointed than ever."

"So now what?"

"Well, so now—" Her voice faltered. "I don't know," she admitted. "What do you think?"

"I think we remember that we are dealing with a thirteen-year-old, and if you're determined not to come for Christmas, then Bella and I will go on to Hawaii as planned. What are you going to do for the holiday?"

This time the length of her silence was alarming.

"Norah?"

She released a strangled little laugh. "I'll be fine. I thought I'd paint Izzy's room and update it—it's still a little girl's room and—"

"Isn't that something you want to do with her? Be sure she likes it?"

"Oh, she's dropped enough hints that I'm pretty sure I can pull it off. It'll be my Christmas present to her."

"You'll hire a decorator," Tom said. "Good idea. How about I pitch in half? I never know what to give her."

"Oh, Tom, she's thirteen. Give her a shopping spree or a gift card or—"

"Because if we go in together on a gift you think she'll take it the wrong way?"

"Something like that," Norah admitted.

"Okay, you win that one. Now tell me what's going on with you?"

Again the laugh that came out was more of a bark. "I'm fine. Just fine."

"Don't tell me we're back to that."

"What?"

"Fine," Tom answered in falsetto.

Norah laughed and it was the laughter he knew so well—warm and rich, rising from somewhere deep inside her. "Get some sleep," she said. "And thanks."

"Good night, Norah."

"You're in a good mood," Izzy noted the following morning as she sat at the kitchen counter eating her breakfast.

"I am," Norah agreed as if she hadn't really noticed until Isabella mentioned it.

"How come?"

I talked to your father and—

Norah shrugged. "It's a beautiful day?"

"Yeah, like just about every other day in Phoenix," Izzy answered, her eyes narrowing. "Has something happened?"

"Does something have to happen for me to be happy? More to the point, does something have to happen to make you happy? And if so, what is it?"

"Whoa!" Isabella threw up her hands in a defensive pose. She scowled as she digested the sudden shift in the conversation's focus. "We were talking about you, remember?"

Norah waved a dismissive hand. "Enough about me. I'm boring. You, on the other hand, have a great many things going on—school, choir, the holiday concert at church...."

"I'm not doing that this year," Izzy mumbled around a mouthful of cereal.

"Why not?"

"Just decided I didn't want to do it."

"Are MJ and Ginny going to be in it?"

A shrug.

"Hey, what's going on?"

"Nothing. I've got to get my backpack. The bus'll be here."

Norah stepped around the edge of the kitchen island and stopped her flight. "Izzy, we need to talk. I know this isn't the right time, but tonight." It wasn't a question.

"Whatever," Izzy muttered and ran out the back door.

Norah watched her trudge down the driveway, shrugging into her backpack as she went. The bus arrived seconds later and Izzy disappeared inside. *Tonight,* she thought. *We're going to work this out. Please, God, help me find the words to make this better.*

As she mentally sent up the prayer, Norah realized that lately she had found renewed comfort and support in a faith she had put on the back burner for so many years. Izzy was right about one thing—Denver had changed her. Seeing Tom in person had allowed her to finally let go of her suppressed anger and bitterness over the divorce. She hoped he'd found similar forgiveness. Maybe it was possible for the two of them to truly share in Isabella's life instead of clinging to carefully laid out guidelines set forth in the divorce settlement.

Next year, she thought. *I'm just not ready to share Christmas—the memories are too precious, too close to my heart still. By next Christmas I'll be ready,* she promised.

Chapter Eight

For Tom weekend days were little different from weekdays. He got up, shaved, dressed, stopped at the local coffeehouse for his usual three-shot extra-hot espresso and headed for the office. On rare occasions he would work from home, telling himself he could use a day off. This was one of those days.

He sat on the terrace of his penthouse condominium and stared out at the Golden Gate Bridge and the sparkling waters of San Francisco Bay. Once—when Norah had been pregnant with Isabella—they'd taken a driving trip into the beautiful northern California countryside. Along the way they had stopped to marvel at the redwood forests and videotape each other striking silly poses comparing their height to the giant trees or mimicking a sea lion's crazy waddle. He wondered if Norah still had those tapes—and more important, did she ever watch them?

They hadn't had a lot of money in those days, so they had camped using a tent and sleeping bags borrowed from friends and cooked over an open fire. Norah had laughed and called this their pioneer period. At night when the temperatures dropped and the fog rolled in damp and chilling, they would snuggle together and plan their future.

A house of their own, kids—lots of kids. Maybe a dog—Norah wasn't so sure about bunches of kids *and* a dog. She had hinted that cats were less work.

"Than kids?" he had teased.

"Than kids and dogs," she had corrected. Then she had sighed and added, "But not half so much fun. Let's start with the kids."

And they had made love under the stars with the sound of the ocean and the crackle of a wood fire, the only background music they needed.

What happened, Norah?

The truth was that he couldn't get Norah's call off his mind. There had been something else—something beyond Isabella. He might have been out of her life for the last five years, but he knew this woman almost as well as he knew himself. They had practically grown up together. On their way to falling in love they'd been the best of friends, confiding and trusting in each other without question. Somewhere along the way in those married years, they'd lost some of that. And certainly during the time they'd been stranded together in Denver there had been times when she'd looked at him with that same distrust, that same questioning of his motives.

On the other hand there had also been times when he'd seen in her eyes the same desire he'd felt—the desire to turn back the clock.

Could they go back? At least to the point where they could once again have that friendship? Not just for the times when they needed to talk about their daughter, but also for the times when they needed a real friend. He could use a friend like Norah. And he had the feeling that there were times when Norah could as well.

"Like now," he muttered aloud. "What's going on with you now, Norah Jenkins Wallace, and why won't you let me help?"

His cell phone vibrated against the glass-topped table, startling him. He stared at it as if willing the caller to be Norah. He flipped open the cover. *Bella.*

"Hi, sweetie. What's up?"

"Daddy, have you talked to Mom lately? Like today?"

"Well no, is something wrong?"

"I don't know. The other day she had me go to MJ's house after school—which is not all that unusual. She's as bad as you are sometimes when she gets to working on a project, but when she came to pick me up she was acting weird."

"Weird how?"

"Like overly cheerful, chattering on about the holidays and how much fun I was going to have with you if we changed plans and went to Wisconsin. She's all, 'Maybe there will be snow, but not until the planes have safely landed,' and stuff like that."

"Sounds pretty normal to me. You know how she's always been about the holidays."

"Yeah, but this was seriously over the top. And then we were supposed to have this big talk—which I had successfully avoided for days—and—"

Tom saw an opportunity to get Isabella to open up. "Talk about what?"

"Just stuff—that's not the important thing, Dad. The important thing is that all of a sudden she suggested we watch a movie together, so I agreed and she puts in this old-time one with Barbra Streisand and Robert Redford."

"The Way We Were," Tom said.

"Yeah, that one, and she starts sobbing about halfway through and doesn't stop. I mean we are talking close to hysterics here. It's a sad story, but it's just a dumb movie."

"It's always been her favorite movie," Tom reminded Isabella.

"Yeah, for times when she's feeling like the world's coming to an end or something," Bella replied. "She must have watched it eighty gazillion times after you guys split up."

"When did you get so smart?"

Bella gave a sigh of relief. "So you see the problem? I mean at first I thought this had to be about something I've done—or not done. Look at the chain of events—need to talk, but first the movie—maybe, so I feel really guilty—and then nothing."

"She's worried about you, sweetie," Tom admitted. "She tells me you've been pulling back from activities you once enjoyed."

"It's not that—well, it is that but not this. *We never talked.* It was like she'd forgotten all about that. I mean something has seriously happened, Dad."

"Have you asked her about it?"

"Dad!" Bella let out an exaggerated sigh of frustration. "Figure it out. One day she goes off to work all happy-happy, then she's practically a basket case. It's like she's waiting for something to happen. It's got to be her job."

"And you want me to do what?"

"Call her. I mean, who are the grown-ups here?"

"You know, Bella, in spite of what happened in Denver, not that much has changed between your mom and me."

"You guys were kissing, Dad."

So she'd seen that and then the following day with her hopes sky high, he and Norah had brought them crashing back to earth by going their separate ways as if nothing had changed.

"She was upset. Don't read anything into that."

"She's still upset and somehow I don't think my kissing her will have the same effect."

"Okay, I'll call her," Tom said. "But if she doesn't open up, Bella, we need to leave it alone."

"It's that boss of hers," Bella grumbled. "I never liked him."

"Luke? I thought the three of you had had some good times together."

"Please," Bella huffed. "He's a user and a loser."

"Your mom seemed to like him."

"Well, yeah, I guess if that's the only game in town."

Tom smiled to himself. "One day when you're older—"

Isabella groaned. "Dad, come into the twenty-first century. Mom went out with Luke because he was available and then he dumped her for Abby who I'll grant you is younger and has a better bod and—"

There's nothing wrong with your mother's body.

"Well, whatever your opinion may be, your mother has a right to a social life and that means she gets to choose the people she shares that life with. Just like I do. You don't get to dictate that, Bella."

"I'm not dictating anything. Is it so hard for you guys to understand that all I want is for both of you to be happy?" She paused. "Please tell me you are not still seeing Tabitha."

"Tamara. And where do you get the idea that your mother and I aren't—content with our lives?" Tom wanted to assure her that he was perfectly happy and he was pretty sure Norah was, but all of a sudden he saw that for the lie it would be—at least for him.

"Content? You're settling for *content?*"

"All right, I'll call your mother," he promised. "But I'm going to need some reason, so let's talk about you, young lady. Now what's all this nonsense about not being part of the youth choir concert?"

"She's fine," Tom assured Norah later that day. "We talked about the choir thing and she's promised to reconsider that. Seems she had decided it was a 'kid' thing."

"She's not fine, Tom," Norah argued. "And this is not about the youth choir. That was simply something I used to illustrate how she's changed since Thanksgiving."

"Okay, so give me another illustration."

"Last night we were watching a movie—"

"The Way We Were."

"Oh, she mentioned that. Well, did she also mention that when I got caught up in the story and started crying, she acted as if I were suddenly having a mental breakdown?"

Tom couldn't help it. He laughed. "That's not exactly her take on the situation."

"Really?" Norah's tone was suddenly overly polite and formal.

"Yeah, really. She's worried about you, Norah—and frankly so am I. What's going on at work?" He could tell that the sudden shift in topics had thrown her and knew that she was taking the time she needed to form her answer—an answer structured so as not to let him in.

"We're talking about Izzy," she said.

"Nice try. Answer the question. Something happened at work. Bella picked up on it and the other night when you and I were talking, I thought there was more going on than just being worried about our daughter. So tell me."

"It's nothing I can't handle," she hedged.

Tom let the silence that followed that remark stretch into several seconds. "Why do you do that, Norah? Shut people out?"

"I don't," she objected.

"You do. You started when we were married."

"You were the one always tied up in other things," she said softly. "There were times when I had to make decisions, had to handle things on my own."

"I was working." Tom felt the long-buried but all-too-familiar bile of his guilt at not having been there more and at the same time the certainty that he had been doing what was best for his wife and child.

This time it was Norah who allowed the silence to linger before she said, "Let's not do this."

"All I'm trying to say is that I'm here now, Norah." It was as close as he was capable of coming to a confession that maybe he could have made better use of his time in the years they were married. "Talk to me—as a friend."

When she didn't say anything right away, Tom pressed his case. "In spite of everything that's happened, Norah, we've always had that—we had that first. The kind of trust between best friends was our foundation."

"Yeah." Her voice was muffled but the single word was clear enough that he knew she'd started to cry.

"Ah, Norah, honey, don't. Just tell me. Maybe I can help."

"It is work," she admitted. "We didn't get the grant I was telling you about when we were in Denver."

"I'm sorry."

"Yeah, well, these things happen."

"But there's more than that—I mean this isn't the first time you've been turned down for a grant."

She sniffed and gave a shaky little laugh. "You're right. Why am I getting so worked up over one lost grant? Must be hormones or something."

Tom frowned. Never in all the years he'd known her had Norah ever blamed an emotional outburst on female physiology. In fact, she had little patience with women who did. She was gently but firmly shutting him out. And why not? It had been five years. Two days stranded in an airport could not erase that, so he decided to back off. "So what's Bella's last day of school before the holiday break?"

He heard her breathe a sigh of relief that he was letting it go and changing the subject. "Tuesday. I've made the airline reservation for Wednesday."

"We could still all go to Wisconsin together." *Why did he keep bringing that up?* She'd given her reasons and he really couldn't argue with them. But ever since he'd watched them get on that plane back to Phoenix, he'd been thinking about when they might see each other again.

"Oh, Tom, let it go."

"It's just an idea," Tom said. "You know, I've got to admit that Bella wasn't the only one who felt a little cheated when we never got that Thanksgiving back home together."

"I know. I felt that too. But trying to re-create that just won't work," Norah replied.

"We'll never know if Bella and I head off to Hawaii."

Her silence spoke volumes and he knew he should let it go. He searched his brain for something he could say that would keep her on the line.

"Well," she said, her voice steady once again. "Thanks for talking to Isabella and for—"

"She's just worried about you," Tom said. "Hey, Norah? Think about all of us getting together with the folks, okay? I can understand why not Christmas, but maybe springbreak or next summer?"

"Maybe," Norah agreed. "Bye, Tom."

* * *

When Norah put down the phone and turned around, Isabella was standing in the doorway. She realized that Izzy had been there for some time and that she'd heard at least her side of the conversation. She met her daughter's sullen glare.

"That was your father," she said unnecessarily.

"No, that was *your* opportunity," Isabella replied and turned for her dramatic exit.

"Isabella, sit down," Norah instructed.

Her daughter flung herself onto the sofa. Norah took the rocking chair across from her. "I am worried about you," she began. "You're setting yourself up to be hurt and I don't know how to stop that."

"You and Dad still love each other," Isabella said tightly.

"Yes, but it's not the kind of love you think. It's not romantic love."

Isabella snorted. "That kiss in the chapel sure looked romantic to me and I was half out of it."

Norah tried turning the tables. "You read that wrong, Izzy."

"Yeah, that's kind of what Dad said when I mentioned it to him."

"Okay," Norah said, slowly buying time as she considered how to navigate this detour in the conversation. "Your father and I kissed. But—"

Suddenly Isabella sat up straight and faced Norah directly. "No buts. Don't try to tell me it was just something that came about because you were worried about me and upset and Dad was just trying to comfort you.

He could have hugged you or patted your hand to comfort you. He could have offered you his handkerchief to comfort you. *He kissed you.*"

And I kissed him back, Norah thought.

"And do *not* tell me it was a mistake."

"Why don't you tell me what you think," Norah said. "Why don't you tell me what you think all of this means—the getting stranded in Denver, the kiss, everything."

Izzy's eyes widened in surprise and disbelief. "You really want to know?"

"I do." Norah leaned back and started rocking as she fought to give every appearance that Izzy had her full and rapt attention.

"Well, after I sort of found out that Dad planned to be in Wisconsin—"

"Sort of?"

"Okay, I knew," she admitted. "So when we were headed there too, well, it was like sort of a sign."

"Why didn't you tell me that your dad was going?"

"Because I just knew you'd change your mind and decide not to go. I mean that's been the pattern, right? Every single time there's been the slightest chance the two of you might actually be in the same place at the same time, one of you found a way to jinx it."

"That's an exaggeration, but go on."

"So then we get to Denver and there's Dad big as life, so sign number two." Isabella held up two fingers to emphasize the point. "*Then* He sends the storm." She raised a third finger and smiled triumphantly.

"He as in God?"

"Well, duh!"

Norah rocked forward and rested her elbows on her knees and her face in her hands before looking up at her daughter. "Izzy, I know your faith in God is very strong. It's also very new. Think about it. Why would God inconvenience thousands of people just so your father and I could be together? Especially when we were all going to be together in Wisconsin anyway? It doesn't make any sense."

"Mom, in Wisconsin you would have found ways to avoid him. In the airport there was no such chance *plus* God gave me just enough of an appendicitis flare-up so the two of you had to bond."

Norah opened her mouth to dissect that logic, but Isabella wasn't done.

"*And* it wasn't just about us. Other people were touched in a good way by that blizzard."

Norah couldn't come up with any argument for that. "Still—"

Isabella stood up, hands on hips. She seemed to tower over Norah. "No. You were almost there—back together but you pulled away. Well, thankfully God is patient. So I will keep praying that there will be another chance for both of you, okay?"

"Okay." Norah smiled up at her beautiful daughter. "In the meantime—"

"In the meantime, you could seriously think about us all three going to Wisconsin and see what happens."

When Norah got to work on Monday she was fully prepared for a showdown with Luke. Instead she was surprised to see Stan Morrison, the agency's founder, in Luke's office. Luke was gesturing wildly, while Stan sat quietly in the single visitor's chair.

"What's up?" she asked Abby.

"Nobody knows. Dr. Morrison was here when Luke and I got here—separately," she added, blushing furiously. "Just at the same time."

"Abby, it's common knowledge that you and Luke are together. If he makes you happy, then there's nothing wrong with that."

"I just—I mean there was a time when you and Luke—"

"Ancient history," Norah assured her. "So did Stan say anything?"

"Not really. He was very pleasant like always and asked if he and Luke could talk in Luke's office."

"Well, whatever it is, I have work to do," Norah said as she headed for her cubicle. She was glad to see that the rest of the staff followed her lead. Only Abby lingered a moment before coming over to Norah's desk.

"Norah, did you call Dr. Morrison?"

"No. Why would I do that?"

Abby shrugged. "It's just that Luke had hinted that he might have to downsize the staff and that you were the person he was thinking of asking to accept a severance and—well, we all know you and the professor are good friends."

Norah raised her voice just enough so that everyone in the small office could hear her response. "It's true that after the news broke that we didn't get the grant, Luke tried to fire me. There was no mention of a severance package and my leaving was not a request. I suggested that he would need to make a valid case based on performance for letting me go. We left it at that and I assumed we would continue the discussion after the afternoon meeting."

"The meeting Luke cut out on and you conducted," said one of the male staff members who no longer pretended not to be listening.

"That's right. When Luke didn't come back, I left the ideas we'd developed on his desk."

Just at that moment the door to Luke's office opened and Luke strode through the front office and out the back exit.

"Ladies and gentlemen, I wonder if you would all join me in the conference room," Dr. Morrison said in his usual calm, even tone.

Chapter Nine

"So Luke's gone?" Isabella said that night as she and Norah shared a supper of spaghetti, salad and garlic toast.

Norah nodded and slurped down a long strand of pasta.

"What did he do and how did the professor know?"

"Well, what I didn't know until today was that Carol Williams of the foundation had already called Stan when I talked to her. I thought her reasons for why we didn't get the funding were vague, but I never suspected this."

"This what?" Izzy said.

"It seems that Luke has a gambling problem himself. And a member of the foundation board had seen him in the casino."

"What was the board member doing there?"

"Well, sweetie, not everyone who enters a casino is a gambling addict. For some people it's just entertainment."

"So Luke could have just been out for some entertainment," Izzy reasoned.

"He could have, but the board member couldn't help noticing that everyone seemed to know him—the dealers, the waitresses and others. The board member asked some questions and learned that Luke was indeed a regular—and that he occasionally lost a great deal of money."

"I knew it," Isabella crowed. "I never liked him. So then what happened?"

"Oh, Izzy, this is a man's life, not some adventure show on television."

"I know." She pasted on a serious and concerned expression and concentrated on her dinner for a minute. Then she looked up, grinned and asked, "But what happened?"

"Carol told Stan that the foundation was willing to reconsider funding the program on one condition—that there be a full audit of the books and that Luke be replaced as head of the agency."

"Fired?"

"Demoted."

"But he's gone."

"He resigned."

"So who's going to head up the agency?"

"Stan will step in temporarily."

Norah cleared the dishes.

"You could do it," Izzy said quietly. "You've practically been doing it ever since Dr. Morrison left. Maybe you should go for it."

Norah stood very still, her hands filled with dirty dishes. "Do you know what you're suggesting?"

Izzy shrugged. "Hey, if God wants us all to be together something like a job is not going to stand in the way. You might as well be happy."

Thank you, Norah whispered, casting her eyes heavenward and then she put the dishes in the sink and hugged Izzy. "Have I told you recently what a terrific kid you are?"

Izzy pulled away, but she was grinning. "Better let me do the dishes while you go dig up the old résumé, Mom."

Norah went to the den and dug through a file drawer until she unearthed her résumé, badly in need of updating. After typing the information on the computer and staring at it for several minutes, she reached for the phone. But who would she call? If she called one of her coworkers or a peer at another nonprofit the word would be out that she was applying for the top post—or worse, that she was actively seeking another position. And for now all she was doing was taking a tentative first step just in case.

I could call Tom.

Norah dismissed the idea out of hand. Why Tom? What did he know of résumés?

He can look at it from the point of view of an employer.

True, but—

And he's not going to spread the word that you might be out there looking or going for the top job. No one will know and you'll still have the option of changing your mind.

Maybe. Norah played with the mouse, rolling the cursor over the screen, bringing up her e-mail. All spam.

Delete. Delete. I could probably find everything I need online, she reasoned.

Sure, but you'd still want somebody to look it over and besides you need to let Tom know that things seem to be back to normal with Izzy. After all, she's the one who encouraged you to go for the job. Hopefully that's a sign that she's finally accepted the way things are.

Before she could change her mind, Norah typed up a message entitled "Good News," attached her résumé—after working it over herself for half an hour, entered Tom's e-mail address and hit Send.

Tom understood that he should be glad that Norah was finally recognizing her own worth. The fact was that the agency should have promoted her instead of hiring Luke, but she hadn't applied. And the news that applying for the top job had been Isabella's idea was good, right? So how come he felt this vague sense of disappointment? What was that about?

Maybe it was that she was moving forward with her life. *And I'm not?*

It was an unsettling idea. Tom had always believed that of the two of them, he was the one who had always had his eye on the future. In the early years the plans he'd made had been for the two of them and then after Isabella came along, he'd felt driven to secure a future for the three of them. But Norah had never shared that drive and they had argued often about his need to make sure that at least financially they had no worries.

"It's the one thing I can control," he'd told her.

"Why do you have to *control* anything?" she'd answered.

And now he couldn't help admitting that while she had looked for work that had meaning and purpose for her, regardless of the pay, early on he had gotten into the habit of considering every career move from the standpoint of what it would mean financially. He wanted the best for his family—the best schools for his children, the best opportunities for travel and—

Tom leaned back and looked around his spacious office. The walls were covered with tastefully framed awards and plaques recognizing his contributions to various organizations in the community. Every one of them represented a business opportunity rather than the kind of altruism they might have illustrated if it had been Norah's name on the certificate.

Beyond the solid Brazilian wood double doors stood a half dozen cubicles housing paralegals, administrative assistants and more staff to handle billing and research. Next door to either side of his office were the offices—almost as luxurious—of the attorneys he had taken on as partners. At the far end of a long hallway was the conference room, surrounded by frosted glass etched with the firm's logo. Everything was a distinct marker of the incredible prosperity he had achieved starting with the day his divorce from Norah had become final and he had bought out his share of the firm and gone into practice for himself. Stung by the finality of the divorce and the feeling of failure that came along with it, he had needed to excel at something. He would show her. And by the time his anger and hurt had subsided into a dull bruise rather than the open wound it had been, working sixteen-hour days had become a lifestyle.

As he reviewed Norah's employment history he saw his success for the hollow victory that it was. He glanced back at Norah's résumé still posted on his computer screen. He knew her to be a woman who had joined the agency because she truly believed she could make a difference for the people the agency served. He knew her as a woman of ideas, who believed anything was possible. None of that came through in the abbreviated sentences that described her responsibilities in each position she'd held. As usual she was underselling herself. Tom turned on the tracker tool and began striking her passive words and adding his own. And as he did he rediscovered that sense of excitement and energy he and Norah had once shared as teenagers and then young adults when everything seemed possible. *When the two of them had dreamed of making a real difference—of changing the world.*

"Wow!" Norah said the next day when she called to thank him. "Who is this woman?"

She's the girl who blew me away when we were the boy and girl next door back in Normal, Wisconsin. She's the one who showed me that even kids from small farm towns can set the world on fire. She's the woman who stole my heart and gave me a daughter who gives purpose to my life.

"It's all true and you know it. If anything, I've understated some of it."

"I doubt it," Norah said and he could hear in her voice how pleased and flattered she was.

"Are you accusing me of bias?"

"Not at all. I am on my knees thanking you," she said laughing. "If I decide to submit this the search committee is going to be superimpressed."

"What do you mean 'if'?"

"It's just that Stan seems to be enjoying being back. He never was very high on the idea of retirement and—"

"So you think he might stay on?"

"The board is accepting résumés, but nothing's going to happen until after the holidays. I just don't want to be in competition with Stan."

"Does he know you're interested?" Tom felt a tug of irritation at Norah's mentor. This was her time, her chance. Stan had had his.

"We really haven't discussed it. Speaking of job changes, did Izzy tell you her friend MJ's dad is being transferred. They'll be moving the first of the year."

"How's she taking that?"

"Pretty well. The transfer is to Minneapolis, so she and MJ are already making plans to get together whenever Izzy comes to Wisconsin. I heard the two of them talking about some music camp in Wisconsin the other night. If I go for the job and get it, then maybe—"

Tom frowned. "If you think music camp is right for Bella, then she should go to music camp. We have the money for whatever Isabella needs, whether you decide to take the job or not, Norah."

"I know," she said softly. "I didn't mean to sound like—I was just thinking out loud."

"Norah? This going for the job? It isn't about whether you'd be doing the best thing for Bella or competing with Stan. Do it—or don't—for only one reason."

"Because it's best for me?" she said.

"That's my girl," he replied. "I've got an appointment. Tell Bella I'll call her later to finalize travel plans."

On the Wednesday before Christmas Norah drove Izzy to the airport. As further proof of her acceptance of the way things were, Isabella had made the final decision about the trip—she and Tom would travel to Hawaii as planned.

"But you promise to seriously think about us all meeting at the grands over springbreak?" Izzy asked on the drive to the airport.

"I promise to seriously think about it," Norah replied. "You didn't gift wrap anything that you're carrying on, did you?" Norah focused on navigating the multiple lanes of the highway.

"Mother, this is not exactly my first flight. I do know the rules."

"Just checking." She switched lanes, waving to the driver who had opened a spot for her. They rode in silence, but Norah was glad to realize that it was not the strained silence of the last few weeks. This time it was comfortable—each of them gathering their thoughts as they looked ahead to the busy day before them.

"Are you going to submit your résumé today?" Izzy asked.

"Probably," Norah hedged. "We'll see."

"Mom! Today's the deadline. Do you want to end up working for another Luke?" She shuddered. "Yuck!"

Norah laughed. It was so good to have things back on track with her daughter.

As Norah parked in short-term near the departure terminal, Izzy was checking her phone for messages, then the weather. "Snowing in Wisconsin," she announced. "Eighty and sunny in Hawaii." She leaped from the car and started pulling her luggage from the trunk. A skycap hovered nearby.

"I've got it, thank you," Izzy said politely as she rummaged through the pockets of her jeans until she came up with two single dollar bills. She handed them to the skycap and grinned. "But Merry Christmas!"

Norah could hardly wait to tell Tom what their daughter had done unprompted. When they reached security, she hugged Izzy hard. "Have a wonderful time and don't worry about anything back here," she instructed. "I'll call you," she shouted as Izzy disappeared down the concourse.

When she reached her office the message light on her phone was blinking madly. Norah dropped her purse on the desk along with the flat briefcase that contained—among other files—her résumé and application for the director's position. She sat down and picked up the receiver, punching in the code for retrieving her messages.

"You have two messages. Message one sent at seven-twenty this morning."

Norah frowned and pulled a notepad closer, prepared for the emergency a call at that early hour might indicate.

"Hi," Tom said, his voice a little thick from sleep and no coffee. "Just wanted to wish you luck with the job thing. I know you won't hear until after the New Year, but this is a big first step, Norah. Just remember, you deserve this and you *are* hands down the best candidate for this job no matter who else applies. I'll call later so you know Bella arrived safely."

Norah's finger hovered over the number that would delete the message and move her forward to message number two. But then she slid her finger to a different key—the one that would save the message so she could listen to it again—listen to Tom believing in her again—and again.

"Message two sent at seven-sixteen this morning."

At first there was silence, although Norah could hear voices in the background, muffled but urgent sounding as if the caller had a hand over the receiver. She turned up the volume and strained to hear. She pulled the notepad closer.

"Norah, this is Eleanor."

Tom's mother. Why was her ex-mother-in-law calling her?

"I called you at home but you and Isabella must have already left for the airport and I don't have the number for her cell."

What's happened? Norah felt her heart skip a beat, then lurch into race mode.

"I'm here with your parents. Earle collapsed while shoveling snow this morning. The paramedics are taking him to the hospital now—possible heart attack. Irene is here with him and I'll follow the ambulance with her. He's conscious and—we're going now, dear. The number at the hospital is—"

Norah waited, pen poised as Eleanor repeated the number someone in the background dictated.

"Everything will be fine," Eleanor assured her. "We'll call as soon as we know anything more."

The recorded voice repeated instructions to follow to delete or save the message—twice. Finally Norah simply hung up the phone.

"Norah?"

Stan Morrison was standing at the entrance to her cubicle. She looked up at the man's kind, weathered face and burst into tears. At the same time, her phone started to ring.

"Somebody get that," Stan instructed as he knelt beside Norah's chair, one hand hovering uncertainly around her shoulders. "What's happened?"

Norah started to tell him, the words coming in between gulps of tears.

"It's your husband," Abby said quietly indicating Norah's phone.

Stan lifted the receiver and handed it to Norah while everyone on the staff gathered around, uncertain of what they should do, but prepared to do anything they could.

"Norah? Mom just called. I'm on my way to the airport to meet Bella, but I've got my assistant working to put everything in place to get you there as soon as possible. Now listen to me." He began rattling off a long list of instructions. *Go home...pack...sending driver... airport....*

"Tom?" Norah said, stopping him. "Bella's going to be so upset. Will you come with her?"

"Oh, honey, where else would I go?"

Chapter Ten

At the airport check-in, Norah was informed that she had been upgraded to first class. *Tom,* she thought. Just before boarding her flight, Norah was finally able to reach the hospital and her mother.

"Yes, it was a heart attack—mild, according to the doctor. A warning, he called it."

"How's Dad doing?"

Her mother sighed. "You know your father. He didn't finish shoveling the front walk and now he's concerned that it will ice over and someone will fall. Eleanor said she would see to it, but now Dad's all worried that she'll ask Dan to shovel and *he'll* end up in the hospital as well."

"Tom and Izzy can take care of it when they get there," Norah said.

There was a beat and then her mother said. "You're all coming? Together?"

It was impossible not to understand the note of hope in those questions.

"We're all on our way," Norah assured her. "Izzy left for California this morning. She and Tom will fly out from there today or tomorrow. I should be there late this afternoon."

"I'll tell your father. That should perk him up."

"Mom? He's going to be okay, right?"

"He'll be fine," her mother assured her, but her tone was too bright, too upbeat. "You just worry about yourself. We'll see you when you get here."

She tried Tom's phone and Izzy's, but got voice mail in both cases. *They must be on their way.* The thought gave her enormous comfort as she settled back in the wide seat and closed her eyes, hardly aware that the plane had started to taxi down the runway.

This trip the flight was smooth and mere background noise for the emotional turbulence Norah was feeling. Anxiety was uppermost—the fear that her father's condition was far more serious than her mother was willing to admit. The sudden panic that she might not make it back to Wisconsin in time to tell him how much she loved him, how much he had meant to her. The uncertainty of what his health might mean for the future.

Then there was work. Stan had suggested she take the remainder of the year off. "Come back fresh after the New Year," he'd said as he walked her out to her car.

Norah thought about the file folder containing her application that was still lying on her desk. All she needed to do was call Stan or Abby and let them know the folder was there. But she didn't. What if her father died? What if he was permanently incapacitated? How would he and Mom manage in a house where all the bedrooms and the single bath were upstairs? As an only child she felt enormous responsibility for the well-being of her parents—she just hadn't thought the need would come so soon.

Underlying everything was an almost suffocating sense of guilt. Guilt that she had chosen to live so far away that her parents rarely had the opportunity to spend time with her or Izzy—their only grandchild. Guilt that there weren't more grandchildren. Guilt that her marriage had failed and that the combination of the end of her marriage and the fact that she and Tom had not had more children and that she had willingly—blithely—continued to reside halfway across the country—for what? Warm weather?

Her parents had never been anything but thrilled for her happiness and concerned for her heartaches. Even though she realized that in the rubble of her own dreams for the future lay their dreams for her and for their own golden years when their friends were intricately involved in the lives of their adult children and grandchildren.

You can always come home.

From the time Norah had been a small child and all through college and her adult years, that had been her mother's message to her. Never said in a whining wishful tone, but rather offered as a haven—an assurance that whatever happened in her life there was this one place where she would be loved unconditionally.

"Ms. Wallace?"

Norah blinked up at the flight attendant.

"I have a message for you." He handed her a folded piece of paper. "I—is there anything I can get for you?"

The young man's expression was sympathetic.

"No, thank you," Norah whispered as she fingered the note, her heart in her throat. Judging by the steward's expression and the unusual delivery of a message in flight, her father must have taken a turn for the worse, but Mom would never handle things this way. Mom wouldn't begin to know how to contact her in midair. She opened the note and read the contents twice, then looked up at the steward.

"I don't understand," she said, handing him the note.

The young man took the empty seat next to her. "Arrangements have been made for you to take a private charter from O'Hare to Madison, Wisconsin," he read, then looked over at her. "I understand you are traveling for a family emergency?"

Norah nodded.

"Apparently someone has arranged to make sure you get there as soon as possible. We're approaching Chicago now. As soon as we land a skycap will be waiting with a cart to take you to the private flight." He stood up and handed her back the note. "I hope everything works out."

"Thank you," Norah murmured.

They landed twenty minutes later, but it took another twenty to reach the gate. Norah was first off the plane once the cabin door opened.

"Ms. Wallace?"

"Yes." Her voice shook and her legs suddenly felt like rubber.

"Hop in," the heavyset woman driver invited, and practically before Norah's feet cleared the floor, they were off. The driver wove in and out of throngs of travelers, beeping her horn and calling out cheerfully, "Stand back. Woman driver on the loose," to the delight and surprise of bored or harried passengers she passed along the way.

"Hang on, sweetie," she said as she made a sharp turn down a narrow passageway, threaded her way through what looked like a warehouse of baggage and out onto the tarmac. "Shortcut," she yelled over the sudden whipping wind. "You warm enough?"

Norah nodded and hung on to the front panel of the golf cart.

"Those your folks there?" The driver nodded toward a small private jet where miraculously Izzy and Tom were waiting—Izzy waving her arms as if directing the cart into a landing.

"Yes," Norah yelled back, her heart suddenly lighter. "Those are my folks."

"Wow, you landed yourself a major hottie, didn't you, girl?" The woman said as she whipped the cart to a halt and eyed Tom's approach.

Norah couldn't help it. She smiled even as tears glistened on her lashes.

"Ah, sweetie, it's all going to be okay," the woman assured her and Norah suddenly realized that the woman's act had been for her benefit to take her mind off whatever trouble she was flying in to face.

"Thank you," she said softly and squeezed the driver's gloved hand.

"This it?" Tom asked as he ran over to the cart and took her small duffel from her. He handed the driver a generous tip.

"Good looking and a good tipper," the woman said to Norah. "This one's a keeper," she advised as she waved and drove off.

Tom wrapped one arm around Norah's shoulders as if protecting her from the elements as he guided her toward the plane. "Get on board, Bella," he called.

As soon as Norah boarded, Isabella burst into tears.

"Oh, Izzy, it's going to be okay. I talked to Grandma and Papa's going to be okay. She says seeing you will be the best possible medicine."

Gently she fastened Izzy's seat belt and then her own as Tom gave final instructions to the pilot and then settled into the seat across from them. As the plane's twin engines revved and the pilot began the slow taxi toward the runway, Tom reached across the narrow aisle and took Norah's hand.

As soon as they landed in Madison, Tom led Norah and Isabella to the car he'd hired. It was waiting on the tarmac and Norah was grateful for Tom's thoughtfulness in getting them to the hospital as quickly as possible. This time instead of riding up front with the driver as he had in Denver when Bella was sick, he got into the backseat. He stretched one arm along the back of the seat so that Bella could rest her head against his shoulder and he could gently stroke Norah's hair with his fingers.

"What if Papa dies?" Bella murmured.

"Papa is not going to die—not yet," Tom said, but until they knew the full seriousness of Earle's condition, he was unwilling to make promises.

He glanced over at Norah. She was staring out the window, but he suspected she was not seeing any of the passing scenery as the driver headed for the medical complex on the campus of the University of Wisconsin. "They're the best, Norah," he said softly. "They've got the best specialists—the best trauma teams. He's in good hands."

Norah nodded but did not look away from the window. She was dry-eyed now, her face looking as if she had aged several years over the hours since she'd received the news. Tom was pretty sure that he knew what she was thinking, for they had often discussed how fortunate they were—and Bella was—that both sets of parents were in good health. Lively seniors who added a generational depth to Bella's life that she might have missed by not having siblings.

The driver turned onto the drive to the hospital entrance.

"Norah?" Tom said quietly and this time she turned to look at him. But her eyes were devoid of anything more than exhaustion. "I'm sorry," he said and understood that under the circumstances she would take the words as comfort for her father's illness. Some day he would find a way to tell her that he was taking steps toward realizing what his pride had contributed to the downfall of their marriage.

A single tear coursed its way down Norah's left cheek. Tom reached over and wiped it away with his thumb.

The receptionist directed them to the cardiac intensive care unit waiting room. Norah hurried down the hall barely aware that Isabella was following reluctantly and that Tom had also held back to reassure their daughter. In this moment Norah was a daughter—an only child—who needed her own mother to calm her fears.

Tom's mother, Eleanor, was the only person in the waiting room other than a volunteer sitting at the desk and reading the newspaper. The minute Norah entered the room Eleanor was on her feet, coming forward, her arms outstretched. Norah did not hesitate to step into the circle of that embrace.

"Where's Mom?" she asked.

"She's in with Earle. The doctor's there now and—"

"I want to hear what he has to say," Norah said, breaking free and heading for the double doors that separated the patient unit from the waiting room. The volunteer made a move as if to stop her, but Eleanor interceded. "This is Mr. Jenkins's daughter," she explained even as she touched the large button on the wall that sent the double doors flying open with a whoosh. "Second room on the left," she told Norah.

Several nurses and a couple of doctors glanced up at the sound of the doors opening, but all but one returned to work. "May I help you?" the woman in a green smock asked.

"My father," Norah said and nodded toward the second sliding-glass door on the left where the curtains were pulled closed. "I—"

"Ah, you must be Norah," the woman replied. "Your parents have been expecting you. Doctor is in with them now—he just arrived, so you haven't missed much." She nodded toward the partially open door.

"Thank you," Norah said.

The news was good.

"You've dodged a bullet this time, young man," the doctor, who looked to be no more than thirty years old, said as he studied the chart and did not look at either of Norah's parents.

Norah saw her father frown and knew exactly what was coming. First he glanced around the room as if trying to figure out who the doctor meant. Then his eyes widened and he pointed to himself. "Are you talking to me?" It was his best De Niro impression and Norah felt a smile tug at the corners of her mouth.

The doctor looked up, startled.

"Because my name is either Earle or Mr. Jenkins—take your pick. If we ever become really good friends I might even let you call me 'Early,' but that's unlikely. I am seventy-two years old—not young—old. Do we understand each other, *young man?*"

"Yes, sir," the doctor replied, all bravado gone.

"So, I've dodged a bullet," Earle prompted. "Define 'dodge.'"

The doctor put down the chart and moved closer

to the bed. He positioned himself so that he included Norah and her mother in the conversation. In clear lay terms, he gave them a detailed diagnosis and then discussed changes and additions to Earle's diet and medications. He suggested that Norah's parents start walking daily or if that was impossible because of weather, then get a treadmill or exercise bike.

"We have one of each," Norah's mother told him. "In the basement."

"They make dandy clothes lines," Earle joked.

The doctor smiled—a real smile and Norah could not help noticing that he was giving no indication that he needed to get this over with and move on to other patients. "You'll be moved to our cardiac care unit this afternoon," he said. "We'll leave the monitor in place, so don't go trying any marathons, okay? But walks up and down the halls every few hours would be good. We'll see how you do for the next twenty-four hours and then talk about getting you out of here."

Norah's father offered the man a handshake. "Thanks, doc. Really. Thanks for everything."

The doctor returned the handshake and laughed. "You aren't getting rid of me that easily, sir. I'll be around this evening to check on you, okay?"

He nodded to both Norah and her mother and left the room. Norah could hear him repeating his orders to the nurse outside.

The minute the doctor was gone her father stretched out his arms to her. His eyes were misty but his embrace was strong. "How's my girl?" he said.

"Better now that I'm here," Norah admitted.

"Isabella off to Hawaii?" Earle asked.

"She's out in the waiting room—with Tom." Norah did not miss the look that passed between her parents—a look she well knew was filled with hope that this was a positive sign.

"Izzy had already left for California when Eleanor called Norah," Irene explained.

"Then Tom called," Norah added, "and—well, you know Tom. He practically hired Air Force One to get us here." Her voice trailed off as she realized she'd delivered this last not with her usual irritation at Tom's ability to buy whatever he needed, but rather appreciation for the fact that he was able to get her here in such good time.

"Do I get to see them or is Doctor Young Man still restricting my visitors?"

"You know the rules, Earle," Norah's mother said. "Only two visitors at a time—at least in this unit. Norah and I will step out so Izzy and Tom can come see you."

"Afraid that'll have to wait," the nurse announced. "Mr. Jenkins is going for some tests and then on to his new digs. You and the rest of the family can meet him up on the fourth floor in room—" She consulted a chart and gave them the room number all the while moving them out the door to make room for the orderlies who had come to transfer Earle.

In the waiting room they filled Eleanor in on the good news. "Where's Isabella?" Norah's mom asked, glancing around.

"She and Tom took a little walk," Eleanor said, glancing at Norah. "Isabella became quite upset. She was crying and Tom was having trouble consoling her. I think he was taking her in the direction of the coffee shop."

Norah looked at her mother. "You should get something to eat as well."

"Don't worry about me. Eleanor and I will get something. You go find Izzy and meet us in Dad's new room."

Tom and Izzy weren't in the coffee shop near the lobby. Nor were they in the cafeteria on the lower level. Spotting the volunteer she had seen in the waiting room, Norah stopped him and asked if he'd seen her daughter.

"You might try the chapel," he suggested. "It's just down the hall from the waiting room. Your little girl was pretty upset and that's a good quiet place to go."

"Thank you." Norah eased open the door to the chapel and heard Tom's low voice. He and Izzy were seated in the front row of chairs. Izzy had her face buried in her hands and was shaking her head vehemently from side to side as Tom tried to reason with her.

"Hey," Norah said as she slid into the seat on the other side of her and looked at Tom for answers. "What's going on?"

"Oh, Mom," Izzy wailed, throwing herself into Norah's arms. "It's all my fault—Papa's heart attack. It's my fault."

"Shh," Norah soothed.

"I tried to convince her," Tom said, his expression helpless and forlorn at his inability to handle this crisis. "I pointed out that she was miles away and had nothing at all to do with—"

This set off a fresh outburst of tears and Norah—relieved by the news that her father would be all right—

suppressed a smile. "She's thirteen," she murmured to Tom. "Reason and logic are not yet part of her repertoire."

"I prayed," Izzy gulped out the words. "I prayed that God would do something that would get us all back together at least for the holidays. I prayed so hard—constantly."

"And you think God made Papa have a heart attack just so we would all be together?"

Isabella nodded and burrowed deeper into Norah's embrace. Tom looked as if he had just heard news beyond comprehension. "But, honey—" he said to Isabella as he rubbed her back.

Norah warned him with a look then started to speak quietly to Isabella. "Well, here's what I came to tell you. Papa is going to be just fine. The doctor is letting him move to a regular room as we speak and then if everything goes okay with the new medicine the doctor is giving him, he'll be able to go home maybe as soon as day after tomorrow."

Izzy grew still and her sobs dwindled to the occasional shuddering intake of breath. She sat up and looked at Norah. "Really?"

"Really. So you see, darling, everything is going to be all right. Your Papa will be home in a few days and we can help Grandma start getting everything set up for Christmas and—"

"We're staying for Christmas?" Izzy asked, looking from Norah to Tom and back again. "All of us?"

"And New Year's," Tom said, then he glanced at Norah. "If that's okay."

"Works for me," Norah said, ignoring the sudden increase in the rhythm of her heartbeat. After all, Tom would say anything right now to calm his daughter. "Of course, I wasn't on my way to Hawaii and the beaches full of cute boys."

Isabella smiled. "There are a couple of cute boys here," she said. "I met them last time I visited—at the church picnic, remember?"

At the church picnic, Norah thought. *Where Tom and I met when I was Izzy's age.*

"Can I see Papa now?"

"In a little while, once he gets back from some tests and settled in his new room. But both your grandmothers are in the coffee shop having lunch and I'm sure they would love to have you join them."

"*Us* join them," Isabella corrected. She stood up and faced the small altar. "You know what I was thinking?"

Tom stood behind her and placed his hands on her shoulders. "I'm almost afraid to ask."

"Daddy! This is serious."

"Okay, what?"

"I was thinking that this is the second time we've all ended up in some strange chapel—not our own church, but just this little place set aside for people in pain to work things out."

"God is everywhere," Norah said softly as she stepped to Izzy's side and took her hand.

"Exactly," Isabella replied, turning to gaze up at her parents. "Can we have a moment of silent prayer to thank God for taking care of Papa?"

"Sure, sweetie," Tom said.

"And feel free to thank Him for other stuff—you know, like us all being together for the holidays," Isabella suggested before bowing her own head.

Norah could not meet Tom's gaze over Izzy's bowed head, so she lowered her eyes and prayed.

Thank You, God, for caring for Dad. I know there will come a day when he and Mom won't be here, but not today—not this time. And, God, thank You for bringing Tom and me together again, but I am so worried that Isabella is going to be hurt. Please help her to see that being together as a family for the holidays is not the same as being back together. Please help her find ways to accept that and for us to move forward.

"Amen," Isabella said aloud, then grinned up at her parents. "Let's eat. I'm starved."

Norah's dad was an instant hit with the staff on the fourth floor. His room quickly became a gathering place for relieved friends and neighbors and Tom found himself observing the scene from a spot near the door. He watched Irene fuss over Earle and Earle lap up the attention at the same time he was chastising her to, "Stop hovering. That's what they pay those folks in uniform to do."

He saw the easy camaraderie between his parents and Norah's—the kind of intimacy that comes with having shared so many of life's adventures—first home, raising children, career triumphs and woes, traveling together and more. Two indestructible marriages made all the stronger because of the friendship between the couples.

His dad was relating a fishing story—one where Earle was the hero, having banished a snake sleeping under one of the seats of the boat once the friends had left shore and had nowhere to run. Tom watched his mother's face, knowing she must have heard this story a hundred times. But her expression showed no irritation at the repetition. Instead she was finishing his sentences, laughing with him. Tom guessed that she was admiring his father's determination to remind them all of other times, better times—times that they could all hope would come again and produce new stories to tell.

He watched Irene and Earle and his parents for several minutes. This was the model he and Norah had grown up with. This was what they had believed they would have. This was what had seemed to come so easily to their parents—and so hard for them.

He glanced over at Norah. She was laughing at the story, finding comfort in it. Some of the tension had gone out of her face and shoulders. She had one hand on the raised head of her father's bed. From time to time her eyes would flick over to the monitor, checking the graph and numbers there, reassuring herself that he was past the crisis. The way the afternoon sun fell across her cheekbones made her look young and vulnerable and he wanted more than anything to go to her, wrap his arms around her and assure her that it would all be okay.

Norah looked up then and her eyes met his. She seemed surprised to find him watching her and ducked her head in that shy girlish way that had always been her trademark. They had loved each other so deeply—like younger versions of their parents.

It wasn't the first time he'd thought about how it might be if they were to get back together. Ever since he'd seen them in Denver his thoughts had repeatedly drifted toward that fantasy. For surely that's all it was—all it could ever be after all this time.

Tom shook himself back to reality. The reality was that he had a law practice—one that employed several other people. Norah had her work—work that she was determined could make a real difference for others. She lived in Arizona. He lived in California. Normal, Wisconsin, was the past and no longer home for either of them. Ever pragmatic, Tom reminded himself that he was seeing everything through tinted glasses—lenses that filtered in the magic of the holidays plus the timely reminder that their parents—and they—were not getting any younger and clocks were ticking for all of them.

He looked down and saw that Norah had moved next to him. "Should we go back?" Norah was asking and at first Tom thought she might have read his mind. She had once been able to do that.

"Back?" *Could they? Was that even advisable?*

"To the house. Drop off our luggage and pick up some things that Mom needs?" She studied him and frowned. "Are you feeling all right, Tom?"

"Yeah. Sure." He moved a step away to avoid her hand raised to check his temperature as if he were Isabella. "Dad? Can we use the car?"

Both sets of parents burst out laughing.

"Have her home by ten," Earle instructed sternly, setting off yet another round of laughter among the four friends.

"I don't get it," Isabella said, then the light dawned. "Oh, like when they were dating?"

Norah gathered her jacket and purse. She looked up at Tom. "Ready?"

"It's a date," he replied, grinning mischievously.

"Cute."

Chapter Eleven

Norah's father came home two days later to a sidewalk and driveway completely clear of ice and snow and strict instructions from his doctor that shoveling—especially by hand—was no longer to be part of his chore assignment.

"What'd you do, Renie? Hire one of those plow services?" he asked his wife when he saw the driveway.

"Two nice young boys from the church youth group did the work and they charged a cup of hot cocoa and some of my peanut butter cookies," Norah's mom replied.

Earle had no response to that and slowly headed up the front walk to the house. But Irene was not finished with the topic. "Of course, there's still the issue of who will do the work going forward. Winter has just begun, you know."

"I know. I know," Earle grumbled.

"Well, no need to think about that right now," Tom said as he held the door open for Earle. "At least through the holidays you've got Isabella and me to handle that kind of thing."

Isabella made a face. "Dad!"

"Hey, it'll build character—not to mention muscles," Tom said and Earle chuckled for the first time since leaving the hospital. Norah could have hugged Tom and saw from her mother's expression that she wasn't the only one.

The phone was ringing when they got inside. "I'll get that," Irene said.

"Come on, Izzy," Norah said. "Let's start some lunch."

"Guess you get stuck talking to the invalid," Earle joked, looking up at Tom as he patted the chair next to him.

"We could play a game of chess," Tom suggested. "I'm a little rusty, but I think I still remember the moves." He took the chair opposite Tom's recliner. The chessboard was set for play on the coffee table between them.

From the kitchen hallway Norah watched her father ease himself into his chair, noting for the tenth time how his movements had become tentative and uncertain overnight. Tom caught her eye and she drew strength from his gaze—one that seemed to say, "It's all going to be okay."

"Thank you," she mouthed.

He smiled and turned his attention back to the chess game. "My first move, right?" he said as he slid a piece forward.

"Whoa!" Earle cried with delight. "You sure you want to start there?" And the game was on.

Over lunch, Irene reported that Eleanor had called to say that the women of the church had organized meals for the family for the coming week. "To give us time to catch our breath, according to Eleanor." Irene shook her head. "People can be so amazingly thoughtful."

The talk turned to preparations for the fast-approaching holiday.

"Fortunately I took care of my shopping before this little episode with my ticker," Earle reported with a wink. "But I could use some help with the wrapping." He turned to Norah and Isabella. "How are you girls at gift wrapping?"

"I'm kind of better at *un*wrapping," Isabella teased.

"We'll teach you," Norah and her father said at the same time and everyone laughed.

"We have to get a tree," Izzy said.

"Oh, darling, we should probably use the artificial tree this year, don't you think?" Irene asked.

"No," Norah said before Izzy could reply. "Let's have a real old-fashioned Christmas. You just leave everything to us."

"And Dad," Izzy added.

"At your service," Tom said with a mock salute to his daughter. He stood up. "Speaking of holiday preparations, I promised Mom I'd haul down the decorations from the attic. Thanks for lunch—and the chess game."

Under protest, Earle agreed to take a nap, while Norah and her mother cleared the lunch dishes and Isabella went upstairs to unpack and settle into her side of

Norah's childhood room. Norah found her there, sitting against the headboard of one of the twin beds, writing in her journal.

Norah knew better than to ask what Izzy was writing. The journal had been part of her assignments as she prepared to join the church. Its contents were for Izzy's eyes only—and God's, of course. For the entries—at least early on—they were to be written in the form of letters to God. That had been the minister's idea as he sought a way to bring the reality of faith into each teen's life.

"Sometimes the concept of prayer can be intimidating to a teen," he had explained to the parents. "A journal seems more in touch with their need to communicate with God." He'd laughed then and added, "If I could come up with a way they could text God via cell phone, I'd use that."

Norah unpacked the few clothes she'd grabbed before heading to the airport. As she pushed back the sliding mirrored doors of the closet, she saw several items of clothing that she had left behind when she and Tom were married. But this time she found that she wanted the memories those clothes might evoke—memories of her youth, of living here with her parents. She pulled out a madras plaid shirt, a pair of cuffed jeans—the wide leather belt still threaded through the loops. Next to that was the silver jersey wrap dress she'd worn the night Tom proposed.

"What's all that stuff?" Izzy asked, putting her journal aside and scrambling to the foot of the bed to watch Norah.

"Memories," Norah said as she burrowed into the far corner of the closet and brought out a double-breasted navy wool coat with fur trim at the cuffs and collar. She slid it off the wooden hangar and tried it on, belting the waist with the wool sash. "What do you think?" she asked as she pirouetted in front of the mirror on the open closet door.

"I think it's got fur trim," Izzy said and made a face. "You wore that?"

"It was my Sunday coat when I was in college." Norah reached onto the closet shelf and pulled down a hatbox. "Wait," she said and then squealed with delight as she pulled out a hat that matched the fur trim on the coat. She put it on and it slid down over her eyebrows. "I had long thick hair in those days," she explained.

"The coat's not terrible," Izzy announced as she surveyed the costume. "But that fur has to go. This is the twenty-first century, Mom. Hopefully we are slightly more enlightened?"

"Okay," Norah said as she replaced the hat in the box and took off the coat. "We'll remove the trim." She took a pair of scissors from a dresser drawer and started snipping threads. "Ta da!"

"Pretty cool," Izzy admitted. "Can I try it?"

"Sure."

They spent the rest of the afternoon trying on Norah's old clothes and rummaging through drawers to see what else Norah's mother had preserved. And there in the far back corner of a dresser drawer stuffed with old photo albums, yearbooks and long-forgotten term papers, Izzy found the prize.

"Ah ha!" she shouted triumphantly as she held aloft a small, green, leather-bound book with a gold-plated closure that locked and a tiny key dangling from a chain like a bookmark. "Your diary!" She hugged it to her chest.

"Hand it over," Norah said, grabbing for it and laughing.

"Do you think Grandma read it?" Izzy asked, dancing out of Norah's reach. "How could you leave your diary here?"

"I forgot it—didn't need it anymore." *Tom and I were married and that was all that mattered to me when I moved out of this room.* "Now give it up."

"Are you going to read it before you burn it?"

"Who says I'm going to burn it?"

"Must be some juicy stuff in here." Izzy mused. "I'll bet Dad would just love to know—"

"That's it." Norah dived for the book and they both ended up in a pile on the bed, laughing and gasping for air.

"Everything okay up there?" Earle shouted from the living room.

"Fine," Izzy and Norah shouted back in unison and then collapsed in a fresh fit of giggles.

"Well, some of the women from the church are coming up the front walk—looks like they're bringing enough to feed the neighborhood. You girls should come down and say hello," Irene called.

"Yes, ma'am," Norah and Izzy chorused.

"You girls?" Izzy whispered and fell back onto the bed laughing.

Norah took advantage of her daughter's distraction to grab Izzy's journal. "Trade you," she said.

"No fair," Izzy wailed, but she was still grinning as she handed over the diary that Norah took and stored inside the fur hat in the hatbox. "I know I can trust you but just to be sure," she said as she tied the ribbons of the hatbox into an intricate bow. "Now brush your hair and let's go make nice with the church ladies."

They had just finished supper when there was a light tap at the back door, and Isabella—now completely at home in her grandparents' house—ran to see who was there. "Dad!"

Then, as Tom entered the laundry room and wiped his feet, Izzy added, "Hey, it's snowing again."

Tom was wearing a black ski jacket that Norah remembered from their years of living in Normal along with a ridiculous pink and purple striped stocking cap. In his gloved hands he held three pairs of ice skates—one black men's pair and two pairs in the pristine white usually preferred by woman.

"Oh no, you don't," Norah said as soon as she saw the skates. "It's December. Is the ice on the pond even solid enough for skating?"

Tom grinned. "They've set up a new skating rink."

"That's right, Norah," her father said. "Just like the professionals. It's downtown in the square—they can freeze it in the winter and then in the summer use it for concerts. It's pretty slick." He grinned at his own joke.

Izzy groaned and then laughed. "You are so weird, Papa," she said and everyone knew it for the compliment that it was. "Where'd you get the skates?" she asked Tom, already removing her shoes. Tom had taught Isabella to skate almost before she could walk.

In those early years of their marriage they had returned to Normal every holiday. Only after the divorce did Norah begin to limit their visits to the summer months. Was that because the memories were too heartbreaking?

"Found them in the attic along with the Christmas decorations," Tom was explaining. "Try these. They're your Aunt Liz's. You might need an extra pair of socks though."

"I'll get a pair," Izzy said and took off.

"Bring an extra for your mother," Tom called as he handed the second pair of skates to Norah. "Seven and a half, right?"

"Right," Norah said, eyeing him suspiciously.

"Clare's an eight—thus, the need for double socks." He handed her the skates.

"All kidding aside," Norah began. "It's Dad's first night home and Mom's exhausted and—"

"And if you weren't here it would be your father's first night home and I would still be tired and we would both settle in to watch our shows and then go to bed," Irene said.

"Your mother's right. You'll do me no favors treating me like a sick old man. Go on. It'll be good for the kid—all that fresh air."

At that moment Izzy came bounding down the stairs and back into the kitchen. She tossed one pair of rolled socks to Norah and sat down and began putting on the second pair. Tom knelt like a shoe salesman and helped her work her foot into one skate.

"How's that feel?" he asked.

"Tight, but I'll get used to it," Izzy said, pulling off the skate and tying the long laces together. She put on her regular shoes then stood and slung the skates over one shoulder. "How do I look?"

"Pretty as one of those Olympic stars," her grandfather said.

"Come on, Mom," she called, heading to the laundry room to get coats, hats and gloves for them both. "It'll be fun."

"I can see that I'm outnumbered," Norah said as she looked at her parents and Tom.

"Yep," her father said. "Might as well face the music."

They walked the short distance to town. Isabella danced ahead of them catching fat snowflakes on her tongue. Norah filled the space between them with chatter about the church ladies and former schoolmates they had both known. Tom let her talk, knowing it was nerves. What he didn't know was whether her anxious chatter was the product of her fear of skating or—like his—the challenge of separating the life they had once shared here from the separate lives they now lived.

"There's your house," he said. He nodded toward a large Victorian structure that sat on the corner overlooking the square. When they were teenagers the house had been owned by the mayor and his large family. It was always alive with lights in every room in the evenings or with children and dogs rushing in and out during the day. Now it was dark and forlorn, badly in need of paint and repair.

"It looks so sad," Norah said, pausing to look at it. "It's been for sale since the last time I was here. I would have thought someone would have bought it by now. It just needs some TLC."

Tom chuckled. "A *lot* of TLC."

"Why do you think it hasn't sold?" she asked as they pressed on toward the lights and music of the rink.

"According to Dad the recession has hit the town hard. Another plant closed last fall. And the population of the town is aging as younger families move on to other places. That house would be a lot to take on even if it were in great condition."

Norah looked back at it and Tom saw by her expression that she was remembering it the way it had been. "Remember how they used to light that big tree with those little white lights every December?"

"I remember that you used to say that if you owned that house, you'd trim that tree in red, white and blue lights for the Fourth of July. Then as I recall the plan was to take out the blue and use the red and white for Christmas."

"And then take out the white and leave the red for Valentine's," Norah said wistfully.

"Mom! Dad! Come on," Isabella called, already seated on a bench and putting on her skates.

"No guts. No glory," Tom said as he placed his hand on Norah's waist and steered her toward the rink.

Within minutes Isabella had attracted the attention of

a group of teens near her age and soon the others were helping her get acclimated to the rhythm of the sport, their laughter like music on the cold night air. Norah envied their ease and spontaneity as they skated to the center of the large makeshift pond.

"Like riding a bicycle," Tom said, watching them as well. "Remember the first time we went skating?" he asked as the two of them glided slowly around the perimeter of the pond.

Norah laughed. "I thought you were going to dump me right then and there, but you were so patient—and I was so…tentative."

"You were a basket case," Tom corrected. "Never in a million years would I ever have guessed that tough little Norah Jenkins might have a hidden phobia about falling down. I mean that was it, wasn't it? It wasn't the ice or the skating per se. It was about not wanting to fall down."

Norah bristled slightly. "Well, people do have their quirks. That was—is mine."

"Is? You mean you never got over it? You were what? Bella's age?"

"I was fifteen and no, I don't believe that you simply outgrow something like that." She eyed the railing that surrounded the pond and saw that he had started to lead them far enough away that it was out of reach. She tightened her grip on his hands.

"Ow!"

"Sorry," she said, glancing at the receding shore that was solid ground and the security of the railing. "We're getting a little far out."

"We're two feet from the edge and the ice is better here—smoother." She could sense him watching her, felt his arm tighten around her waist. "I'm not going to let you fall, Norah," he promised. "Just trust me, okay?"

There was an edge to his tone. The matter of trust—or the lack thereof on her part—had been a major factor in their divorce. "I am doing what I believe is necessary to secure the future for us and our children," he would argue when she challenged his long hours at work, his absence from home and all the benchmarks of Isabella's first years that he had missed. "You need to trust me on that," he would add.

And Norah would flinch at the implication that he knew what was best for her—the same way she had flinched if anyone suggested such an idea. After their divorce she was the one who had thrown herself into work, telling herself that it was vital that she build a secure career, a secure financial base for her life with Isabella. Not that she ever doubted that Tom would be there for their daughter. He had college covered by the time Izzy was seven. But Norah had been determined to make her way, provide for her child....

"Better?" Tom asked now as they started their second lap around the pond.

Norah nodded and forced herself to relax. But the minute she did, her ankle buckled and she started to fall.

"Got you," Tom assured her, hauling her upright.

"This can't be much fun for you," she said. "Why don't I sit over there and you go get Isabella and skate with her?"

Tom glanced to the center of the ring where Isabella

was obviously having a great time with her newfound friends. "I'll make you a deal," he said. "Go one more round with me and I'll buy you hot chocolate and we'll both sit on the sidelines with the rest of the old folks."

"I'm not old," Norah sniffed.

"Do we have a deal or not?"

"Does the hot chocolate come with marshmallows?"

Tom's laugh was filled with pure merriment. It rang across the pond and Norah saw Izzy glance their way and smile. "Come on," he said. "Longer strides—not those short little baby steps. No wonder you fall down. Glide. Glide. Glide. That's better."

Norah could not deny the pure pleasure of sailing along as if her feet had sprouted wings. She closed her eyes and visualized the grace and beauty of the skaters she'd watched on television. "Don't let go," she begged as she concentrated on following Tom's rhythm.

"Right here, Norah."

There was something in the way he said those words that made Norah open her eyes and look up at him. She searched his face for some underlying meaning, but just then he pulled her closer and spun slowly around. Once again she stiffened and stumbled. This time she fell against his hard chest and felt his arms tighten around her as he lifted her just enough so that her skates were off the ice. "Home base," he said quietly, nodding toward the warming house with the promised hot chocolate.

"Oh. Well, good," she said. "Put me down. I can make it from here."

"And risk having you turn an ankle three days before

Christmas? I don't think so," he replied as he scooped her into his arms and glided to the edge.

Over his shoulder Norah saw Izzy headed their way. "Put me down," she urged. "Izzy's coming and she'll take this the wrong way."

Tom shrugged. "She's already seen what she wants to see—no changing that." But he set Norah on the end of a bench and turned to greet their daughter. "Hey, kiddo, I was just getting your mom some hot chocolate. Want some?"

"With marshmallows?"

Tom laughed. "Like mother like daughter. No promises, but I'll ask."

While Tom headed for the warming house, Izzy plopped down next to Norah. "Looked like you and Dad were having fun," she commented, her eyes focused on the other teens.

"I almost fell and your dad was helping me and—"

"Whatever," Izzy replied, dismissing Norah's feeble attempts to explain. "Guess what?" Her eyes brightened and she turned to face Norah directly. "No, I'll wait until Dad comes. I've got a surprise for you both."

"Who are your new friends?"

"You remember Darcy and Heather. They're the sisters who live on the block behind Grandma and Papa. I met them last year at church."

"Oh, that's right. Their mother is the artist, right?"

"And their dad owns the hardware store."

"Hot chocolate with marshmallows," Tom announced as he distributed the steaming cardboard cups.

"Izzy was just telling me about her new friends," Norah said. "And I believe she has some news to share."

Tom sat down on the other side of Isabella and blew on his hot chocolate. "Good news?"

"Good for me—not so good for Darcy and Heather's friend." She glanced from side to side, then stood up and moved to the end of the bench, forcing Norah to slide closer to Tom. "I feel like I'm at a tennis match," she muttered. "There. That's better. Now I can look at you both at the same time." She gave them an innocent grin.

Norah gave her a look of warning that shouted *Stop matchmaking!* which Izzy ignored.

"So the girl who was to play Mary in the church's Christmas Eve pageant fell while skating a couple of days ago. She broke her ankle and banged up her face some. She'll be fine but not by Christmas Eve, so Darcy and Heather asked me if I would do it."

"Do what?" Tom asked.

"Play Mary. Of course, I'd have to rehearse pretty much all day tomorrow, which sort of messes up helping Papa wrap his presents but—"

"I think it's wonderful," Norah interrupted her. "I can help Papa. It'll be like old times—like when I was a kid."

"Dad? Okay?"

Tom set down his cup and held out his arms to her. "It's better than okay. It's great," he said.

"Cool," Izzy said as she buried her face against Tom's shoulder and then pushed away and headed back out onto the ice. "It's a go," she shouted and the teens waiting for her cheered. Izzy turned back. "Oh, and how about I walk home from here with Darcy and Heather? I mean, unless you two want to hang around."

"Nine o'clock curfew," Norah instructed.

"Oh, Mom," Izzy moaned. "Nine-thirty?" she bargained, her eyes shifting to Tom.

"Nine," Tom said firmly.

Once again Tom noticed that Norah was unusually talkative on the way home. She chattered on about everything from how great the new ice rink was for the teens in town, to how much she had always liked Darcy and Heather's parents, to the need to pick up wrapping paper and ribbon the following morning.

"Dad always wants his gifts for Mom to be wrapped in a special way, so it's important to give him a lot of options," she explained as if Tom had questioned the need for more gift wrap.

It dawned on him that she was nervous. And if she was nervous, didn't that mean that maybe she was experiencing some of the same feelings he was? Feelings that perhaps they'd been given this opportunity to take a step back and reexamine past decisions?

Past decisions? Like what?

Tom dismissed the thought as part of the nostalgia of the season and being back in the town where they'd grown up—and fallen in love. He shook off the thought and tried to concentrate on Norah's chatter, but she had fallen silent.

"Look," she said, her voice low as she pointed to the old Victorian house. "Somebody's coming down the front walk."

"That's Keith Olsen, Darcy's dad," Tom said as he picked up the pace. "Keith! Tom Wallace," he said, offering his hand.

"Hey, good to have you home," Keith said, nodding to Norah.

"Are you thinking of buying the mayor's house?" Norah asked, calling the property by the name given to it in its heyday.

Keith laughed. "No. I just check on it now for the bank to make sure there's no broken pipes or vandalism." He glanced back at the dark house. "It's a pity it hasn't sold. Good bones on this one," he observed.

"Can we see it?" Tom asked. *Now where had that come from? He wasn't in the market for a house—certainly not a house in Normal, Wisconsin.* "Not that I'm in the market. It's just I've never been inside and it was a landmark even when we were kids."

"Sure." Keith handed him the key and a large flashlight. "Just lock up when you leave. You can drop the key and light off at the hardware store tomorrow—coffee's always on."

Chapter Twelve

"I don't believe you did that," Norah said, but her voice was filled with excitement and wonder as they climbed the front stairs to the wraparound porch and the worn front door with its panels of etched glass to either side.

"You don't have to come," he teased.

"Try and keep me out." She held the flashlight while Tom worked the key in the lock and pushed open the door. "Oh, wow!" she whispered reverently as she scanned the light over the broad curved stairway and the wide front foyer.

"They've kept it in good shape," Tom observed. "I would have expected cobwebs and dust bunnies to have taken over by now." He walked across the hall to the double pocket doors that led into the front parlor and pushed them apart.

"Look at that fireplace," Norah said, shining the light over the decorative tiles that bordered the opening. "And those windows," she added as the moonlight reflecting off the snow spotlighted the large triple window capped by stained-glass panels. The room ran the length of one side of the house. "You could have a television area at one end and a reading and conversation area there," Norah said, mentally arranging furniture.

"Floors need refinishing," Tom observed as he led the way back across the hall to the dining room with its built-in china cabinet, and on to the butler's pantry and the ancient but charming kitchen.

"Look at this," Norah squealed, having made her way back to the front hall. She was standing in a small room to one side of the front door.

"Coat closet?" Tom guessed.

"Ladies' powder room."

"No men allowed?"

"Well, look at it." Norah flashed the light over the wallpaper trimmed with pink roses, the plaster cherubs mounted above the pedestal sink and the ruffled lace skirt of the dressing table.

"You've got a point." He stepped back into the hall and opened a door on the opposite side of the front door. "Ah, separate accommodations," he announced and Norah hurried over to see the men's cloak room complete with wallpaper that featured hunting scenes and furnishings that were decidedly masculine. "Want to go upstairs?"

Four large bedrooms and two bathrooms surrounded the center stairway that continued on to the third floor where they found a large ballroom and three small bed-rooms, plus a tiny bathroom near the back stairs that led back down to the kitchen. "Servants?" Norah marveled. "In Normal?"

"It's a big house," Tom observed. "And the mayor and his wife had, what—eight children?"

They walked back down the front stairs, their footsteps silenced by the Oriental runner anchored on each tread with a brass rod. Outside, Norah waited for Tom to lock the door and check to be sure it was secure, then she switched off the flashlight. "That was a real treat," she said. "Thank you."

"If you could buy that place what would you do with it?"

"Oh, I would have—"

"Not when you were a kid. Now." He couldn't imagine why it was important to make the distinction. They were dreaming, after all and weren't the dreams of their youth really all they had when it came to being in this town again?

"I would live in it—with Izzy," Norah replied quietly.

Tom tried to read her expression, but her features were in shadow. "You always missed living here, didn't you? I mean even before we—that is, before we decided to split up."

"Just a small-town girl," Norah said with a laugh. "That's me." They walked along in silence and then she added, "Seriously, though, I did think about moving back after you left, but I had a good job and you'd made sure we had a house."

Tom bristled at her assumption that he was the one who had left—abandoned the marriage and his daughter. He reminded himself that she had credited him with providing them a place to live, but still the unconscious accusation hurt. "I didn't want to leave," he said quietly.

Norah looked up at him. "Oh, Tom, I didn't mean it that way. Of course you didn't. We just—well, it was a two-way street, right?"

"Would you come back here now?" he asked.

"I've been thinking about it," she admitted. "Dad's heart attack was a kind of wake-up call. Even if they're doing all right now, down the road, they might need more help—more care."

"What about applying for the director's job?"

She shrugged. "I never handed in the application. It's still on my desk. Depending on who they hire, I might not even have a job."

"You know better than that."

"And I have to think about Izzy," she continued as if he hadn't spoken. "She's an Arizona girl. Her friends are there and she's gotten so involved with the church."

"She's thirteen. You need to think about what you want—what you need to be happy."

"I'm happy," Norah protested as they reached her parents' house.

No, you're not really, he thought to himself. He watched Norah go up the porch steps and into the house. *And neither am I.*

The following morning Isabella was up and out early.

"Went to meet the other kids at the church," Irene said when Norah came down for breakfast. "Isn't it wonderful that they've included her in the pageant?"

"It is," Norah agreed. "How's Dad?"

"Dad is fine," Earle boomed from the hallway. "Wondering if he might find an elf around here to help with some wrapping today."

"At your service," Norah said, giving him a bow.

"I could help," Irene offered with a wink at Norah. "But I have some last-minute shopping to do."

"Good," Earle replied. "Do you good to get out of here. You've been hovering like a mother hen ever since I got home from the hospital."

"I'll be here," Norah assured her mother. "You go ahead."

Earle rolled his eyes. "Now let's get one thing straight, Norah. You are helping me wrap presents—not playing nursemaid."

"Got it."

"How was the ice-skating?" Irene asked.

"Oh, Izzy had a lovely time."

"Your mother didn't ask about Isabella," her father said.

"It was fun."

"Did Tom walk you home?"

Norah burst out laughing. "How come suddenly I feel as if we've done a time travel thing and I'm back in high school?"

"It was just a question," Irene huffed as she got up to get more coffee.

"Yes, Mom. Tom and I walked back together and Isabella came later with her friends." She picked at her toast and added. "We ran into Keith Olsen. He was checking the mayor's house."

"That white elephant has been on the market for well

over a year," her mother said, shaking her head. "It's so sad. None of the heirs want the place and there it sits, getting older and more decrepit every day."

"Like us," Earle joked.

"It's not so bad," Norah said and did not miss the way her parents glanced at each other across the breakfast table. "I mean it's well-built and the rooms are so large and lovely. I always loved that house."

"You looked at it?"

"Yeah. Keith let us borrow a flashlight. I'd never been inside."

"You and Tom?"

Norah's head shot up as she realized the thoughts that must be running through her parents' minds. "Now don't go getting the wrong idea. It was pure serendipity."

"If you say so," Earle muttered, but Norah saw him grin at her mother.

"So, Dad, how about we work on getting those gifts wrapped?" Norah didn't wait for an answer as she hurried up the stairs to gather paper, ribbon and trims for the gift-wrapping project. *It was serendipity. Pure coincidence.*

But, oh, what a lovely coincidence it had been. Long after Isabella was asleep, Norah had toured the old house once more in her mind. Room by room she had imagined—as she had when she was a teen—what it might be like to actually live there.

On his way to return the flashlight and keys to Keith at the hardware store, Tom took a real look at his hometown and what he saw was a town redefining itself.

Most of his visits to Normal had been brief and if he got into town it was to run errands for his mom. But the unexpected opportunity to have a look inside the mayor's old house had triggered his curiosity.

True, there were still too many vacant storefronts on Main Street and the factory that had been the town's primary employer when he and Norah were growing up had shut down. But other than the mayor's house and one or two others, the homes were occupied, well-tended and not for sale.

He walked past the high school—boarded up and deserted ever since students from Normal had transferred to a larger consolidated high school several miles away. But a large sign in front of the school told of the coming of a trade school and education center in the spring. Everywhere he turned it seemed as if the community was gearing up for rebirth.

Main Street bustled as merchants swept drifted snow away from their front doors, freshened holiday window displays or headed to the post office to pick up the morning mail. He shook off the cold as he pulled open the door to the hardware store. An old-fashioned bell jangled.

"Be right there," Keith called from somewhere in the back.

The heavy door to the loading dock slid shut. "Hey, Tom," Keith called.

"Brought back the key and flashlight."

"Come on back. I was just going to have a cup of tea. There's the promised coffee, but Meredith's got me drinking this green tea. She's gone all healthy on me," he said with a laugh. "Great having you home, Tom," he added.

Normal will always be home. Norah had said that to him more than once in the days when he'd been determined to move them all to California. "Not Arizona," she'd declared, "and certainly not La La Land. That is not who we are, Tom Wallace."

But is it who we have become? He accepted a mug of tea and sat down to visit with Keith. "Town seems to be humming. Is it the holidays or is this normal for Normal?"

"Business has started to pick up. I have to tell you, when the plant closed we all thought we were going to have to go to work for one of the monster stores out near the freeway."

"What happened?"

Keith shrugged. "Some of us got together. Meredith is an artist, you know, and she and some of her colleagues got together and rented space in the old railroad station. They renovated the place and set up galleries and studios there. It's become quite a draw. Then there's the bike trail slash cross-country ski trail. Brings folks into town." He glanced around. "Of course, we've got a ways to go yet, but it's a good time to be living here."

A customer came in and Keith excused himself. Tom sipped his tea and listened to the exchange between Keith and his customer, the sound of someone calling out to a neighbor from the street, the honk of a car horn that sounded more friendly than irritated as it would have in California. Everything about the place throbbed with possibility.

Keith's words echoed through Tom's mind as he picked out some new lights for the tree at his parents' house and added a special ornament for his mom.

"Ever think about coming back?" Keith asked as he rang up the sale.

"Haven't you ever heard the old adage about not being able to go home again?"

Keith handed him his receipt. "That's just a book title. The town could use a good lawyer—and social workers are always in demand," he added.

"Norah and I are..."

Keith shrugged. "It's not like they carve divorce papers in stone, you know. Every couple goes through rough patches. You and Norah—well, everybody was stunned to hear you two had split up."

Made for each other. That's how the locals used to talk about them. "Me too," Tom muttered and realized Keith had heard him.

"Like I said, nothing's carved in stone."

That idea stayed with Tom as he helped his Dad set the large Douglas fir into the stand and position it in front of the bay window.

"They're here," his mom called from the hall and hurried to open the front door to welcome Isabella, Norah and her parents.

For all the years that their parents had been friends they had shared the tradition of trimming each other's trees together. In fact Tom had proposed to Norah one night after they had trimmed the tree at her house and they had shared the news the following night when everyone was gathered at his house. There had been so many shared moments like that. How many more were they likely to have? Earle's heart attack had been more than a health scare—it had been a real wake-up call for all of them.

He watched as his dad hugged Bella and then Norah, saw his mom wrap her arm around Bella's shoulder and lead her toward the kitchen. Heard Norah's parents protest that they couldn't possibly eat another bite having just finished supper as they followed his parents down the hall. And there was Norah. She was standing uncertainly in the doorway looking at the giant tree.

"Wow!"

"Yeah," Tom replied. "Can we say overkill? We already had to cut six inches off the bottom, but Mom was adamant that this was the one."

"It's beautiful and smells fabulous. Like—well, like Christmas," she said, laughing as she ventured farther into the room.

"Help me get these lights on it. I want to surprise Mom," Tom said as he unwrapped the packages he bought from Keith.

"Oh, look at them. Snowmen and candles and—oh, this one is wonderful. Little trees and poinsettias."

"Keith had a good selection." *Good time to be living here. Nothing's carved in stone. Made for each other.* Tom plugged in the lights and started draping them on the tree. "Do you ever think about coming back here—to stay, Norah?"

"I hadn't until...."

"Yeah, your dad has always seemed indestructible to me."

"I think about being their only child—I mean your folks have you and your sisters, but…"

"Oh, Tommy!" Eleanor squealed. "What lovely lights!"

Just before noon on Christmas Eve Isabella kicked off her boots on the mat in the laundry room and shrugged out of her ski jacket, scarf and mittens. "Mom?" She spotted a folded note on the kitchen table.

Gone with Grandma to help decorate the church. Papa is napping. Lunch in the fridge. Love, Mom

The phone rang and she hurried to grab it before it could wake her grandfather. "Hello?"

"Isabella? Is that you?" Stan Morrison's gravelly voice was unmistakable and usually welcomed, but Isabella had the strangest feeling she wasn't going to like what he had to say.

"Hi, Dr. Morrison."

"How's everything up there in the north woods? Have you got a white Christmas?"

"Fine. Yes. Mom's not here."

"Oh, well, ask her to give me a call, would you?"

"Could I take a message?"

"Sure. Let her know we found her application. I guess in all the trauma of hearing about her dad—how is he anyway?"

"He's doing just fine, thank you," Isabella said, her mind racing with the fact that in spite of her mother, the application had been found. What did that mean?

"That's good. Well, might as well say this outright—kind of an early Christmas present. Let her know we've considered the applications—all of them—and the job is hers if she wants it. We're going to close up early since it's Christmas Eve, but I'll be at home. Have her call me, okay?"

"Yes, sir. Thank you."

"Merry Christmas, Isabella."

"Happy New Year," Isabella added automatically before placing the phone back on its charger. Her lunch forgotten, she paced the downstairs of the house. She paused in front of the tree that they had all decorated the night before, just after doing the same thing at her other grandparents'. What a fun day it had been. So filled with memories and stories triggered by the ornaments—stories about her dad as a boy, her mom when she was Isabella's age, the two of them the year they got engaged and Isabella's first Christmas. And best of all had been the way her parents and grandparents had all laughed together and teased each other—like a real family.

Her cell rang and Isabella grabbed it.

"Hey," Darcy said without preamble. "Heather and I are going to town for some last-minute shopping. Wanna come?"

She could tell her Mom about the call later. "Sure."

"Fifteen minutes," Darcy replied and rang off.

The church was electric with anticipation, from the children gathered in the hallway behind the altar to parents, friends and neighbors crowded into the pews.

Angel wings got caught on shepherds' crooks while mothers tied bathrobes and straightened foil-covered cardboard crowns. It was Christmas Eve in Normal, Wisconsin, and a tradition that went back to before Norah was born was about to begin—the annual reenactment of the Nativity story.

Isabella peeked out from behind the burlap backdrop that served as the stable. "There's Dad," she said excitedly, "and the grands—all sitting together. They've saved you a seat on the end," she told Norah. "Right next to Dad," she added with a mischievous grin.

"I brought you something," Norah said, ignoring her daughter's last comment. She unfolded a woven rose-colored shawl as light as air as she floated it up and over Izzy's long hair. "Your grandmother and I thought this would be exactly what Mary might choose," she explained as she arranged one end over Izzy's shoulder and then adjusted the edges to frame Izzy's face.

"Oh, Mom, it's beautiful," Izzy exclaimed. "Darcy, look," she called to her friend who was going over her part as narrator for the evening's performance.

"Perfect," Darcy said.

"Thanks, Mom. I love it." She threw her arms around Norah and added, "I love you."

"Places!" Darcy's mom called and Norah gave Izzy a final squeeze and sent her on her way.

The Christmas Eve service was a wonderful symphony of all that reminded worshippers of life's true blessings. The children—some of them not more than four or five years old—played their parts to perfection. Darcy was the perfect narrator, her strong precise voice giving fresh interpretation to the timeless scripture. But when Izzy came down the aisle, Norah heard Tom's breath catch and she knew that he was probably thinking the same thing she was. Their daughter was growing up, evolving into a lovely young woman and in the blink of an eye they might find themselves in a church somewhere watching her come down another aisle toward a young man waiting at the altar.

It seemed the most natural thing in the world to slide her hand into Tom's as they stood beside each other singing an old carol while Izzy took her place at the altar and gently laid a doll in the manger. The pageant played out and the service moved on to its final moments—the lighting of the candles everyone had been given upon their arrival. At the far end of their pew the usher lit Eleanor's candle. She turned to Tom's father and he in turn lit Irene's and so it went until it was Tom who turned to Norah. He steadied her hand as he bent the flame of his lighted candle to hers.

And when she looked up and into Tom's eyes, Norah felt a kind of peace come over her, a sense that in this moment her life had taken a turn for the better. They would be all right. Whatever the future held, they were once again the friends they had been from the first day they had met at this very church. It was that friendship she had missed most of all, that one person she knew she could go to with anything—no matter how ridiculous or far-fetched it might seem.

There was a short reception following the service before everyone headed home to enjoy the rest of Christmas Eve with family and close friends. Norah couldn't help noticing how quiet Isabella became on the ride home.

"Are you feeling all right, Izzy?"

"Sure."

The smile was too bright, the single word answer way too chipper. Norah placed the back of her hand on Izzy's cheek. No obvious fever. "You did a terrific job tonight."

"Thanks."

"Best Mary I've ever seen and I've been going to that pageant for over fifty years," Norah's dad assured her.

"Oh, Papa, I bet you said the same thing when Mom played Mary."

Her grandmother laughed. "She knows you too well, Earle."

"Can we open a present tonight?" Izzy asked as they pulled into the garage.

"It's tradition," Irene said. "But first we need to put out some milk and cookies for Santa and some carrots for his reindeer."

"Oh, Grandma," Izzy giggled.

"What? You don't believe in Santa?" Papa said. "You do realize that those who stop believing no longer get presents?"

"I believe. I believe," Izzy shouted as they all crowded into the laundry room to remove their outer garments and boots.

They were just opening the traditional one present—the ones from Norah's Aunt Helen who lived in Florida—when there was a knock at the back door.

"Just me," Tom called.

"Too bad," Earle replied. "We had our hearts set on Santa being early."

"Well, I brought a few more packages for under the tree."

"For me?" Izzy squealed as she took the gift-wrapped boxes from him and examined the tags. "Ooh, Mom, this one's for you." She held up a box and rattled it vigorously.

"Stop that," Norah said, but she was laughing as she took the package and shook it gently. "Something to wear," she guessed.

"Who's it from?" Izzy asked, her eyes on her father.

"To Norah, Love Eleanor and Dan," Norah quoted. "Ah, that's so nice." She placed the package under the tree, then relieved Izzy of the rest of the gifts and added them to the pile. "You, young lady, have had a very full couple of days. Time for bed."

"Dad?"

"You heard your mother. Hey, how about having an early breakfast with me in the morning and letting these old folks sleep in?"

"Can Mom come?"

"No, you go with your dad. It'll be fun—a new tradition," Norah hurried to say. The truth was that there had already been so much togetherness that she was very afraid that Izzy's dreams of a true reconciliation were working overtime. Besides, she still wanted to talk to Izzy about the possibility of them moving permanently to Normal.

Tom studied Norah for a second, then grinned at Isabella. “Like I said, let’s let the old folks sleep in. Just you and me, kid.”

“Okay. Eight?”

“Seven,” Tom said and everyone laughed when Isabella groaned. “Best time,” he assured her.

“Then I’m going to bed,” she announced. “Merry Christmas—” she paused on the stairway and raised one hand dramatically “—and God bless us, every one.”

“Well, speaking of bedtime,” Irene said, “Earle, it’s well past yours. We’ve got a busy day tomorrow.” She flicked her eyes toward Tom and Norah.

Earle yawned and stretched. “Be sure you turn out the tree lights, Norah.”

“Good night,” Norah and Tom said in unison.

Left alone with Tom, Norah was suddenly shy. “Sorry about that. Everyone seems to be matchmaking these days.”

“They mean well,” Tom said. He stood in front of the tree for a long moment while Norah scurried about, clearing away the wrappings from the gifts the family had opened earlier. “Well, I’d better let you get some rest as well.”

“Do you have a minute?” Norah asked.

Tom looked taken aback but pleased. He took a seat on the sofa that faced the tree and patted the space beside him. “I always have time for you, Norah.”

She perched on the edge of the sofa and pressed her fingers over the fabric of a throw pillow. “I don’t know where to start,” she said with a nervous laugh.

“Can’t help you there. What’s this about?”

She looked at him. “It’s about something Dad said

about me marking time ever since—well, for a while now." She took a deep breath and plunged in. "Tom, what would you think about the idea of Izzy and me moving back here—to Normal?"

"I'd start by asking you why you might do that," he answered, his eyes riveted on hers.

Norah stood and paced the small area between the sofa and the tree, pausing every now and then to reposition an ornament or light. "It's a terrible idea, right? I mean, I have a good job in Arizona and a house and Izzy has her friends and her life there. I mean, what would I do here?"

"Okay, you've given me reasons why not to do it. What about the other side of the argument?"

"Once a lawyer," she murmured and Tom shrugged. "First, there's Mom and Dad."

"Get back to what Earle said—about 'marking time.'"

"He struck a chord," Norah admitted. "After—when you and I—went our separate ways, all of my energy was focused on Isabella. Making sure she was happy. Making sure things stayed as normal as possible for her. And even after time passed and she moved on—I didn't."

"What about your work? That's important."

"It's not what it was. The focus changed. My role in it changed. I went there to make a real difference, but lately—"

"That was Luke's doing. He's gone now. Maybe when the new person takes over—"

Norah shrugged and turned back to the tree.

"What else?"

"Izzy," Norah replied. "How can I expect her to just pull up stakes and move here? Normal is my hometown, not hers."

"Maybe you should ask her how she'd feel about it," Tom suggested.

"Would you? I mean, would you feel her out maybe tomorrow when you two have breakfast? Just raise a what-if situation? Then if she was totally turned off, I'd have my answer."

"And based on that you'd go back to Arizona to a job that no longer inspires you? And what about Irene and Earle?"

Norah sighed. "I know. Maybe I could get them to move to Phoenix." She saw by Tom's expression that such an idea didn't even merit a comment. She collapsed back onto the sofa, hugging the throw pillow to her.

"Hey," Tom said, gently removing the pillow and putting his arm around her shoulders. "Let's not get the sleigh before the reindeer here. Let me feel out Bella in the morning and then you can decide your next step."

Norah sighed with relief and allowed her head to drop onto Tom's shoulder. "Thank you," she murmured.

"Want to know what I think?" he asked, tightening his hold on her.

Norah looked up at him and nodded.

"I think it's a good idea," he whispered and kissed her forehead.

"You have no idea what that means to me," she said and curled her feet under her as she snuggled more securely into the curve of his arm. "This has been a good Christmas, Tom."

"It's not over yet," he reminded her with a chuckle.

Suddenly she sat up. "You didn't get me anything, did you? I mean ever since we—since the divorce—we've never—you didn't?"

Tom shrugged. "Seems like we're moving on to a new plateau. I thought a gift was a good marker for that."

"But I didn't get anything for you and now it's after midnight and all the stores are closed and—"

Tom touched a finger to her lips. "You have given me your trust," he said.

"You always had that. Well, maybe not *always,* but certainly when it comes to Izzy."

"Okay, then. Just remember you're the one with the need to match me gift for gift," he said and before she could respond, he leaned over and kissed her.

Not just a holiday peck on the lips, but he pulled her into his arms and kissed her with all of the passion they had shared as teenagers. A kiss that left her stunned, breathless and wanting more.

"There," he said, setting her gently away from him and standing. "Now we're even."

She blinked up at him as he reached under the tree and handed her a heavy shoebox-sized package. "My present to you," he said. "Afraid it doesn't quite measure up to that kiss, but as you used to say 'it's not a contest,' so Merry Christmas."

He waited while she opened it. Inside was a pair of ice skates with double blades—the kind children wear when learning to skate. "Got you the training wheels model," he said with a grin.

Norah laughed. "They're perfect. Thank you."

He held out his hand to her and she walked with him to the door. "Be sure Bella is up for our breakfast," he said. "I'll talk to her."

Norah nodded and pulled open the front door. "Thanks, Tom—for everything." She stood on tiptoe and kissed his cheek and when he looked surprised, she indicated the sprig of fresh mistletoe her mother had hung over the doorway. "Merry Christmas," she called as he headed down the front walk. "I…"

Tom turned and looked back at her, but she waved him away and closed the door. She leaned against the door and realized that she had almost added, "I love you."

Chapter Thirteen

Isabella barely slept. If she had been younger and still believed in the magic of Santa and his reindeer, her insomnia might be understandable. The truth was that Darcy's invite to go shopping had given her all the excuse she needed to put the call from Dr. Morrison out of her mind. Of course, she had remembered it several times through the evening but convinced herself the timing wasn't right to blurt out that her mother had been offered the director's job.

Face it, she thought as she pulled on jeans, a bulky turtleneck sweater sent by Aunt Helen and heavy socks, *you found every reason not to tell her.* She glanced at the other twin bed where her mother was sleeping, her mouth slightly open, her eyelids twitching with dreams. *You don't want to tell her because that would mean it's all decided. You and Mom will go back to Phoenix and Dad will go back to California, and maybe by the time you get out of high school, the two of them will finally realize they were meant for each other.*

She tiptoed to the door and slowly turned the knob. The smell of fresh brewed coffee wafted up the stairs and she heard her father's familiar laughter and the clatter of a spoon in a ceramic mug. It was so good being here—almost like being a real family again. Sometimes with just Mom and her in Arizona, it seemed really lonely.

"Merry Christmas," she said as she entered the kitchen and kissed her grandmother's cheek. Grandma was still in her bathrobe—last year's model—and slippers, but Isabella's dad was dressed for the snowy morning.

"Ready?" he said as he drained the last of his coffee.

"Sure, but nothing's open, so maybe Grandma's oatmeal wouldn't be terrible. I mean, it would be great," she amended, seeing her grandmother's look of mock offense.

"Nope. You'll have to settle for day-old bagels and a thermos of hot chocolate. We're going on a breakfast picnic."

"Uh, Dad, it's like freezing out there?"

"So bundle up." He kissed Irene's cheek. "I'll have her back by nine," he promised.

"Take your time," she said. "Have fun."

Tom pulled an extra wool scarf off a hook in the back hall and wrapped it several times around Isabella's neck until it covered her chin, then he plopped an old knitted toboggan on her head.

"Dad!" Isabella protested, "I look like a dork."

"This is not a fashion moment," he declared and

pulled open the back door. "Your chariot awaits," he added, pointing to a large sled.

Isabella giggled as she sat on the sled and pulled the blanket Tom handed her over her legs and knees. "Mush!" she cried.

Tom picked up the sled rope and pulled her across the yard and on into the woods behind her grandparents' house. "Oops," he said as they came to an open space that overlooked a frozen pond below. "Here's the dilemma," he announced scratching his head as if he hadn't set up this whole thing. "Breakfast is down there and we're up here and I don't know about you but I am starving. If only there were some way to get down there faster."

"Oh, Dad, do not pretend you didn't plan this whole thing. Come on." She scooted forward and wrapped the blanket around her shoulders as Tom positioned the sled on the brink of the hill. Then he climbed on behind her, pulled her tight against himself.

"Ready?"

"Set! Go!" Isabella cried raising her arms high and shouting with joy as they flew down the hill.

The sled came to a stop several feet from the edge of the pond and a rattan picnic basket. "Breakfast is served, my lady." He pulled out the thermos, two cups, cloth napkins, and bagels sandwiched around cream cheese and Grandma Eleanor's famous peach jam.

"Heavenly," Isabella sighed as she took the first bite.

They sat straddling the ends of the sled using the middle as a table between them. "So, talk to me," her dad said.

"About?"

"Whatever's on your mind—Christmas, the pageant last night, your mom, whatever."

Isabella felt her throat tighten. "Can't we just enjoy the morning?" she said quietly and feigned an interest in the silent woods in the distance. Without warning the tears came. Isabella tried to sniff them back, pretend they were from the cold, not her culpability in keeping Dr. Morrison's news a secret.

"Hey, what's this? Has something happened?"

She sighed. Dad would know what to do. "Dr. Morrison called yesterday."

"Oh."

"Yeah. He found Mom's application and he's offering her the job."

"Is she going to accept it?"

"She doesn't know. I never gave her the message."

"I see."

"At first I forgot—truly. Darcy called and well, anyway I forgot. But then I remembered."

"And still didn't tell her?"

"I remembered when we got to the church and she was there with Grandma Eleanor finishing up the decorations and I had to get ready for the pageant and it just seemed like the wrong time."

"Okay, but there was time later."

Isabella ducked her head. "I know. But we were having so much fun and it felt so—like a real family and I just—"

"You have to tell her, Bella."

"I know."

"You should be proud of her—happy for her. She's worked hard for this."

"I'm proud of her. It's just if she takes this—and why wouldn't she? It's just we'll all be back where we were—us in Phoenix, you in San Francisco."

Tom lifted her face to his. "Honey, us all being here isn't the real world," he said. "It's wonderful but—well, it's more like a wonderful accident, a kind of special gift."

"Exactly," Isabella argued. "It's as if God brought us here. Admittedly Papa's heart attack was maybe overkill, but we're here. There's a reason for that—a plan in action."

"Bella, are you saying you could live here—permanently?"

"It wouldn't be terrible."

"But Mom's been offered the job she's always wanted."

Isabella made a face.

"Maybe we're becoming a holiday family—no more splitting time between us. We could do all the holidays together. I'll bet she would go for that."

"So, I have to tell her about the call." It was a statement not a question.

"Yeah, and the sooner the better."

Isabella packed up their picnic and stood up, her back to her father. "I was just so sure that God had this plan for us to be together." Her shoulders shook and Tom was on his feet with his arms around her in seconds. That brought on the full flood of tears. "Why can't we be a real family?" she wailed.

"We are," he assured her. "Hey, glass half-full, remember? Think about all the progress we've made in just a few short weeks. Don't spoil what's left of our time together by looking at the dark side, honey. We're sharing Christmas and then New Year's—that's a huge step forward, Bella."

She looked up at him and smiled. "I guess when you look at it that way. Okay, let's go. I'll tell her as soon as we get back—right after we open the presents—" She saw her father's frown and sighed. "As soon as we get back."

Isabella wasn't the only one who had spent a restless night. It wasn't visions of sugarplums dancing in Norah's head. It was her father's heart attack, the aging of both parents, the draw she felt to be there for them, and more than she was willing to admit, the draw she had been feeling toward being back in Normal.

And it's Tom.

She tried to tell herself that the season with all its memories and good tidings of peace and joy had created a false sense of what might have been. But the truth was from the moment she had gotten the call about her father's heart attack, her first instinct had been to turn to Tom. No, it had really started with Denver and Izzy getting sick. And then later when she'd needed to talk to someone about Izzy's change in attitude, it had been perfectly natural to call Tom. After all, it was how they had always handled things with bringing up Isabella.

But when she had decided to contact him about her résumé and the idea of applying for the new job, something had clicked into place like a puzzle piece that had once seemed impossible and then slid into place so perfectly. And even though she told herself that the way they were interacting with one another now that they were here in Normal had to do with not wanting to upset their parents or Izzy, the truth was it felt so right—so absolutely genuine.

"Mom?"

When Izzy returned. Norah was sitting up in bed. She grinned at her daughter's red cheeks and nose. "Dad did a picnic?" she guessed.

"Like at the bottom of this giant sledding hill," Izzy giggled. "He is so weird sometimes."

Norah saw that statement for the compliment it was. She held back the covers and patted the bed beside her. "Come on. Warm up with me, then we'll go rip through all those presents."

Izzy snuggled in next to her. Norah wrapped one arm around her daughter and pulled her close. "That's nice," she said.

"I have to tell you something, Mom, and I don't want you to get mad or upset. I mean, you couldn't have done anything about it with today being Christmas and all so—"

"What's happened?"

"Dr. Morrison called—yesterday. He found your application and you've got the job. Congratulations."

"What!" Norah tried digesting this flood of information. "You mean they want to interview me?"

"Nope. He said if you want it the job's yours." Izzy looked directly at her for the first time since blurting out the news. In her eyes Norah saw a message that was even more unsettling than the fact she had the job.

Please, don't, Izzy's eyes seemed to plead.

"Wow," Norah murmured. "Well, that's something, isn't it?"

"Yeah." Izzy slid off the bed.

"Something for us to consider," Norah added and saw Izzy freeze. "See, I was going to talk to you about something today once we'd gotten through the gift opening and church and Christmas dinner. But maybe now's the best time."

"For what?" Izzy stared out the window.

"I've been thinking maybe we could consider moving back here, Izzy."

"Here? In this house?"

"No. In Normal—in a house or apartment of our own."

Izzy turned. Her eyes were enormous. "What about the job?"

"That does bring a new element to the discussion," Norah acknowledged. "But we have to consider everything, After all it would be a big change. This isn't Phoenix. It's much smaller and it gets cold here and—"

"Let's do it." Izzy clapped her hands with delight, then hopped onto her own bed and started listing the pluses. "We'd be near both sets of grands. I could help them. Oh, and we're not that far away from Minnesota so maybe MJ could come for a weekend or I could go there. And there's Darcy and Heather and—"

"Slow down," Norah warned. "Take some time to

think it over. We don't need to make a decision right this minute. It's just an option."

There was a loud knock at the door and Earle called out. "You girls decent?"

"Come in, Dad," Norah called and put a finger to her lips to warn Izzy not to say anything about them possibly moving just yet. Izzy nodded and flung herself at her grandfather. "Oh, Papa, this is just going to be the best Christmas ever. Let's go open presents."

They made short work of the pile of gifts, ate a second breakfast and then piled in the car for church services traditionally held at noon on Christmas Day. While the evening before the sanctuary had hummed with excitement and conversation, on Christmas Day everyone entered in silence. They might nod and smile at neighbors and friends, but no one spoke as the old pipe organ belted out carols and the scent of fresh evergreens, and dozens of lit candles filled the air. Everyone was dressed in the festive colors of the season and a mantle of love and serenity seemed to cover every shoulder, fill every heart.

Norah sat with her parents and Izzy in one of the side pews. She glanced around and saw that Tom and his parents had not yet arrived and every pew was nearly filled. Just then she spotted them standing at the back of the church. Tom smiled at her and time stood still. How many times in this very church had she thought of Tom only to look up and see him there, smiling at her, watching her?

As his parents hurried down the opposite aisle and

took their places with the rest of the choir seated in the side pews, Tom raised one eyebrow at Norah. She nodded and then pressed closer to Izzy so Tom could squeeze in with them.

The hour-long service consisted of a series of responsive readings, choir anthems and organ solos that served as background for silent prayer and meditation. Norah was surprised to find that these times for prayer came as naturally to her as breathing. Maybe it was being back in the church of her youth. And maybe Izzy was right. God was reaching out to her—or more likely she was reaching out to God.

Dear God, thank You for the wealth of blessings You have bestowed on our families—for health restored and for bringing us all together here at times in our individual lives when we truly need the support and caring of each other. Please help us to make the right decisions as we go forward. We all know what Isabella wants. Over these last weeks so much has changed for us. Izzy believes Your hand is guiding all of that. Forgive me, but I'm not that sure. Please don't let her heart be broken again. Please help me—and Tom—see what's real and what's fantasy. It is blessing enough that we have found our way back to being friends. Help us show our beloved daughter that sometimes friendship is enough—help me accept that it can be enough.

Norah swallowed. The truth hit her. In her heart of hearts she hoped Izzy was right and that God did intend for her to be with Tom again. She was in love with him, had always loved him, would always love him. It was not Izzy who needed to come to terms with the idea that friendship might be the extent of it—it was Norah.

Help me, she silently prayed. *Open my eyes. Show me Your way.*

The organ music swelled to a crescendo and the congregation rose as one for the final carol, "Joy to the World."

Tom sang with gusto as if he believed every word, as if he had suddenly recognized the truth of every word. Norah felt her heart open to the sheer beauty of the moment. The three of them a family again if only for these few days. She would talk to Tom about the job in Phoenix versus the idea of moving back to Normal. She trusted him. Oh, how she had missed being able to talk about things like this with him.

"...and heaven and nature sing," she bellowed so loud that Tom and Izzy both looked at her and grinned.

"I think moving back here is a great idea," Tom said that afternoon as they walked back to her house after both families had shared a traditional brunch at the home of Tom's parents. "It's good for Irene and Earle. For Isabella. Not so sure it's the best thing for you."

"How so?"

"You've practically built the program at the agency. This would be your chance to really do the things you've always wanted to do there."

Norah shrugged. "Maybe I've been a little too invested in my work," she said. "Maybe Luke did me a favor that day when he tried to fire me. It certainly made me look at the job in a new way."

"But Luke's not part of this anymore."

"It doesn't matter. It occurred to me that trying to find your identity in the work you do is at best a moving target."

"You don't need to find your identity," Tom argued. "You're you."

Norah stopped walking and looked up at him. "And who is that?" she said quietly. "Once I was your wife. Then I was Izzy's mom. Then I was whatever my title of the moment was at the agency. I've been a lot of things to a lot of people, but who is Norah?"

"And you think coming back here is the right place to find answers?"

"It feels—safe. It feels familiar."

"You can't turn back the clock, Norah."

"Sure you can," she said half-jokingly. "We do it every fall when we go off daylight saving time."

But Tom remained serious. "You know what I'm saying."

"I know. I'm not going into this with blinders on," she assured him. "I know the difference between being Izzy's age and growing up here and the realities of making a life here. I'll have to find work and there are bound to be moments when Izzy—and I—think we made the wrong choice."

"Want my best advice?" He placed her hand in the crook of his arm.

"That was the point of sending the others ahead and walking home with you," she said with a smile.

"Okay, here it comes. Don't turn down the job in Phoenix yet. Call Morrison and tell him you'll have a decision when you get back after New Year's. Then while you're here explore what the reality of moving back here might be—check out job opportunities, schools, housing, the works."

"That sounds like a wonderful plan. Izzy is ready to put a down payment on a house, but you're right. We need the whole picture."

"Okay, so now that we've solved that, I had an idea." He told her of his idea that going forward they would spend all holidays together. "Either here or in San Francisco—or Phoenix if you decide to go back. We could maybe travel some—springbreak in Washington so Izzy gets a taste of her nation's capital. What do you think?"

Norah laughed. "Oh, Tom, I thought it was just Izzy and me who were getting caught up in the fantasy of the holiday. Do you know what you're proposing? I mean what if you want to spend a holiday with someone else?"

"Who else?"

"A girlfriend?"

Tom shrugged and grinned. "I'll bring her along and you'll bring your guy. If they can't handle it, then they aren't the right ones. Let's be a family—at least to the extent we can be."

It had always amazed Norah how Tom could take the most complex situation and winnow it down to the simplest terms. It was one of the things she had loved most about him. And, she couldn't help remembering, it was also one of the things that had left her stunned and furious when he had left her.

She glanced up at him as he opened the front door to her parents' house and waited for her to precede him.

"Are you happy, Tom?"

He seemed surprised at the question. "Of course."

But the answer had come automatically and the assurance in his smile did not reach his eyes. She touched his cheek.

"You mean in general?" Tom shrugged. "This isn't about me." He kissed her fingers. "You're doing the right thing, Norah. Take your time. Gather the facts. Then decide."

"And in the meantime?" Norah couldn't seem to take her eyes off his fingers entwined with hers. "Will you help me make sure Izzy doesn't get her hopes too high? I mean, she's likely to see this as the next step in God's grand plan—for us."

"I can't stop her from praying for what she's always wanted, Norah."

"In church today it occurred to me that maybe we're the ones who should be seeking God's guidance."

"Great minds," he tapped her forehead and then his own. "I was praying hard during those silent meditations this morning."

Norah was surprised. "Me too," she admitted. "Think it's possible for two former holiday-only churchgoers to change?"

"It's worth a shot—when we were teens we were pretty into our faith."

"Like Izzy," Norah said.

"And a little child shall lead them?" He wrapped his arm around her shoulders. "Don't sell yourself short, Norah. You've raised a fabulous kid. You've built a career you can be proud of, and yet you're still thinking about coming back here for your parents' sake."

"Don't put me up for sainthood yet," Norah cautioned. "Starting fresh has some really selfish appeal to me right now." She looked up at him. "I don't want to some day look back at my life and have the best I can say about it is that I made do."

Tom pulled her to him and hugged her. "Lady, you may be many things but selfish is not on the list, okay? In fact, I would applaud selfish. For once in your life make a decision based on what's best for you. Isabella will be fine whatever you decide."

"Thanks," she whispered as she hugged him back and drew strength from his embrace. *If only...* She pulled away a little. "How about a turkey sandwich?"

He grinned and then kissed her.

"Tom!" she protested when he broke the kiss.

He grinned and pointed to the mistletoe. "Blame your mom," he said and headed down the hall toward the kitchen.

"We should have a New Year's Eve party," Isabella announced as they sat around the kitchen table later that night picking at the remains of their supper.

"What a good idea," Irene agreed. "Why don't you start a guest list, Isabella, and then we can plan a menu."

"And games," Isabella said.

"Parlor games," Earle said.

"Oh, stop sounding like you were born in Victorian times," Irene chastised him but she was laughing.

"How about a scavenger hunt?" Isabella suggested.

"Scavenger hunt and then all meet at the church for midnight services, then come back here and see who found the most things on their list and eat dessert and—"

"And by that time it'll be nearly time for breakfast," her grandfather teased her. "Might as well not go to bed at all."

Izzy eyes and smile widened. "We could watch the sunrise—the dawning of the first day of a new year—cool!"

"Well, I can see I'd better rest up for this grand affair," Earle said. "Come on, Renie, let these young folks clear away. That holiday movie you like is on the family channel—starts in five minutes. Want to snuggle up in bed and watch it with me?"

Irene smiled and pulled off her apron. "Now how could I possibly refuse an offer like that?"

"I'm going to call Darcy and Heather," Isabella said. "It's okay to invite them and their parents, right?"

"It's fine, but don't get too ambitious with your guest list," Norah warned. "It's not that big of a house."

Izzy frowned as she scanned the living room and small dining room visible through the kitchen pass-through. "Yeah, that could be a problem." And she was off, cell phone already to her ear as she bolted up the stairs and shut the door to the bedroom she and Norah were sharing.

"I should go," Tom said.

"Oh no you don't." Norah tossed him the dish towel. "You're not leaving me alone to clear up this mess. I'll wash. You wipe."

"They have this marvelous invention called a dishwasher."

Norah pulled open the dishwasher door to show him it was already filled. "Unless you want to add unloading this to clearing up?"

"I'll wipe," he said as he stacked plates and flatware and carried them to the sink. "Remember that first apartment in Arizona?"

"Yeah. We could barely turn around in that kitchen."

"But it was fun. We had some good times in that place."

"Seems like a long time ago." Norah handed him a plate and he wiped it dry and put it in the cupboard. His actions brought back memories of nights spent washing dishes in that first apartment, nights when they had talked about the future—their future. *You can't go back—only forward.* "Last plate," she announced brightly and handed it to him as she drained the water and wiped out the sink. Their chore completed, there was an awkward silence in the kitchen.

"Well..." Tom said, making the first move. Norah followed him into the front hall and waited by the door while he put on his jacket and gloves. "See you tomorrow?"

Hundreds of times when they were in high school and college they had stood in this very place. He had asked the same question. She had made the same reply, "Sure."

She pulled open the front door and made sure she stood well out of range of the mistletoe. It had been an emotional roller coaster of a day. One more kiss—even a “mistletoe peck” as Tom had once called it—would put her over the edge. Tom glanced at the mistletoe and her position and laughed. “Coward.”

Chapter Fourteen

The next day Norah searched various Web sites for job postings. While there were some possibilities in the Madison area, that would mean an hour's commute each way—unless she and Izzy moved closer to Madison.

"But then what's the point?" Izzy said with maddening logic. "I mean, isn't the idea to be closer to the grands?"

"We would be. Just not in the same town."

"So you're talking really starting over—like totally?" She flopped onto the sofa. "I mean here at least I've got some friends and the church youth group and—"

"Don't get ahead of yourself," Norah said, fighting to keep her own frustration out of her voice. "Nothing's been decided, okay?"

"What about a place to live? Does that look any better?"

"First I need to find gainful employment."

"Hey, what about that cool old house you like so much?"

"The mayor's mansion? Oh, Izzy, we could never afford that and even if we could, it would need a ton of work and it's a huge house for just the two of us."

"We could turn it into a bed and breakfast," Izzy suggested, her eyes alive with what she clearly saw as the brilliance of that suggestion.

"We could," Norah said as if she might seriously consider the idea. "So you're saying that you would be willing to make beds and clean guest rooms and bathrooms for tourists while I cook them elaborate breakfasts and prepare afternoon tea—assuming we have guests?"

Izzy made a face. "We could hire help?"

Norah shook her head.

"Okay, bad idea. You're not that good of a cook anyway," she reasoned.

"Isabella Wallace," Norah protested, but she was laughing because it was true. Tom had been the better cook. She wondered if he still tried new recipes from time to time. *You could ask him,* she realized and felt a warm spot in her heart because Tom was right down the street, not halfway across the country.

"We could at least look at the place," Izzy was saying. "Come on, Mom. Let's just look at it. It'll be fun—and educational for me to see a house like that."

"It would also be a waste of time—and time is not something we have a lot of right now. Besides don't you have things you need to do for the party?"

The phone rang and Norah grabbed it before Izzy could. "Go," she whispered to her daughter before greeting the caller.

"Norah? Meredith Olsen."

"Hi."

"I hope I'm not out of line here, but it's a small town as I'm sure you know and news tends to travel fast." She paused for a breath and added, "Is it true you're thinking of moving back?"

"How did you know?"

"I was in the chair next to Irene at Sadie's this morning."

After Tom had left the evening before, Norah had stopped by her parents' room and told them she was thinking about coming home to Normal. Her mother had gone to the hairdresser earlier that morning and Sadie Evanston's shop had always been gossip central.

"Isabella and I are thinking about it," Norah admitted.

"Great. Irene said you were checking out jobs and I may have a position for you to consider. Maybe you heard the old hospital is being converted into a wellness center?"

"I did. That's such a good use for that wonderful old building."

"Well, I'm on the planning board and we're just beginning the search for an executive director. Interested?"

"Maybe."

"At the Christmas Eve pageant Tom was going on and on about all the programs you created for that place you work for in Phoenix. That kind of innovation is exactly what we need here—not to mention someone who knows how to go after grant funding and keep the doors open."

Norah had stopped at *Tom was going on and on,*

savoring the idea that Tom would show such obvious pride in the work she'd done.

"Are you available to meet with the committee day after tomorrow?"

"Sure. Just let me know what time and where."

"Let's meet at the hospital at ten. That way I can give you a tour and then the others can come at ten-thirty and we can talk. If nothing else we'd love to just pick your brain for ideas."

"That would be fine."

Norah hung up.

"Well?" Isabella huffed.

Norah had almost forgotten her daughter was there, hearing only her side of the conversation. "I have a job interview—here in Normal." Together they squealed with delight and hugged each other.

"Let's go house hunting," Izzy said as she grabbed for the phone. "I'll call Dad and see if he's free."

Caution replaced the euphoria Norah was feeling. "Iz, even if this works out for us, Dad's not moving back—you get that, right?"

Isabella gave a dramatic elongated teenaged sigh. "Mother, he *is* a real estate attorney, remember?"

Norah couldn't argue that. But was she ready for Tom to know things were moving forward so quickly? On the other hand, who better to celebrate such good news with than your best friend? "All right, call your father."

When Tom picked them up he handed Norah a folder. "Copies of your résumé," he explained. "I still had it on my laptop."

"Thanks. Izzy, you ride up front with your dad and navigate since you've got the listings," Norah directed as she climbed into the backseat. But as soon as Izzy was in the car and Tom had started down toward town, Norah sat forward in the middle, her face between them as she filled Tom in on the details of her conversation with Meredith.

Tom could smell the faint scent of the perfume she'd always worn. It suited her—it was fresh and woodsy. Totally natural. He watched her face in the rearview mirror. Her expression was animated and youthful as she recalled every word Meredith had said. And it struck him that while she had always been pretty with a sort of gamine quality to her features, maturity had made her beautiful.

Isabella called out the address for the first house and Tom obediently followed streets he knew by heart to their destination.

"Yuck," was Isabella's immediate assessment of the place. "Total drive-by. Keep going."

Tom couldn't disagree and Norah's silence said she wasn't eager to look any closer at house number one. Houses two through five were not much better. After that Norah—always determined to find the positive in any situation—began working overtime trying to find something good to say about the places.

"It has a nice yard," she commented.

"Mother, we are not going to be living in the yard," Bella reminded her as she sank lower in the seat and threw one hand over her forehead as if exhausted. "Bor-r-r-ing," she moaned.

"It's not so bad," Norah said, but even her voice rang with doubt and when Tom cocked an eyebrow at her in the rearview mirror she smiled. "Okay, it's bad. Shall we abandon this exercise for today? It's premature."

"There's still the mayor's place," Bella murmured.

"Yeah," Tom said as he turned the car away from the street that would take them home and headed back toward town.

"We've had this discussion," Norah told Isabella firmly. "It's a fabulous house, but it's way too big and too expensive—"

"Doesn't cost anything to look," Tom said with a wink at Bella. "I'll just borrow the key from Keith." He left the motor running while he ran to the hardware store. This time Keith handed him a fact sheet on the house.

"For Norah," he explained. "Can't hurt."

Tom returned to the car and handed Norah the sheet, but Isabella grabbed it first. "Wow! There are a gazillion rooms."

"You realize this is a terrible idea," Norah told Tom.

"Hey, we saw it in the dark. Let's see what the place looks like in daylight."

"You two were there? At night?" Bella was all ears now. She sighed and returned to her scrutiny of the flyer. "That is *so* romantic."

Tom saw Norah roll her eyes and sink back onto the seat, her arms folded across her chest as she met his apologetic gaze in the rearview mirror. *Great work not getting the kid's hopes up,* her expressive eyes said.

"Look at this!" became Isabella's mantra as she

bounded from room to room once they were inside the house. Within a matter of minutes she had selected her room—the third floor corner that overlooked the street. "A canopy bed would be so perfect," she announced.

"Your bed at home is a trundle," Norah reminded her.

"Oh, Mom, surely you aren't planning to move that modern stuff here."

"Oh, Izzy," Norah parroted her daughter's exasperated tone, "surely you don't expect that I can afford a mansion like this *and* all new furniture?"

Tom could not help laughing out loud at Isabella's next plan. "Grandma Eleanor has a canopy bed in her third bedroom."

"Stop laughing. You're only encouraging her," Norah warned as she brushed past Tom and started back down the stairs.

"Don't blame me. She learned this stuff from you," he replied as he followed her, leaving Bella to continue her exploration of the third floor and on to the attic.

"Meaning?"

"Meaning that from the day I met you there was never a problem you faced that you couldn't solve. Bella has a lot of that can-do side of you in her. It's one of the things that makes her instantly attractive to other kids—that confidence and assumption all things are possible."

He saw Norah soften slightly. "That's more of you," she said. "You were the one we all turned to as kids when it looked like we were facing some impossible situation. You were the leader."

"Maybe. But we're not talking about leadership, Norah. We're talking about the ability to take lemons and turn them into lemonade. That's what you do and Bella has picked up on that from you."

"Thank you," Norah said. "That's one of the nicest things you've ever said."

And suddenly he knew that she, like he, was remembering all the hurtful things they had said to each other in the months leading up to and following their divorce. Would it always be this way? Tom wondered. Would they ever reach the point where the memories that sprang to mind weren't neatly divided between before and after their split?

Only one way that's going to happen, he thought. *Heal the split.*

He shook off the thought as well as one that had kept him awake most of the previous night—an idea not yet fully formed. An impossible idea made all the more intriguing by the sheer impossibility of it becoming reality. *What if he came back to Normal—started a little practice in town?*

"You know what I think?" he asked. "I think you need a time-out."

Norah laughed. "From what?"

"From everything. You've been worried about Isabella and then your dad and now you're thinking of making a huge life change. How about we take this evening and just put all of that on the back burner for a couple of hours?"

"You, me and Izzy?"

"You and me. Not Izzy," he replied and realized he was practically holding his breath the way he had the first time he'd officially asked her for a date when they were in high school.

"I don't know," she hedged.

"There's a new film version of that Broadway musical you like so much playing at the movies. Two or three hours of mindless entertainment with a big bucket of popcorn and a soda?"

"Tempting," she agreed. "Buttered popcorn?"

"Is there any other kind?"

"It might not be terrible," she said, mimicking their daughter.

Tom thought his heart might actually hammer right out of his chest. *Do not blow this,* he mentally ordered. "Hey, Bella," he shouted up the stairway. "Tour bus leaves in five minutes, okay?"

Norah deliberately dressed down for the movies in jeans and an old turtleneck. She was relieved when Izzy asked permission to spend the night with Darcy and Heather so they could work on the party plans.

"Going out?" her mom said when she came downstairs and laid her jacket and purse on the hall table.

"Tom and I thought we'd see a movie," she said, hoping she sounded as if this was no big deal. "Do you guys want to come?"

"Nope," her father replied. "Basketball game I want to watch. Renie, you go if you want."

"No, I'll watch the game with you."

Norah was well aware that her parents were trying to remain as casual as she was and that not one of the three of them didn't see this for what it was. Norah and

Tom were going on a date. Norah heard Tom's car on the drive and was out the front door before he had a chance to come in. "See you later," she called.

"Next time, tell that young man to call for you properly," her father shouted.

On the short drive to the theater they talked about people they'd run into that they both knew from before, amazed at how many of their old friends and classmates had moved back to Normal or never left in the first place. At the movie, Tom bought the tickets and the promised popcorn and they hurried to find seats in the already crowded theater.

"Remember when movies didn't have commercials?" Tom said as they sat through several minutes of ads for cars, sportswear and local businesses.

"You make us sound like we're a hundred and two," Norah said, reaching for more popcorn and all too aware that her shoulder and Tom's were pressed together in the tight space. To her relief the lights were lowered the rest of the way as the feature started.

For the next two hours she was lost in a world of fantasy—the one up on the screen where people burst into song at the oddest moments. And the one in the darkened theater where she was sitting next to Tom as she had dozens of times before, laughing at the same lines, their hands touching as they reached for more popcorn at the same time. And when as usual the happy ending of the film touched Norah and brought on tears, Tom shook his head, grinned and offered her his handkerchief.

The movie was exactly what she had needed—an escape from everything she'd been dealing with these last several days. As the credits rolled she reached over and took Tom's hand. Surprised, he looked at her.

"Thanks," she whispered.

He laced his fingers through hers and held on. "You're entirely welcome."

On the way back to the car they talked about stopping for ice cream only to discover that nothing was open in town.

"What happened to the Hob Nob?" Tom asked.

"It closed at least five years ago," Norah told him. "We had some good times there," she added and immediately wondered if Tom had taken that the wrong way when he didn't reply. "I didn't mean that..."

"I know. I was just thinking."

"About?"

"Old times and maybe some not-so-old times," he said as he drove the deserted streets and parked in front of her parents' house. He cut the engine and turned to her. "Norah, do you ever think we might have made a mistake?"

All the time lately, she thought. "Sometimes," she admitted. "But I think that's probably to be expected. I mean we were both so sure—each in our own way. And being back here—especially at Christmas—well, it's a little like the movie we saw. Not the real world." She leaned over and kissed his cheek. "We've come a long way, Tom," she said softly. "Whether it was Denver or my dad or some combination, it feels as if we've turned an important corner, don't you think?"

"Yeah, I..."

She reached for the door. "Thanks, Tom," she said. "For knowing this was exactly what I needed tonight—mindless entertainment with no pressures of job or family or anything else to think about. It was great."

She was deliberately letting the moment pass. *Opportunity missed,* she could practically hear Izzy protesting, but the truth was that she was still caught up in the romance of a world where people wore colorful gowns and sang and danced to express their joys and sorrows. That wasn't real—and neither was this.

Chapter Fifteen

The day of the party, Tom chauffeured Isabella and her friends around town to buy decorations and other party supplies.

"Aren't you coming in?" Isabella asked when Tom pulled up at the Jenkins house and left the motor running as Norah came out to help unload the car. "We need help with stuff for the party."

He kissed the top of her head. "I'm sure you and your friends have everything under control. I've got an errand to run. See you later at the party."

"Well," Izzy huffed as she and Norah stood on the sidewalk watching Tom drive away. "That errand must sure be important."

"It's probably something for his work, Izzy. Give him a break. He's been away from the office for over a week now. I can't remember the last time he did that, can you?"

"Well, it's not like anyone's forcing him to stay here. He seems perfectly happy, don't you think?"

"It's always good to come home," Norah said as she put her arm around Izzy and headed up the front walk. "Now, what are my assignments, Ms. Party Planner?"

Norah had to give her daughter credit. She and her friends had thought of everything. Although the guest list had grown to the place where the venue had been moved, Izzy had accepted every guest's offer to "bring something" and created a kind of smorgasbord of favorite dishes without either of her grandmothers having to lift a finger. The event was now scheduled to be held in the large open gallery space shared by Darcy's mom and the other artists who had studios in the same building.

"Of course, we had to invite her artist friends as well," Izzy had explained, "but the more the merrier, right?"

Before they were inside the house Izzy was already on the phone and half an hour after that Norah and Izzy had loaded her parents' car with decorations and supplies and driven to the gallery. A crew of teenagers arrived to arrange tables and hang decorations for the party. The place was alive with laughter and chatter and as she watched Izzy with her new circle of friends, Norah came to a decision. The interview had gone well and if Meredith and the rest of the planning committee offered her the job, she would take it. She and Izzy could continue living with her parents for the time being while they waited for the perfect—and affordable—house to come on the market. It was all coming together. Norah could hardly believe the changes that had come their way these last several weeks. It was like living life in fast forward, but she had to admit that it all felt right—as if some force greater than all of them was in charge.

Maybe Izzy is right, Norah thought as she watched her daughter.

"What are you going to wear?" Izzy asked that afternoon.

Norah laughed. "I don't have a lot of choices," she said as she laid out the one pair of black wool slacks, a blue silk shirt and the short charcoal tweed jacket she'd been wearing the day the call about her father had come.

Izzy moaned. "For the party?"

She had a point. Norah considered the outfit. "Maybe lose the jacket?"

Izzy wrinkled her nose. "Let's go shopping. I have the gift cards Dad put in my stocking."

"Those are for you, honey."

"And therefore I get to use them the way I want," Izzy countered.

Norah placed her palms on either side of her daughter's face. "Has anyone ever told you that you are the dearest and most generous child?"

"Not in those words." Izzy squirmed free. "I'll take that as a yes."

"Okay. We'll go shopping—maybe a scarf or necklace for the blouse?"

Izzy made a face. "Or we could start from scratch and have you wear something really hot for a change."

"Isabella Wallace! I am almost forty years old. I do not do 'hot.'"

Izzy shrugged. "You might want to rethink that."

* * *

In spite of Izzy's determined efforts to upgrade Norah's fashion, in the end she had to agree that the silver wrap dress hanging in Norah's closet was better than anything they'd seen in the shops.

"But you must have decent shoes," she'd insisted, leading Norah to the shoe department.

"It's going to snow. I can't walk through snow in these," Norah had argued admiring the way the strappy evening sandals Izzy had selected for her looked in spite of herself.

"Dad will bring the car right up to the door."

"Dad is meeting us there, remember?"

"Oh yeah," Izzy said. "He had 'something to do.' Like he couldn't put that on hold for one day?"

"Izzy," Norah warned.

But later that evening after everyone else had arrived at the party, Norah couldn't help but admit that Izzy wasn't the only one watching the door. Then just when she'd decided he'd gotten wrapped up in work as usual and felt a twinge of the irritation that had been at the root of many of their arguments in the last days of their marriage, he was there. He stood at the door shaking off the snow that clung to his hair and jacket.

Izzy's face lit up as she raced across the room to him. Norah watched Tom follow their daughter's motions as she obviously showed off all that she had put together for the party. Izzy tugged at his hand, but he spotted Norah across the packed room. He said something to Izzy, gave her a hug and moved through the throng of guests as if a path had been cleared that led straight to Norah.

"Hi." He was nervous. "Sorry I'm late."

"Hi," she replied. "They offered me the job." She hadn't meant to blurt that out, but realized she'd been wanting to tell him ever since Meredith had told her when she arrived at the party.

He grinned. "That's great, honey. Just terrific."

There was an awkward moment when she realized he wanted to hug her but instead just took her hands. He stepped back and looked at her. "Wow," he murmured.

Norah was suddenly shy under the spotlight of his gaze. *Did he recognize the dress? Remember she'd worn it when he proposed? Probably not.*

"Can we get out of here for a bit?"

Norah looked up at him. "You just got here and..."

"I know, but it's important. I've got something I want to show you."

"Outside?" She glanced at her flimsy shoes and laughed. But when she looked into his eyes she saw that whatever this was, it was something really serious—something that Tom could discuss only with her. For that she would walk barefoot through slush and snow. "Sure."

Tom found her coat and held it for her. Outside, he picked her up and carried her across the snow-covered street. She didn't protest mainly because he seemed so tense—so intent on whatever mission he was on. He helped her into the car and closed the door.

"What's happened, Tom? Where are we going?" she asked.

He forced his fingers into a more relaxed grip on the wheel. "It's a surprise—a good one, I hope."

He made turns at the next two corners and then pulled to a stop in front of the old mansion. From the glove compartment he took out a remote control and fiddled with it as he made the speech he'd obviously worked out and practiced earlier.

"Norah, five years ago I made an enormous mistake—I think we both did. But sometimes people get a second chance." He raised his eyes to hers. "I love you, Norah—have loved you even when I was so angry at you I couldn't speak. In fact, it was because I loved you that I got so angry. But it takes two—two to be together and two to come apart." He drew in a shaky breath and released it with a nervous half laugh. "I guess what I'm trying to say is that it will also take two to come back together."

"Tom, I..."

"Let me get through this, okay? Then however you decide, I'll accept. After all, like you said the other night, we've come a long way and if I'm pushing things then..." He paused as if trying to find his place in the mental notes he'd obviously worked out. "Okay, here's what I'm saying. I love you—can't say that enough. But I also love who we were when we lived here. I love the dreams we had, the plans we made, the way we were." He smiled. "Like the movie title—only real life, you know?"

Norah nodded. She felt as if she'd been holding her breath ever since he'd started to speak. She was afraid if she released it she might blow away the miracle of what she hoped and prayed he was trying to say.

He turned toward the house. "It's a big old monster of a place, but I was thinking maybe I could open a law office—"

Norah tried to quell the disappointment that pressed against her chest until she couldn't breathe. He was going to use the old house for his law practice. He was talking about moving back to Normal, but not about moving into her heart. "You're right," she said, forcing the words through a tight smile. "It would make a wonderful law office—so close to town and all."

Tom looked confused, then he started laughing and she was ready to punch him.

"I've rented office space down the street from Keith's hardware," he said. "The house—well, here." He handed her the remote control. "Press it," he coached.

Norah pressed the control and the house came alive. There was a large lighted tree in the front window. Two leafless crab apple trees in the front yard were ablaze with small red and white lights, and along the front walk and stairs gold lights glowed from under the accumulating snow. On the door there was a large wreath decorated with a wide red velvet bow.

"Oh, Tom, I don't know what to say. You did this for me?"

"For us." He pulled Norah into his arms as they looked at the grand old house. "Let's live there, Norah. Let's go back and start over and make all those grand plans we had before we got so caught up in making a fortune—me—and saving the world—you—and build the life we always wanted."

"What about your work? I mean you can't just walk away from everything you've built there in California."

"It's a global world, Norah," he said with a grin. "Cell phone, laptop. Besides, there's something exciting about the way this town is reinventing itself."

Norah couldn't help herself. This was just beyond her ability to accept at face value. There had to be a catch. "Look, if this is about Izzy—I know she's been pressuring us, but don't change your life for a thirteen-year-old."

"I'm not. I'm talking about both of us changing our lives for us. Honey, from the moment I spotted you in that airport in Denver, there's been something eating at me. When I got back to California I realized how in spite of everything I had believed, I wasn't happy. None of my success made any difference without you."

"And Izzy," Norah reminded him.

"I had Isabella," he said, cupping her face and drawing her closer to make his point. "What's been missing in my life is you—us. I love you, Norah. I have always loved you even when I thought you were being stubborn and unreasonable. The fact is that you were right. Money and success mean nothing without people you love to share them with. Please give us another chance."

Norah touched his cheek, felt the single tear that coursed the deep lines of his face and her heart broke free of the last remnants of what had been. "Okay," she said and saw that he was waiting for her to continue that with a *but.* She grinned. "No buts," she told him. "I'm saying yes."

He stared at her, disbelieving. "Really? The whole package? Marriage and all? I mean if you need some time..."

"Really," she said and then she hugged him and they were kissing and the next thing they knew a police officer was tapping on the window.

Tom broke free of kissing Norah and greeted the officer, who was clearly taken aback to discover two adults rather than the teens he'd obviously been expecting to see. "Everything okay, folks?"

"Everything's perfect," Tom assured him.

Isabella kept glancing back at the entrance to the church. Her parents had disappeared from the party shortly after her dad arrived. *Where were they?* She had the terrible feeling that maybe this was not a good sign. Her dad had been so distracted and looked so serious. *Please! We've come this far. Mom's agreed to come back here to live and I'm more than okay with that. In fact even if You decide they shouldn't get back together—and sometimes I know You decide that's not for the best—still— Please?*

The service ended in silence as the bell tolled twelve beats. Izzy tried to keep her head bowed, but she could not resist one more look back. And there they were. Her dad with his arm around her mom, their heads bowed. And then as the last toll of the bell echoed across the peaceful calm of the midnight hour, there was a moment of absolute silence and then the organist played the celebratory chorus from Handel's *Messiah.*

The church throbbed with laughter and conversation and wishes for the New Year as Isabella made her way through the throng to her parents. "Well?"

Her dad pulled a key from his pocket. "How would you like to take another look at that third-floor bedroom?"

"We're getting the house?"

Her mom looked up at her dad and Isabella was positive there were stars in both their eyes. "Yes, we are," they said at the same time. Then the miracle of miracles, her dad kissed her mom right there—right in front of God and half the town. And as if everyone had suddenly realized the significance of the moment, they broke into applause and pressed forward to offer congratulations and best wishes.

Isabella closed her eyes tight. *Thank You! Thank You sooo much for the best present ever.* And when she opened them, her parents were watching her.

"Told you God had a plan," she reminded them, then squeezed in between them to complete the circle.

* * * * *

Dear Reader,

I remember one December when it began snowing in Wisconsin on December 1 (and didn't much stop for three months!), I began to think about the idea of travelers getting stranded in airports. I remembered one time when I had gone to the mountains of Virginia to visit my family. A snowstorm shut down the small airport that was a couple of hours from my hometown. So, along with several fellow passengers, we hiked over to the nearby motel, only to find that they could not get their staff in to run the place. But never underestimate American ingenuity! Within an hour, we passengers were doling out linens (make your own bed!) and handling kitchen duty (short-order breakfast items only, please!). We not only made it through the night—even after the electricity and heat went off—but the following day, as we all trooped back to the airport and gradually got out on our flights, we realized just how much our lives had been enriched by the experience. Like Isabella in this story, I firmly believe things happen for a reason, and we only need to give ourselves over to the adventure of that incident to come away a stronger and better (and sometimes happier) person. I hope you enjoyed this holiday story and that you and yours have a joyful and peaceful holiday season, and the very happiest of next years!

All the best,

Anna Schmidt

Please stop by my website, at www.booksbyanna.com, and sign up for my eNewsletter to receive advance notice of upcoming books.

Questions for Discussion:

1. What part did coincidence appear to play in reuniting Norah and Tom?

2. Do you believe that even random coincidences happen for a reason? Why or why not?

3. What occasions in your life can you recall where it seemed as if things were happening to send you in a different direction than you first thought?

4. What might have happened if Tom and Norah had decided to simply remain friends?

5. How might Isabella have dealt with their decision if the family had remained separated?

6. What were the factors that ultimately led Norah to decide to return to Normal—even if she and Tom did not remarry?

7. How did Norah and Tom handle parenting Isabella even though they were estranged?

8. What positive ways have you seen separated or divorced couples deal with parenting?

9. In a world where blended families are common, how can faith help?

10. How was Isabella's faith tested, and how did she deal with each challenge?

Love Inspired
CLASSICS

SPECIAL EXCERPT FROM

Love Inspired

Bygones's intrepid reporter is on the trail of the town's mysterious benefactor. Will she succeed in her mission? Read on for a preview of COZY CHRISTMAS by Valerie Hansen, the conclusion to

THE HEART OF MAIN STREET *series.*

Whitney Leigh rolled her eyes. "Romance! It's getting to be an epidemic."

Because she was alone in the car she didn't try to temper her frustration. Fortunately, this time, the editor of the *Bygones Gazette* had assigned her to write a new series about the Save Our Streets project's six-month anniversary. If he had asked her for one more fluff piece on recent engagements, she would have screamed.

Parking in front of the Cozy Cup Café, she shivered and slid out.

As a lifelong citizen of Bygones she was supposed to have been perfect for the job of ferreting out the hidden facts concerning the town's windfall. Too bad she had failed. Instead of an exposé, she'd ended up filling her column with news of people's love lives. But she was not going to quit investigating. No, sir. Not until she'd uncovered the real facts. Especially the name of their secret benefactor.

She stepped inside the Cozy Cup.

"What can I do for you?" Josh Smith asked.

Whitney was tempted to launch right into her real reason for being there. Instead, she merely said, "Fix me something warm?"

"Like what?"

"Surprise me."

She settled herself at one of the tables. There was something unique about this place. And, truth to tell, the same went for the other new businesses on Main. Each one had filled a need and become an integral part of Bygones in a mere five or six months.

Josh Smith was a prime example. He was what she considered young, yet he had quickly won over the older generations as well as the younger ones.

He stepped out from behind the counter with a steaming cup in one hand and a taller, whipped-cream-topped tumbler in the other.

"Your choice," he said pleasantly, placing both drinks on the table and joining her as if he already knew this was not a social call.

"I see you're not too busy this afternoon. Do you have time to talk?"

"I always have time for my favorite reporter," he said.

"How many reporters do you know?"

"Hmm, let's see." A widening grin made his eyes sparkle. "One."

Will Whitney get her story and find love in the process?
Pick up COZY CHRISTMAS to find out.

Available December 2013 wherever
Love Inspired® Books are sold.

LIEXP1213

Love the Love Inspired book you just read?

Your opinion matters.

Review this book on your favorite book site, review site, blog or your own social media properties and share your opinion with other readers!

Be sure to connect with us at:
Harlequin.com/Newsletters
Twitter.com/LoveInspiredBks
Facebook.com/LoveInspiredBooks

HLIREVIEWSR